**Two brand-new stories in every volume...
twice a month!**

Duets Vol. #57

Popular Jill Shalvis serves up a delightful duo—
the disaster-prone Anderson twins and the sexy men
they meet!—in a humorous special Double Duets!
Rendezvous says this author is "fast, fanciful
and funny. Get ready for laughs, passion
and toe-curling romance."

Duets Vol. #58

Two talented new writers make their Duets debut
this month. Look for Candy Halliday's playful romp
about a bad boy who has a soft spot for his pooch—
and the gorgeous dog owner next door!
Then nurse-turned-writer Dianne Drake will tickle
your funny bone and send temperatures rising
with a fun story about a small-town medical practice.

Be sure to pick up both Duets volumes today!

Lady and the Scamp

"Your place or mine, Counselor?"

Dumbfounded, Cassie almost dropped the phone. "You, Mr. Hardin, have to be the most arrogant, insufferable man I've ever met."

"Well, nobody's perfect," Nick agreed, "but you're the one who said we had a problem to solve. I'm just suggesting we settle things over a bottle of wine and a sensible conversation."

"Oh, I'm sure you handle all your problems with a bottle of wine and a sensual conversation..."

"I said *sensible* conversation," Nick corrected.

Cassie ignored him. "I left Duchess with the vet earlier, but we won't know for a few weeks if she's going to have puppies."

"Then what?" Nick quizzed.

"Then you can save yourself a lot of trouble and pay for the damage your mutt caused, or we can go to court."

"You're really serious about this, aren't you, Counselor?"

"What do you think?" Cassie challenged.

He laughed. "Lady I think if you'd let nature take its course the way your fancy show dog did, you'd have a much better outlook on life."

For more, turn to page 9

The Doctor Dilemma

"Don't you touch my zipper!" Jack protested.

Lacy shook her head at him. "Let's play pretend, Dr. Sutton. You be the doctor and I'll be the patient with the aching knee acting just like you. What would you do?"

"I'd send my nurse to handle the situation."

"Well, I *am* the nurse and I *am* handling it."

"Oh, all right. You take them off," he grudgingly replied.

His jeans were tight, but it took her only one tug to discover he wasn't a boxer man. Every inch of him was devilishly sculpted and it took every ounce of restraint to avert her eyes from the rich shape of his manhood beneath the cotton fabric, to the scar she was supposed to be examining.

"Now that you've taken a good look at everything, Nurse," Jack snapped, "don't you think you should get on with he real exam?"

"You owed me one, Jack. Now I've been repaid."

"Just check the knee, Lacy," he sighed, "just check the knee."

For more, turn to page 197

HARLEQUIN DUETS

ISBN 0-373-44124-X

LADY AND THE SCAMP
Copyright © 2001 by Candace Viers

THE DOCTOR DILEMMA
Copyright © 2001 by JJ Despain

This edition published by arrangement with Harlequin Books S.A.

® and TM are trademarks of the publisher. Trademarks indicated with
® are registered in the United States Patent and Trademark Office, the
Canadian Trade Marks Office and in other countries.

Visit us at www.eHarlequin.com

Printed in U.S.A.

Lady and the Scamp

Candy Halliday

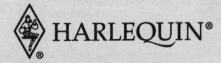

HARLEQUIN®

TORONTO • NEW YORK • LONDON
AMSTERDAM • PARIS • SYDNEY • HAMBURG
STOCKHOLM • ATHENS • TOKYO • MILAN • MADRID
PRAGUE • WARSAW • BUDAPEST • AUCKLAND

Dear Reader,

You might say I'm living proof that love has a lighter side. I met my husband on a blind date to, of all things, a Halloween party. Dressed as a punk rocker with purple streaks in my hair, who knew I'd meet the man of my dreams? His incredible sense of humor overlooked my ridiculous costume and two years later we walked down the aisle. This time, however, I had baby's breath—not purple streaks—in my hair.

A big fan of romantic comedy even before my own personal episode, I got the idea for *Lady and the Scamp* while watching a telecast of the Westminster Dog Show. The Best In Show winner was all puff and fluff and the poor trainer was having a terrible time keeping her away from the big red-bone hound who won runner-up. "Don't you know the trainer would have a fit if those two got together?" my husband asked, and by the time we both stopped laughing, the story was already forming in my head.

I had such fun writing *Lady and the Scamp*. I hope you have just as much fun reading it.

Best Wishes,

Candy Halliday

I owe special thanks to my husband, Steve,
for putting up with the crazy life of a writer.
I also owe special thanks to my agent, Jenny Bent,
and my editor, Susan Sheppard, for believing in me.

This book is dedicated to my wonderful daughter,
Shelli, who has always been the pride of my heart
and the joy of my life.

Prologue

CASSIE COLLINS STIFLED a groan as her perfectly groomed mother paced dramatically around the foyer in a full-blown snit. "I still think your father and I should postpone our trip to Europe entirely," Lenora Collins said with a pout. "The three of us have been taking family vacations together since you were born, and I certainly don't like the idea of leaving you behind to supervise something as important as seeing Duchess mated to the proper sire."

Cassie looked down at the pampered pooch she was holding in her arms and absently stroked the dog's soft white fur. Her mother's champion bichon frise had finally offered Cassie the perfect excuse to forgo the dreaded family vacation from hell, and Cassie didn't intend to give in without putting up a fight.

"You were the one who said it would be too traumatic to leave Duchess with a total stranger at a delicate time like this, Mother," Cassie said. "I know you were counting on Duchess's trainer to handle everything, but emergencies do come up. All we can do now is make the best of it."

Lenora made several phony kissing noises toward the recent winner of the prestigious Westminster Dog Show, then again pursed her lips in a surly pout. "Well, I can assure you of one thing. If Duchess's trainer thinks I'm going to forget the trouble he's caused us, then he's sadly mistaken. As far as I'm concerned, it was totally unprofessional of him to leave us in the lurch like this."

Cassie rolled her eyes. "I hardly think having an acute

attack of appendicitis qualifies as being unprofessional, Mother," Cassie argued. "Besides, you've already paid an enormous fee to see that Duchess is bred to a champion sire and the breeder arrives from London next week. It's only logical that I stay behind and handle matters here."

"Cassie's right, Lenora," Howard Collins chimed in as he picked up the last of their luggage and headed through the foyer. "Our daughter didn't graduate magna cum laude from law school for nothing. She's perfectly capable of handling things here."

Lenora Collins snorted at her husband's statement, then shot another dubious look in Cassie's direction. "Well, at least promise me you'll be careful, Cassandra. I can't say I'm not equally concerned about you being here alone with a hoodlum living right down the street. There's no telling what a man like that might be capable of doing. Lock your doors and keep the security system on at all times."

Cassie sighed. Her mother was, of course, referring to their incorrigible new neighbor who had scandalized their exclusive neighborhood from the moment he'd arrived. A cross between Howard Stern and TV's Frasier, the outspoken radio talk-show host had refused to conform to any of the genteel southern traditions most people in Asheville, North Carolina, still held sacred. To date, Nick Hardin had been banned from the country club, thrown off the golf course and had even been levied a heavy fine for parking his monstrous Harley-Davidson motorcycle on the country club's manicured lawn.

"I don't care for Nick Hardin any more than you do, Mother," Cassie said, "but I hardly think the man is a rapist."

"Well, one never knows," Lenora argued in her usual authoritative voice. "Especially since that horrid man could be harboring a grudge against you. You really were foolish to call in to that disgraceful program of his and make a complaint, Cassandra."

That's right, Mother, Cassie thought. *Make sure you deliver at least one more reprimand before you leave.*

Not that Cassie didn't regret her own lapse in judgment, because she did. She usually let the standard jokes that attacked her noble profession roll off her back. But it had been one particular lawyer-of-the-day joke on Nick Hardin's radio program that had pushed Cassie over the edge. Stating on the air that "the only difference between a lawyer and a vulture was that a vulture waits until you *die* to pick your bones clean" had, in Cassie's opinion, taken things a bit too far. She had called in to the popular morning radio program and politely suggested that Mr. Hardin do a little research on what was considered humorous and what was considered in bad taste.

The creep, of course, had laughed at her comment, but when he insulted her further by suggesting that *even* a lawyer should be smart enough to turn the dial if she didn't like the program, Cassie had promptly slammed the phone down in the arrogant jerk's ear.

"Okay, Mother. I promise I'll be careful," Cassie conceded when a blast from her father's car horn inched her mother a little closer to the front door.

"Well, just remember, you can't let Duchess out of your sight for a moment," Lenora cautioned. "I'm still having panic attacks over the ridiculous stud fee I had to pay to that overrated thief from England. After what that snooty man charged me, I'd better come home to a litter of champion puppies."

With that said, her mother sashayed out the door. Cassie followed, then remained standing on the porch of the rambling old Victorian where she'd lived all her life. "Send me lots of postcards," Cassie called out as her father's car pulled out of the drive, but it wasn't until the black Lincoln disappeared from view that Cassie let out a liberating scream and danced across the porch with her mother's prize-winning show dog held high above her head.

"We're free at last!" Cassie cheered as she whirled the tiny dog around in circles.

For Cassie, six weeks home alone would be sheer heaven on earth. And even the fact that she had to play nursemaid to a world-class-champion fur ball didn't dampen her spirits.

1

"THIS IS CASSIE COLLINS over on Crescent Circle. There's a rapist in my backyard! Hurry, I need your help."

Cassie tossed the portable phone aside when the intruder made another advance in her direction. "Get out of here, you filthy beast," she yelled, then turned the tables and charged *him* instead.

Unfortunately, all Cassie accomplished was another futile chase through the trees. Having as much success as snaring a feather in a hurricane, she was no match for the speed demon who darted out of reach every time she lunged in his direction.

After another unsuccessful romp around the yard, Cassie bent over and rested her hands on her knees, drinking in deep drags of air as she tried to catch her breath. When a reddish-gold curl fell across her face, she sent a frustrated puff upward, blowing the curl out of her eyes. It was then that she noticed the gaping hole by the side of the high wooden privacy fence that surrounded the backyard.

His eyes locked with Cassie's for a brief moment, and as if the culprit could read her mind, he immediately darted in the direction of his escape hole.

"Come back here, you coward," Cassie screamed, but the sound of the security cruiser's siren screaming toward the house forced her to temporarily abandon the chase.

Shaking her fist at the black-and-white terrier who had now distanced himself at the far end of the yard, Cassie actually thought she saw the little criminal grinning back at her through his sharp, pointed, doggy-type teeth. Knowing that the chase was pointless without help from her neighborhood troubleshooters, Cassie stomped to the front foyer where a concerned security officer was already pounding his fist on the door.

"Are you hurt, Miss Collins? Did the goon lay a hand on you?" demanded the older of the two officers as he lumbered into the foyer with his weapon drawn.

Annoyed at the sight of the revolver, Cassie frowned at the two rent-a-cops who were affectionately known as "Andy and Barney" in her luxurious neighborhood. "I don't want you to shoot him, Joe. I just want you to help me catch the rascal."

"I'll go first," the portly officer announced, then sent an official look toward his baby-faced partner, who was anxiously turning the knobs on his handheld police radio.

"Should I call Asheville PD for backup now, Joe?" the rookie asked in a voice that was still struggling with puberty.

"No!" both Cassie and Officer Joe shouted simultaneously.

Pushing past both officers, Cassie took the lead and stomped back through the house with her nervous defenders following closely at her heels. As soon as they reached the wicker-filled sunroom at the back of the house, she pointed through the doorway to the furry assailant the officers had come to arrest.

"There he is," she said, fuming. "The filthy little beast dug his way under the privacy fence and assaulted Duchess before I even knew what was happening."

Both officers followed Cassie's gaze through the door to the terrier, who immediately cocked his head in their direction and showed them the same silly doggy grin Cassie had seen earlier. And then as if to mock her, the mutt wagged his stubby tail, obviously pleased by what he'd been able to accomplish before help arrived.

"You said *rapist,* Miss Collins," Joe scolded as he shoved his revolver back into its holster and sent Cassie a stern look.

Cassie glared back. "I'm in no mood for a lecture about a minor technicality, Joe," Cassie warned. "You know as well as I do, you guys wouldn't have rushed right over here if I'd called to report a stray dog in my yard."

Neither of the officers denied Cassie's accusation, but both men continued to stare at her as if she were some alien life-form who had purposely been sent to invade their peaceful domain. And Cassie really couldn't blame them. They were used to seeing the calm, collected, professional Miss Collins going to and from her respected law firm every day, not some wild-eyed maniac whose hair was still in a lopsided ponytail from her shower, and who had grabbed the first thing she found in her bureau when she glanced out her bedroom window and saw the lewd tango that was being conducted across her lawn.

"Look, Joe," Cassie said, trying to appease the man. "You of all people know how difficult it is to deal with my mother."

When the officer paled at the mere mention of such a trying experience, Cassie pointed to the tiny white bichon frise, who was now scampering across the yard to join forces with the enemy. "Well, I'm warning you. No one in this entire neighborhood will be safe when Lenora Collins finds out her famous show dog crossed paws with the first stray mutt who came along. She'll blame *me* for not watching Duchess more closely. And she'll blame *you* for allowing some nasty mutt to roam free through the neighborhood."

Joe's heavily browed eyes immediately grew wide with concern. Sending a quick glance over his shoulder, he absently patted his holster as if he might need the gun for his own protection. "But y-your m-mother *is* still in Europe, isn't she, Miss Collins?" Joe stammered.

"Yes, but I can't keep Lenora in Europe forever, Joe,"

Cassie said, and sighed. "And if we don't get that mutt out of here before he does any more damage, we'll *all* be buying tickets to Europe to save our own lives." .

Joe dragged a meaty hand over his face, then pointed to the woo-some twosome who were currently engaged in what appeared to be another premating ritual. "You mean that little white dog out there is the one who just won all those awards in New York City?"

Cassie nodded, glaring at the poodle-looking paramour whom she'd vowed to protect and keep safe in her mother's absence. The little witch was her mother's pride and joy, but now that the current diva of the dog world had succumbed to the charms of a mutt whose only credentials seemed to be an overdose of testosterone and an attitude, Cassie suspected those dog-food and pet endorsements her mother planned to glean from winning Westminster would disappear faster than a pack of antacids at a federal tax audit.

"Man, I don't blame you for being upset, Miss Collins, but—"

"Oh, I zoomed way past *upset* when I found them doing an intimate bunny-hop across the backyard," Cassie interrupted. "Now, are you guys going to help me catch the mutt before they engage in another close encounter of the *fur* kind, or aren't you?"

Both men seemed a bit embarrassed by her graphic outburst, but the Barney Fife lookalike finally stepped forward to take up the challenge. "I'll help you catch him, Miss Collins. I've always been good with dogs."

Cassie held her breath as the lanky officer left the sunroom and strolled across the yard in the perpetrator's direction. To Cassie's surprise, instead of leading the officer on another exhausting game of hide-and-seek through the trees, the scruffy little scamp inched toward him and sniffed at the man's outstretched hand. In a flash, the officer snatched the mutt up. Mission accomplished, he returned to Cassie's side with the little bandit tucked safely under his arm.

"Peanuts always work," he said proudly, sending Cassie a wink. "I always keep loose peanuts in my pocket for between-meal snacks."

Cassie shuddered at the sight of the lint-covered peanuts the mutt was happily munching from the officer's hand, then looked around the yard for the other half of the dissolute duo. Obviously sated by the wild display of carnal acrobatics Cassie had witnessed earlier, the little floozy trotted obediently toward the house in search of her lover. Cassie grabbed the pampered pooch and marched Miss Duchess into the sunroom. When Cassie placed Duchess in her traveling crate and fastened the latch, the shameless hussy actually had the nerve to look annoyed.

When Cassie joined the officers back on the patio, she smiled and said, "Thanks, guys. Now you need to help me find this mutt's owner. And when you do, I want you to make an immediate arrest for violating the neighborhood leash law."

Both men exchanged nervous looks. Joe actually laughed. "Hey, you're not really serious about making an arrest over this, are you, Miss Collins?"

Cassie frowned, but let out an exasperated sigh. "Probably not, but it really would serve the owner right if I did. If that dog has left Duchess with a litter of mongrel puppies, I'll be facing a death sentence."

"Hey, I really sympathize with your predicament, Miss Collins," Joe mumbled, "but I sure wouldn't want to be the one to make the arrest."

"Me, neither," interjected Barney Fife's twin. "He wasn't real happy the last time we had to serve him with a complaint."

Hands on her hips now, Cassie sent both men a puzzled

look. "You mean you guys already know who owns this mutt?"

Barney swallowed, sending his pronounced Adam's apple roaming up and down his throat several times before he managed to spit out the answer. "The little fellow belongs to Nick Hardin. You know, that radio talk-show host who's caused all the trouble since he moved into Biltmore Forest."

Hearing that Nick Hardin owned the mutt responsible for her current nightmare affected Cassie like a slap across the face. She immediately reached for the wiry terrier and snatched the little Casanova from the officer's grasp.

"I really do appreciate your help, boys," she told her cohorts, then sent both officers a sinister smile. "But if Nick Hardin owns this guy, I'm going to pay him a visit he won't soon forget."

"Give him hell, Miss Collins," Barney said on a giggle.

"You can count on it," Cassie promised, then turned on her heel and headed for the garage with the relieved security officers trailing after her.

After waving goodbye to her obliging dream team, Cassie opened the door to her silver Lexus sedan, placed the black-and-white scoundrel on the passenger's seat, then slid behind the wheel.

"So, you belong to the famous Nick Hardin, do you?" she said, looking over at the mutt who was responsible for turning her peaceful Saturday morning into a full-blown disaster. "Well, thanks to you, my scruffy little friend, we'll see if your obnoxious master still has a sense of humor after this *vulture* picks *his* bones clean for the damages you've caused this morning."

IT TOOK LESS THAN five minutes for Cassie and her hostage to make the short trip to the old Tudor mansion Nick Hardin had purchased some six months earlier. When she reached the gate to the aging estate, Cassie pulled into the winding driveway that led up to the house. She had always loved the charm of the old place, especially the brilliant rhododendrons and the multicolored azaleas that lined both sides of the driveway. The old Jeep and the big Harley-Davidson motorcycle that were parked haphazardly in the driveway, however, looked as out of place as the radio talk-show host had been since he moved into her neighborhood.

Eager to give the cocky old coot an up-close-and-personal look at the legal system he was always complaining about on his stupid radio program, Cassie switched off the engine and grabbed the furry scamp sitting next to her. Marching straight to the front door, Cassie paused on the stoop and pressed the doorbell long enough for the blast to wake the dead. When her adversary failed to appear from within his fortress, Cassie reached for the bell again, but the squirming captive in the crook of her arm saw his chance and wiggled from her grasp.

"You come back here this minute," Cassie yelled.

The naughty little maverick bounded around the side of the house and Cassie dashed after him. Charging through the back gate in hot pursuit, she almost had the miniature monster in her grasp, but a loud splash from the backyard pool brought her to a sudden stop. When she looked up, her eyes widened in disbelief as the lower half of a nude male body slipped beneath the surface of the shimmering blue water.

Ignoring her own gasp, Cassie willed herself to move, but the instincts that kept screaming *run* didn't relay the message to her addled brain fast enough. Before she could flee, a bronzed phantom with an upper torso reminiscent of the Incredible Hulk's broke the water's surface gracefully with muscled forearms stretched out before him.

Cassie watched in awe as Adonis himself made long, purposeful strides across the water in her direction. *This can't be Nick Hardin,* she kept assuring herself, but she'd never actually *seen* Nick Hardin before, not even a picture of him.

It was his politically incorrect attitude that led Cassie to believe he would be much older than this Greek god she had just caught in the buff. In fact, the mental picture Cassie had always put with that deep baritone voice on the radio was one of a middle-aged hippie who was still trying to cling to the lost age of sex, drugs and rock and roll.

Please, God, let this Chippendale refugee be Nick Hardin's pool man, Cassie prayed silently, aware that the naked stranger was now swimming dangerously close to the shallow end of the pool.

To her relief, he stopped when the water was still waist-high, ran a hand through his unfashionably long hair, then stared back at Cassie with eyes the color of midnight. "Well, good morning," he called out boldly. "I'd given up hope of the Biltmore Forest welcoming committee dropping by, but if *you're* the representative it was well worth the wait."

The second she heard that too-familiar baritone voice, Cassie felt a searing flush spread straight to the center of her cheeks. Squaring her shoulders, she sent him the type of icy stare that she usually reserved for the courtroom. "You're Nick Hardin?" she managed to say, already knowing the answer.

"Guilty as charged," he admitted with a cocksure grin. "And you are?"

"Sorry to disappoint you, Mr. Hardin, but I'm definitely not the welcoming committee," she informed him curtly, then pointed to the black-and-white half breed who was running up and down the edge of the pool, yapping at his master. "I brought your dog home, because…"

"Hey, if the mutt's been in your garbage, I'm sorry," Nick interrupted. "I found the little bandit at a garbage dump when he was only a pup. It's a bad habit of his I can't seem to break."

The overwhelming knowledge that the degenerate dog had credentials even worse than she imagined instantly erased any curiosity Cassie had about the part of Nick Hardin's body that was still under water. "Oh, I assure you, your dog's crime is much more serious than raiding trash cans," she remarked tersely. "Your *mutt,* as you call him, dug a hole under my fence this morning and accosted a world-champion show dog."

Cassie watched an amused look cross his painfully handsome face while he digested her statement. At about the time Cassie decided Nick Hardin was actually contemplating the seriousness of the situation, he burst out with the same gregarious laughter he'd exhibited when she called to complain about his stupid lawyer jokes.

How dare he laugh about his own negligence! Reaching for the first thing that caught her eye, Cassie grabbed a towel from a nearby deck chair and flung it in her tormentor's direction. "If I were you, I'd get out of the pool and get dressed, Mr. Hardin," she informed him curtly. "I doubt you're going to find things so funny when we discuss the extensive lawsuit I intend to file against you."

NICK CAUGHT THE TOWEL easily, but remained in the center of the pool, watching his exquisite guest stomp back around the side of the house. He'd always been a sucker for cutoffs, and this lady had a delectable little fanny that filled out the short cutoff jeans to perfection.

When he'd first surfaced from his dive, Nick decided his fuzzy head from his night out with the boys the previous evening was responsible for conjuring up the vision of loveliness he found standing beside his pool. When he started swimming in her direction, however, the shocked deer-in-the-headlights look she gave him convinced Nick that his visitor was real.

In no longer than it took to shake the water from his face, he had absorbed every detail of her more-than-pleasing appearance. She was literally stunning, even in cutoff jeans and a baggy T-shirt that had Run for Fun splashed across the front. Not that the loose-fitting T-shirt concealed her well-endowed bosom from Nick's prying eyes, because it didn't. No more than her extremely short cutoffs kept him from committing her long, perfectly shaped legs permanently to his memory.

The only problem seemed to be her age. Though her manner of speaking and the way she carried herself suggested she was older than she looked, her teenager-type attire and her slightly askew ponytail made Nick suspect she was barely past twenty. Enticing or not, women on the low side of twenty were much too young, even for a thirty-something rake such as he.

Pulling himself out of the pool, Nick wrapped the wet towel around his waist, then wandered into the house, oblivious to the dripping water that trailed across the expensive parquet floors. The last thing he needed to start his weekend off was another irate neighbor. He had left the rat race in Atlanta, seeking peace and solitude in the Blue Ridge Mountains, only to find when he arrived in Asheville that he'd traveled back in time fifty years. The upper-crust socialites who shared his lovely locality had been appalled by his long hair, outraged by his refusal to adhere to their silly rules and dress codes, and mortified by the big Harley-Davidson that had always been Nick's pride and joy. Now it seemed even his choice of pets didn't meet with their approval.

From the den, he grabbed the faded polo shirt and jeans he'd worn the night before, then tossed the dripping towel into the sink on the well-stocked wet bar that took up one side of the sparsely furnished room. Droplets of water still clung to his lean, muscular body, but Nick donned his clothes without toweling off, then slipped his feet into a pair of well-worn Birkenstock sandals. After raking his fingers though his sun-streaked hair, he pulled the wet mass to the back of his head, then used a leather strip he pulled from the back pocket of his jeans to secure his hair in a short ponytail.

His first instinct was to throw the irate beauty off his property, but Nick decided maybe it was time he took a more amicable approach where his fellow neighbors were concerned. He had, after all, invested a huge chunk of his financial reserves in the aging estate he now called home. If spreading a little harmony around the neighborhood could give him a reprieve from the scorn he'd been receiving to date, showing his good side might make life in Biltmore Forest a little more pleasant for everyone concerned.

"Stay," Nick told his unwanted shadow when the frisky terrier followed him faithfully down the hallway to the front door. "It appears you've already caused enough trouble for one day."

MINUTES LATER, NICK found his exquisite visitor propped against the luxury sedan that was sitting in the driveway next to his classic '47 flat-fender Jeep. Arms folded stubbornly across her chest, she still wore the same surly look on her face. Nick hooked his thumbs in the pockets of his jeans, then sauntered down the steps in her direction, wondering if he still had what it took to cajole his agitated visitor into a friendlier mood.

He attempted his most winning smile. "I was just getting ready to fill the espresso machine. If you'll join me, maybe we can discuss this dog situation over a cup of coffee."

Lifting her chin defiantly, his visitor glared in his direction. "This isn't a social call, Mr. Hardin. Everything we need to discuss can be discussed right here."

"Well at least drop that 'Mr. Hardin' crap," Nick said, trying to get at least one smile out of his attractive guest. "I'm Nick."

"And I'm what I think you referred to as a vulture on your

program several weeks ago," she replied, ignoring his out-stretched hand.

Nick paused, vaguely remembering the incident. But he stifled a laugh when he recalled the entire situation. "Ah, so you're the attorney who didn't particularly care for my joke about…"

He watched her aqua-blue eyes immediately turn a shade darker and several degrees colder. "About vultures and lawyers?" she quizzed, finishing his sentence.

Nick grinned in spite of himself. "Hey, I'm sorry you didn't particularly care for that joke, counselor. But like I told you when you called, you can always tune me out if you don't like my program."

"Oh, I've tuned you out, all right," Cassie retorted. "I suspect hundreds of other women who don't care for your chauvinistic attitude have done the same."

"Chauvinistic?" Nick moaned, pretending to be hurt. "Hey, you're way off base on that one, counselor. You see, I've always been extremely fond of *women.*"

"As long as they're barefoot and pregnant, and know their place, you mean?" she challenged.

Nick flinched. In all fairness, he could understand that his lawyer jokes, and now the incident involving his dog, might be responsible for launching a bumblebee up the legal eagle's attractive little behind. But he was quickly growing weary of being attacked in his own driveway. Determined to make his snotty visitor vanish as quickly as she'd appeared, Nick deliberately let his coal-black eyes travel over her body with a look that even this uptight attorney couldn't misinterpret.

And only when she flinched did Nick break his ill-mannered leer.

"Sorry if my appraisal made you uncomfortable," Nick lied. "But since you're already barefoot, I was just trying to imagine the *pregnant* part."

Cassie gasped and looked down at all ten of her hot-pink

polished toes. In her haste to get retribution for the heinous crime Nick Hardin's dog had committed, she had completely forgotten that she left home looking like some reject from a bargain-basement sale. She hadn't even realized that she wasn't wearing shoes.

Clenching her fists to keep from slapping him, Cassie struggled until she finally regained her ability to speak. "If that was meant to shock me, it didn't," she huffed. "In fact, that's exactly the type of statement I would expect from a man like you."

Raising one eyebrow slightly, Nick grinned. "Hey, I hate to point out the obvious, but you're standing in my driveway, counselor, I'm not standing in yours. If you find me so offensive, you can always leave."

His comment brought an even deeper shade of pink to Cassie's cheeks. "Oh, believe me, I'll be more than happy to leave once we come to an understanding about the damage your idiot dog…"

"Let's see. How did you so aptly put that before?" Nick interrupted, bursting out laughing again. "Didn't you say he *accosted…?*"

"That's exactly what I said," Cassie snapped, cutting him off. "But your mutt didn't assault just any dog. I'm talking about a priceless dog. A dog that would put a dent in any bank account. Even one as healthy as yours."

She paused then, giving Nick a chance to comment on the significance of her statement. Instead, he remained silent, keeping his eyes fixed permanently on her full, moist lips. The same type of lips he would have preferred tasting and teasing, instead of watching them spout out a bunch of silly nonsense about some famous show dog.

"Since I'm sure you do little else than listen to your own voice on the radio," Cassie accused, "you obviously failed to read the front page of the *Asheville-Citizen Times* a few weeks ago when they did a feature story about the local bichon frise who won Best-in-Show at the Westminster Dog Show in New York City.''

"Let me guess," Nick scoffed, thinking that even the name of the damn dog sounded pretentious. "This...*be-shon free-za,* or whatever name you called the silly dog, just happens to be..."

"How clever of you to figure it out," Cassie snapped.

Stalling for time, Nick let out a long sigh, then removed the leather strip from his ponytail and forced his fingers through his still-damp hair. "So let me get this right. Your fancy show dog didn't bother to ask for credentials before she lifted her manicured little tail for the first stray male who came along, and you think that gives you the right to sue *me?* Get serious, counselor. How do I know my dog wasn't in line behind some other hound who got to her first?"

"That's so typically male!" Cassie shrieked. "That's always a man's first line of defense, isn't it? Always try to pawn it off on someone else."

Nick shrugged, unwilling to admit or deny the accusation. "Then what about calling in a vet if you're so appalled that your dog didn't hold out for a champion stud? I've heard they have this shot you can give..."

"You, Mr. Hardin, are even more disgusting than I imagined," Cassie interrupted. "How brilliant of you to come up with a man's second line of defense!" Shaking her finger wildly in his direction, Cassie added, "If you think for one minute I'd risk harming a priceless show dog and possibly prevent her from having *champion* puppies someday, you're crazy."

Unimpressed with her tirade, Nick leaned against the fender of the Lexus while the hyped-up attorney paced back and forth in his driveway, stewing over his unhelpful suggestions. He was tempted to grab her and hold her in a bear hug until she finally calmed down, but he was actually enjoying watching her flounce around his driveway with her fists clenched at her sides. Most women he met were all over him before he had a chance to say hello, but Nick already knew this sexy spitfire would probably scratch his eyes out if he even took a step in her direction. And the fact that she might intrigued him.

"And don't you dare say something stupid, like requesting a doggy paternity test," Cassie warned, wheeling around to face him again. "I caught your dog in the act, remember? And if I end up playing nursemaid to a litter of unregistered puppies, I intend to hold you and your worthless dog totally responsible."

With that said, she marched to her car, opened the door and slid behind the wheel. "I'm taking Duchess to the vet the second I get back home," she announced as she fumbled with the ignition. "I realize you have little use for legal advice, but it would be wise if you obeyed the leash law and keep that flea-bitten mutt at home where he should have been in the first place."

Nick suppressed a laugh, then quickly placed his hand on the driver's side door. Leaning down, he sent his beautiful but angry visitor a slow, seductive smile. "Hey, just for the record, counselor, it might ease your mind to know that our dogs may be better suited than you think."

"Not in this lifetime," Cassie assured him, grinding the Lexus into reverse.

"But didn't you just say your dog's name was Duchess?"

"What does that have to do with anything?" she snapped, taking the bait.

Nick laughed the same hearty laugh she had heard on the radio and by the pool. "Because my dog has a royal name, too. I named him Earl."

"After one of your motorcycle-riding, beer-swilling friends, I'm sure," Cassie shot back, then roared out of the driveway, coming dangerously close to hitting the big Harley Hog that was parked at the edge of Nick Hardin's paved drive.

2

IN LESS THAN AN HOUR after she roared out of Nick Hardin's driveway, Cassie drove into the parking lot of an elaborate brick building and pulled in beside a lone red Porsche, thinking that she should have taken her best friend's advice and gone into veterinary medicine instead of law. Dee had been savvy enough to tap into the gold mine that surrounded the movers and shakers in the dog world. Limiting her practice to champion canines only, Dee wouldn't have allowed a cur like Nick Hardin's to place a grimy paw on the pavement in the parking lot, much less receive treatment at the chic canine facility appropriately known as Pedigree, Ltd.

Cassie hopped out of the car, dragged Duchess's crate from the passenger's seat, then hurried to the glass front door of the building that had Your Champion Is The Heart Of Our Business stenciled in gold letters across the front.

"Dee...we're here," Cassie yelled the second she stepped inside.

"Well, hello Daisy Mae," Dee Bishop teased as she appraised Cassie's appearance.

Cassie frowned at her friend's attempted wit. She still hadn't taken time to change from her shorts and T-shirt, but she *had* grabbed her sandals this time. "Don't start with me, Dee," Cassie warned. "I've already had a morning straight from hell and it's only ten o'clock."

"Well, your reason for dragging my butt in here on a Saturday better be a good one," the tall blonde said as she pulled on a lab coat. "I don't ruin my weekends for just anyone."

"Spare me the poor pitiful-me act," Cassie grumbled. "As much as my mother pays you to take care of this fancy dog of hers, I think you can afford the sacrifice."

"Touché," Dee conceded. "Follow me."

Crate in hand, Cassie followed her friend down the hallway to the first doggy examining room. "I know I was vague on the phone, Dee, but I wanted to get here as fast as I could."

Dee waited until Cassie placed the crate on the table before she unfastened the latch and gently lifted the tiny dog out. "Hey there, Miss Duchess," Dee cooed. "What's wrong, sweetie? Are you under the weather today?"

"No. She was *under* the sex-crazed terrier who lives down the street."

Clutching Duchess to her breast as if Cassie had arranged for the lewd rendezvous herself, Dee glared in Cassie's direction. "That isn't even funny, Cassie. The champion sire your mother arranged for will be here on Monday. If you've allowed another dog to get to Duchess first, your mother will *kill* you."

Cassie's deadpan look spoke volumes. "Of course Lenora's going to kill me, you nitwit. Why do you think I was practically in tears when I called you?"

Ignoring the shocked look on Dee's perfectly made-up face, Cassie began pacing around the room, talking more to herself than to her judgmental friend. "Believe me, Dee, if you think I'm taking this lightly, you're badly mistaken. I'm the one who insisted that I should stay behind to keep Duchess and make sure everything went as planned with those breeders from London. 'I can handle it, Mother,' I kept saying until I was blue in the face. And do you know what's so funny?" Cassie added with a hysterical giggle. "For once, Lenora actually trusted me to have enough sense to take care of things. Leave it to me to screw it up and only reinforce my mother's opinion that I'm not capable of doing anything right.''

"Lenora doesn't think anyone's capable of doing anything right but herself," Dee mumbled.

Cassie's eyes narrowed. "Don't you think I realize that?"

"You already know what I think," Dee insisted. "I think it's way past time for you to cut the apron strings and stop trying to live up to Lenora's expectations, Cassie. You're twenty-eight years old. Get a life and put that dutiful-daughter act to rest."

Cassie frowned. "Spare me your dutiful-daughter speech, Dee. You've been delivering it since we were in grade school."

"And I'll keep delivering it until you get a little backbone and at least move out on your own," Dee insisted.

Circling the room again, Cassie sighed, thinking about her overbearing, hypochondria-impaired mother whom she loved in spite of everything. "You know as well as I do the minute I left home, Lenora would take to her sickbed like she did the last time I mentioned moving out. She expects me to live at home until I get married, Dee. It's Mother's twisted form of punishment for me being twenty-eight and still single."

"Well, if I were you, I'd risk it," Dee argued. "Call Lenora's bluff about that phony heart murmur of hers."

The image of her mother, left hand to her forehead, right hand draped dramatically over her heart instantly crossed Cassie's mind. "Oh, Lenora definitely has a heart murmur, Dee. It murmurs *suck-er* every time I play along when she fakes another siege with her imaginary angina."

Dee laughed, but shook her head in disgust. "I've never been able to understand the hold Lenora has over you, Cassie. You're one of the most talented, confident and self-reliant women I know—except when it comes to your mother."

When Cassie didn't bother to respond, Dee realized the

subject was closed. Taking a pair of rubber gloves from beneath the examining table, she snapped them into place and transformed from best friend into Dr. Bishop, canine caregiver. She began feeling along Duchess's hindquarters.

Looking up at Cassie, Dee said, "And you're positive Duchess and this stray male made contact?"

"Oh, they definitely made contact," Cassie confirmed. "If I'd found them sharing a cigarette when I finally got over the shock, it wouldn't have surprised me a bit."

"Surely you weren't letting her run loose knowing her condition?"

Cassie felt like slapping the dear doctor across the face. "Of course I wasn't letting her run loose, Dee. I had the little witch in the backyard. Her boyfriend was just aroused enough to dig a hole under the fence."

"You'd be surprised how inventive dogs can be when they're ready to mate."

"Oh, I've been surprised enough for a lifetime," Cassie wailed. "Just tell me what we can do about it now."

"There isn't much we can do, after the fact."

"But don't you have one of those pee-on-a-stick doggy tests or something? Surely you have some space-age method that can tell me if I should start knitting little mongrel puppy booties by the dozen."

Dr. Bishop finished her exam and tossed the gloves in the waste can. "I can do an ultrasound later, but it will take at least nineteen days before I'm able to detect any fetuses."

"Nineteen days!" Cassie exploded. "And what am I supposed to do in the meantime? The grand stud from London is supposed to arrive on Monday."

"And that may be your salvation, Cass. If Duchess is receptive to the champion male bichon, and the mutt didn't impregnate her first, you may get your champion puppies, after all. It isn't uncommon for a bitch to mate with more than one dog, you know. In fact, I've seen litters that have two entirely different sires.''

Cassie groaned. "Must you dog people always use the *B* word so causally?" Cassie scolded. "Even though I'd like to strangle the little floozy myself right now, I feel like a traitor allowing you to refer to Duchess as a bitch."

"Well, you'd better get used to the sound of the *B* word, Miss Priss," Dee teased. "I'm sure *bitch* will certainly cross Lenora's mind if Duchess ends up with a litter of unregistered puppies."

"That's what I love about you, Dee," Cassie scolded. "You're always so supportive."

Cassie made several more laps around the small room before she said, "I hate to even mention this, Dee. And don't start throwing things, but I've heard there's some type of shot…"

Dee sent Cassie a look that stopped her midsentence. "Yes, there is a 'mismating' shot available if that's what you're referring to, but I'd never use it personally. It can be detrimental to the bitch's health."

Cassie frowned. "So, what are we going to do now?"

Dee leaned against the examining table, displaying her best I'm-the-doctor-you're-the-buffoon face. "Well, we certainly can't take a chance that Duchess might be exposed again before the proper sire arrives," Dee said. "I think you should leave Duchess here with me. I know one of the breeder's stipulations was that you keep the dogs in a home environment instead of a kennel, but it makes much more sense for me to supervise the breeding here. I have the facilities to keep the dogs confined, and I can keep an eye on both of them in case there are any complications."

Cassie rolled her eyes. "And what am I supposed to tell the breeder? The man was rude enough when I called to inform him that Duchess's trainer was in the hospital and that I'd be taking care of the dogs in his absence."

"Let me handle that part. I can come up with a long list of valid reasons why I should monitor the breeding."

When Cassie nodded in agreement, Dee added, "And by the way. I'll also need to examine your neighbor's dog. I don't want to take any chances where Duchess is concerned, Cassie. The dog could even be diseased, plus if he's a mixed breed and their little rendezvous was successful, the puppies could be too large and Duchess could have trouble whelping."

Cassie's laugh was cynical. "Fat chance of that happening. I just had a screaming fit in the man's front yard less than an hour ago."

Ignoring Cassie's comment, Dee turned to the small basin next to the examining table and lathered her hands. "Then call him back and apologize, Cassie. Do whatever it takes. Like I said, Duchess is the one we have to think about now."

Cassie shook her head furiously. "The day I apologize to Nick Hardin, is the day..."

Dee whirled back around, ignoring the soap that splattered on the floor. "Get out!" she gasped. "Surely you don't mean the stray belonged to your neighborhood's resident Hell's Angel?"

"Oh, he's an angel straight from the gates of hell, all right," Cassie remarked, chewing at her bottom lip. "I just didn't expect him to be..."

"A cross between Antonio Banderas and Brad Pitt—with a body better than Sly Stallone's?" Dee quizzed, exercising the ability all close friends have of finishing each other's sentences.

Cassie's interest perked slightly. "So? You've met my infamous neighbor."

"Yeah, several months ago. I know you were livid after his smart reply about his lawyer jokes, Cassie, but he's really a great guy. He and Ron are organizing a committee to help children deal with the problems they face after a divorce. Ron says he's really great with the kids, and he's real generous with his time.''

Disturbed by the news that Nick Hardin might have even one redeeming quality, Cassie said, ''Well, he's an arrogant ass, if you ask me.''

Dee shrugged her shoulders, then turned back to rinse the soap from her hands. ''Well, you know what I always say. Nick Hardin's one man I sure wouldn't...''

''Kick out of bed,'' Cassie finished with a groan, then added, ''You're incorrigible, Dee. If I had a hunk like Ron for a fiancé, I'd never look twice at another man.''

''But you do have a hunk, remember? Or has your *in*significant other finally given up on the ice maiden who won't share his bed, *or* accept his proposal to become Mrs. Mark Winston?''

At the mention of Mark Winston's name, Cassie grabbed her friend's arm and stared in disbelief at Dee's fancy Lady Rolex watch. ''Damn! Mark's supposed to pick me up in less than an hour, Dee. I'm supposed to attend one of those stupid fund-raisers with him at noon.''

''I know you say you aren't in love with Mark, Cassie, and even if Lenora did handpick him as your perfect mate, you have to admit he's a very ambitious man. Assistant D.A. now. Senator Mark Winston tomorrow. You could have a great life playing hostess in Washington to all those dignitaries from around the world.''

Ignoring Dee's boring assessment of Mark Winston's credentials, Cassie blew a kiss toward the little strumpet in the crate. ''Take care of Duchess, Dee,'' Cassie called over her shoulder as she ran from the room. ''I'll see you Monday when the Brits arrives. And once this is all over I want you to send Nick Hardin a huge bill for your services.''

WHEN CASSIE TURNED INTO her driveway thirty minutes later, Mark Winston was standing on her front porch with a scowl on his face. Looking down over the top of his designer glasses, her insignificant other, as Dee called him, reminded Cassie of a disapproving schoolmaster waiting for a tardy student.

Forcing a smile she certainly didn't feel, Cassie stepped from the car, aware that Mark's scowl quickly changed to a look of total shock when he noticed her untidy appearance. "What's going on, Cassandra?" he demanded, glancing at his watch as if God had suddenly appointed him official time-keeper. "You aren't even ready and it's time to leave."

Cassie walked past Mark as he stated the obvious, deciding she preferred extensive root canal therapy to sitting through another luncheon while Mark made a boring speech. "I'm sorry, Mark, but you'll have to go without me," she said over her shoulder as she entered the house. "Not that you bothered to ask, but I've had an emergency this morning."

Having entered the foyer behind her, most women's version of "tall, dark and handsome" followed Cassie down the hallway. When he marched into the Collinses' rambling kitchen, he removed the jacket of his expensive Italian suit, slung it over the back of one of the kitchen chairs, then stood with his hands at his waist, waiting for an explanation. Cassie could see the crisp cut of his freshly starched Brooks Brothers shirt from the corner of her eye, but she continued to ignore him while she poured herself a much-needed glass of iced tea.

"Well? Don't keep me in suspense, Cassandra. What was the big emergency?"

Mark's insistence on always using her formal name, the way her mother did, had the same effect on Cassie as hearing fingernails scrape down a blackboard. Feeling like a child being interrogated by an angry parent, she whirled around and said, "I'll tell you what the big emergency was, Mark. A mongrel dog from hell dug his way under the fence and seduced Duchess this morning before I could even swallow my first sip of coffee.''

"And?" he exploded.

Bracing herself to keep from grabbing Mark by his two-hundred-dollar tie and tightening the knot until his eyes bulged, Cassie answered through clenched teeth, "*And,* after I rescued Duchess, I tracked down the dog's owner and gave him a huge piece of my mind. And then I had to take Duchess to Dee's office to have her examined.''

Mark frowned, mulling over her words. "You said you gave *him* a huge piece of your mind. I certainly hope you haven't said something to offend anyone in the neighborhood, Cassandra. Your father has personally introduced me to everyone in Biltmore Forest and you know I'm depending on every vote I can get when I run for office this fall.''

"Believe me, Mark, Father didn't introduce you to this joker. It was Biltmore Forest's biggest outcast, Nick Hardin.''

"Nick Hardin?" Mark repeated, his dark brows knitting in a frown.

"Yes, Nick Hardin. Like I said, I've already given him a huge piece of my mind, and if Duchess turns up pregnant, I'm going to sue that worthless...''

"And you went to Nick Hardin's looking like that?" Mark interrupted, letting his eyes travel over Cassie's under-clothed body. "Good grief, Cassie. I'm surprised he didn't drag you into the bushes and ravish you the same way his dog did Duchess.''

Cassie met Mark's cold stare, unimpressed with his attitude or with his sudden show of jealousy. "Is it some written rule that a man starts thinking with his family jewels the second the woman he's dating comes in contact with another man?" she demanded.

Mark's face reddened. "Well, how do you expect me to

react when you go traipsing off to some hoodlum's house looking like the current playmate of the month?''

When Cassie refused to answer, Mark eventually broke the silence. Using a much softer tone he said, ''Look, I don't like the idea of you living in the same neighborhood as an outlaw like Nick Hardin, much less you showing up at his house in that outfit. He's trouble, Cassandra. Leave him alone.''

And he's also gorgeous, Cassie thought to herself as the memory of her neighbor's tight naked buns flashed through her mind. When she noticed Mark glance at his watch again, she said, ''You'd better go, Mark. You'll be late for your speech.''

''You know how important these functions are to my campaign,'' Mark grumbled, unwilling to be dismissed without having the last word.

''Which is exactly why you should go,'' Cassie told him. ''It would take me at least another hour before I could be ready.''

Mark's jaw muscles tightened as he sent her a scathing look. ''Did it ever occur to you that I deserved the simple courtesy of a phone call, Cassandra?'' he asked, his temper flaring again. ''Who knows? Maybe I would have asked someone else to the luncheon. You obviously forgot all about me the second you had the opportunity to show up on Nick Hardin's doorstep practically naked.''

''Oh, for God's sake, Mark, you're blowing this out of proportion and you know it,'' Cassie snapped back. ''And excuse me for having the misguided notion that I meant a little more to you than just some warm body sitting at your elbow when you took the podium.''

Mark glared back at her, then ran a hand through his dark, perfectly groomed hair. ''You *are* special, and you know it,'' he mumbled halfheartedly. ''Maybe I would feel more secure if you were willing to make a commitment.''

Cassie stared at the man who was her grandfather's senatorial protegé and her mother's answer to who's who on the social roster. "I've told you a million times, Mark, when I decide to accept a marriage proposal, it will be based on love. Not because it will benefit my future husband's political career."

Mark frowned, but he didn't deny her accusation. "Well, it certainly won't benefit my career or my campaign if word gets out that my girlfriend is hanging around with a bum like Nick Hardin."

"Why on earth are you so obsessed with Nick Hardin?"

"I told you. He's trouble. Surely you aren't naive enough to think he won't have a field day with your tirade about this dog problem on his damn radio program, Cassandra. I can't afford a scandal like that this close to election, and you know it. Maybe you should call him and apologize."

"I'll do no such thing!"

Mark's face turned crimson. "Listen, Cassandra, either you apologize to that idiot and head off the obvious disaster you'll face if you go to war with him, or you can forget about me. It's up to you. Make your choice now."

Cassie felt every drop of blood in her body drain to her feet. "If Duchess does turn up with a litter of unregistered puppies, Mark, I *will* sue Nick Hardin for damages, campaign or no campaign. So, *you* make the choice now."

Grabbing his jacket from the kitchen chair, Mark sent her a final disapproving look. "Remember, this was your call, Cassandra."

"No, this is your *loss,* you self-centered…" Cassie groped for the right word as Mark stormed out of the room. "Politician!" she finally screamed, but her brave words rang hollow when she heard the front door slam in the distance.

Kicking the refrigerator, which only resulted in scraping the bare toes her sandal left exposed, Cassie let out a yelp, then limped to the kitchen table and, with an exasperated sigh, flopped down in one of the chairs. As amazing as it seemed, only twenty-four hours ago Cassie thought she had the entire world by the tail. Who would have guessed that the wag of a particular little tail would turn her world upside down?

In the short span of one morning, she'd allowed a priceless show dog to do the wild thing with a mutt straight out of the garbage heap. She'd practically been arrested for making crank calls to the security police. And now she had willingly liberated her mother's idea of the perfect husband to go off and find a more suitable mate.

Well, that's two major strikes against me as far as Mother is concerned, Cassie thought. *First Duchess, and now Mark.*

The disastrous turn of events would certainly be good for at least one month of sickbed silence from her mother. And though Cassie should have been near tears, oddly, she wasn't. In fact, the insane irony of the situation actually struck her funny. She had separated Duchess from her boyfriend, and now Duchess had indirectly returned the favor.

Letting out a long sigh, Cassie rolled her head from side to side, trying to loosen the huge knot of tension that was now trapped between her neck and her shoulders. Praying that a hot shower might relieve at least the muscle-related part of her problem, Cassie started for her bedroom on the second floor. She had just reached the kitchen door when the shrill sound of the telephone sounded through the room.

Deciding it was Mark, calling from his cell phone to apologize, Cassie let the phone ring several times. An apology from Mark was the last thing she wanted. In fact, Cassie didn't want Mark period. Although her mother had visions of monogrammed towels and dirty diapers where she and Mark were concerned, Cassie had known from the beginning she would never let things go beyond dating with Mark. She had only kept up the pretense to keep Lenora off her back.

After the fifth ring, Cassie answered the kitchen extension, prepared to tell Mark it was definitely over between them. Instead, she almost dropped the receiver when a familiar voice floated over the line.

"Look, counselor, I know we both got a little hostile earlier, but I'm sure this is something we can settle over a chilled bottle of wine and a sensible conversation. How about eight o'clock? Your place or mine?"

Cassie was dumbfounded. "You have to be the most arrogant, insufferable man I've ever met," Cassie informed him.

"Well, nobody's perfect," Nick agreed, "but you're the one who said we had a problem to solve. I'm just suggesting that we settle things in a much more pleasant atmosphere than a courtroom."

Cassie laughed in spite of herself as a vision of Nick Hardin ushering dozens of women into his "much more pleasant atmosphere" danced through her mind. "Oh, I'm sure you handle all of your problems with a bottle of chilled wine and a *sensual* conversation, Mr. Hardin...."

"I said *sensible* conversation."

"But we both know you meant *sensual,* don't we?" Cassie chided.

When Nick didn't answer, Cassie added, "I left Duchess with the vet earlier, but it'll take several weeks before the vet can determine if she's pregnant."

"And then what?" Nick quizzed.

"Then you can save yourself a lot of trouble and pay for the damages your dog caused, or we can settle this in court."

"You're really serious about this, aren't you, counselor?"

"What do you think?" Cassie challenged.

He laughed. "Lady, I think if you'd let nature take its course the way your fancy show dog did, you'd have a much better outlook on life."

NICK JERKED THE RECEIVER away from his ear when she slammed down the phone, breaking their connection. Chuckling to himself, he tried to imagine the flustered look on her perfect face, but his thoughts eventually switched to more important details. Details like whether or not she was still wearing those Daisy Dukes that had driven him crazy.

Tossing the phone on the cushion beside him, he stretched out his long legs and leaned back on the sofa with his hands clasped behind his head. He hadn't really expected the enraged Miss Collins to accept his offer, but he couldn't resist calling the sexy wench, if only to rattle her chain a little. After all, this was the second time Cassandra Collins had gotten in his face. First with her complaint about his lawyer jokes, and now by storming into his life making threats about suing him over some stupid show dog.

Glancing back at the notepad in his lap, Nick looked over the composite of information he'd been able to collect on the feisty female only minutes after she'd left him standing in a cloud of dust in his driveway. A single phone call to one of his buddies at the *Asheville-Citizen Times* had given him all the information he needed.

According to his buddy, the dog actually belonged to a Mrs. Lenora Collins, the attorney's mother. The guy also knew enough about the Collins family to give Nick the full scoop. Cassandra Collins was the only child of parents who both came from old money, born with the proverbial silver spoon in her mouth. Her maternal grandfather, now deceased, had been a respected judge. Her paternal grandfather was a retired United States senator, still alive and still very active in politics.

After graduating at the top of her class from the University of North Carolina, the lovely Miss Collins had returned home to Asheville and joined her father at the family firm of Collins and Collins. Without a doubt, the pretty lady's pedigree was every bit as impressive as the silly dog she was so upset about. Nick pored over the rest of her vital statistics, which included everything from her age to the fact that she was currently dating the assistant district attorney.

He kept telling himself that he was only interested in the information because the legal barracuda might possibly hit him with the ridiculous lawsuit she was threatening. And despite the hassle it would cause him, Nick wished the lovely lady would make that silly mistake. After all, his syndicated radio program did have the ears of thousands of listeners who thrived on controversy. Taking her down a peg or two over the air would be fairly simple. Unless, of course, those long tanned legs of hers kept turning up in his memory to interfere with his usual killer instincts.

She was definitely attractive. No, when he thought about it, she was downright beautiful. But she was also the epitome of everything Nick *didn't* want in a woman. He would never settle down with some hoity-toity socialite, any more than he would marry some career-driven female who would probably refuse to share his last name.

And especially not a woman who had chosen law as her profession.

His own mother's obsession with her career had been responsible for making Nick gun-shy where career-oriented women were concerned. Her preference for a career over being a wife and mother had resulted in a nasty divorce between his parents when Nick was only ten. He'd been bounced back and forth between his parents until he turned sixteen and put an end to the madness himself. It was the endless steam of court battles that had fueled Nick's hatred for the legal profession. Even the superb strawberry-blonde who was threatening to sue him now didn't change Nick's opinion that greed, more often than justice, was the main reason most people embraced the law as their chosen profession.

Letting out a loud groan when Earl sailed through the air and landed in the middle of his stomach, Nick wrestled the squeaky toy away from his playful partner, then tossed it to the far end of the room. After pulling himself up from the sofa, he strolled through the patio doors, then slumped into one of the deck chairs scattered around the pool.

"If you end up being a daddy, Earl, we'll have one hell of a fight on our hands," Nick told his faithful companion when Earl returned with his squeaky toy and nuzzled against Nick's hand.

But even as Nick sat in the afternoon sun planning his defense strategy, he couldn't shake the feeling that his perceptive sixth sense was somehow alerting him to danger. Could matching wits with the leggy lawyer be menacing enough to trip his intuitive powers?

Possibly.

And in more ways than he cared to admit.

3

To Cassie's horror, the scheduled rendezvous with the expensive English prince from London was a total calamity. Not only would Duchess not let the courtly stud get near her, she also bit the yapping powder puff squarely on his royal nose, prompting his snooty owner to threaten a lawsuit of his own. Thankfully, when Cassie upped the already preposterous stud fee, which had to be paid whether the dogs mated or not, she'd managed to calm the man's ruffled feathers.

Now the only hurdle that remained was the ultrasound Dee was going to perform to see if Earl had been successful in making Duchess a mommy.

Forcing thoughts of fleeing to South America from her mind, Cassie reluctantly handed her keys to the valet parking attendant at Asheville's impressive Grove Park Inn. The last thing she'd wanted to do that evening was attend the annual fund-raiser for the local historical society. Especially since Mark Winston would be there in all his glory with his new lady on his arm.

Cassie's pride, however, wouldn't allow her to stay at home. She knew the rumors would be bad enough if she made an appearance. But if she stayed away, she figured she would forever be dubbed as "the idiot who let Mark Winston get away."

Crossing the lobby, Cassie took a deep breath before stepping into the large ballroom that was housing the charitable event. As luck would have it, the first person she saw was Evelyn Van Arbor, Asheville's biggest gossip.

Hurrying to the cocktail bar on the far side of the room, Cassie purposely ignored the old snoop, and thought she'd been successful until the woman's shrill voice rang out behind her.

"Cassandra, darling. Wait up."

Steeling herself, Cassie turned to face the blue-haired piranha, knowing Evelyn would feast on her every word. After the old woman kissed the air on both sides of Cassie's face, Cassie said, "You look glamorous as usual, Evelyn."

"And so do you, dear," Evelyn gushed, then added, "I can't tell you how delighted I am that you decided to come, Cassandra. I was afraid you'd let this horrible misfortune with Mark Winston turn you into a bitter recluse."

It took all of her composure, but Cassie managed a smile. "I'm not sure I know what you mean, Evelyn."

The woman patted Cassie's shoulder sympathetically. "You don't have to act so brave with me, you poor little thing. Mark's an idiot. And you're so much prettier than that flighty Dianna Nugent."

Cassie's smile was now so forced it threatened to make huge cracks in both sides of her face. "I know there's been a lot of speculation about me and Mark the last few months, Evelyn, but we've never been anything more than good friends. I assure you, I couldn't be happier for both of them."

"Oh, you're much too gracious for your own good," Evelyn complained as she nodded toward Mark and Dianna, who were twirling around the dance floor. "Besides," she whispered, leaning close enough to make Cassie nauseous from her overpowering perfume, "Dianna's father might be a doctor, but he isn't a *good* doctor, judging from the malpractice suits that have been filed against him. Mark would have been better off staying with you, where he belonged. At least your father and your grandfather share his interests in politics."

Cassie started to comment, but froze when a pair of black eyes she hadn't counted on seeing at the fund-raiser locked with her own. As if her evening hadn't started out badly enough, she now found Nick Hardin standing at the opposite end of the bar.

Her heart skipped a beat when he sent her a cordial nod, then graciously lifted his glass in her direction, offering a toast. *God, please don't let him come over here,* she prayed silently, then quickly dismissed him by turning her back.

Aware that her hands were shaking when she accepted a glass of champagne from the attentive bartender, Cassie swallowed most of the expensive liquid in one easy gulp, then reluctantly turned her attention back to the lesser of two evils. "I'm sorry, Evelyn. What was your question again?"

"I asked what part of Europe your parents were touring now?"

Before Cassie could answer, the old woman leaned forward and grabbed her arm. "Don't look now, but that horrible Nick Hardin is headed our way. I can't believe he had the nerve to show up here, can you? Especially after that episode at the country club. Why, the very nerve of him riding his filthy motorcycle up on the country club lawn and parking—"

"Good evening, ladies," Nick interrupted, silencing Evelyn Van Arbor's rant.

Cassie took a deep breath, reluctantly turning around to face Nick. Immediately, she felt her knees buckle. Dressed in a snazzy designer tux with his shoulder-length hair slicked back in a perfect Steven Segal queue at his nape, he looked like a cross between Cinderella's Prince Charming and a modern-day action hero. And despite her first impulse, which was to punch him in the nose for the lewd comment he'd made on the telephone about "letting nature take its course," he was so wickedly handsome Cassie wasn't sure she could trust herself in his presence.

Ignoring the cold reception he was receiving from the upper-crust matriarch standing beside her, Nick nodded a cordial greeting to Evelyn, then openly appraised the strapless black cocktail dress that fit Cassie like a second skin.

"You certainly look ravishing tonight, counselor," he drawled in his deep, honey-smooth voice.

The fact that he was openly undressing her with his eyes while a room full of her peers looked on made Cassie curse herself for giving into a whim and wearing the extremely short frock that was capturing his attention. She'd only worn the stupid thing because Mark detested her in anything flashy. Now it seemed her silly attempt at revenge on Mark had ultimately backfired in her face.

When his eyes left her cleavage long enough to look her in the face, he asked, "How about a spin around the dance floor, counselor? It is, after all, for a very noble cause."

"I'd rather walk barefoot on hot coals, Mr. Hardin," Cassie assured him through clenched teeth.

She'd meant to insult him, but instead he laughed goodnaturedly at her rebuff, then shrugged nonchalantly. "Well, you can't blame a guy for wanting at least one dance with the sexiest lady in the room, can you?"

"Of all the nerve..." gasped Evelyn Van Arbor.

Cassie ignored the old snob's outburst and sent Nick a lethal look that said "go away." It was bad enough that everyone in the room was already buzzing about Mark throwing her over for Dianna Nugent. But if the elite of Asheville caught her conversing with the devil himself, she knew the rumors would take on a whole new life of their own.

When she sent him another frosty glare, it seemed to do the trick. Nick smiled, made a cordial little bow, then said, "Since it's obvious I can't interest you in a dance, then I'll do the honorable thing and clear the way for someone you might find more suitable."

When Cassie refused to comment, Nick sent her another mocking grin. "Have a nice evening, ladies."

He turned and walked away, leaving Cassie feeling extremely guilty. Especially since he'd been so gracious when she'd purposely tried to embarrass him. Normally, she wouldn't have acted so rude, but her gut instinct told her it was safer if Nick Hardin thought she was a kindred spirit to the mass of insufferable snobs who were gathered together for the evening. The taunting look in his sultry black eyes told Cassie he already knew she found him attractive. And she did. Even though they were complete opposites.

She almost smiled, thinking that referring to her and Nick Hardin as opposites was certainly the understatement of the century. They were like oil and water. Like fire and ice. They were the most unlikely match Cassie could possibly imagine. And for her own sake, she knew it was better to keep it that way.

Still reeling from the close encounter, she motioned for the bartender again. The man quickly refilled her glass, but as Cassie brought the glass to her lips, Evelyn Van Arbor leaned forward and said loud enough for the entire room to hear, "You did the right thing, Cassandra. It's time a derelict like Nick Hardin realizes that he'll never be accepted at a social gathering in this city."

Cassie sputtered in her champagne and jerked her head around in time to see that the woman's rude comment had brought Nick to a mid-stride stop. Turning slowly back to face them again, he wore the same cocky grin she remembered from the morning she first found Nick swimming naked in his pool. She shivered.

"Oh, by the way, counselor," Nick called across a room that was now so quiet Cassie could hear her own breathing. "You never did telephone me with the results of that pregnancy test."

"Dear Heavenly Father…" Evelyn Van Arbor wailed, and dropped the champagne glass she was holding in her wrinkled, diamond-laden hand.

Cassie instantly sprang forward and grabbed Nick by the

arm before he could slither off into the sea of people, who were all now staring in their direction. Pulling him toward the exit door, she managed to push Nick outside onto the large veranda that ran along the back side of the inn. But by the time she hurried out the door behind him, Cassie could already hear the excited whispers skipping across the crowd.

"Yeah, I like this much better," Nick announced when Cassie stomped up beside him. "Excellent choice, counselor. And it's such a beautiful night, too. Much too pleasant to waste inside with all those stuffy friends of yours."

"How dare you say something like that in front of that old gossip." Cassie fumed.

"What? Did I say something wrong?"

"You know perfectly well you said something wrong," Cassie snapped. "And by the time Evelyn Van Arbor spices up the story, it'll be all over Asheville tomorrow that I'm pregnant with your illegitimate child."

"But that's how I prefer my women, remember? Barefoot and pregnant."

"You're impossible," Cassie said, resisting the urge to reach out and strangle him. "How did you get invited to this benefit in the first place? You know these people despise you."

Nick winked, unruffled by her comment. "You'd be surprised what the right amount of money can buy in this world, Miss Collins."

Cassie sent him a murderous glare. "I hate to disappoint you, Mr. Hardin, but all the money in the world can never buy you class."

"My sentiments exactly," Nick assured her. "Take that rich old bat you're so worried about now. If she had one ounce of class, she wouldn't dream of repeating any gossip about you."

The truth in Nick's statement kept Cassie silent for a moment. Knitting her perfectly arched eyebrows together in a deep frown, she leaned back against the old stone wall that surrounded the veranda, wondering how long it would take her mother to hear through the grapevine that Nick Hardin had sired her first grandchild.

Cassie feared that, with that kind of news, Lenora Collins really *would* have the coronary she'd been threatening all these years.

"You know what you need?" Nick asked, studying Cassie's grave expression.

"A submachine gun might come in handy at the moment," Cassie shot back, but her caustic wit didn't discourage Nick from lending his advice.

"You need to lighten up a little, counselor. Don't take life so seriously. You'll never get out of it alive, anyway."

Cassie rolled her eyes. "Spoken like the true scholar you *aren't*," she chided.

"I might not be a scholar," Nick agreed, taking several steps closer than Cassie felt was necessary. "But I'm smart enough to know that old biddy will believe you over a...what did she call me?"

"I believe it was 'derelict,'" Cassie provided gladly.

Nick grinned. "Yes, I'm sure she'll believe you over a derelict like me the minute you go back inside and tell her I was only talking about your prissy dog."

Cassie didn't bother to tell Nick she only wished it were that simple. She would rather have the entire city of Asheville think *she* was pregnant than have her mother find out that her precious dog with the award-winning genes had accepted a bad seed under Cassie's supervision.

Ignoring the splendid full moon that was shining above them and the dreamy music that was now floating out to the veranda, Cassie glared at the incorrigible man who was directly blocking her path. "For your information, I'd rather face a firing squad than walk back through that room," Cassie told him. "And since you've already done enough damage to my reputation for one evening, if you'll move your obnoxious self out of my way, I plan to get out of here before you pull another stunt that makes us both the topic of conversation for the night.''

To her surprise, Nick's ink-black eyes instantly flickered with anger. "Now, wait a minute, counselor. Don't try to blame me for making you the topic of conversation in that room this evening. Your boyfriend, old Markie, did that all by himself when he showed up with a different lady on his arm.''

Cassie reached out to slap him, but her heel caught in a crack in the flagstone porch and landed her face-first against Nick's massive, rock-hard chest. Angry looks flashed between them as he gripped her bare shoulders with his powerful hands to steady her fall. Entwined in an awkward embrace, neither of them expected the wave of passion that erupted between them.

But it did.

And it carried both of them along like a fast-moving train.

Before Cassie knew what was happening, Nick crushed her even closer to him and sent a tingling explosion rippling through her body. When he brushed his lips against the sensitive hollows of her throat, he left her defenseless, lost in a magical place that Cassie never knew existed. Helpless, she surrendered, but only momentarily. When his hungry mouth inched closer, threatening to claim her own, she finally came to her senses.

"I can't do this,'' Cassie gasped, forcing herself to push him away.

Their eyes locked briefly before Nick released her, allowing her time to see desire fade and a look of mischief take its place. "But we both enjoyed it, didn't we, counselor?''

The weak "hah!'' Cassie mustered was almost as shaky as the two legs that were trying to keep her standing. "The only thing I'm going to *enjoy*, is taking a huge chunk of your bank account if Duchess ends up pregnant,'' Cassie lied, tossing Nick a smirk of her own. ''I'll know the test results tomorrow,'' she added, ''and if Duchess *is* pregnant, then we'll see if *you* don't start taking life a little more seriously.''

Before Nick could answer, she pushed past him and marched toward the outside stairway at the opposite end of the veranda.

Within seconds, she disappeared into the darkness without looking back.

CASSIE'S HANDS WERE still shaking when she accepted her keys from the uniformed parking attendant. She quickly handed the man a crumpled bill, then slid behind the wheel of her Lexus, trying to slow her thumping heart and regain her lost composure. Afraid her current rattled state of mind might result in destroying half of the luxury automobiles that lined both sides of the lot, she eased cautiously out of the parking lot, cursing the day she'd been stupid enough to stomp up Nick Hardin's front steps.

How the man had the ability to arouse her one second and make her capable of murder the next was totally beyond her comprehension. He was the most arrogant, the most insufferable, the most exasperating man she'd ever met in her entire life, yet he had the power to reduce her to a sniveling schoolgirl with one glance from those wicked eyes of his.

Oh, he excited her, all right. He excited her more than she ever thought possible. But the type of raw desire he aroused inside her was pushing her into uncharted waters. Waters she knew could be extremely dangerous. To say her experience with the opposite sex had been limited was putting it mildly. Oh, she'd had her share of pimple-faced boyfriends in high school. She'd dated occasionally in college, and she'd even spent the past few months fighting off the unwanted attentions of a would-be senator. But the male persuasion had never been powerful enough to steer Cassie away from the personal goal she had set for herself the summer she turned sixteen.

It had all started with a conversation she overheard between her father and her famous senator grandfather. The realization that the distinguished Senator Edward Collins resented her for not being a grandson had hurt Cassie deeply. Referring to her as "a silly female who would care more about her coming-out party than she would about the family law firm" had devastated her to the point that her mission in life had become her determination to prove the old man wrong.

She had graduated at the top of her class both in college and in law school, and had surpassed any of the academic records either her father or her grandfather held. When Cassie proudly joined the family law firm, she had also brought with her enough expertise in contract and corporate law to add an impressive number of new clients to the firm roster. Until now, she had always believed that her professional accomplishments would be sufficient to sustain her throughout her safe, predictable life.

But that had been before Nick Hardin had arrived on the scene and punched a gigantic hole in her silly facade.

Leaving the Grove Park Inn far behind her, Cassie headed for the south end of town, preoccupied with the way Nick had made her dizzy the minute he took her in his arms. She let her fingers find the warm flesh of her throat and marveled that her skin still tingled from the ravishing kisses he'd placed along her neck. Just thinking of him now, in fact, made her pulse lurch again and sent even a warmer glow straight to the center of her stomach.

Shuddering, Cassie tried not to think what might have happened if she hadn't somehow found the strength to push him away. A few hasty kisses on her neck had rendered her defenseless. If his fiery mouth *had* captured her own…

She snapped out of her fantasy when an oncoming car

blasted its horn. Somehow, she managed to get the Lexus back into her own lane, but the quick movement slid the car sideways and promptly landed it in the ditch. Shaking now from fright, instead of her brief fantasy about Nick, Cassie gripped the steering wheel and took long measured breaths until she could force her heart back into her chest.

"Dammit," she said, pounding her fist against the steering wheel. "What else can possibly go wrong tonight?"

After flipping on her emergency signal lights, Cassie launched herself from the Lexus and stomped to the back of the car. Glaring at the right back tire that was currently sitting in the deep rut by the side of the road, her first impulse was to take her frustration out on the car. Pretending it was Nick Hardin's mocking face she was abusing, she gave the tire a swift kick and promptly broke the heel of her four-inch stiletto pump.

"Would someone please tell me what I've done to deserve so much grief?" Cassie howled. "This was supposed to be my six weeks of fun-filled freedom. Remember?"

When she didn't get an answer, she jerked the shoe off her foot, then let out a loud yelp when the sharp gravel shredded her new panty hose and took a quick bite out of the bottom of her foot. "Just shoot me now and get it over with," she mumbled, glaring at the shoe whose heel was now twisted at a silly angle and just as useless as Cassie felt standing by the side of the road, shoe in hand.

After several cars passed without slowing down, Cassie was prepared to throw herself across the pavement when the next pair of headlights appeared in the distance. Fortunately, her sacrifice wasn't necessary. What appeared to be a small sports car suddenly slowed down, then pulled off the road and stopped a few feet behind her.

"There is a God," she mumbled under her breath.

Shielding her eyes against the bright headlights with her right hand, she saw the silhouette of a man get out of the car and start walking in her direction. "Hey, thanks for stopping," she called out, putting on her brightest smile. But her smile quickly faded when she saw who it was.

Sauntering up beside her, Nick leaned against the Lexus, then sent her a silly grin. "This must be your lucky night, counselor. You've had the pleasure of seeing me twice in one evening."

"Are you following me?" Cassie snapped.

"Think about it, sweetheart," Nick jeered. "We both live in the same neighborhood, remember? Or did you think this highway was for your exclusive use only?"

Cassie's only answer was a she-devil glare.

Pushing himself off the car, Nick bent down and examined the tire. Glancing back over his shoulder, he grinned again. "What happened? Did you run off the road daydreaming about me?"

The truth in Nick's statement reddened Cassie's cheeks faster than a blistering arctic wind. "The only dreams I have about you are of the nightmare variety," she informed him.

Nick chuckled, then stood up and held out his hand. "Give me your keys and I'll see if I can get you out of this ditch."

"Don't bother, I'd rather walk."

Nick's eyes swept from the shoe in her hand to her one bare foot. "That should be amusing, since you seem to have only one workable shoe."

Cassie was tempted to take off her one workable shoe and make a neat hole in the center of Nick's forehead with its knife-sharp heel. Instead, she nodded toward the car. "The keys are in the ignition."

Nick opened the car door and slid behind the wheel, then motioned for Cassie to step away from the car. He pulled the Lexus forward a few feet, then backed it up, and as if by magic, drove it safely up on the graveled shoulder beside the highway.

Cassie waited until he opened the door and got out before

she hobbled in his direction doing a perfect imitation of a peg-legged pirate with a sawed-off wooden leg.

"Thanks," she mumbled, choking on the word.

"Hey, what are neighbors for?" Nick teased, but Cassie refused to look at him again.

When he remained leaning against the driver's side door blocking her escape, Cassie made a dramatic production of looking at her watch. "Look, it's getting really late, and..."

"I owe you an apology for what I said in front of Evelyn Van Arbor," Nick interrupted. "I couldn't care less what those idiots think about me, but I shouldn't have put you in that position."

Cassie slowly raised her eyes to meet his, deciding she was much safer in his presence when he was being rude and nasty. "Well, there's nothing you can do about it now."

"For what it's worth, I did try," Nick told her. "I went back inside to explain the situation to the old bat, but she was too busy giving an Academy Award performance for anyone who was willing to listen."

Caught off guard by his sudden show of sincerity, Cassie managed a tiny smile. "Careful, Mr. Hardin, your bad-boy image is losing out to those fine Georgian manners of yours."

Nick instantly raised an eyebrow. "Why, counselor, if I didn't know better I'd think you'd been checking up on me."

Trapped by her own smart remark, Cassie felt the heat penetrate her cheeks again. "Don't flatter yourself," she sputtered. "It's no big secret that you moved here from Atlanta. I simply read in the paper that you..."

Nick interrupted Cassie's explanation when he reached out and pulled her to him. She did a little hip-hop dance across the ground when he dragged her into his arms. After kissing her so thoroughly that the cloud walk she was doing didn't require the aid of both shoes, he opened the car door and guided her safely into the driver's seat.

Leaning down, he whispered close to her ear, "Now, this

is the part where you say 'Follow me home, Nick, so we can finish what we started earlier on the veranda.'"

Outraged that the oaf would have the audacity to think she would hop into bed with him the minute he crooked his little finger, Cassie pushed him backward, then promptly slammed her car door shut. "No, this is the part where I say 'You'll come closer to being served Popsicles in hell than you will to finding me in *your* bed, Nick Hardin!'"

Cassie tore off down the highway while Nick blew her a sweet little kiss.

NICK WAS STILL CHUCKLING to himself as he walked back to his classic '57 Corvette, which he kept covered in the garage except for special occasions. Feeling the lower half of his body stir at the thought of how good the angry Cassandra had felt in his arms, Nick removed his tux jacket and noticed it still held the faint sent of her expensive perfume. Tossing his jacket on the passenger's seat, he slid behind the wheel, trying to remember when he'd ever been so taken with a woman.

He couldn't.

Cassandra Collins had entered his life like a menacing whirlwind, and since the day he found her standing by his swimming pool, everything about her confused his thoughts and made him doubt what he thought were his deepest beliefs. He'd only attended the fund-raiser in the hope of seeing her again, though he had expected her to be on the arm of the stuffy senatorial candidate she'd been dating. To find out she was no longer involved with anyone both pleased him and bothered him that it did.

Nick certainly hadn't been prepared for their collision on the veranda earlier. In fact, he couldn't even remember pulling her to him—only that he had. And once her voluptuous body was pressed against his own, nothing else seemed to matter.

For one brief moment, Nick had actually felt complete.

But is this spitfire attorney typical wife and mother material? Nick kept asking himself as he drove along the highway. Not a chance. She was, after all, twenty-eight and still single, which led him to believe that her career came first in her life. She would probably even be the type of woman who refused to damage her perfect figure in order to give him the children he so desperately wanted.

No, Nick already had an image of the type of woman he wanted for a mate. She would be down-to-earth, fun-loving, warm and giving. And she would love him beyond all reason, always placing him first in her life, preferring to raise a family instead of having a career. Even if he had preferred the social, career-oriented type, everything about the sassy attorney's actions told Nick she wasn't interested.

Or was she?

Despite her silly protests, Nick hadn't missed the wanton look his kisses had produced in those blue-green eyes of hers. Or how visibly shaken she'd been when she finally managed to get control of herself and push him away. As different as they were, Nick knew Miss Uptight Socialite couldn't deny the electricity that existed between them any more than he could. He only hoped Cassandra Collins would continue to keep her distance if they *were* forced to deal with the dog issue.

Heaven knew he wouldn't have any control over his actions if fate kept throwing them together.

Nick passed the street address he remembered from the notes he'd taken on the feisty female and caught a glimpse of taillights turning into a driveway. He was tempted to follow her home and try his luck again, but this woman had a strange power over him Nick couldn't fully explain.

She'd even invaded his thoughts to the point that Nick was afraid he was developing a conscience. Rarely, if ever, had he apologized to anyone for his brusque behavior. Yet, he'd apologized to *her* without a second thought. And the fact that he'd apologized so easily scared him more than he cared to admit.

Turning into his driveway, Nick punched the remote button for his garage door opener, then guided the Corvette into the safety of the garage. Grabbing his tux jacket from the seat beside him, he brought the jacket close to his face and took another deep whiff of her intoxicating perfume.

And then he laughed.

Despite the havoc the woman was currently wreaking on his emotions, Nick couldn't help but enjoy the mental picture that kept flashing through his mind of the captivating Miss Collins running naked through a fiery ring of hellfire and brimstone to hand him the multiflavored Popsicle she held in her outstretched hand.

4

CASSIE LEANED CLOSE to the blurred ultrasound screen, thinking that the squiggly image on the monitor was probably what her brain looked like on this particular Saturday morning. She hadn't slept well at all, waking several times after having extremely erotic dreams involving the man who was responsible for getting her into this mess in the first place.

"Bingo," Dee Bishop chirped as she moved a tubelike instrument across Duchess's furry stomach.

"Please tell me you're referring to a parlor game, and not a name for a puppy," Cassie gasped.

"Sorry, old girl, but it looks like you're going to be Auntie Cassie after all," Dee assured her.

"Look again," Cassie demanded. "You've made a mistake."

Dee shook her head adamantly. Using the mouse on the computer to draw a circle around a small mass Cassie thought resembled a bowl of Jell-O, she pointed to the vague object. "I don't have to look again, Cass. I see at least two puppies here. There could even be a third one hiding behind the others."

Restraining herself from smashing her fist through the expensive screen, Cassie began pacing around the examining room. "God, Dee, this can't be happening. What am I going to do now?"

Dee switched off the screen and wiped a mass of gooey jell from Duchess's fur with a gauze square. "Well, for one thing you're going to give this little cutie the attention she deserves while she's carrying her puppies,'' Dee announced. ''Once they arrive, Duchess can take care of everything else herself.''

''You know what I mean,'' Cassie snapped.

Taking a doggy treat from a canister on the counter, Dee rewarded Duchess for her cooperation during the test. ''No, I don't know what you mean. You've been obsessing over this ordeal for over two weeks now, Cassie, and I really can't understand what you're so upset about.''

''Does Lenora's wrath ring a bell?''

''Oh, please. Lenora will get over it,'' Dee scoffed as she placed Duchess back in her crate. ''Besides,'' she added, ''Duchess isn't the first champion to whelp a litter of mongrel pups, and her little indiscretion can't take away the title she earned at Westminster.''

''But what about all those endorsements Lenora's been bragging about all over town?'' Cassie quizzed.

Dee rolled her eyes. ''You of all people know how your mother likes to exaggerate. Lenora may get a few requests from suppliers wanting to use Duchess's picture to promote their products, but the pictures they'll want are the ones taken at Westminster. Duchess's real earning power will come from providing champion breeding stock.''

Cassie slumped onto Dee's examining stool. ''Current litter excepted, of course.'' Cassie grumbled.

Dee sighed. ''Yes, current litter excepted, but it's the current litter that we have to be concerned about now. I wasn't kidding when I said I wanted to examine the male. I hope you took my advice and patched things up with Nick Hardin.''

Cassie winced. ''I'm surprised you haven't already heard about the horrible episode he created at the Grove Park Inn last night.''

Dee raised an eyebrow in Cassie's direction, then listened intently as Cassie recounted the entire gruesome story. And

Cassie wasn't the least bit impressed when her best friend burst out laughing.

"Oh, come on, Cassie. You have to admit it's hysterically funny. I'd have given anything to see the look on Evelyn Van Arbor's face."

"Well, it wasn't funny to me," Cassie argued. "And it isn't funny that everyone in Biltmore Forest thinks I'm carrying that idiot's child, either."

Dee's mouth twisted in a knowing smile. "You can call Nick all the names you want, Cass, but you can't fool me. You have the major hots for this guy, and from what you just told me the feeling seems to be mutual."

Cassie blushed, thinking about the scoundrel's warm lips against her neck and the toe-curling kiss he gave her by the side of the road. "I've never met anyone like him, Dee. He makes me swoon one minute and infuriates me the next. It's like having a crush on Dr. Jekyll and Mr. Hyde."

"Sounds serious to me," Dee teased.

"Seriously dangerous," Cassie said, and sighed.

"Well, you can't stay a virgin the rest of your life, silly," Dee goaded. "Maybe if you let Dr. Jekyll jump your hide, you'll find out you like him just the way he is."

"You know I'm not a virgin, Dee. You were in the other room swapping spit with that oily-haired geek who gave you mono."

Dee laughed. "I take it you're referring to our senior year at summer camp?"

"No, I'm referring to the most horrible two seconds of my life," Cassie groaned.

"Sorry, my friend, but that little disaster doesn't qualify you as being totally devirginized. You need a real man to show you what it means to be a woman, Cass. And from where I'm standing I think you've already found him."

"And wouldn't Lenora be pleased if I came home with some motorcycle-riding moron on my arm?" Cassie sneered.

Dee frowned. "When are you going to get a real life and stop worrying about what your mother wants, Cassie? Geez, you're twenty-eight years old and you still let Lenora call all the shots. This man is educated, he's funny, not to mention being gorgeous. What more do you want?"

Tired of the lecture, Cassie placed her hands to her temples and tried to massage away the tension headache that had grown to a monumental roar inside her head. "I don't know what I want, Dee, but I just can't deal with Nick Hardin right now. If you really have to examine his mutt, *you* call him."

"Okay. I can do that," Dee agreed. "I'll call him at the radio station first thing Monday morning."

"And I wasn't kidding about you sending him an itemized bill for Duchess's care. Including this ultrasound you just did," Cassie added.

"That certainly won't score you any points with the guy," Dee grumbled. "The ultrasound alone runs close to a thousand dollars. And if you add in all the other charges, including my treating the champion sire for the big bite Duchess took out of his nose..."

"I don't need a rundown of the charges, Dee," Cassie interrupted. "And I'm not trying to score any points with Nick Hardin. His cur is responsible for this mess. The least he can do is pick up the tab for the trouble he's caused me."

Throwing her hands up in defeat, Dee grabbed a notepad from the counter and began scribbling across the page. "Fine. But I'm writing down some instructions for the special diet I want Duchess on while she's carrying the puppies. She's hardly eaten a thing since she's been here and it's extremely important for her to have the proper nutrition during her gestation period. She'll also need to be exercised regularly, at least three times a day...."

"Hel-lo," Cassie interrupted. "Have you forgotten that I put in twelve hours a day at the office? What do you expect me to do, Dee? Take a family leave of absence until the puppies are born?"

Dee paused. "I'd say you could leave Duchess here, but I don't think it's wise, Cass. Dogs occasionally get depressed when they're left in a kennel for long periods of time. That's probably what's causing her poor appetite now. I really think she'll do much better at home."

"And who's supposed to baby-sit her all day?" Cassie demanded.

Dee thought for a moment. "You can always call her trainer. I'm sure John's recovered enough now to help out, but he sure isn't going to be pleased about her current condition."

"Absolutely not," Cassie argued, shaking her head. "John has five other dogs that he boards on a regular basis. Duchess won't get any special attention if she's put back in that situation."

"Then, what about Louise?"

Cassie paused, thinking about the woman who'd been the closest thing Cassie ever had to a grandmother. "I guess I could ask her to come every day and stay until I get home. But only if you really think it's necessary."

"I wouldn't have mentioned it if I didn't think it was necessary," Dee insisted. "We can't afford to take any chances with Duchess's health now. Especially since she may have trouble whelping these off-brand puppies."

Making a mental note that Louise's salary would be another bill she would forward straight to Nick, Cassie nodded in agreement. "I'll call her tonight and arrange things."

"Good," Dee said, handing Cassie the page of instructions. "I want you to call me if Duchess's appetite doesn't improve, or if you notice even the slightest change in her behavior."

"I may have to call you from the emergency ward when Nick gets your bill," Cassie mumbled.

Dee laughed. "Well, if nothing else, I think it's safe to say that it won't be boring in Biltmore Forest for the next few months."

Cassie frowned, longing for the days when things *were* boring. Days when she didn't know that one glance from a particular scoundrel could make her pulse race faster than a locomotive. And nights when her dreams weren't invaded with visions of her and that same outlaw entwined in every position outlined in the *Kama Sutra.*

Dee headed for the door, but stopped when she noticed Cassie's forlorn expression. "Hey, cheer up, Cass. You *are* okay, aren't you?"

"I'm okay," Cassie lied as she lifted Duchess's crate off the examining table.

But as Cassie followed Dee out the door, she wondered if she'd ever really be *okay* again, now that Nick Hardin had kissed her senseless.

"GOT A MINUTE, NICK?"

Leaning back in his chair with his feet propped up on his desk, Nick motioned for the station manager to enter his office. When the man walked through the door, Nick swung his feet to the floor and returned to a sitting position, still thinking about the informative call he'd received from a Dr. Dee Bishop some thirty minutes earlier.

"I've been looking over your rough draft for tomorrow's program, Nick," the man said, bringing Nick's attention back to the present.

"Cut to the chase, Bob," Nick growled. "What's the problem?"

The bald man took a pencil from behind his ear and began tapping it against the printout he was holding in his hand. "I guess I'm just a little puzzled."

"About what?"

"About your show over the last two weeks, Nick. What's

happened to the spice? The wit? Hell, you haven't even included any of your trademark lawyer jokes in your monologue lately.''

Nick flinched, unwilling to admit that he hadn't found those jokes so funny since he'd tangled with a certain long-legged attorney. ''You can run anything into the ground, Bob. I'm sure my listeners were getting tired of my attack on lawyers. It was time for a change.''

''And you think this mumbo-jumbo about Congress passing a law to make *gossip* a felony is funny?'' the editor demanded. ''Hell, you're attacking just about everybody on the planet.''

Nick shifted in his chair, then sent his boss an angry glare. ''So, it's okay to attack lawyers, just leave the gossips alone, right?''

Nick watched as his boss's ears turned a light shade of pink. ''Hell, boy, you'd better stop and think who it is you're attacking. Those faithful listeners out there are mainly just regular people, going off to work every morning and depending on you to lighten their mood and give them something to chat about at the water cooler. It's your humor that's got you this far, son. Don't throw that success away by attacking the little guy.''

''And you learned that in Broadcasting 101, I suppose.''

Leaning over the desk until his face was only inches away from Nick's, the older man said, ''Now, listen here, Nicky, I don't know what's had your shorts in a knot over the last few weeks, but I expect you to get over it and start giving me the type of show that got you syndicated in fourteen states and put all that damn money in your fat bank account. Now, get to work and give me an outline that will keep me laughing all day. Understand?''

When Nick refused to answer, the station manager stomped out of the office and slammed the door behind him, leaving Nick sitting at his desk in a stew. *Damn, but this week has already gotten off to a rotten start,* he thought. He hadn't been at his desk long enough to take his first sip of coffee when the vet called to inform him that Earl *was* going to be a daddy. The woman also insisted on examining Earl as soon as possible. For what, Nick had no idea.

But with the way his luck had been running lately, Nick wouldn't be surprised if Earl didn't have some dreaded doggy social disease.

Caught off guard by the call, Nick hadn't objected when Dr. Bishop gave Earl an appointment for eleven o'clock that morning. Of course, once he thought things over, he was thoroughly p-o'd that the lovely Miss Collins hadn't bothered to contact him herself. Nick resented being ordered around by a hired associate, and he intended to tell Miss Collins so himself before the day was over.

Glancing at his watch, Nick sighed, knowing he barely had time to dash home and grab Earl, then hurry back downtown to make the damn vet appointment. Calculating he probably wouldn't return to the office until well after noon, he figured he'd have only a few hours to do the new outline his surly station manager had just requested.

"Damn, I hate Mondays," Nick grumbled to himself as he grabbed his leather jacket from the back of his chair.

Heading for the elevator, Nick ignored the scowling station manager and banged against the down button with the ball of his fist.

"And where the hell do you think you're going?" yelled his boss from across the cluttered radio station.

"I'm going to see a lady about a dog," Nick yelled back, then disappeared into the elevator, cutting off a string of angry curses when the doors finally slid together.

"CALM DOWN, DEE, I can't understand a word you're saying," Cassie said as she listened to the excited voice on the other end of the telephone line. However, when it finally registered what her best friend was trying to tell her, Cassie's eyes grew wide with concern.

"I mean it, Cassie, get out of that office before Nick Hardin gets there. I've never seen anyone so angry."

Cassie jumped from her chair and hurried to the window behind her desk. Peeking through the miniblinds, she searched the parking lot below her second-story window. She would have laughed if the situation hadn't been so serious. Pulling into a parking space near the building entrance was Nick on his big Harley, with Earl perched between the handlebars looking like Snoopy in his Red Baron pose.

"It's too late, Dee," Cassie gasped. "He's already here."

Hurrying back to her desk, Cassie rummaged through her top drawer, searching for her compact. A madman was on his way to her office possibly to end her life, yet her first instinct was to make sure she'd make an attractive corpse. Satisfied with her appearance, she slipped the compact back into the drawer, then quickly flipped the intercom switch.

"Sally, a man in a black leather motorcycle jacket is going to burst through the door any minute carrying a dog under his arm," Cassie told the law student who was her assistant for the summer. "Give him an appointment if you have to, Sally, but don't, and I repeat *don't* let him into my office under any circumstances."

"I beg your pardon?" came a shocked reply from the voice box on Cassie's desk.

"Just do it, Sally," Cassie begged, knowing that the young woman who had promptly adopted Cassie as her role model was probably now making the assumption that the usually professional Miss Collins had suddenly resorted to taking heavy doses of some mind-altering drug.

Trying to quiet her rattled nerves, Cassie forced herself to pick up the brief she'd been working on, but tensed at the sound of raised voices filtering through her closed office door. Within seconds, her office door burst open and Nick stormed inside, holding his fuzzy companion in the crook of his arm.

"I'm sorry, Miss Collins, he rushed past me before I could stop him," the freckle-faced student wailed as she hovered in the doorway.

"That's okay, Sally," Cassie said, then forced a smile at Nick when Sally quickly closed the door and sealed Cassie and the enemy inside the room alone.

Show no fear, Cassie told herself, then calmly rose from her desk. "Is there a problem?"

"I'd say that's putting it mildly," Nick growled.

After plunking Earl down on one of the expensive leather chairs that faced Cassie's desk, Nick pulled a crumpled piece of paper from his inside jacket pocket. When he tossed the paper on Cassie's desk, she saw the name Dr. Dee Bishop printed across the top of the page.

"Is this some kind of a joke?" Nick demanded.

"Do you see me laughing?"

"What I see is a woman who has a vivid imagination if she thinks I'm going to fork over fifteen hundred dollars for one vet appointment."

Cassie glared at Earl, who had not only spent the past few minutes digging at the expensive leather of her chair, but who now held one leg high in the air while he expertly licked himself where no human could. "The cost of passion runs high these days, Mr. Hardin." Cassie nodded toward Earl. "If your dog had spent more time engaged in the activity he's enjoying now, none of us would be in this mess."

Slightly embarrassed, Nick thumped Earl on the head, prompting the dog to stop the lewd performance and sit obediently in the chair. Locking eyes with Cassie again, Nick said, "Excuse the pun, counselor, but as far as I'm concerned, there's never been a piece of *tail* worth fifteen hundred dollars.''

Cassie blanched slightly but quickly recovered. "I have no doubt you're well versed in what the going price for human flesh is these days," she said, pleased when his eyes narrowed to tiny slits. "But I warned you from the very beginning that your negligence would be expensive."

"Negligence?" Nick shouted. "You seem to be forgetting it takes *two* to tangle, counselor. What I don't understand is why you think you're automatically exempt from being negligent. If you'd been keeping an eye on your precious show dog, Earl couldn't have jumped her in the first place."

Cassie placed both hands on her hips, her lips puckered in annoyance. "Excuse me for bringing it up, but Duchess was in her own *fenced* backyard."

Nick's eyes hardened. "Just as Earl was in his *fenced* backyard when I let him out that morning. I had no more control over him digging *out* of my yard and *under* your fence than you had when the queen of the dog world decided to lift her groomed tail when Earl sniffed in her direction."

His heated glare left Cassie slightly singed and more than a little shaken. She watched as he ran his hands through the long, sun-streaked strands of his hair. When he looked at her again, his eyes had lost a little of their anger, but the tension in the room was still bouncing off the walls like supercharged Ping-Pong balls.

"Look," Nick said. "We can stand here and insult each other all day, or we can try to settle this problem like two rational adults. You tell me. What's it going to be?"

Cassie had no intention of giving an inch, but she *was* willing to hear what her opponent had to say. Giving a tense nod to the leather chair that *wasn't* currently being occupied, Cassie took her own seat behind her desk. "I'm open to suggestions if you have any."

Nick dropped into the seat facing her, but Cassie found she had trouble ignoring the way his muscled thighs strained against the faded material of his jeans. The way his leather jacket was unzipped low enough to expose the golden hair peeking over the top of his V-neck polo shirt didn't do much for her concentration, either. Feeling her willpower ooze out of her like air from a leaky balloon, she had to use every ounce of her self-control to keep from grabbing the lapels of his jacket and dragging him across her desk for another one of his mind-blowing kisses.

Unaware that he was on the verge of being attacked, Nick sent her a semifriendly smile that was a hair short of being a smirk. "Before we go any further, do you think you could humor me during this conversation and stop calling me Mr. Hardin?"

"If you'll stop calling me 'counselor.'"

"Okay, Cassandra."

"Cassie," she corrected him.

He seemed surprised. "Cassie," Nick repeated in that deep southern drawl that drove her crazy. "Yeah, I like Cassie much better." The smile he gave her this time was breathtaking, weakening her defenses even more.

"Well, the way I see it, Cassie, we're both victims of circumstance in this situation. I happen to know this famous show dog belongs to your mother."

"That doesn't have anything—"

Nick held his hand up. "Now, wait a minute. All I'm saying is that I've already figured out the main reason you're so upset about this dog siring a bunch of unregistered pups is because it was your responsibility to take care of her while your mother is in Europe. Am I right?"

Cassie couldn't disagree. "And you're a victim because…?"

"Like I said before. Neither of us have any control over

Mother Nature. The dogs got together. All we can do now is deal with it.''

Cassie licked her lips involuntarily when Nick leaned back in his chair and stretched his long legs out in front of him. Despite her determination not to look, the healthy bulge between his legs caught Cassie's attention faster than if a flashing neon sign had been sewn to the metal tab on his zipper. Forcing herself to look away, Cassie realized he was still talking, but she only caught the tail end of his next sentence.

"...so, I think it's only fair that we work together on this, and split the expenses fifty-fifty."

Cassie leaned forward and rested her arms on her desk. "You realize, of course, this one vet bill won't be all of the expenses incurred during this ordeal."

Nick shrugged. "Sure, I figured the dog would have to be seen regularly by the vet while she's carrying the puppies. And then I guess the puppies will need shots—"

"There's also a weekly fee for the sitter," Cassie interrupted without thinking.

A dark cloud crossed Nick's face as he sat upright in the chair. "What did you say?"

"I've hired a sitter to stay with Duchess during the day until I get home from the office," Cassie answered nonchalantly. "I do work for a living, you know."

"But a sitter? I mean, we are talking about a dog here."

"A world-class champion," Cassie reminded him. "Besides, I leave home at seven in the morning and usually don't get home until seven or later in the evening. Duchess is going to have to be fed properly and exercised at least three times a day."

With that said, she reached for the calculator on her desk. "That will average out to the sitter working about twelve hours a day. At $6.50 per hour, that will be..." Cassie started punching in the numbers, but Nick's quick mind did the math before she could finish.

"That's seventy-eight dollars a day," Nick barked in disbelief. "That's the most ridiculous thing I've ever heard. You're talking about over fifteen hundred dollars a month. And the dog still has to carry those puppies for..."

"At least one more month, maybe a little longer," Cassie provided. "The vet says there's no way to know when she'll deliver. This is Duchess's first litter. The puppies could be early or they could be late."

Nick stood up and unzipped his jacket the rest of the way, giving Cassie the impression that he suddenly found the room much too warm. After walking back and forth in front of her desk several times, he stopped and shook his head in disbelief. "So what you're telling me, is that on top of these outrageous vet bills, you expect me to pay someone to come to your house and sit with a dog?"

"You said fifty-fifty, *Nick*," Cassie reminded him smugly, using her first opportunity to call him by name.

A muscle twitched along his lower jaw. "I know what I said, *Cassie*," he snapped, "and I *will* pay my half of the vet bills, but paying a personal nursemaid to sit for a dog is where I have to draw the line."

Cassie bristled. "Then I'm afraid we're back to square one, aren't we?"

Instead of trying to negotiate a plan B as Cassie had expected, Nick snapped his fingers, prompting Earl to propel himself from the chair and into his master's arms. "Then sue me," Nick said, his voice full of confidence.

Cassie was so shocked, she couldn't seem to find her voice. Before she was able to respond, Nick strolled to the door with his furry friend tucked under his arm. But when he reached for the doorknob he looked back over his shoulder and sent Cassie that cocky grin she was quickly growing to despise.

"But I'll make you one wager, counselor. This will be the damnedest fight you've ever had in a courtroom."

As furious as she was, Cassie wouldn't permit herself to dignify his last remark with a comeback. And even before the big Harley-Davidson thundered to life and roared out of the parking lot, Cassie's fingers were already pounding her computer keys, typing up the paperwork that would put Nick Hardin's latest challenge to the test.

5

"ALIMONY, PALIMONY…but *pet-imony?* Remember, you heard it here first, folks. It looks as if the world really is going to the dogs. As if our courts aren't already overloaded with senseless lawsuits that clog the system and stand in the way of justice, it seems yours truly has been hit with a ridiculous lawsuit that will make all others pale in comparison. In fact, I'm willing to conduct a public-opinion poll here at the radio station to see if my faithful listeners don't agree that the lawsuit I'm sharing with you today shouldn't win first prize in the Stupid Lawsuit of the Year Contest…"

Cassie switched off the kitchen radio and began devouring her bagel with the ferocity of a man-eating tiger. Her only satisfaction was the fact she'd been the one to draw first blood. Thanks to modern technology and that wonderful little invention called the fax machine, his truly had been served with her lawsuit less than four hours after he strolled confidently out of her office.

"Stupid Lawsuit of the Year Contest, my elbow," Cassie mumbled under her breath, then whistled for the ball of white fluff that was lying in the middle of the kitchen floor. When Duchess refused to acknowledge her, Cassie left her chair and drew the tiny bundle into her arms. "You have to eat something, sweet girl," Cassie cooed as she stroked the dog's soft fur. "You have little puppies to think about now."

The old woman standing beside Cassie sent Duchess a worried look of her own. "I prepared her food just like Dee instructed," she said.

"I know you did, Louise. I've tried to get her to eat this morning, but she won't even take a nibble."

"Well, the poor little thing's gonna have to eat something." Louise sighed, wiping her wrinkled hands on her bright-colored apron. "She's as limp as a dust mop now. She sure can't go on like this much longer."

Cassie gave the dog a final pat and smiled when Duchess rewarded her with a halfhearted kiss on the chin. After handing the dog over to her new nursemaid, Cassie picked up her attaché case from the kitchen table and glanced at her watch.

"I'm running late, Louise, but I'm going to call Dee as soon as I get to the office. In the meantime, you might try tempting Duchess with those milk-bone treats she likes. I bought her some new toys, too. They're in a box in the sunroom."

"Don't you worry about us. I'll take good care of her," Louise said as Cassie headed down the hallway. "Me and Miss Duchess will do whatever it takes to get some food inside that little tummy of hers."

Cassie pulled out of the driveway minutes later, feeling a twinge of guilt for running off to work when Duchess was in such a fragile state. After the initial shock had worn off, Cassie was actually looking forward to having a few more bundles of white fur romping through the house. Or was her ticking biological clock just using this opportunity to bring out her maternal instincts?

Sliding her hand over her taut stomach, she wondered briefly what it would be like to have another life stirring inside her. She'd never given much thought to marriage or to motherhood before, especially since her work had always been the driving force in her life. But now that she thought about it, she realized that she would want a large family. Possibly because being an only child had been such a tremendous burden to bear.

More than once Cassie had wondered if having brothers

and sisters may have made life with Lenora a little easier. Dee scolded her on a regular basis for being the "dutiful daughter," and she had been, but Cassie had done so out of love, not fear. Despite Lenora's overbearing personality, Cassie loved her mother dearly. And like her father, she had just found it much easier to bend to Lenora's will.

Thinking about her parents now, Cassie realized how quickly things had gotten out of hand in their short absence. Duchess *was* pregnant, and Cassie may as well have been pregnant since everyone in Asheville was buzzing about the rumor Evelyn Van Arbor repeated to anyone who would listen. Cassie hadn't missed the snide looks people sent her way, or the fact that everyone she ran into lately had their eyes focused directly on her stomach.

"Oh, well, I don't have time to worry about the rumor now," Cassie said aloud as she pulled into her reserved parking space. She had more important things to occupy her mind at the moment.

Things like whether or not Dee had the ability to pull a magic potion out of her bag of doggy tricks and make Duchess well again.

"NICK, OLD BOY, you've really hit pay dirt this time."

Nick barely grunted when the station manager strolled into his office with a silly grin plastered across his fleshy cheeks. Ignoring Nick's cool regard, the man perched a hip on the corner of the desk, looking like the Cheshire cat who followed Alice around in Wonderland.

"I'm not kidding, Nick," his boss said when Nick still failed to respond. "The damn phone's been ringing off the hook all morning, and the e-mail's piling up faster than a bar tab at a Shriners convention. Everybody in town seems to have an opinion about this lawsuit of yours, and so far, those *for* you outnumber the nay-sayers ten to one."

"I'm flattered," Nick mumbled, though he really couldn't care less.

Sure, he'd been fired up when he went on the air that morning, especially on the heels of receiving that lawsuit. But by the end of the day Nick's rage had evaporated around him like the lifting of an early morning fog. And what settled in its place was much worse than anger.

Like a multimega amplifier, the same name kept reverberating through Nick's mind in an endless chant: Cassie. Cassie. Cassie.

"Are you listening to me, Nick?"

"Sure, I'm listening," Nick said as he reluctantly met the man's gaze.

"I'm serious about this, boy. I want you to milk this story for all it's worth. I mean, I want this story broadcast right down to the minute when the judge bangs his gavel and ends the courtroom proceedings."

"I'm hoping the judge will throw the damn case out of court," Nick grumbled.

"Even better," the station manager assured him. "Think about it, boy. You'll be an instant hero to all those little people out there who have their doubts about their ability to fight city hall and win."

Deciding his boss had evidently lost a few shingles since the last storm, Nick shook his head. "Let's not get ahead of ourselves on this, Bob. I talked to my attorney yesterday and he said there's a good chance I'll lose this case." Pointing to the legal document on his desk, Nick added, "Those papers charge me with being in flagrant violation of the City of Asheville's leash law. And whether I like it or not, my dog *was* running loose."

The manager frowned for a moment, but the frown quickly faded. "Hell, who cares whether you win this case or not? The way our ratings are going up, I'll pay your damn court costs myself. We're on a roll, son. Don't drop the ball now."

Nick should have felt comforted by the friendly slap on the back before his boss left the room, but he didn't. Leaving his chair, he walked to the window at the end of the room and stared out at the majestic Blue Ridge Mountains that surrounded Asheville like a protective barricade. He'd fallen in love with the sleepy town several years earlier when he'd attended a radio convention as the guest speaker. Though his friends in Atlanta declared him insane when he turned his back on the big-city lights and headed for a town with a population of less than 100,000, Nick hadn't regretted his decision once since his arrival.

In fact, it was almost as if some outside force like an imaginary magnet had drawn him to the mountains.

Of course, he hadn't exactly been welcomed with open arms. His neighbors didn't care for his unconventional ways. But despite the fact that he would never conform to their ridiculous social protocol, he secretly admired the old families who held their traditions sacred, and who were determined to preserve a heritage for upcoming generations. Nick had been bounced back and forth over the entire nation by the time he turned sixteen. Now, for a reason he still couldn't explain, it seemed as if he'd finally come home.

Deciding a long ride on the Blue Ridge Parkway might lift his spirits, Nick walked back to his desk and glanced at the outline he'd drawn up for the next day's early morning program. Despite his foul mood, he had to admit the material was extremely funny. He intended to thoroughly explore what he'd called ''Earl's Day in Court,'' complete with a scenario where Earl would have to raise his right paw when he took the witness stand in his own defense.

After stapling the papers together, Nick motioned to one of his co-workers who was passing by his door. ''Make sure Bob sees this outline for tomorrow's program,'' he instructed, then grabbed his jacket and headed for the door.

A long ride through the mountains had never failed him

in the past. And with any luck, the mountains would come to his rescue again this time and permanently erase Cassie Collins's name from his memory.

"DEE BISHOP ON LINE ONE for you, Miss Collins."

"Dee?" Cassie asked the second she punched the appropriate number on the phone pad.

"Yes, it's me. But before you say anything else, if you're making plans to string the jerk up, I'll go out and buy the rope myself."

"Who are you talking about?"

"Who do you think I'm talking about? Nick Hardin, of course. I thought that was why you called me."

"I called you because Duchess still won't eat anything."

"I thought you were calling about Nick's talk show this morning?" Dee replied. "Everyone else in Asheville is sure talking about it. I've heard it's even going to make the evening news tonight."

Cassie lowered her coffee cup from her mouth to her desk, suddenly feeling sick to her stomach. "I only listened to the first part of his monologue, and then I turned the stupid thing off," she admitted.

"Then you mean you don't know?"

"Know what?" Cassie demanded.

"Oh, Cassie," Dee whined. "Nick Hardin didn't use your name, but he left no doubt about who filed the lawsuit against him. He said things like, and I quote 'I really can't blame old Earl. After all, his new lady love did just win Best-in-Show at the Westminster Dog Show in New York City.'"

Cassie gasped.

"It gets worse," Dee assured her. "He also said, 'I know I should find some comfort that the lady suing me looks more like a model than an attorney, but even so, I admit I was a little shocked that she expected me to pay seventy-eight dollars a day for someone to sit with her prissy pooch....'"

"I'll kill him," Cassie screeched.

"Not if I get to him first," Dee vowed. "He took a cheap shot at me, too. During the last part of his program the jerk had the nerve to say that 'the only highlight of this whole episode might be uncovering yet another predator who is greedily feasting on Asheville's unsuspecting citizens.' And then he went on to ask everyone if they'd checked their veterinarian bills lately and pointed out that 'the vet who takes care of Earl's girlfriend drives a red Porsche.'"

Cassie glanced at the waste can sitting beside her desk, deciding she may to use it if the wave of nausea plaguing her stomach washed over her again. After several seconds of silence, she blew out a deep breath and dabbed at her clammy forehead with a tissue she'd taken from her purse.

"I'm really sorry I've dragged you into this, Dee," she finally managed to say. "I should have known better than to go up against a crazed militant like Nick Hardin. Especially since he's willing to use the media as his weapon."

Dee remained silent a little longer than usual. "Oh, what the hell. I'll weather the storm far better than you will, my friend. But maybe you should think about dropping this lawsuit. Do it while you still have time."

It was Cassie's turn to remain silent a little too long. "You're right. Maybe I will drop the suit. But I'm more concerned about Duchess right now. She still won't eat a thing and she's listless. I'm really worried, Dee. Do you think I should bring her in and let you check her?"

"Is she drinking any water?"

"A little, but she just mopes around. I swear it's almost as if she's grieving over something. Does pregnancy do that to dogs?"

"Now, don't go into orbit, Cassie, but I don't think her condition is physical."

"You mean you're saying you think the dog is a nut case?"

"No, I'm saying I think it would be a good idea to have that behavior therapist Lenora has on the payroll to stop by and evaluate Duchess. He's worked with her in the past. Especially before some of the major dog shows. And he knows Duchess's temperament. Do you have his number?"

"Yes," Cassie groaned. "But I don't even want to think about what Nick will say on the air when I add a doggy psychiatrist's bill to the list of expenses."

"You asked for my advice, Cassie, nobody said you had to take it," Dee reminded her curtly.

Cassie removed the clasp from her hair and let the long tresses topple down her back. Along with the upset stomach, it seemed she was now developing a throbbing headache. "Sorry, Dee," Cassie said with a sigh. "You know I value your opinion. I'll call the guy the second we hang up."

"I promise this man knows what he's doing, Cassie. And he always insists on seeing his patients in their home environment," Dee added. "See if you can make the appointment for around seven tonight. I'd like to be there myself when he examines Duchess."

"Will do," Cassie agreed. "And I'll even call Louise and see if she won't fix us a pan of her award-winning lasagna."

"And after dinner, maybe we can sneak over to Nick Hardin's house and smother him in his sleep."

Cassie snorted. "I'd rather see his head roll out from under a guillotine blade, myself, but that wouldn't be torturous enough for the creep."

Dee laughed. "See you at seven. I'll bring the wine."

Cassie returned the receiver to the holder on her desk, then propped her elbows on her blotter and placed her head in her hands. After massaging both of her temples for several seconds, she searched through the numbers her mother had compiled for Duchess's care before she left for Europe. When Cassie found the name she wanted, she decided Houston Baumfarger was an appropriate name for a man who devoted his time delving into the minds of the animal world. And had Cassie's own mental state not been so rattled from the morning's hectic events, she may have found a little humor in the response she gave when the shrill voice of the renowned dog psychiatrist answered his private line.

"Houston?" Cassie said. "We have a problem."

IT WAS DARK WHEN NICK pulled into his driveway. He'd ridden all the way to Mount Mitchell which, at an elevation of more than six thousand feet, was the highest point in the state. Embracing the great outdoors usually cleansed his inner demons and left his soul restored, but nature had failed him this time. The experience hadn't purged Cassie Collins from his thoughts. Instead, her memory had ridden right along with him as if she'd been sitting behind him on the bike with her arms clasped tightly around his waist.

In a far worse mood than when he'd left his office that morning, Nick lifted the flap on the saddlebag at the back of his motorcycle and retrieved two containers of spicy takeout he'd bought from a quaint little Chinese restaurant he'd discovered on the west side of town. A wide variety of eating establishments was the one thing Nick missed most about Atlanta, but that was all he missed. He didn't miss the traffic, the fast pace or the wild lifestyle he'd left behind when he made the decision to head for the peace and solitude of the mountains.

The turning point had actually arrived when Nick awoke one morning at his sprawling Atlanta home and found that he didn't know half of the people who were already milling around his pool. When he noticed several people snorting cocaine from the neat little rows they'd skillfully lined up on the glass top of his patio table, however, Nick went into orbit.

Nick loved his brandy and savored the taste of fine wine. He even had a passion for imported beer, but he had never indulged in taking drugs, nor would he tolerate drug use in his presence. Within the space of five minutes, he'd cleared the place out, and he put his house on the market the same day. Within two months, he was on his way to Asheville in search of a better life.

"Hey, buddy," Nick said when Earl tore into the foyer and began jumping around his legs. "Did you realize you've become a celebrity overnight?"

Greetings exchanged, both Nick and Earl headed for the den. But as Nick walked toward the bar, it crossed his mind that other than the bedroom, the den was really the only other room he used in his rambling sixteen-room abode. He'd known from the beginning that he didn't need such an enormous house, but the Realtor had shown Nick documented proof that his favorite author, Thomas Wolfe, had rented the old Tudor mansion one summer while he finished his celebrated novel, *Look Homeward, Angel.* Being the hopeless romantic and sucker for nostalgia that he was, Nick had bought the house on the spot. And he finally justified his purchase by rationalizing that the house would provide plenty of room later for him to raise the big family he had always wanted.

But what is my definition of later? Nick asked himself as he filled Earl's bowl with a healthy portion of dog food. He would soon be thirty-six, and was no closer to starting a family now than he had been at eighteen.

Moving aside when Earl lunged at his bowl, Nick wondered if it hadn't made him feel a little inferior that his own dog would become a father before he would. When his own stomach growled in protest, however, he decided his stomach took precedence over trying to sort out warped emotions. Without another thought to parenthood, he grabbed one of his favorite brews from the refrigerator and settled himself decidedly at the bar.

Using a plastic fork that was left over from some other evening's fine dining experience, he dug into the cardboard

containers of rice and Szechwan beef, then turned on the TV
and channel surfed. When he landed on a particular channel,
a loud bark from Earl made Nick pause a little longer than
usual. He almost choked on his food when a life-size picture
of the current winner of the Westminster Dog Show filled
the wide-screen.

Yapping excitedly, Earl put his front paws on the television, trying to lick the image, but his sullen master was far
from being impressed.

"Damn reruns," Nick cursed under his breath, then
switched off the television and threw the remote halfway
across the room.

"ARE YOU OUT OF YOUR MIND?" Cassie shouted as she
vaulted from her chair.

The slender man sitting primly on the edge of Cassie's
sofa jumped at her outburst, causing some of the hot tea he
held in his lap to slosh over the rim of the china cup and
puddle in his saucer. After sending Cassie an annoyed look,
he quickly glanced at Dee for support. "You asked for my
expert opinion, Miss Collins. I'm sorry it wasn't to your liking."

Cassie glared into the man's watery eyes, eyes that were
the same color as the wiry sprouts of gray hair that seemed
to spring from the top of his head in every direction. Tired
of having expert opinions from veterinarians and haughty
doggy shrinks shoved down her throat, Cassie stood her
ground. "No, Dr. Baumfarger, your expert opinion *isn't* to
my liking. In the first place, you'll have a hard time con-
vincing me it's possible for a dog to be lovesick. And in the
second place, it would be next to impossible to arrange for
the father of Duchess's puppies to pay her a *conjugal* visit."

The man actually gasped. "Now, really, Miss Collins,
there's no point in being vulgar."

Cassie ignored the reprimand and launched into her usual

pacing mode. *When is this nightmare going to be over?* she kept asking herself. She stomped around the room several times, but when her pacing brought her back to face the two esteemed doctors who were sitting on her sofa like stone statues, she brought her hands to her hips and asked, "You're absolutely certain you can't come up with any other reason for Duchess's behavior?"

Dr. Baumfarger sent Dee a conspiratorial look, then placed his teacup and saucer on the silver tray sitting on the coffee table. Rising from his seat, he smoothed an imaginary wrinkle from his sharply creased trousers, then lifted his chin until he was literally looking down at Cassie over his beaklike nose. "I'm not in the habit of having my diagnosis questioned, or of making mistakes, Miss Collins," he retorted curtly. "I've told you how to solve your problem with Duchess. It's up to you whether or not you choose to follow my advice."

With that said, the man took a step forward in Cassie's direction. Cassie moved aside to let him pass and made no objection when Dee offered to show the smug canine collaborator to the door. As their muffled voices echoed back from the foyer, however, Cassie strained to listen. "Don't worry, I'll convince her" was all she could make out.

"I'll convince her, my foot," Cassie mumbled under her breath, then stomped toward the kitchen, heading straight for the bottle of white wine that was already chilling in one of Lenora's fancy silver ice buckets.

"I'm ashamed of you, Cassie. I've never seen you act so rude," Dee scolded minutes later when she stormed into the kitchen.

Cassie ignored the comment and took another long sip of wine from her glass. "And I've never heard such a ridiculous diagnosis in my entire life," Cassie shot back.

Dee walked over and a poured her own glass of wine from the bottle. "Well, Miss Priss. I guess you'll never really know if Dr. Baumfarger's diagnosis is ridiculous, will you? You've already made it exceedingly clear that you don't intend to follow his suggestion.''

Still seething, Cassie attacked the pan of lasagna Louise had left for them, then grudgingly pushed a plate full of the luscious concoction in her best friend's direction. "Don't even start with me, Dee. You know full well there's no way to test that nitwit's theory, short of kidnapping the mangy mutt from Nick Hardin's yard.''

"You've obviously forgotten we have that terrific little invention called the telephone," Dee snapped back. "Call the man, Cassie. It might not be as impossible as you think.''

"And say what?" Cassie demanded. "Sorry I just filed a lawsuit against you, but the dog psychiatrist just informed me that Duchess is lovesick. Would you mind letting old Earl come over and sit in the parlor with her to cheer her up?''

Dee grimaced as Cassie's voice grew higher with each word she said. "Very funny," Dee tossed back. "I was thinking you might call and explain the situation, and tell Nick you were willing to compromise. You'll drop the lawsuit if he'll allow Earl to make an appearance.''

They both took their plates to the kitchen table and sat down, but Cassie only toyed with her food. She'd halfway decided to drop the lawsuit, anyway, but she certainly hadn't counted on having to call Nick Hardin. Much less apologize and ask him for a favor. Just the thought of seeing him again face-to-face was enough to put her into a tailspin. But asking for a compromise? And one that would undoubtedly mean they would be seeing each other off and on over the next few weeks? Cassie knew spending time with that man would be as dangerous as playing a game of Russian roulette with six bullets in the chamber. She'd never survive it.

Pointing her fork in Dee's direction, Cassie moved it up and down as she talked. "Okay, Miss Expert," she scoffed. "Let's say Nick *did* agree to a compromise, and that he *did* let me borrow his dog for a few hours. What am I supposed to do if Earl's princely presence doesn't change Duchess's attitude?''

Dee shrugged. ''I guess you won't know until you try it, will you?'' she mumbled with her mouth half full.

Cassie let out a long sigh, then left the table and went back to the kitchen for the wine bottle. After refilling each of their goblets, she looked at Dee and managed a feeble smile. ''You realize you may have to go out for more wine. I've heard drinking large quantities of alcohol makes it much easier to grovel at someone's feet.''

Dee's look turned serious. ''No one's expecting you to grovel, Cassie. But that little dog in there can't take many more days without any food. I'll even go with you for moral support if you want.''

''Oh, and that should go over real big,'' Cassie quipped. ''Nick doesn't exactly hold either of us in very high esteem at the moment, remember?''

''You're right,'' Dee admitted, polishing off her last bite of lasagna. ''He'd probably be defensive and think we were ganging up on him.''

Although she could feel an impending cloud of doom gathering above her, Cassie knew this was one time she had no choice in the matter. Dropping her head in her hands, she let out an agonized groan. ''I'd rather have hot needles poked through both of my eyelids than apologize to that man, Dee.''

Dee laughed despite her friend's anguish. ''I know you would, but you're a tough old girl, Cass. And for Duchess's sake, I think you can handle it.''

6

NICK TOSSED THE ARMLOAD of dirty clothes he'd collected from the den into the hall closet, then forced the door shut with his elbow. Hurrying back to make one last survey around the room, he made a mental note to have his cleaning lady come weekly instead of monthly. When he noticed a stack of old magazines still peeking out from under the stereo cabinet where he'd stuffed them, Nick used the sharp toe of his cowboy boot to kick them out of view, then proclaimed his cleaning spurt over.

Whether he liked it or not, the den looked as presentable as he could make it, given the short distance his unexpected guest had to drive from her house to his.

Heading for the bar, Nick poured himself a stiff drink, trying to imagine what Cassie had on her twisted little mind. "We need to talk," she'd said in a voice as sweet as sugar. "Is it too late to drop by your place for a few minutes?"

Nick was tempted to tell her it was too late to talk the day she filed the lawsuit against him, but something in her voice told him she was nervous. And nervous was good. Nick knew it meant that, for some reason, he now had the upper hand.

He suspected she'd taken so much heat from the publicity his talk show was receiving that she'd made the wise decision to drop the lawsuit while she still had time. He'd hoped as much when he did everything but scream her name out over the air. He just hadn't expected her to give up so soon.

Finishing off his Scotch, Nick prayed the smooth liquid would calm his jittery nerves. *And why shouldn't I be a little jumpy?* he asked himself. The woman had caused him nothing but trouble from the first day he met her. He only hoped she wouldn't show up wearing those damn Daisy Dukes of hers again. If she did, Nick knew he'd be a goner.

Not that having her fully clothed seemed to diminish her power to send his libido into orbit, because it didn't. Besides her infamous short-shorts, Nick had also seen her in a sexy party dress. She was even wearing a man-tailored suit the day he barged into her office. Yet each time her saw her, Nick found she aroused him to the point that he felt like throwing her over his shoulder and dragging her off to his cave.

At the sound of Earl's shrill bark, Nick's thoughts snapped back to the present. Bracing himself, he waited for the knock, then lingered a few seconds longer than necessary before he made a move toward the foyer. "Stay, Earl," Nick ordered, then made the long trek down the hallway where his gorgeous opponent was waiting on the opposite side of the door. This would be the fifth time the two of them had met face-to-face.

Nick only hoped round five would put an end to their fight, and declare him the winner.

He opened the door, and the minute he saw her, he knew his instincts about him now having the upper hand had been correct. The lady had pulled out all the stops for this bout in the ring. The white jeans she was wearing immediately shot his blood pressure up several notches. And she had chosen a tight-fitting teal-colored sweater that not only showed off her well-endowed bosom, but also complemented her thickly lashed aqua-colored eyes. She had even resorted to using her hair as a weapon against him. Instead of having it pulled up in a silly ponytail, or slicked back in the severe French twist she seemed to favor, her magnificent russet-colored tresses flowed over her right shoulder and almost to her waist like shining waves of amber.

Nick was lost before she even said hello.

Thrusting an ornate silver ice bucket in his direction, complete with a chilled bottle of Dom Pérignon, she said, "I hope you aren't opposed to receiving peace offerings after nine o'clock in the evening, Nick."

This time her smile even seemed genuine. A first, if Nick's memory served him correctly.

Their fingers brushed lightly when he accepted the present, but he forced himself to maintain his resolve. "If this really is a peace offering, then I guess I can make an exception," he told her, then stepped aside so she could enter the foyer. "The bar's in the den at the end of the hall," he added, and thankfully she took the lead.

Unfortunately, her backside didn't give him any reprieve, either. And sweet mama, how the lady did fill out a pair of tight jeans. Feeling the beginnings of an erection he certainly didn't want, Nick positioned the ice bucket a little lower so the cold canister could take care of his problem. To his relief, the trick worked. At least temporarily.

When she entered the den ahead of him, he nodded toward the cream-colored sofa that was facing the fireplace. She ran her slender fingers along the low back, taking in the overstuffed cushions, then looked up and smiled at him again. "I've always loved a sectional sofa. It's great you have a room large enough to accommodate one."

Nick glanced at what he usually referred to as his "sexual" instead of sectional sofa, but decided his little play on words probably wouldn't amuse her. Instead, he said, "Make yourself comfortable. I'll pour us both some champagne."

She kicked off the sandals she was wearing and settled on the sofa with her knees drawn beneath her in a comfortable pose. *Like a spider waiting for a fly,* Nick reminded himself, but the sight of her curled up there seemed right somehow. She didn't even object when Earl bounded onto the cushion beside her and began sniffing tentatively at her clothing.

"I think he smells Duchess," she offered, and actually allowed Earl to climb onto her lap.

"Don't bother the lady, Earl," Nick called, afraid Earl would disgrace him at any moment by launching into a wild fit of humping Cassie's leg.

For once, Earl obeyed his master, but hearing Cassie mention the fancy show dog's name sobered Nick enough to remind him that his guest was there on a mission, not a social call. Unwilling to let her get the upper hand, he took the lead.

"I have to admit the two of us being neighborly is much better than being at each other's throats," Nick said as he poured the expensive bubbly into two champagne glasses. "But I'd prefer to skip the game playing, counselor. Exactly what's on your mind?"

Nick's heart lurched when she unwound her long legs from beneath her and left the sofa. Padding barefoot across the carpet with the grace of a gazelle, she chose a bar stool directly in front of Nick, then took the champagne glass he handed her. "I guess you can say I've come here to propose a compromise," she said, then took a long sip.

Nick raised an eyebrow slightly. "I'm listening."

She toyed with a strand of silky hair for a moment, then took a deep breath and calmly met his gaze. "I won't lie to you, Nick. I'm willing to make a compromise only because I've run into a problem."

Nick grinned broadly. "Let me guess. You're afraid the notoriety you're receiving from my talk show will be bad publicity for your law firm."

"That, too," she admitted, "but it's Duchess I'm worried about. She's become so despondent she won't eat or drink a thing."

Now Nick *was* amused. "And?"

She paused for a moment and shook her head, as if she herself couldn't believe what she was about to say. Sending

Nick a look that dared him to laugh, she finally blurted out, "And as ridiculous as it sounds, the doctor thinks Duchess is lovesick."

Nick tried to constrain his facial muscles, but he couldn't. "You've got to be kidding me," he said with a grin.

Her blue-green eyes narrowed as she polished off her champagne in one easy gulp. "Believe me, I wish I were kidding, but I'm afraid this isn't a joke."

Nick didn't ask permission to refill her glass. Her expression told him she needed another drink. "Now, don't get defensive on me, counselor," Nick said, watching as she lifted the glass to the full, red lips he found irresistible. "But did you ever stop to think this vet of yours might have a screw loose somewhere?"

Cassie took another long sip. "Dee Bishop didn't make the diagnosis," she said quietly as she returned her glass to the bar. "My mother has an animal behavior therapist on the payroll. He's the one who examined Duchess."

This time Nick laughed out loud. "A dog shrink? Now I've heard everything."

Instead of being annoyed, Cassie surprised him by nodding in agreement. "And this is one time I have to agree with you."

Taking a sip from his own glass, Nick sent her a puzzled look. "You still haven't told me how I figure into the latest chapter of our little saga."

"I need a favor," she said without hesitation.

Nick braced himself. *Here it comes, buddy.* Pointing to the sofa, Nick grinned. "Something tells me I'd better sit down for this one."

Cassie followed after him and reclaimed her original spot, but Nick flopped down a good three feet away, trying to distance himself from the enchanting perfume he still remembered from the first night he'd kissed her. "You did mention words like 'peace offering' and 'compromise' earlier, didn't you?''

Cassie managed a smile. "I did. And I'm willing to drop the lawsuit and dismiss you from any financial obligation whatsoever where Duchess is concerned.''

"If?"

"If you'll allow me to borrow Earl until Duchess delivers their puppies.''

Her statement could have knocked Nick over with a feather. They'd literally been in a backyard brawl since the day Earl placed a grimy paw on her lawn, and now she expected old Earl to come to the rescue? Nick didn't think so.

Before he could voice his outraged opinion, Cassie hurried on. "Dr. Baumfarger insists that some domestic dog breeds inherit strong instincts similar to their ancient cousin, the wolf. Wolves run in packs, but the leader, which they call the alpha male, usually takes only one mate...."

"I've studied wolves myself," Nick interrupted, his black eyes now flashing with anger. "And I know all about the alpha male and the alpha female.''

"Then you know they work together as a team to raise their young...."

Nick interrupted again. "All I know at the moment is that I find your request a little hard to swallow. Especially after all the fuss you've made about a mutt like Earl being the father of your fancy show dog's puppies.''

Cassie dropped her eyes for a moment, then returned his gaze with a pleading look. "I deserved that, Nick. But all I can do now is apologize for my behavior and beg you to put aside our personal differences so Duchess can deliver a healthy litter of puppies.''

Beg?

The word echoed through Nick's mind like a musical note. Suddenly drunk with power, he forced himself to suppress a menacing smile. "Has it slipped your mind that those puppies will still be *mongrels,* not champions?"

The color in Cassie's cheeks deepened. "Only half-mongrel," she corrected him, lifting her chin slightly. "They'll be half-champion, too."

"Well, give the little lady a big round of applause," Nick said, placing his wineglass on the coffee table long enough to clap his hands together several times. "She's finally seeing the glass half full instead of half empty."

"Don't push it, Nick," Cassie warned, but there was no stopping him now.

Leaving the sofa, he strutted around the room for several seconds, then stopped to face her. "Okay, counselor, you've made your request, but before I agree to this compromise of yours, I have a few stipulations of my own."

"I thought we agreed to call each other Nick and Cassie," she reminded him.

"Okay, *Cassie.*" Holding up his index finger, Nick said, "Number one. I'll expect daily visitation rights with Earl."

Cassie's mouth dropped open, but Nick ignored her shocked look as he held up a second digit. "Number two. I have no intention of leaving my listening public hanging after I've piqued their interest about Earl's love affair. I hate to admit it, but right now my ratings are soaring through the roof, so I *will* continue to broadcast what the dogs are going through while they wait for the blessed event."

Cassie frowned. "At my expense, I'm sure."

Nick shook his head. "No, I promise I'll keep the tone funny and friendly."

The fact that she was now clenching her fists until her knuckles turned white only increased Nick's pleasure as he held up the third and final finger. "And number three. Since my schedule dictates that I can only visit Earl in the evenings, it would be nice if my generosity was rewarded with an occasional home-cooked meal."

Nick fully expected Cassie to run screaming from the house at the last part, but she didn't. Instead she closed her eyes and swallowed deeply, as if she were letting the bitter pill he'd just given her slide down her exquisite, creamy throat. "Okay," she said when she opened her eyes and looked at him again. "I agree to everything you said."

Only because you have no choice, Nick thought sarcastically, then walked back to the bar for more of the peace offering Cassie had brought with her to seal the deal. After refilling their glasses, Nick lifted his arm in a toast. "To compromises."

Their glasses touched, producing a magical tinkle, and though Nick knew he should be jubilant that he'd finally won their fight, a nagging little thought kept pulling at him.

"Just one other thing," Nick said as his eyes searched Cassie's lovely face. "What happens if Earl showing up doesn't do the trick?"

Raising an eyebrow, Cassie sent Nick a wry little smile of her own. "I won't go back on my word about dropping the lawsuit, Nick," she assured him, "but you can bet your buns we won't be sharing any home-cooked meals."

WHEN EARL BOUNDED into Cassie's sunroom, all that was missing was a camera crew and a commentator from one of the daily TV talk shows to capture the joyful reunion on film. Duchess darted from her crate the second she saw her lover and wagged her tail furiously while Earl delivered a series of lavish doggy kisses across her tiny face. Duchess then led Earl on a merry chase through the room, circling around Cassie's ankles several times before they both dashed into the hallway for an excursion into the rest of the house.

Now she plays hard to get, Cassie thought bitterly, then glanced behind her and found Nick propped against the doorjamb of the sunroom in a perfect James Dean pose.

"Should I make a list of my favorite foods before I leave?" Nick teased.

"As long as they come in a package that has Lean Cuisine written across the top," Cassie retorted, then walked past the cheerful victor and headed for the kitchen.

What she needed now was a hot pot of coffee to dilute some of the alcohol she'd already consumed that evening. She didn't trust herself alone with Nick in the first place. But having that warm, fuzzy feeling weaken her defenses was a chance she didn't intend to take.

Filling the coffeemaker with her favorite brew, she cursed herself for not protesting harder when Nick insisted on bringing Earl himself. Of course, it *had* made more sense. Had Duchess not responded to Earl's charms, Cassie would have been required to take the mangy mutt back home.

But respond, Duchess certainly had, Cassie thought as the dogs charged through the kitchen on their way back to the sunroom. She was tempted to reach out and grab Duchess by the scruff of the neck and shake the little traitor until her doggy teeth rattled. But Cassie was so relieved that the ditsy dog psychiatrist had been right, she knew she should count her blessings. And it could have been worse. If she'd spent the entire evening licking Nick Hardin's boots for naught, Cassie would have been really ticked off.

When she felt her tormentor's presence in the room, she turned around to find he had followed her into the kitchen. Making a grand display of sniffing the air in a truly canine manner, he grinned at her and said, "Don't tell me that's homemade lasagna I smell."

Cassie rolled her eyes. "You're really going to play this to the hilt, aren't you, Nick?"

"Hey, Italian's my favorite," he told her, disarming Cassie temporarily with the little-boy look that crossed his face when he peeked into the covered baking dish that was still sitting on the stove.

Their eyes met briefly, then locked in a meaningful stare. In the space of a second, even the bantering they kept tossing back and forth couldn't disguise the underlying emotions they were both trying to conceal. Nick knew it. And Cassie knew it. They were sitting on a giant powder keg, waiting to see who would make the first move to ignite the imaginary fuse.

Cassie's heart stopped when Nick took a small step in her direction. *You can't go there,* Cassie pleaded with herself, but her willful heart already knew the next time Nick took her in his arms she wouldn't have the strength to push him away.

"Cassie," Nick said, his voice husky with emotion, "I..."

The dogs suddenly thundered through the kitchen again, and as they chased each other around Nick's and Cassie's legs, Cassie quickly took advantage of the situation. "I think these guys need more room to run," Cassie said, sidestepping Nick's advance. "I'll make you a deal. I'll fix you a plate of lasagna, if you'll take these little monsters outside while I get things ready."

Her attempt at changing the subject wasn't successful. Instead, Nick moved forward, closing the distance between them, forcing Cassie to retreat until she found her back against the kitchen sink. With less than an inch of space left between them, Nick reached out and brushed a loose tendril of hair away from her cheek. Amazed at his gentleness, all Cassie could do was stare.

"It's not lasagna I'm hungry for and you know it," Nick whispered hoarsely.

"Nick, p-please," Cassie stammered, but he was so close his warm breath tickled the side of her face.

"Don't get so jumpy, counselor," he whispered, then lifted her chin and forced her to meet his gaze. "The only way anything will ever happen between us, is if *you* ask me."

She started to protest, but Nick cupped her face in his

hands and brushed her lips with a kiss so gentle Cassie wondered if she had only imagined it.

He stepped away from her then and turned to leave, but he looked back over his shoulder when he reached the kitchen door that led into the hallway. "Oh, by the way, counselor," Nick added, sending Cassie a wink, "Earl likes to sleep on the foot of the bed. And I sure wouldn't be unhappy to find pot roast waiting on the table when I stop by to see you guys tomorrow night."

CASSIE FLIPPED OVER on her stomach and covered her head with her pillow, trying to block out the persistent howling that was coming from the sunroom. When a particularly mournful howl penetrated the thick down feathers pressed against her ears, she threw the pillow across the room and switched on her bedside light.

Glaring at the clock as if *it* were responsible for keeping her awake until 2:00 a.m., Cassie kicked off the covers, then stomped out of her bedroom, thinking that Nick Hardin's dog was even more obnoxious than his master. Not that Nick hadn't played his own part in the reason she hadn't been able to drift off to sleep. In fact, their latest little rendezvous in the kitchen had left her with enough mixed emotions to keep her awake a lifetime.

It continued to amaze her that Nick had the ability to arouse her one minute, and infuriate her the next. She'd always heard there was a thin line between love and hate. And from the moment she'd walked into Nick Hardin's life, Cassie was beginning to believe it.

"*I'll* be the one to ask *him,* my grandma's girdle," Cassie mumbled under her breath as she descended the stairway on a mission to both bind and gag her tormentor's dog.

Traipsing through the house wearing nothing but a T-shirt and her skimpy bikini panties, Cassie jerked the French doors open and switched on the light. As she expected, two intent

little faces stared back at her. "What's the problem down
here?" Cassie demanded, glancing toward the malleable bed
of old quilts she'd made for the two lovers in the far corner
of the room.

Of course, she didn't get an answer, but she wasn't prepared when Earl darted around her and ran from the room
with Duchess scurrying after him at warp speed. Throwing
her hands in the air in disgust, Cassie stomped after them,
then chastised herself for being so mean. *I'm sure the little
guy's homesick,* Cassie thought. *Maybe he'll settle down if I
pay him a little attention.*

Expecting to find Earl standing by the front door, waiting
to be taken home to his beloved master, Cassie reached the
foyer in time to see two little doggy tails disappear up the
stairs.

"Now, wait just a minute you little rascals," Cassie called
after them, then took the stairs two at a time.

Practically sliding through the doorway when she reached
her bedroom door, Cassie groaned when she saw both dogs
curled into comfy little knots in the middle of her bed.
She started to protest, but thought better of it when the dig-
ital flaps on her clock flipped over, declaring it was now
2:15 a.m.

"Well at least move over," Cassie grumbled, too tired to
argue and too softhearted to make them leave.

After retrieving the pillow she'd tossed to the floor earlier,
Cassie switched off the light, then slid into the bed beside
her two new bed buddies. As she resumed her favorite fetal
sleeping position, both dogs immediately inched closer and
made a nest for themselves in the vacant space left by the
bend of her knees.

Cassie let out a long sigh of resignation as they snuggled
against her, then promptly closed her weary eyes. But the last
thing that crossed her mind before sleep mercifully claimed

her was an appropriate line Nick had said on the air the first morning he complained about her lawsuit.

"You heard it here first, folks. It looks like the world really is going to the dogs."

NICK GLANCED AT the luminous dial on his bedside clock, then returned his stare to the ceiling. It was after three o'clock in the morning, yet he still hadn't closed his eyes. He kept replaying the words he'd said earlier to Cassie over and over in his mind, knowing from the angry look she'd given him before he left that the meaning of his statement had been totally misinterpreted.

What I said did sound rather cocky, Nick admitted to himself. But that hadn't been his intention.

He'd merely been trying to tell his nervous adversary that she didn't have to worry about him forcing himself on her against her wishes. Instead, his statement made it sound as if he couldn't care less if they ever acted on the high-voltage impulses that sparked between them every time they got together.

"You idiot, you should have explained what you meant," Nick said aloud into the darkness.

Hell, of course he wanted her. He wanted her more than any woman he'd ever met. And she wanted him, too. Nick knew it in his heart, whether Cassie realized it yet or not. Why else would he have insisted on daily visitation rights with Earl? Sure, he cared about his dog, but the main reason he used the ploy was so he and Cassie could spend as much time together as possible.

Suddenly wondering if the aristocratic attorney was so highly educated she didn't have any common sense, Nick pulled himself into a sitting position and switched on the light by his bed. And as he sat on the side of his king-size water bed, it occurred to Nick that he might as well take advantage of this bout of insomnia.

Deciding to do something more constructive with his time than brood about a silly female, Nick kicked aside the crumpled pair of jeans lying on the floor, then strolled naked across his bedroom to the huge rolltop desk that housed his computer. And as he waited for the screen to come to life, Nick's mind was already spinning with the task at hand.

As his fingers caressed the keyboard as if it were a familiar old friend, a broad smile erupted across his face. And then he began typing.

"When you think about it, folks, now that Earl has his Duchess, this story is shaping up to be a dog lover's version of Romeo and Juliet. I'm happy to report that unlike Shakespeare's star-crossed lovers, who were kept apart by their feuding families, Earl and his lady, Duchess, won't have to resort to suicide in order to be together. Yes, quarreling owners that we previously were, the lovely attorney and I have finally put aside our petty differences. Especially once it became obvious that these two dogs were determined to be together..."

Nick's fingers flew across the keyboard, stopping only when a particularly funny line made him chuckle out loud. Of course, had anyone been able to peer inside his bedroom window, they would have found it rather amusing to see a grown man sitting naked in front of a computer, laughing to himself.

But work had always been Nick's personal therapy for blotting out the world, and his work didn't fail him this time, either. Despite the fact that he hadn't had any sleep, Nick looked up and smiled when the alarm clock went off at 5:30 a.m.

To Nick, it seemed like a miracle.

For the first time in more days than he cared to remember, he had managed to spend two splendid Cassie-free hours, not thinking once about the erotic things he intended to do to her voluptuous body if she ever gave him half a chance.

7

"TELL ME HOW the groveling went," Dee demanded the instant Cassie answered her private line. "From what Nick said on his program this morning you've obviously buried the hatchet. Did you happen to hear his Romeo-and-Juliet analogy?"

"Yes, I heard it," Cassie groaned.

"Well?" Dee snapped. "Don't keep me in suspense, Cassie. Tell me what happened."

Balancing the phone between her shoulder and her ear, Cassie waded through a detailed account of the previous evening's events while she opened her morning mail.

"Now, that's where I'd draw the line," Dee insisted when Cassie got to the part about the home-cooked meals.

"I have everything under control," Cassie assured her best friend. "I've instructed Louise to stuff Nick every night until his ears bleed. I just don't plan to be there when she does it."

"Don't you let that man muscle you out of your own home, Cass," Dee warned.

Cassie stiffened at the remark. She hadn't told Dee about the kiss-in-the-kitchen scene, knowing it would only set her friend off on another tirade. Unfortunately, Dee always had the uncanny ability to read between the lines. "Why would you say that?" Cassie asked, a little sharper than she intended. "If you could see my desk right now, Dee, you'd know what I mean. With Father away, I have more work than I could handle if I moved into the office full-time."

Dee didn't try to disguise the "harrumph" she snorted at Cassie's statement. "You might fool someone else with that explanation," Dee scoffed, "but you're talking to me, remember?"

"I'm sure I don't know what you mean."

"Yeah, and George Clooney didn't look great in those Batman tights, either," Dee said. "You know as well as I do that you think you can ignore what's going on between you and Nick by keeping your distance."

"I told you from the beginning, Dee. I don't intend to let myself get involved with that man."

"You don't believe that any more than I do," Dee argued. "And whether you *intend* to get involved with him or not, it's just a matter of time, Cassie, until you come to your senses and jump that gorgeous hunk's bones."

Cassie rolled her eyes. "Are you on that doggy-treat diet again, Dee? You obviously have the word *bones* embedded in your brain."

Dee laughed but wouldn't drop the subject. "Give Nick a chance, Cassie. It might turn out better than you think."

"Fat chance of that happening," Cassie scoffed. "Nick and I are as different as night and day."

"Like Ron and I aren't?"

Cassie had to admit that a Methodist minister was the last person she'd expected the party-girl of Alpha Delta Pi to fall for. Yet it had happened. Dee and Ron were even dancing around the issue of setting a date. Imagining Dee as the humble parson's wife, however, seemed as farfetched as picturing herself walking down the aisle on Nick Hardin's arm.

Choosing to end the conversation before Dee started making sense, Cassie crossed her fingers and told her best friend a tiny white lie. "My other line's ringing, Dee. I'll call you later."

Returning her attention to the stacks of files waiting on her desk, Cassie rearranged several groups into neater stacks, then placed several other files on the floor beside her desk. Once her desk was suitable for working again, she forced herself to concentrate on the corporate merger contract that loomed before her. Unfortunately, she never got a chance to read the first word.

"Mr. Hardin on line one for you, Miss Collins."

Cassie stared at the blinking phone for several moments, deciding a call from Nick was probably fit punishment for lying to Dee. Rather than have the brute think she spent a second thinking about the kiss, or about his final arrogant words, Cassie mustered her most cheerful, phony voice and picked up the phone.

"Hi, Nick, how are you this morning?"

"Good morning, counselor. Thought I'd call and see how things went last night."

"You mean before or *after* I relented and let the little creep sleep on my bed?"

Nick laughed. "Hey, I told you Earl slept on the foot of my bed."

"I know you did, but I thought you were kidding."

"When you get to know me better, counselor, you'll realize I never kid about important things." His voice grew huskier with every word.

Cassie waited out the pregnant pause with her eyes closed, but managed to summon her phony voice again. "Well, don't worry about Earl, Nick," she said, struggling to control her gag reflex. "The lovebirds were sharing a bowl of dog food when I left the house this morning."

"Glad to hear it," Nick told her. "See you tonight."

Not if I have anything to do with it, Cassie thought as she slammed down the phone. Unwilling to go through another phony performance in case Nick *did* decide to call again, Cassie flipped the intercom button on her desk and waited until her assistant answered in response.

"Please hold my calls, Sally," she instructed. "Especially

any calls from Nick Hardin. I don't want to be interrupted again."

NICK DROPPED THE RECEIVER back in the holder and looked up to find the station manager strolling through the doorway of his office. "Show me the money," the bald man chanted, doing a comical dance around Nick's desk.

"I take it you're pleased with this morning's program?" Nick mused.

The bald man grinned. "Pleased? Nicky boy. The listeners ate that Romeo-and-Juliet stuff up with a spoon. I'm telling you, this damn dog affair of yours is hotter than a tabloid exclusive. Our ratings are up almost fifty percent. The phones are still ringing off the hook. And I just got a call from that local TV morning show wanting Earl and Duchess to appear on the program next week."

Nick frowned. "No deal."

"Who says so?" the station manager demanded.

"I do," Nick said. "Think about it, Bob. Like you just said. We have an exclusive here. Let the damn television media find their own hero and heroine. If the public gets a peek at Earl and Duchess, it'll be because the station holds its own party and invites the public to attend."

"Damn smart thinking," Bob said, rubbing his hand over his fleshy jowls.

"Then maybe you'd better show *me* the money," Nick replied.

"Like you're not overpaid as it is," his boss growled, then made a hasty exit, which was exactly what Nick wanted.

Leaning back in his chair again, Nick propped his feet up on his desk, resting cowboy boot over cowboy boot. Despite his fear that she would still be angry over his arrogant comment from last night, Cassie had certainly been pleasant enough on the phone. In fact, she even sounded cheerful. Was it possible he was beginning to wear down her defenses?

Or could it be he'd done the right thing by telling Cassie it would be her idea if they ever made love?

Nick knew some women preferred being the aggressor, even to the point of taking complete control in the bedroom. Was it possible Cassie Collins was that type of woman?

Grabbing a pencil from behind his ear, Nick chewed on the end, trying to anticipate how Cassie would react when he saw her later that evening. Letting his imagination run wild with possibilities, he pictured them sitting in the kitchen, enjoying a cup of coffee after the delicious meal she'd just served. Maybe they'd even take their coffee outside so the dogs could romp around the yard while they looked on from the moonlit patio. And then, when it was time for him to leave, Cassie would stop him. "Oh, Nick," she would say, slipping her arms around his neck and—

"Dammit, Nick, where's your head, boy? I've been yelling at you for at least five minutes."

Startled from his fantasy, Nick jumped to his feet. "What?" Nick shouted.

"There's a herd of TV reporters downstairs demanding an interview with you, that's what," Bob shouted back.

Nick shook his head with determination. "No interviews. Tell them it isn't possible."

"March your fuzzy ass down there and tell them so yourself," his boss hollered. "I'm not your press agent, boy. I've got a damn radio station to run."

NICK WASN'T PLEASED when he drove his motorcycle into the circular drive of the Collinses' house and found the silver Lexus missing from the driveway. Checking his watch, he was relieved to see it was only a little after seven. Nick faintly remembered Cassie saying that she rarely got home before seven, and then, like a lightbulb going on over his head, he recalled the entire conversation.

"The dog sitter," Nick mumbled under his breath.

Dismounting his faithful metal steed, he removed his gloves and helmet, then glanced around the property, trying to decide if he should knock on the door or wait in the yard until Cassie arrived. His dilemma was settled for him, however, when an elflike woman with silver-white hair appeared at the Collinses' door wearing a brightly colored apron.

"Mr. Hardin?" she called, waving in his direction.

Nick walked cautiously up the steps of the elaborate old Victorian, then stood towering over the woman who had beckoned him to the porch. "Please call me Nick," he said when the woman granted Nick a brilliant smile.

Taking his outstretched hand in both of her tiny ones, she gazed at Nick, a twinkle in her pale blue eyes. "And I'm Louise. Cassie told me to watch for you."

I just bet she did, Nick thought, as all of the pieces in the puzzle silently fell into place. Before Nick could comment on exactly when Louise expected the piquant trickster home, Louise ushered him inside, where Nick was instantly greeted by both dogs at once.

Kneeling down to scratch Earl's ears, Nick soon found that the queen of the dog world didn't intend to be ignored. He had never cared for poofy, prissy dogs, but he had to admit that Earl's lady did have a sweet little face. He didn't even object when Duchess vaulted onto his bent knee and showered him with a series of sloppy doggy kisses.

Her Majesty's actions, however, resulted in a quick reprimand from her royal sitter. "Duchess. Leave the poor man alone," Louise scolded, then shooed both dogs away from their victim.

Nick stood up when the dogs scampered back down the hallway. "I hope Earl hasn't been too much trouble today," Nick said as he followed Louise toward the kitchen.

Louise laughed. "Lordy, no, Earl's been a blessing to this household, Nick. And the change in Duchess has been amaz-

ing. We were really getting worried about the little thing's
health, you know,'' she added when they reached the kitchen.

Nick did know, but he only nodded.

Steering him toward the kitchen table, Louise motioned
for him to sit. ''Cassie told me to feed you until you
'popped,''' Louise said, letting out another musical giggle.
''I've set your place here in the kitchen, Nick, but if you'd
prefer eating in the formal dining room, it'll only take me a
second to change things.''

By now Nick was livid. So Cassie had it all figured out,
did she? She'd meet his requirements by having Louise fix
his dinner, then avoid coming home until she was positive
he was gone. *Well, it's not going to be that easy, sweetheart.*

''It's really no trouble if you'd prefer the dining room,''
Louise insisted, jarring Nick from his thoughts.

''No. No, the kitchen's fine, Louise,'' he told her, and
quickly took his seat.

Nick watched the spry little woman bustle around the
kitchen. ''I'm sorry you've gone to all this trouble,'' he told
her, but the overwhelming aroma of the delicious-looking pot
roast she was serving up quickly turned his statement into a
lie. He hadn't taken time for lunch and he was famished.
Cassie or no Cassie, Nick's mouth involuntarily watered as
the tiny woman began filling his plate.

''Lordy, cooking isn't any trouble for me,'' Louise said
over her shoulder. ''I usually cook something for Cassie
when I'm here, anyway, and we have dinner together. It isn't
much fun eating alone, you know.''

''Then join me, please,'' Nick told her.

Her eyes lit up with the same sparkle he had first seen on
the porch. ''Well, thank you, Nick. I don't mind if I do.''

They ate in silence for several seconds, Nick fully enjoying
the tender meat that virtually melted in his mouth every time
he took a bite. But after a few minutes, he decided he would

do a little prying. And who better to get information from than the hired help?

"Have you worked for the Collins family long?" Nick asked casually.

"Since Cassie's mama was knee-high to a grasshopper," Louise said, then dabbed daintily at the corner of her mouth with her napkin. "I started working for Cassie's grandpa, Judge Parker, two weeks after his wife died and left him alone with a small daughter to raise."

"I'm sure he felt lucky to find you," Nick told her.

"Well, I hope so. I never left the judge's side until the day he died," Louise confided, her voice fading away on a sad note. After a few seconds of reverent silence she added, "This was Judge Parker's house, you know. Cassie's parents moved in with the judge the same day they were married. The judge wouldn't have it any other way. Lucas Parker was a very formidable man."

Nick thought about her statement, then took another bite before he asked, "And you stayed on with the family after Judge Parker died?"

"Of course I did," the old woman said, lifting her chin slightly. "Cassie's mama is like my own daughter. The judge spoiled Lenora rotten, of course, but I'll tell you one thing, Nick," she added, shaking her finger in Nick's direction, "Lenora Parker Collins knows better than to pull any of that big-shot socialite stuff with me. Old Louise spanked her bottom plenty when she was little. I might be close to seventy now, but I still have a mighty quick hand."

Louise burst into another long giggle as she swatted her hand through the air for effect. Nick found her laughter infectious, and laughed along with her for a few seconds before he finally got down to the heart of the matter.

"And Cassie. Is she spoiled, too?"

"Why, that child is an angel straight from heaven," Louise protested, obviously alarmed that Nick had even asked such a question. "You'll never meet a sweeter girl in your life, I can promise you that." She paused then, her look turning reflective. "I just wish Cassie would find a nice boy and make a life for herself. She's been under Lenora's thumb way too long."

Already knowing the answer, Nick couldn't resist hearing Louise's version of the question he was about to ask. "But I thought Cassie was serious about the assistant district attorney?"

"Oh, pooh," Louise spat. "Mark Winston is a sniveling snot Lenora and her father-in-law tried to force down Cassie's throat. I'm glad Cassie finally got the nerve to tell him to—" Louise paused before she finally whispered, "Shove it," then giggled behind her hand.

Deciding he liked this woman better by the minute, Nick dug a little deeper. "I take it you aren't very fond of Senator Collins."

Louise's eyes narrowed. "That pompous toad always looked down his nose at the judge. And he wouldn't give Cassie the time of day. Too busy living in Washington rubbing elbows with the big shots," Louise said with a frown. Her face broke into a wide grin when she added, "I'm here to tell you, though, Lucas Parker didn't mind putting him in his place. One of the darnedest fights I ever saw, happened right here in this kitchen when Lenora and the senator made noises about sending Cassie off to boarding school in Switzerland. The judge wouldn't stand for it. Cassie stayed right here."

Nick nibbled on a roll. "What about Cassie's father? Didn't he have a say in the matter?"

The old woman's eyes softened. "Howard Collins is a good man, Nick, but he's never been very good at standing up to his father, or to Lenora. I always thought it was ironic that the judge wanted Lenora to marry Howard, thinking some of his kindness would rub off on her, and Senator Collins pushed Howard to marry Lenora, because she's every bit as snooty and phony as he is.''

"The world's a strange place, isn't it?" Nick reflected, then polished off his last bite of pot roast before he pushed himself back from the table.

Smiling at the old woman who had already won his heart, Nick said, "You certainly outdid yourself, Louise, so let me return the favor by cleaning up the kitchen.''

At first, Nick thought Louise was going to reject his offer, but her tiny face suddenly broke into a wide smile that smoothed away the wrinkles at the corners of her mouth. "Well, praise be to God," she said, bursting out with another musical laugh. "I've finally found a man who's willing to do the dishes.''

CASSIE FROWNED WHEN she pulled into her driveway and found a motorcycle sitting in the space where Louise's hatchback should have been. *And why isn't Louise's car still in the drive?* Cassie wondered. She'd told Louise only that morning to plan on spending the night because it would be extremely late before she got home that evening. Cassie didn't like Louise being out on the highway by herself late at night. It wasn't safe.

Slamming the door when she left the car, she wished she'd taken time to freshen makeup before she left the office. But since it was midnight now, she hadn't expected to have company—especially not *his* company—waiting when she returned home.

She heard a faint bark from inside the house when she put her key in the lock, then frowned when she found the front door wasn't locked at all. *Not that the big muscle-bound brute waiting inside would be afraid of a burglar,* Cassie thought angrily as she pushed the door open and stepped into the darkened foyer.

The light glowing from beneath the library door made it

easy to determine where her unwanted guest was hiding. *That's all I need,* Cassie thought, grimacing as she pictured her mother returning home from Europe and finding something amiss in the sacred room. Lenora had preserved the library as a shrine to the judge since the day Cassie's grandfather died.

Tossing her purse and keys on the cherry table by the door, Cassie headed for the room that even *she* wasn't allowed in, fully prepared to give her unwanted guest a huge piece of her mind. When she opened the double doors and entered the library, however, the sight Cassie beheld left her frozen in horror. *Now wouldn't Lenora faint dead away if she saw a picture of this?*

"Hi," he said casually, looking up from the leather-bound book that was balanced on his stomach. "I told Louise she could go ahead and leave since I volunteered to clean up the kitchen."

Cassie was speechless. Not only had Nick evidently taken the liberty of giving Louise the night off, but he was also stretched out on the judge's antique horsehair sofa with his boots off and both dogs curled around his feet. It was just too much for her to process. Knowing there was no way she could make a civil word roll off her tongue, she turned on her heel and marched out of the room.

"Hey, was it something I said?" Nick called from behind her.

Seething by the time she reached the kitchen, which happened to be immaculate, Cassie grabbed the glass pot from the coffeemaker. Turning the faucet as if it were Nick's neck she held in her hand, Cassie was surprised when the knob didn't twist off and fly across the room by itself.

Of all the bold, insolent, unmitigated nerve! Cassie thought as she ticked the words off in her mind.

Trying to ignore the two dogs who had followed her into the kitchen, Cassie soon found they wouldn't permit her to disregard their attention. Kneeling down, she accepted a few wet kisses from the determined canine couple, hoping the unconditional love they were showing her now would some- how put her in a better frame of mind. Unfortunately, from her crouched position, Cassie saw a pair of stocking feet walk into the room.

Her chances for a better mood were instantly blown straight to hell and back again.

She jumped up, hands flying to her hips. "I agreed you could spend a few hours in the evening with Earl, Nick," she spat in his direction. "I don't remember saying anything about you spending the night with him."

Nick's black eyes immediately narrowed. "Well, excuse th' hell out of me," he snapped back. "Louise mentioned she usually played bingo at the nursing home with her sister on Wednesday nights, so I volunteered to stay with the dogs until you got home. I thought I was doing both of you a favor."

Cassie's mouth dropped open, then closed again. Praying for a giant hole to suddenly appear in the kitchen floor and swallow her up, she called out, "Hey, Nick, wait."

Her words fell on deaf ears. Nick marched from the room without so much as a backward glance, followed by the two dogs, who seemed to understand that Cassie had just made a gigantic faux pas. She found all three of them in the library several minutes later. Both dogs were perched on the sofa beside Nick, watching while he pulled a reptile-skinned cow- boy boot over his foot.

"Nick, I'm sorry, but it's been a really long day and I…"

"And you jumped to the conclusion that I was hanging around until you got home so I could drag you off to bed," Nick growled, tugging the leg of his jeans down over the top of his boot. "But I thought we had that discussion last night, counselor."

If that's your definition of a discussion, buster, then we need to have a serious talk! Cassie wanted to shriek, but for once she bit her tongue and swallowed her words. Making the dogs move over, she sat down on the sofa beside Nick. As she and the dogs watched, Nick pulled on the other boot. "You can't make me feel any worse than I already do," Cassie said. "I really am sorry. What more can I say?"

"Forget it." Nick snapped the jeans down over the second boot, but when he started to rise from the sofa, Cassie grabbed his arm. He lowered himself back onto the sofa, then sent her an angry stare.

"Please don't go away mad," Cassie pleaded, sending him her most apologetic look.

"Just go away?" Nick replied, but this time he refused to look at her.

Cassie studied his strong profile, admiring his square jaw, which now sported a faint shadow from a new growth of beard. Reaching out, she wanted to touch his face, but she let her hand drop at the last minute and picked up the book he'd left lying between them instead. "So, you're a Stevenson fan?" she inquired, leafing through the pages of *Treasure Island.*

When Nick let out a long sigh, Cassie knew he was responding to her soft approach whether he wanted to or not. Propping his elbows on his knees, he turned his head in her direction and glanced at the book. "Yeah, I've always loved Stevenson. I hope you realize how valuable that first-edition copy is."

Cassie glanced at the large floor-to-ceiling bookcases that lined three sides of the dark-paneled room. "There are a lot of classic first editions in those bookshelves," Cassie mused with a smile. "They belonged to my grandfather and he cherished every one of them." She flipped the book back to the front page and pointed to a distinct male scrawl that was written in faded ink. "The judge wrote this in every volume he had," she added, and handed the book to Nick. "He didn't care that it reduced its resale value."

"'A good book is like an old friend. Treat it kindly, and see it safely home,'" he read aloud. To Cassie's relief, some of the irritation faded from his face.

"And how many of those first editions have you read?" he challenged.

"All of them," Cassie answered truthfully.

He seemed amused. "Seriously?"

"Not all women think *Moby Dick* is a social disease, Nick," Cassie scolded without thinking, but then she held her breath, waiting for his reaction to her smart remark. She didn't exhale until she saw the laughter reach his eyes.

When his hearty laugh filled the room, Nick licked his finger and chalked up an imaginary point. "Lawyer one, disc jockey zip," he said, sending her a genuine smile. "You never cease to amaze me, counselor. And here I thought people in the legal profession didn't have a sense of humor."

Cassie relaxed then and leaned back against the sofa, remembering happier days when her grandfather's laughter had warmed her heart the same way Nick's had now. *Oh, my God. That's one of the reasons I'm so attracted to Nick*, she suddenly realized. When she thought about it, Nick's personality wasn't really much different from that of the judge's. And Judge Lucas Parker *had* been a rascal in his day.

Not only had the powerful man been outrageously outspoken, but he had also thumbed his nose at the social sector, preferring instead the company of the farmers in the field to that of the snooty bigots who lived around him. The judge had even insulted his own profession more than once by discarding his black robe when his courtroom became too hot, and conducting sessions while he sat on the bench in his bib overalls.

Staring at Nick as if she'd just seen him for the first time, Cassie realized what her heart had been trying to tell her all along. She had fallen hopelessly and helplessly in love with Nick Hardin. And there wasn't anything she could do to change it.

Closing the book, Nick handed it back to Cassie, then gave Earl a fond pat on the head. "Well, I guess I'd better go," he said, and started to stand.

Fighting back the tears that were quickly pushing to the surface, Cassie knew it was time to put an end to their silly game playing. She grabbed his arm again, refusing to let him go. "I wasn't afraid you'd try to go to bed with me tonight, Nick," she admitted, biting her lower lip to keep it from trembling. "I was afraid I *would* go if you asked me. I've been fighting whatever this is that's happening between us, because I already know if I let myself, I'll fall head over heels…"

She bit her lower lip. She just couldn't bring herself to finish her sentence.

Nick's black eyes softened when a single tear betrayed her and slid down her cheek. Reaching out, he gently wiped it away with the pad of his thumb. "Hey, sweetheart, don't cry," he whispered. "Don't you realize I've been fighting the same thing? You turn me inside out, Cassie. I know it doesn't make any sense, but I'm in love with you. I have been since the day I found you standing beside my pool."

Nick's sudden tenderness tore through Cassie like a herd of wild horses, instantly freeing a life's worth of pent-up passion. Without any reservations, she leaned forward and brushed her lips lightly across his.

But it wasn't enough for either of them.

No one would remember later exactly who slid off the narrow sofa first, but Nick and Cassie both ended up on the floor, touching each other everywhere at once, as kiss after sweltering kiss left them both panting, breathless and begging for more.

"Stop me now or don't stop me at all," Nick warned, his voice hoarse with desire.

Cassie answered Nick's challenge by literally ripping the silk blouse off her shoulders and tossing it over her head.

Articles of clothing began flying through the air at lightning speed, sending the dogs into a barking frenzy as they ran around the room, playing catch at what they thought was a delightful new game. One of Nick's cowboy boots hit the bookshelf with enough force to send an entire row of first editions toppling to the floor. And one of Cassie's heels sailed into oblivion, striking the antique cuckoo clock hanging on the wall in just the right place to awaken the feathered little thespian inside.

Stuck in a locked position, the once-silent clock now allowed the cuckoo freedom to run from his house every few seconds to announce his punctual call. The room suddenly plunged into darkness when Nick's other cowboy boot sent the table lamp crashing to the floor, but the little bird's confident warble continued to cheer the enraptured couple on.

And on.

And on a little longer.

After fifteen minutes of what had to be the most urgent sex known to modern man, the dust finally settled in the room, leaving Cassie and Nick lying naked in the darkness, entwined in each other's arms while they listened to Earl and Duchess howl every time the determined little cuckoo yodeled its cheerful call.

"I'll strangle the dogs if you'll do something about that damn cuckoo," Nick whispered, sending Cassie into a fit of hysterical laughter.

When she finally stopped laughing, she rolled on top of Nick and began teasing his earlobe with the tip of her tongue. "We can always pretend we don't hear them," she whispered, then abandoned his earlobe and began making little circles down his neck with the tip of her tongue.

"Baby, that does feel good," Nick moaned, putting an end to her torturous activity when he pulled her head down and tucked it safely under his chin. "But I don't think even Superman could get an erection with that noise in the background."

Cassie giggled and rolled on her side, then slid her hand boldly down the length of his naked thigh. "Oh, yeah? Well, it sure didn't seem to bother you a few minutes ago, cowboy."

Nick laughed. "You should have warned me there was a sex-crazed monster hiding beneath that professional disguise of yours," he teased, then aimed a kiss at what he thought were Cassie's lips.

He missed and caught her in the corner of the eye.

"Sorry," Nick said, then sat up when Earl let out another blood-curdling howl. Smacking his hand firmly against the sofa cushion, Nick ordered, "Earl, hush."

Earl stopped howling instantly, but both dogs quickly joined Nick and Cassie on the floor. Cassie squealed when a cold, wet nose pressed against her bare side. Putting her hands out in front of her, she tried to locate at least one article of her clothing, but she only succeeded in scraping her fingernail across Nick's left ear.

"Ouch!" Nick groaned.

"Sorry," Cassie said, grimacing when the cuckoo screamed out again from his lofty perch in the pitch-black room.

"How much glass do you think I'll have to walk through before I find the light switch?" Nick asked.

"I'll go," Cassie said, holding on to the edge of the sofa as she pulled herself up. "You'd never find the overhead switch."

Stumbling through the dark room with her panties still tangled around one ankle, Cassie finally reached the wall and slid her hand along the smooth paneling, searching for the evasive switch. When she finally found it, she balanced herself on one foot long enough to yank the panties off her foot, then darted from the room the second she flipped on the light.

"I'll be down in a minute," she yelled over her shoulder.

Nick laughed when Cassie made a mad dash for the stairway with both dogs yapping at her heels, but she hadn't been fast enough to prevent him from getting a quick glimpse of her creamy-white bottom as she bolted from the room. Still chuckling to himself, he remained sitting on the floor for several seconds, totally amazed at the mass destruction that surrounded him.

The room resembled a war zone after a major battle. Replacing the sound of enemy fire was the irritating screech from the infernal little cuckoo as he continued to burst through the door of his house every two or three seconds.

Nick didn't bother to look around for his jeans. Restraining himself from jerking the clock off the wall and adding it to the rubble lying on the floor, he marched across the room and whacked the bird square in the nose when it made its next appearance. To Nick's relief, the door to the miniature alpine house slammed shut, sealing the cuckoo safely back inside its prison.

"Thank God. Peace at last," Nick said triumphantly, but as his heart filled with love for the woman who'd just attacked him with the ferocity of a wild tigress, he knew he'd never find true peace again.

At least not until the little vixen responsible for the current carpet burns on both of his knees agreed to share more than his bed.

CASSIE STEPPED INTO the shower, humming to herself as she lathered her hair. And then it hit her. *Oh, my God. What have we done?*

As she stood staring into space for several minutes, it took the shampoo burning her eyes to bring Cassie back from her zombielike trance. Though the shower blast quickly rinsed the irritant from her eyes, the steaming hot water did nothing to wash away the mounting fear that was now surging through her body.

How did I let this happen? she kept asking herself.

They didn't use protection. They didn't even take time to have the "talk" first.

The overwhelming knowledge that her glorious few minutes of unbridled passion could possibly have major repercussions made Cassie's knees buckle. "What on earth is happening to me?" she groaned aloud.

Hadn't she always been the responsible one? The "Ice Maiden," as Dee called her, because she never slept around? Maybe Lenora had been right, after all. Maybe she really wasn't capable of taking care of herself. From the moment her parents had left for Europe, her six weeks of blessed freedom that she'd been looking so forward to had turned into an apocalyptic asperity.

After at least thirty minutes of serious lamenting, Cassie pulled herself together long enough to go back downstairs. Not caring that her hair was still wet, or that her face was now void of any makeup, she pulled on a pair of faded jeans and an equally washed-out T-shirt. If Nick was now rested enough for a repeat performance, Cassie decided her unsightly appearance would quickly put him out of the mood.

She found him in the library wearing nothing but his boxer shorts and his cowboy boots, tossing splintered pieces of glass into a trash can he'd found somewhere in the room. He grinned when he looked up and saw her standing in the doorway.

"I still haven't found my jeans," Nick said, but a closer look at Cassie's ashen face told him something was wrong.

"Leave the mess. I'll vacuum later," she said, but remained by the doorway with her arms folded across her chest.

Nick dropped a final piece of the broken lamp into the trash, then flopped down on the sofa and patted the cushion beside him. "Come on, counselor, the look on your face tells me we need to have a little talk."

"Don't you think it's a little late for that?" Cassie asked, but she did cross the room and sit down beside him.

Nick took her hand and kissed the tips of her fingers, obviously reading her mind. "I know we got carried away a few minutes ago, but you have my word, Cassie. I'm completely healthy."

She sent him a tearful look. "I'm healthy, too, Nick, but that's only half of our problem."

It was Nick's turn to have the color drain from his face. "You mean…you mean you're not…?"

"On the pill?" Cassie snapped, then broke eye contact before she added, "There's never been any reason to take birth control before, Nick."

A certain amount of pride filled Nick's heart knowing Cassie hadn't taken a regular lover before him, but it was quickly replaced with concern over their current predicament. Squeezing her hand, he sent her a meaningful look. "I don't want you jumping to conclusions over any smart remarks I might have made about the dogs, Cassie. I've always wanted a large family. If it turns out we do have a problem, I promise you, we'll handle it together."

Cassie wanted to ask Nick exactly what his definition of *handle it* was, but she didn't. When she didn't respond, Nick squeezed her hand again, trying to joke her into a better mood. "Hey, we've already admitted that we love each other, right? And our dogs are even soul mates. It can't be that bad, can it?"

Glancing at the two dogs who were currently lying together in a knot at their feet, visions of doctor's appointments, ultrasounds and special diets flashed through Cassie's mind. "Yeah, it's just like déjà vu all over again, isn't it?" she sighed, making a lame joke with her redundant statement.

Neither of them laughed.

8

IT WAS NOON THE FOLLOWING day when Cassie pulled into her office parking lot. Nick had stayed long enough the previous evening to help her repair the havoc they'd wreaked on the judge's precious library, but after he left, Cassie fell into a deep sleep shared only by the dead. She would have still been asleep now, if Louise hadn't kept pestering her until Cassie finally surrendered and rejoined the world of the living.

As she left her car, Cassie noticed several camera crews and a group of television reporters gathered around the entrance to the Flat Iron Building. As she wondered briefly which of the other five law firms that were housed in the building had captured the media's attention, it never crossed Cassie's mind that the reporters were waiting for her.

"Miss Collins! Miss Collins," one of the reporters yelled when Cassie approached the door. "Is it true that Duchess went on a hunger strike because you wouldn't let her see Earl?"

"When are the puppies due?" a female reporter screamed from the center of the crowd.

Aghast, Cassie pushed through the mob yelling "No comment!"

She finally made it to the big revolving door that led into the office building, but before she could escape to safety, a male voice echoed from behind her, "What about you and Nick Hardin? Is there any truth to the rumor that you're pregnant with Nick Hardin's baby?"

Cassie stopped and wheeled around to face the man. "That, sir, is none of your business."

The reporter sent Cassie a leering grin. "Can I take that comment as a 'yes'?"

"You can take it and shove it for all I care!" Cassie shouted, then stormed through the revolving door, colliding with none other than her recent "ex," the assistant district attorney himself.

Straightening his suit jacket with a curt little jerk, Mark Winston then bent down and retrieved the attaché case Cassie had dropped when she bumped into him. After handing the briefcase back to her, he sent a friendly wave toward one of the camera crews that had followed Cassie through the revolving door. Though he was putting on his usual politician smile for the benefit of the cameras, Cassie didn't miss the vengeful look in Mark's eye.

Purposely turning his back on the reporters so they couldn't hear what he was saying, he folded his arms sedately across his chest and sent Cassie the smug little grin she had always despised. "Well, Cassandra," Mark said, looking her up and down as if she were last week's garbage, "you have no one to blame for this fiasco but yourself. I tried to warn you about the bad publicity you'd get if you linked your name with a man like Nick Hardin, but you wouldn't listen, would you? And to think I wasted all that time treating you like some vestal virgin because I thought you had morals. You wouldn't sleep with me at all, much less on our first date."

"No, I slept *through* my first date with you, Mark," Cassie hissed, "and whether or not I choose to link my name with Nick Hardin's is *still* none of your business."

Mark's eyes narrowed as he sent Cassie an evil smirk. "Then it's true, isn't it? You really *are* carrying that hoodlum's child."

Without a second thought, Cassie's fist came from nowhere and landed precisely in the center of Mark Winston's nose.

Temporarily addled, Mark stumbled backward several steps. "You'll regret this, damn you," Mark growled as he jerked a handkerchief from his inside jacket pocket to stop the spurt of blood that was threatening to stain his crisp Brooks Brothers shirt.

"Don't bet your campaign on it," Cassie snarled.

"Did you get that on film?" an excited reporter yelled from behind them.

Cassie didn't wait to hear the answer. Turning on her heel, she headed for the elevator, relieved that the rest of the media rushing into the large marble lobby had found a much bigger fish to fry. When the elevator doors slid shut, sealing her safely inside, Cassie brought her throbbing hand up for inspection and actually smiled.

Bruised knuckles were well worth the satisfaction she'd gotten from punching Mark Winston in his arrogant nose.

NICK SAT AT THE COMPUTER in his office putting the finishing touches on the outline for his next program, which was a comical little piece about his unsuccessful search for a Lamaze class that would accept Earl and Duchess. He looked up for a second when his boss stuck his head around the door, then returned his eyes back to the screen, typing in the final line.

"Hey, Nicky, Charlie just came back from lunch and said the word on the street is that your girlfriend just punched the assistant D.A. in the nose. Call her up and get the scoop."

"She did *what?*" Nick screeched, jerking his head around, but Bob had already disappeared down the hallway.

Nick sat at his desk for several minutes thinking that twenty-four hours ago he would have argued adamantly about Cassie Collins being his girlfriend. But now the word seemed too trivial to describe what she meant to him.

Then what is she? he asked himself. *The possible mother of my unborn child?*

"My child," Nick repeated aloud to himself, amazed at how protective he felt just uttering the unfamiliar phrase.

His protective feelings toward Cassie and his possible baby were quickly replaced with anger, however, at the thought of Mark Winston having any contact whatsoever with either of them. Knowing he would personally beat the man to a pulp if the idiot so much as laid a finger on Cassie, Nick rifled through the papers on his desk until he found Cassie's office number.

"Cassie Collins, please," Nick said when the pert voice on the other end of the line answered.

"Miss Collins isn't taking any calls at the moment," the efficient voice announced.

"She'll take one from me. It's Nick Hardin," Nick said, tempted to throw in *the possible father of her unborn child.*

"NICK, I'M FINE... NO, HE didn't...no, you won't!" Cassie shook her head in disbelief at the angry voice on the other end of the line. *And how had Nick heard about any of this so soon?* Cassie wondered as she glanced at her watch. It was only 2:00 p.m.

"Nick, if you'll hush for a second, I'll tell you what happened." When Nick paused long enough for Cassie to get a word in, she took a deep breath. "A bunch of TV reporters ambushed me in front of the Flat Iron Building earlier, asking questions about Earl and Duchess."

"Dammit, I told the media yesterday that we wouldn't be granting any interviews about the dogs," Nick grumbled.

"Well, they obviously didn't listen," Cassie said. "Anyhow, things turned ugly when one reporter couldn't resist throwing in a little dig about the rumor that's been circulating ever since you mentioned Duchess's pregnancy test in front of Evelyn Van Arbor."

They both remained silent for a few seconds, each thinking that their little escapade the previous night had possibly validated the woman's gossip.

"Sorry about that," Nick said, then added, "but how did Winston get involved?"

"Mark was coming out of the building as I was going in. He insulted me, and I lost it. I swear, Nick, I didn't even realize what I'd done until I saw the blood spurt from his nose."

"How did he insult you?" Nick demanded, suddenly angry all over again.

Cassie paused. "Let's just say Mark referred to the rumor as 'carrying that *hoodlum's* child.'"

Instead of being outraged, Nick laughed, thinking how degrading it must be for the arrogant D.A. to think he'd been cuckold by a hoodlum. "That's priceless. I love it." He chuckled. "Thanks for defending my honor, counselor."

"I was defending my own honor, you jerk," Cassie insisted, unwilling to admit that Mark calling Nick a hoodlum had enraged her almost as much as Mark asking the question in the first place.

"Are those vultures still hanging around the building?" Nick asked, changing the subject.

Cassie was tempted to remind Nick he usually reserved the term *vultures* for lawyers, but she left her chair instead and peeked out the window. "They're…here."

"Then I'm coming to get you," Nick said. "Meet me at the back of the building in ten minutes."

"You'll do no such thing," Cassie insisted. "I have a ton of work on my desk that won't wait."

"Then call me here at the station when you're ready to leave," he ordered. "I won't let you face those reporters alone again."

"I'll probably be here until six or after," she warned, praying it wouldn't matter. The thought of facing the nasty man with the leering grin again didn't appeal to her at all.

"Call me," Nick said, and broke their connection before Cassie could argue.

CASSIE WAS JUST FINISHING her paperwork that evening when her office door burst open and she looked up to find none other than her grandfather, Senator Edward Collins himself, standing in the doorway. In a split second, Cassie knew Mark Winston had made good on his threat to make her regret that punch in the nose.

As always, the senator was impeccably dressed. His salt-and-pepper hair was perfectly coiffed, complete with a sufficient amount of spray to hold every strand in place, and though he would soon be seventy, thanks to his skillful plastic surgeon, no wrinkles or jowls marred his handsome face.

Cassie braced herself, then forced a smile for the pretentious man who considered her chromosome-deficient because she hadn't been a male. "I didn't realize you were in town, Grandfather," she said casually.

Slamming the door behind him, the senator wasted no time shaking his finger in Cassie's direction. "I don't have to tell you why I'm here, Cassandra, so don't pretend that I do."

Cassie bristled at his sharp tone. Her jaw set with determination, she folded her hands on top of her desk, then inclined her head toward one of the leather chairs opposite her desk. "Then at least sit down while you give me the lecture you came to deliver. I'm sure your flight from D.C. was both unexpected and tiresome."

His rich man's perpetual tan paled slightly before his face turned a brilliant blood-red. Stomping up to her desk, he glowered down at her with both hands at his waist. "Don't you dare use that insolent tone with me, young lady," he bellowed. "You've disgraced this entire family and I won't have it."

Cassie struggled to maintain her courage. "I admit striking Mark, especially in public, was a stupid…"

"Stupid?" Senator Collins screamed. "'Stupid' is putting it mildly, Cassandra. You could face disbarment for that little episode. But thank God, Mark had the good sense to call me first. Together we've come up with a plan that should get you both out of this mess."

She tried to squeak a protest, but the senator held his hand up for silence. "I met with Mark's press agent before I came here. We've decided it's best to pass this entire nightmare off as a silly lover's spat."

"Oh, no you won't," Cassie warned, shaking her head in protest.

The senator slammed his fist down on the top of Cassie's desk, causing her to jump. "Oh, yes I will, Cassandra," the senator snarled. "I've already arranged for a press conference. The sooner we clear up any speculation about your outlandish behavior, the less chance the media will have to ruin Mark's campaign."

After glancing quickly at his watch, the senator looked Cassie up and down, obviously displeased with her haggard appearance. "Go make yourself presentable," he ordered. "Mark's agreed to meet me here in thirty minutes. We'll all three attend the press conference and formally announce your engagement."

More angry than she'd ever been in her life, Cassie jumped up from her chair. "You'll do no such thing, Grandfather," she said through clenched teeth. "I'll take disbarment any day of the week before I'll even *pretend* to be engaged to Mark Winston."

The senator's lips pressed into a thin line. "If you'd really make such an asinine choice, Cassandra, then I have to assume that incorrigible disc jockey you've been slumming around with really has put a little bastard in your belly."

Cassie blanched at his crude statement, but to her surprise, a deadly calm settled over her as she pointed to the door. "Get out of my office, Grandfather. Get out now, before I say something I'll regret later."

"Get out?" the senator bellowed. "You can't throw me out of my own offices, you ungrateful little fool. Whose names do you think are on that door?"

When Cassie refused to answer, the senator's smile turned lethal. "Collins and Collins refers to me and your father, Cassandra, it has nothing to do with you. In fact, *you*, my dear, have never been anything more than a necessary inconvenience."

Cassie knew the statement should have crushed her, just as her grandfather had crushed her more than a decade ago by admitting he was disappointed that she hadn't been male. But surprisingly enough, she suddenly felt totally, completely and wonderfully liberated.

Sending the senator her brightest smile, Cassie grabbed her office keys from the top drawer in her desk and tossed them in the old man's direction. "Thank you for pointing out that I'm such an inconvenience in *your* office, Grandfather. Because as of this moment, I quit."

IT TOOK NICK ONLY five minutes after Cassie's call to make it from the radio station to the Flat Iron Building. Frowning at the crowd assembled at the front entrance, Nick was tempted to stop when he saw Mark Winston and an older man smiling for the TV cameras that were pointed in their direction.

"Hey, isn't that Nick Hardin?" a voice from the cluster of people yelled.

Nick revved the engine of his big Harley and darted down the alley, praying that Cassie would be waiting at the back door as he'd instructed. To his relief, she stepped from the doorway the second he screeched to a halt.

"The place is crawling with cameramen," Nick said as he

pushed back the visor on his helmet. "I thought we'd be able to make it to your car, but we don't have a chance."

Glancing nervously at the huge motorcycle, Cassie bit her lower lip. "Then what are we going to do?"

Nick grinned. "It's your call, counselor."

Without another moment's hesitation, Cassie hiked the tight skirt of her tailored business suit to her waist and climbed behind Nick as if she were a veteran biker. "Just get me out of here," she told him as she wrapped her arms tightly around his waist.

The big Harley jerked to life and started down the alley, but Nick slid to a sideways halt as a camera van appeared from nowhere, blocking their path. Without warning, the van door slid open and a cameraman hopped out, pointing a lens in their direction.

"Hold on," Nick yelled.

Doing a fancy U-turn in the narrow space, he then darted back the way he'd come. Unfortunately, an even larger group of people were waiting when they burst out of the alley. Slowing down as they approached the crowd, Nick contemplated the risk, then launched ahead full speed and forced the crowd to scatter as he and Cassie roared past the rolling cameras, looking like a knight in shining armor rescuing a beautiful damsel in distress.

As they zoomed safely past the crowd, Cassie didn't see the shocked looks on her grandfather's and Mark Winston's faces when they realized it was Cassie on the back of the big Harley with her arms around a hoodlum and her skirt hiked to her waist.

"Cassandra Collins! You get back here this instant!" the senator screamed.

Startled by the sound of her name, Cassie looked back over her shoulder in time to see the senator waving his fist in the air and Mark Winston standing beside him slowly turning a light shade of green.

"Who was that?" Nick yelled.

"Only my grandfather," Cassie yelled back, but she laughed in spite of herself.

Nick picked up speed, causing the wind to whip through her hair and send it toppling down her back in a cascade of reddish-gold curls, and Cassie laughed even louder.

"Hey, are you okay back there?" Nick yelled.

"I'm won-der-ful," Cassie yelled back, knowing that despite the terrible shambles she'd made of her once predictable life, racing through the wind with her arms around the man she loved was the only thing that mattered at the moment.

Feeling free for the first time in her life, she leaned her head back and screamed like a banshee.

"Hey, counselor, you're getting a little carried away back there, aren't you?" Nick called, laughing himself.

Cassie snuggled closer to Nick and shouted in his ear, "Shut up and take me home, you handsome hoodlum. You're stuck with me now."

PROPPED UP IN THE BIG canopy bed that Cassie had slept in since childhood, Nick and Cassie passed a bowl of buttered popcorn back and forth between them while both dogs slept on the foot of the bed.

"Flip back to the local news," Cassie gasped, then grabbed the remote from Nick's hand and performed the task herself.

"It looks as if senatorial candidate Mark Winston may have more than political woes to keep him awake at night," the handsome WTCV anchorman announced with a semi-straight face.

Cassie sat straight up in the bed, ignoring the fact that Nick whistled when the sheet slipped below her bare breasts. The film footage flashed to a picture of Cassie punching Mark in the nose, then melted into a shot of Cassie's bare legs from the back of Nick's motorcycle. She watched in horror.

Nick let out a loud wolf whistle again. From the angle of the shot, it appeared as if Cassie was completely nude from the waist down.

"Winston and his biggest supporter, retired Senator Edward Collins, called a press conference late this evening stating that the altercation you just saw of Winston being punched in the nose by attorney Cassandra Collins was only the result of a lover's spat between Winston and the senator's granddaughter...."

By now Nick was laughing so hard, Cassie finally pushed a pillow over his face so she could hear what the anchorman was saying.

"However, only minutes after Senator Collins announced the happy couple's engagement, the attractive bride-to-be roared away from the press conference astride a Harley-Davidson motorcycle, driven by popular radio talk-show host, Nick Hardin. Miss Collins's name has been linked with Hardin's this past week over the charming story we've been running about their two dogs, Duchess and Earl. And just for the record, folks, though you couldn't tell from the footage we shot, Miss Collins really was wearing a skirt..."

Cassie switched the television off, flopped back on the bed with an agonized groan and promptly pulled the sheet completely over her head.

"Hey, come on, counselor," Nick teased, punching her playfully in the ribs. "You quit, remember? Your grandfather can't do anything to you now."

Jerking the sheet off her head, Cassie glared at Nick as if he'd suddenly sprouted two heads. "I'm not worried about my grandfather, Nick, it's my mother. You can bet my grandfather is trying to locate Lenora as we speak."

Nick pulled her to him and began stroking her hair. "Even if your grandfather does reach your parents, they're in Europe, remember? It'll take a few days before they can get home and by that time all of this hoopla should have settled down.''

''You don't know my mother.'' Cassie sighed, then practically jumped out of bed when the telephone's shrill ring echoed through the room.

''Let your voice mail answer that,'' Nick urged, pulling her closer and nuzzling her neck. ''I have more important things for you to do than answer the phone.''

Cassie snuggled against him, enjoying the hard feel of his body as it pressed against her own. ''And just how many of those little protection packages did you bring with you, Mr. Hardin? Two? Three? Maybe even four?'' she teased.

Nick growled low in his throat. ''Let's just say I don't plan to stop making love to you until I hear you scream like you did earlier on the back of the Harley.''

''Prove it,'' Cassie challenged, then tangled her hands in his hair and brought his mouth down hard against hers for a lingering kiss.

CASSIE GENTLY MOVED Nick's arm so she could slip out of his bear hug, then held her breath when he moaned in his sleep and rolled over on his side. When two little heads popped up from the middle of the bed to see what she was doing, Cassie drew her finger to her lips to shush them, then grabbed her robe from the bottom of the bed and sneaked out of the bedroom.

It was already after 1:00 a.m., making Cassie envy Nick's ability to drop off to sleep the second he closed his eyes. And though Nick's ardent lovemaking had left her both immensely satisfied and physically drained, she couldn't stop worrying about the persistent caller who had tormented them to the point that Nick had finally left the bed himself and unplugged her bedroom extension.

Once downstairs, Cassie hurried to the kitchen and punched in the access code to receive her voice mail. And before she listened to the first of the sixteen messages the animated operator said were waiting, Cassie already knew Lenora's angry voice would be on each and every one of them.

"I'll never be able to hold my head up in Asheville again, Cassandra. And poor Mark. You've probably ruined his chances…"

Cassie erased the first message before it concluded, then waited for the second one.

"The very idea you'd even speak to a man like Nick Hardin, much less…"

Erased.

"I've been so upset ever since your grandfather called me, that the ship's doctor had to give me a sedative…."

Erased.

"And what is this silly nonsense about Duchess that has everyone laughing through their teeth…?"

Erased.

Cassie continued to erase each of the messages until she got to the final one.

"We're cutting our trip short, young lady. We'll be home Sunday afternoon and the first thing I intend for you to do is…"

Cassie punched the erase button before Lenora finished her sentence, wishing she would have that same luxury once her mother arrived home. It was official, then. Her parents were actually cutting their trip short and coming home on Sunday. And since it was technically already Friday, Cassie knew she only had two days left before Lenora returned and put an end to her freedom.

And to me and Nick, Cassie realized with a panic. Lenora would rather show up at the country club in an outfit from some discount mall than allow Cassie to continue to see Nick.

Unless? Cassie decided, trembling at the mere thought.

Unless I finally stand up to Mother and start making my own decisions.

Movement from the doorway caused Cassie to look up. Wearing nothing but a pouting look, Nick stumbled into the kitchen with his hair tousled and his eyes still heavy from sleep. Despite the fact she had just spent hours engaged in the most intimate union possible for a man and a woman, Cassie blushed at his nakedness.

Stretching languidly, Nick sent her a sleepy smile. "Hey, what's up? I reached for you and you were gone."

"Have you always been this modest?" Cassie asked, trying to mask her embarrassment.

Nick ran his hand over his hairy chest and grinned. "Yep. But you still haven't answered my question. What's wrong, sweetheart?"

Cassie left the kitchen chair and walked straight into Nick's open arms. "That was my mother calling earlier."

"I figured as much. That's why I unplugged the phone."

"They'll be home Sunday," she said, exhaling with an exasperated puff.

"Then let's not waste a minute of the time we have left," Nick whispered as he kissed the top of her head.

Cassie didn't object when he took her hand and led her back to bed.

9

BOTH CASSIE AND NICK rose fairly early Friday morning. He rushed off to do his morning talk show but he promised to return with Cassie's car before noon. She, on the other hand, found herself at home with nothing to do for the first time since she graduated from law school.

Wandering around the big house alone, she wished she hadn't excused Louise from her dog-sitting duties the previous evening, but she also knew Louise had only been doing her a favor. It didn't seem right to keep the woman confined to a daily job she didn't need when Cassie no longer had one of her own.

"You guys want to go outside?" Cassie quizzed.

Taking her coffee cup with her, she followed Earl and Duchess out into the sunny morning and lounged at the patio table while the parents-to-be romped playfully around the yard. *Parents-to-be*, Cassie thought to herself. She and Nick had been extremely careful the previous night, but being responsible then couldn't erase their irresponsible behavior during their first fit of wanton passion.

And what if I am pregnant? Cassie asked herself. Nick had said they would handle things together. But if his idea of "handling" things meant anything other than having his child, Cassie never wanted to see or hear from Nick Hardin again.

Worried that her heart may have led her down a traitorous path, Cassie hated to admit that she hardly knew Nick at all. They hadn't had time to get to know each other. They'd either been *at* each other's throats or had their tongues *down* each other's throats since the moment they met.

Yet, Cassie knew beyond all reason that she loved him. The problem, however, was did she love him enough?

She left the patio table and wandered around the yard, trying to keep her old doubts and fears from invading her mind. Yes, she and Nick were different, but they also fit together like the intricate workings of a Swiss watch. Cassie knew love sometimes wasn't enough, but now that she'd found love with Nick, she also knew she'd rather have a few days of bliss than a lifetime of nothing special. And "nothing special" was exactly what she'd end up with if she allowed Lenora to keep running her life.

"I've danced the dance," Cassie told the dogs when they ran up beside her. "Now I guess I'll have to pay the piper."

Both dogs barked simultaneously, seemingly in agreement with her statement, but their efforts did little to boost Cassie's self-confidence. If she wanted a future with Nick, she would have to confront Lenora.

The thought was terrifying.

"DAMMIT, NICK, I TOLD YOU to get the scoop from your girlfriend, I didn't say a word about you becoming a CNN celebrity."

Nick sent a scowl at his boss as he headed for his office, but it didn't discourage the man from following him into the room. "Don't give me that, Bob. Publicity, good or bad, will keep our listeners tuning in and we both know it."

The balding manager dragged a hand over his flabby face, trying to wipe away a silly smirk. "Well, I just wanted to be sure you weren't planning to mention your coup d'état on your program this morning."

"And have Winston's lawyers slap me with a six-figure libel suit?" Nick scoffed. "Give me a little more credit than that."

"Hey," Bob said, "lust does strange things to a man's head. Especially when he's in lust over a woman with legs like those."

Nick shot his boss a look of warning, then handed him the outline for the morning chapter in the Earl and Duchess saga. Titled Mongrel Takes on AKC in Discrimination Suit, it was a whimsical account of Earl's intention to have his half-champion puppies recognized by the American Kennel Club, even if it meant facing a court battle to do it.

"Satisfied?" Nick demanded.

His boss was still chuckling when he walked out.

After his morning show, Nick left his motorcycle in the radio station parking lot and walked the five blocks to Cassie's office building. To his relief, he found the sidewalk in front of the entrance vacant and no reporters lurking in the parking area. He suspected Senator Collins had pulled more than a few strings in the past twenty-four hours. North Carolina, after all, was predominately a Republican state. And the powers that be would waste no time putting an end to any story, sensational or not, that might damage the campaign of their golden boy, Mark Winston.

Whistling as he unlocked the door of the Lexus, Nick slid behind the wheel, thinking he should send Senator Collins a thank-you note himself. Whether the old goat realized it or not, calling off the heat on Winston also made Nick and Cassie off limits to the media. It was a break they both needed. Especially with Cassie's parents on their way back from Europe.

But as Nick eased out of the parking lot, his euphoria at having the media off their backs was overshadowed by his concern over where he would stand when Cassie's parents did return home. They hadn't had the opportunity to discuss Cassie's relationship with her parents, but it didn't take a rocket scientist to figure out if Cassie was twenty-eight and

still living at home, that Ma and Pa Collins had enough in-
fluence to keep their little bird close to the nest.

Not that Cassie still living at home bothered Nick, because
it didn't. Many single women her age already had at least
one live-in lover under their belt. Nick had never been serious
enough with anyone to move them into his home. He was
actually pleased Cassie hadn't chosen that route, either.

Although, Nick thought as a half smile formed on his lips,
Cassie and he might be taking that live-in step sooner than
they thought, if there was a baby in the making.

Neither of them had mentioned the possibility of a baby
since their first night together, but the thought had never been
far from Nick's mind. They'd be married as quickly as possible, of course, and raise their child together in a loving,
caring home. The type of home Nick always wanted as a
child but never had.

Nick laughed, thinking how much he'd changed in such a
short period of time. Nick Hardin, the man who swore he'd
never get involved with a career woman, and especially not
a lawyer, was suddenly thinking about wedding bells and
baby booties.

In fact, waking up that morning and finding Cassie sleeping peacefully next to him had only confirmed what Nick
already knew. Career woman or not, Cassie Collins had sto-
len more than his heart. As if by osmosis, she was now part
of his soul.

And what more could I ask for in a woman? Nick asked
himself. She had spunk, yet she was witty. She made love to
him with wild abandon, yet she still managed to retain the
innocence of a child. She was beautiful *and* intelligent. And
she wasn't anything like his mother.

Just thinking of his mother jerked Nick's brows into a
deep-furrowed frown. His father had remarried several years
ago and was happy now. But his mother still lived for her
California-based real-estate business and for the hordes of

rich and famous celebrities that kept her business thriving. She always called Nick on his birthday and at Christmas, but he saw her rarely. Mainly because having a thirty-six-year-old son hanging around damaged the youthful image she tried to portray to her jet-set friends.

But Cassie isn't like my mother, Nick reminded himself again. Or was she?

The haunting question made Nick realize it was time to find out.

Whipping into the parking lot of the quaint little fresh market Biltmore Forest residents relied on to provide them with the gourmet items most supermarkets didn't carry, Nick decided he would pick up a great bottle of wine, some fruit and cheese, and then he'd take this mystery woman he'd fallen so hopelessly in love with on an old-fashioned picnic.

"It's time we got to know each other," Nick mumbled as he hurried into the store.

And what better way to accomplish his goal than sharing a romantic picnic in the mountains where they could both have a long, serious talk?

CASSIE GIGGLED AS NICK delivered a series of silly kisses over her forehead and down to the tip of her nose. "I'll have to send you rushing off to the radio station more often," she teased.

Pulling her to him, Nick ravished her with a long, lingering kiss, then swatted her playfully on the bottom. "Get your shoes on and find the dogs, woman," he ordered. "We're going on a picnic."

Cassie squealed in delight. "Really? Where?"

"To the mountains, of course," Nick said, then whistled for Earl and Duchess.

"But don't we need to fix—"

"You're burning daylight, counselor," Nick interrupted as he pushed Cassie toward the doorway. "I have everything we need. Now, put that gorgeous little butt of yours in the car.''

Laughing, Cassie ran upstairs for her sneakers, glad she'd chosen a comfortable pair of shorts and T-shirt as her outfit for her first day at home without a job. ''I'm hurrying,'' she yelled when Nick whistled again.

Bounding out of the house, she laughed when she saw Nick shepherding Earl and Duchess into the back seat of her Lexus. Pulling the door closed behind her, she hurried to her car, then saluted Nick when she slid into the passenger seat.

''I'm at your disposal, Captain Hardin. Carry on.''

Nick rolled his eyes, but steered the Lexus skillfully out of the driveway. ''How's it feel to be unemployed?'' he teased, but then he squeezed her hand.

''I'll tell you after I see what you purchased for my lunch,'' Cassie replied playfully, but his hand over hers warmed her heart.

She knew it was Nick's way of saying he understood how nervous she must be at the uncertainty of what the future held for both of them. Still holding his hand, Cassie relaxed as Nick took the exit for the Blue Ridge Parkway. It had been years since she'd ridden along the parkway, much less headed off for a picnic.

''What gave you the idea for a picnic?'' Cassie asked as she ran her fingers along the top of Nick's strong, bronzed hand.

He glanced at her and grinned. ''You can't keep me chained to the bedpost every minute we're together, counselor.''

Cassie pinched him. ''If memory serves me correctly, *you* were the one going for a marathon record last night. I was begging for mercy.''

''That isn't all you were begging for.''

Cassie blushed.

Nick brought her fingers to his lips. "I just think it's time we got to know each other better, that's all," he confessed.

Cassie glanced in his direction. "What do you want to know?"

Nick smiled. "Everything. Your favorite color. The type of music you like. Whether or not you love Christmas as much as I do. Things like that."

Absently playing with a strand of hair that had escaped her ponytail, Cassie took a deep breath. "Well, my favorite color is any shade of green. I'm partial to the oldies music of the sixties and seventies. I love rocky road ice cream. I'm crazy about Chinese food. I'd rather read than watch TV...."

"And Christmas?"

Cassie wrinkled her nose, thinking how Christmas had never been the same since the judge died. "Let's just say Christmas usually leaves me feeling lonely."

They rode along in silence for a few seconds before Cassie turned the tables. "You've heard my story, now how about you?"

"My new favorite color is strawberry-blond," Nick said, making Cassie laugh. "I love all music, from classical to country and western. And you can keep your rocky road, counselor, because if memory serves me correctly you owe me a Popsicle."

Cassie laughed. "And food?"

"I love food, period," Nick said, "and I, too, would rather read than watch TV. Unless, of course," he added, "it's football season."

"And Christmas?" Cassie asked.

Nick sent her a thoughtful glance. "I guess I love Christmas more than any other time of the year," he admitted. "It's the one time people seem to put all their petty differences aside and embrace one another."

It was Cassie's turn to squeeze Nick's hand. "Why, Mr. Hardin, I do believe you have a sensitive side."

"Just don't take advantage of it," Nick said, then pulled off the parkway onto a narrow gravel road.

Cassie was amazed at how quickly they disappeared into the forest. The huge canopy of trees allowed only fractured rays of the summer sunlight permission to peek into the pine-scented forest. Giant ferns brushed against the side of the car as Nick took another turn, then crossed a wooden bridge. A delightful little brook babbled up at them, spewing frothy white foam in places where the swift water careered over rock and fallen limb.

"We'll have to walk from here," Nick said, switching off the engine.

Cassie left the car and laughed when Earl and Duchess darted off through the forest, sniffing everything they saw like seasoned hunters. "It's absolutely beautiful here. How did you ever find this place?"

"My dear, you haven't seen anything yet," Nick informed her, then handed over one of the three sacks he had taken from the trunk of the car.

Making a big production of peeking inside all three of the sacks, Cassie grinned. "Wine, cheese and fruit? Is there anything you *didn't* think of?"

Nick shrugged, but Cassie could tell he was pleased with her praise. She followed along behind him, picking her steps carefully as they climbed up a steep ridge. "Wait for me," she called when Nick disappeared from view, but once she finally made it to the top of the ridge her mouth dropped open in sheer amazement.

The view was breathtaking.

She lowered herself onto the plastic tablecloth Nick already had spread out on the ground and stared in awe at the majestic Blue Ridge Mountains that seemed to reach into infinity. Turning to him, she asked, "Have you ever seen anything this beautiful in your life?"

"Not until I ran into you," Nick said truthfully.

When he took her in his arms, Cassie knew the wine, cheese and fruit would have to wait their turn.

"WHO WOULD HAVE THOUGHT a snazzy attorney like yourself would be willing to give up her career for a loving husband and a house full of kids?" Nick teased as he fed Cassie a plump grape.

"I think the word I used was *postpone* my career until my children were older," Cassie said after she swallowed the sweet fruit. "And who would have thought a motorcycle-riding rebel like yourself would want a conventional family with a stay-at-home wife and a dozen little kiddies calling him Daddy?"

Nick laughed. "We're quite the pair, aren't we?"

"I'm beginning to think so." Cassie leaned forward for a quick kiss, then added, "You already know my life story, but you still haven't told me how you ended up in Asheville."

Nick took a deep breath. "Well, I moved to Atlanta at the ripe old age of eighteen and adopted it as my hometown. I intended to live there forever until I looked around one day and decided I needed a better quality of life. I'd been in Asheville before and it seemed like a good place to find myself."

"And have you found yourself, Mr. Hardin?" Cassie urged.

"I found I had the ability to actually listen when someone criticized my work."

"Meaning?"

"Don't even pretend you aren't aware that I've dropped the lawyer joke of the day from my program, counselor. Hell, I've even refrained from suggesting that working women were largely responsible for putting an end to America's traditional family way of life."

Cassie wrinkled her nose. "I just assumed you were so

wrapped up in the Earl and Duchess saga that you'd put your other pet peeves on hold.''

"Not so," Nick assured her, shaking his head. "You were right to call me on the carpet about the jokes. I'm just sorry I didn't take your comments seriously until you stomped up on my doorstep. I was letting my personal feelings leak over into my professional life. That's never a good thing."

Cassie ran her finger down the top of his arm. "Well, despite the fact that I dreamed of strangling you after you insulted me on the air, if it makes you feel any better, you knocked a giant hole in my defenses that first evening on the veranda."

"And do I dare say I told you so?" Nick asked. "I distinctly remember telling you I knew you enjoyed our little encounter as much as I did."

She sent him a sheepish smile, then pulled her knees to her chest. "Yes, I hate to admit it, but you were right all along." Turning her face back to him, Cassie couldn't hide her tear-glistened gaze. "And now that I've found you, I just can't bear the thought…"

"Hey, hon," Nick whispered, pulling Cassie close. "Now, don't go and spoil our picnic by getting morose on me. We both know this relationship of ours will be a real challenge, but it isn't anything we can't work out together."

She nodded and tried to send Nick her bravest smile. "We're definitely the perfect pair of book ends for a psychological study, aren't we? We're both educated, intelligent adults, yet we're still struggling with the infamous 'mother' complex. Your mother never had time for you, and my mother still won't let me out of her sight."

Nick filled each of their plastic cups with sparkling burgundy and handed one to Cassie. "I know you're not looking forward to a fight with your mother, Cassie, but I can't imagine you not holding your own. You've never had a problem putting me in my place."

Cassie let out a long sigh as she toyed with the red liquid she was swirling around in her cup. "That's what's so crazy about our twisted mother-daughter relationship, Nick. I can argue contract law with the best corporate attorney available. I've always been outspoken. I've even taken up for myself with my peers and my enemies, but when it comes to standing up to Lenora Collins, I regress to a sniveling five-year-old."

Kissing the top of her head, Nick said, "But this time you'll have someone else on your side, hon. I just hope you'll decide fighting for our relationship is worth being at odds with your parents."

When Cassie didn't comment, Nick pulled her to him and cradled her head on his shoulder. "Maybe that's why fate kept throwing us together. We'll both know what mistakes *not* to make with our own children."

Cassie flinched at his statement. "Let's don't even go there, Nick," Cassie begged. "I have enough on my mind right now. I've disgraced the family's good name, quit the family law firm and I'm way past crazy knowing I have to face my mother in two days. If I start thinking about the possibility that there might be a baby on the way, I'll blow every circuit in my not-so-stable body."

"You're right," Nick said, squeezing Cassie's shoulder affectionately. "Let's not give a second thought to anything else but that beautiful sunset hovering above the mountains right now, and the entire night of lovemaking we can look forward to when I take you home tonight."

"I love you, Nick," Cassie whispered as Earl nudged his head under her arm.

"Not half as much as I love you," Nick told her, allowing Duchess to curl into a tiny ball in his lap.

But as the sun slowly slipped out of sight, Nick wondered if the sudden chill he felt was due to the uncertainty that awaited them about the baby, or the fact that he couldn't be sure how Cassie would react when her mother did return home.

Did Cassie love him enough to risk severing ties with her powerful family? Or would she be the second woman in Nick's life to break his heart by making him the last priority on her list?

10

NICK MANAGED TO GET one eye open the next morning, only to find Earl sitting on his pillow and sending Nick that panicked I-have-to-go-out-now look. Glancing at Cassie's bedside clock, Nick didn't blame Earl. It was 8:00 a.m.

"Okay, okay," he groaned as he slipped from the bed. "I'm taking the dogs out," he whispered, then leaned over and kissed Cassie on the shoulder.

Her only response was to snuggle deeper under the covers.

He stumbled along behind Earl and Duchess, who darted for the stairs the second he opened Cassie's bedroom door. Raking a hand through his long hair, Nick started down the stairs himself, saddened by the fact this would be their last day together. At least until Cassie had time to smooth things over with her parents.

They had discussed their relationship at length the previous evening as they sat on the ridge top watching the sun slip behind the fog-tipped mountains. But nothing had been settled completely. Cassie assured him that she didn't intend for them to be apart. But as simple as it sounded, Nick had a deep gut feeling that nothing about their relationship would be that easy.

Reaching the bottom of the steps, Nick started down the hallway, but Earl's shrill bark brought him to an abrupt halt. Turning around to see what all the commotion was about, he froze when the front door suddenly burst open and an elaborately dressed woman with platinum-blond hair rushed into the foyer with a scowl on her face.

Automatically covering his privates, Nick tried to run for cover, but Lenora Collins let out a blood-curdling scream and promptly wilted into a tidy heap on the expensive Oriental carpet that covered her marble foyer floor.

CASSIE SAT STRAIGHT UP in bed the second she heard the piercing scream.

"Oh, my God! It's Mother!"

Jumping from the bed, she danced around on one leg, trying to pull on her shorts and her T-shirt at the same time. Bolting through her bedroom door, she reached the top of the stairs only to collide with Nick, who was naked as usual and obviously flustered.

"I think she fainted," Nick gasped. "You'd better call 911."

Cassie pushed Nick aside and flew down the steps in time to see Lenora wielding her favorite Gucci purse at the two dogs, who were taking full advantage of finding a helpless victim lying in the floor.

"Get these beasts away from me!" Lenora screamed, swatting mostly at Earl. "I mean it, Cassandra. These are two-hundred-dollar silk stockings straight from Italy. I won't have them ruined."

Cassie herded the dogs down the hallway, flung the sunroom doors wide open, then ran back to the foyer, only to find that Lenora was gone. Fearing her enraged mother had marched upstairs in search of the naked man who'd been copulating with her saintly daughter, Cassie started up the stairs. When she heard a low moan coming from the direction of the living room, however, a long sigh of relief took most of the breath from Cassie's body and flung it into the tension-filled air around her.

"Welcome home, Mother," Cassie mumbled under her breath, then squared her shoulders and strolled toward the laborious monody coming from the living room.

Lenora was draped artfully on the living room sofa looking like some femme fatale straight out of one of the old silent movies. As usual, one hand was placed dramatically over her forehead and the other hand placed protectively over her heart. Though Cassie suspected Lenora already knew she was there, she cleared her throat to announce her arrival.

"Call an ambulance, Cassandra," Lenora managed to say in a weak-sounding voice, but she kept her eyes squeezed shut for the optimum effect.

Cassie crossed her arms and glared at the fraudulent heart patient, suddenly tired of playing an extremely old game. "I know you've had a shock, Mother, but we both know you don't need an ambulance."

Opening one eye briefly, Lenora jerked herself to a sitting position. "How dare you talk that way to me! First, I walk into my own house and find a naked man standing in my foyer, and then my daughter informs me that I'm not having the heart attack I know I'm having. Call the ambulance, Cassandra. Do it now!"

For the first time in her life, Cassie remained glued to the spot. "It won't work this time, Mother. You've been controlling me for years with that phony heart murmur of yours, but those days are over."

"Have you completely lost your mind?" Lenora wailed.

Before Cassie could answer, Lenora jumped up from the sofa and began pacing around the room, waving her arms wildly in the air as she raved. "Your grandfather was right. I think you've suffered a serious nervous breakdown, Cassandra. That's the only reason either of us can come up with for your outrageous behavior."

Cassie let out another long sigh, which only brought more wrath her way.

"And don't you dare roll your eyes like I'm some kind of a lunatic. You're the crazy person here. You should be ashamed of yourself. Punching Mark Winston in the nose. Quitting the firm. And worst of all…''

Faking another attack, Lenora pretended to stumble back to the sofa, then promptly covered her face in her hands and burst into tears.

"Tears won't work, either, Mother," Cassie warned, stopping her mother's tears as quickly as they'd started.

Jerking her head up, Lenora shook a manicured finger in Cassie's direction. "I'll tell you what isn't going to work, young lady. Having that bum, Nick Hardin, strolling around my house buck naked isn't going to work a second longer. Now, get that charlatan out of this house, before I do it myself."

"That won't be necessary, Mrs. Collins," Nick announced from the hallway. "I'm already leaving."

Cassie stiffened at the sound of Nick's voice, then turned to find him standing in the doorway. She'd never seen Nick look so angry. She knew Nick would leave, but the look in his eye told her he wouldn't leave peacefully.

"I want you to come home with me, Cassie," Nick said, keeping his gaze strictly on Cassie.

"She isn't going anywhere. Especially not with you," Lenora spat.

"You don't have to take this, Cassie. You're not a child anymore."

"How dare you stand in my own house and tell my daughter what she does or does not have to take. Who do you think you are? Do you think just because you coerced her out of her panties once or twice you can tell her what to do now?"

"Mother, stop it!" Cassie shouted.

Wheeling around to face Cassie, Lenora's eyes flashed with anger. "I have every intention of stopping it, Cassandra. And if I'd been here, your relationship with this social outcast never would have started in the first place."

Glaring at Nick, Lenora gave him a casual once-over before lifting her nose in total disgust. "I'm forbidding my daughter to so much as look at you again, Mr. Hardin. Now, leave my house this instant before I call the police and have you arrested."

Nick's eyes were blacker than Cassie had ever seen them. Standing with his legs slightly apart, he folded his arms across his chest and sent Lenora a deadly look. "You can have me arrested, Mrs. Collins, but you'd better understand something right now. I intend to see Cassie as long as she's willing to see me."

Cassie winced as both pairs of eyes impaled her at once.

"Well?" Lenora demanded, indignation radiating from her drawn-up face. "Tell this idiot to his face that you're never going to see him again, Cassandra."

"Get your things now and come home with me, Cassie," Nick insisted.

Cassie was saved for the moment when Earl and Duchess bounded into the room, but her brief reprieve ended when her mother made the mistake of kicking at Earl. "Get that ugly animal away from me," Lenora squealed, then jumped back when Earl growled in protest.

"I'm outta here," Nick fumed, then stomped across the room and picked Earl up in one easy swoop. As he headed for the door, he looked back over his shoulder and said, "If you're coming with me, Cassie, you'd better do it now."

Cassie took a step forward and actually jerked her arm away when Lenora reached out to stop her. "I'm taking Nick home, Mother."

"You'll do no such thing!" Lenora screamed.

Surprising Lenora as much as she surprised herself, Cassie turned her back on her mother for the first time in her life and walked out of the house.

"JUST WHAT DO YOU THINK you were doing in there?" Cassie demanded when she slid into the driver's seat of her

Lexus where Nick and Earl were already waiting.

"In case you didn't notice, I was taking up for you," Nick retorted.

Cassie pushed her foot down on the gas pedal and tore out of the driveway. "You said yourself I wasn't a child anymore, Nick. You didn't need to defend me."

"Oh, yeah? Well, you were doing a pretty lousy job of it yourself."

Cassie sent him a look that would kill. "Whether I was handling things to your satisfaction or not, Nick, my relationship with my mother is none of your business."

"Oh, so that's how it's gonna be," Nick yelled, pounding his fist against the panel of the car door. "All that sweet talk last night about how much you loved me goes right out the window the minute Mommy comes home and scolds you for falling into the clutches of someone who's unworthy of your precious social standing."

Cassie slammed on the brakes, then pulled the car over onto the side of the road. "How can you even make such a ridiculous statement, Nick? You know how I feel about you. You just didn't help things by confronting my mother in her own house."

Nick's cold glare stopped Cassie's heart. "Who do you think you're kidding?" Nick shouted. "I saw how much you loved me when you stood there saying nothing while your mother called me everything but a human being."

His harsh words sliced through Cassie's heart like a fine-honed knife. "Nick," she pleaded, "all I'm asking for is a little time. You have to admit it was quite a shock for Mother to come home and find you strolling around her house naked."

Nick's eyes bored into Cassie like the tip of a hot poker. "You can take all the time you want, Cassie, but as far as I'm concerned you've already shown me where I fit into your neat little life. And just for the record, I've never enjoyed being low man on the totem pole.''

Before Cassie could answer, Nick jerked the car door open and pulled himself out of the passenger's seat. ''I know my way home. You don't need to take me.''

''Nick, please...''

Tears spilled over Cassie's lashes, but Nick snapped his fingers, signaling for Earl to follow. ''Come on, Earl. Now!'' Nick ordered, but Earl only crouched down further in the seat next to Cassie. ''Well, that's just damn perfect.'' Nick cursed, then kicked the car door shut with the heel of his boot.

And without another word, he tore off down the street with his hands in his pockets and a scowl on his face.

Cassie and Earl remained sitting by the side of the road long after Nick disappeared from view, and when she finally composed herself enough to control the tears, she turned the car around and headed home. Lenora would be waiting.

And whether Cassie was prepared or not, she knew it was time to sever the umbilical cord.

BY THE TIME NICK MADE the short trek back to his house, he was feeling totally rejected. *And why shouldn't I feel a little sorry for myself?* he thought as he stomped into his front yard. Not only had the woman he loved sent him packing so she could smooth things over with her condescending mother, but his own damn dog had betrayed him, as well.

Times like these usually found Nick roaring away on the Harley until he calmed down, but he'd left his motorcycle at the radio station, which only irritated him even more. He glanced briefly at the Jeep, but the nagging thought that Cassie might still roll up in his driveway kept Nick from driving off in a huff.

Instead, he lowered himself onto the stone steps in front

of the house and sent an anxious glance toward the main road like a hopeful child.

He'd been praying with every step he took that Cassie would drive up behind him and tell him she didn't need time to think things over. But, of course, she hadn't. And when he thought about it now, Nick guessed he really couldn't blame her for being so angry. Maybe he should have slipped quietly out of the house like some thief in the night, instead of initiating a shouting match with her mother. But the very thought that the snooty woman would try to put an end to their relationship had made Nick furious enough to fight back.

Raking a hand through his hair, Nick tried to suppress the same type of disappointment he'd felt as a child, but he couldn't. For the first time in ages, memories of unattended soccer games, missed holidays and even his mother's absence at his college graduation ran through his mind like a slow-moving film strip. The betrayal he'd always felt from his mother was the same type of betrayal he felt now from Cassie.

Only this time his heart had a much greater stake in the outcome.

His gut instinct told him to end the whole fiasco himself before Cassie trampled his heart more than she already had, but he knew that he loved the woman beyond all reason. And all she had asked for was a little time to work things out.

"Okay, counselor, I'll give you a few days to work things out," Nick mumbled to himself. "But as much as I love you, you'd better make a quick decision."

With that said, he pulled himself up from the front stoop. But before he entered his deadly silent house, he sent another wistful look at the main road, still hoping to see the silver Lexus pull in his driveway.

It took driving around the block twice before Cassie mustered the nerve to pull into her own driveway. And it took another five minutes before she could make herself leave the car.

Despite Earl's whining, Cassie left him in the car scratching wildly on the driver's side window. She would figure out what to do about Earl later. First, she needed to settle things with Lenora.

Opening the front door, the first thing Cassie saw was Duchess's traveling crate sitting on the foyer floor. Apparently as frustrated as Earl, Duchess was scratching madly at the wire mesh of her cage. Cassie bent down, then reached out to unfasten the latch, but never got the chance.

"Leave Duchess where she is," Lenora ordered.

Cassie looked up to find Lenora coming down the stairs with a brown cigarillo extending from the end of her fancy lacquered cigarette holder.

"I thought you quit smoking," Cassie said.

Blowing a perfect smoke ring over her sleek platinum head, Lenora met Cassie's gaze with a cold stare. "And I thought you were a lady, Cassandra."

"Oh, save it, Mother," Cassie groaned.

Stomping down the remainder of the stairs, Lenora took a short puff on the holder, then pressed her red-painted lips into a thin, straight line. "Are you suddenly obsessed with shocking me? Is this some latent rebellious period you're going through now?"

"Mother, please," Cassie began, but Lenora turned on her heel and sashayed into the living room.

Cassie followed behind her, waiting until Lenora perched herself in a perfect pose on the sofa. When Lenora met Cassie's gaze again, Cassie said, "I'm sorry I've upset you, Mother, but…"

"I'm not listening to anything that starts with 'but,'" Lenora announced, taking a longer drag off the cigarette holder.

"Just look at you, Cassandra, standing there with your hair in a mess and your shirt on wrong-side-out."

Automatically responding to her mother's critical tone, Cassie raked a hand through her tangled hair. Unfortunately, there wasn't much she could do about her shirt. "I, uh…well…"

Obviously pleased that she hadn't completely lost the ability to fluster her daughter, Lenora leveled a deadly glare at Cassie and said, "The first thing I want to know is how this rumor Evelyn Van Arbor is spreading all over town got started."

Cassie hesitated. If she answered her mother's exact question, there wouldn't be any need to mention that what *had* been a rumor might now be true. "Evelyn overheard Nick ask me about Duchess's pregnancy test. Of course, the old witch took it from there and came up with a much more interesting version which she happily passed along."

Apparently satisfied with the explanation, Lenora pointed her rank cigarillo in Cassie's direction. "Well, I didn't believe you'd be that stupid, especially not in this day and age. I mean, really, Cassandra, there's a birth control pill you can take before, after and probably even during sex these days."

Biting back the urge to mention it was a little late for the mother-daughter sex talk, Cassie sent Lenora a sheepish smile. "Too bad veterinary medicine isn't that advanced. I really am sorry about Duchess, Mother, and…"

Lenora waved her hand through the air, sending a stream of blue smoke snaking in Cassie's direction. "I'm not concerned with Duchess at the moment," Lenora snapped. "What I'm concerned about is this nonsense with you and Nick Hardin and the mess you've gotten yourself into with Mark Winston. I forbid you to see Nick Hardin again, ever. I insist that you call Mark and make a formal apology. And I expect you to return to the law firm first thing Monday morning."

After blowing another puff of smoke into the air, Lenora raised a stenciled-in eyebrow in Cassie's direction. "Do I make myself perfectly clear?"

Cassie lowered herself into the high-backed chair closest to the sofa, imitating her mother's pose by sitting only on the edge of the chair. "You've made yourself clear about what *you* want, Mother. Unfortunately, this is *my* life you're talking about."

Lenora opened her mouth to speak, but for once, Cassie's look silenced her. "I love you, Mother. I always have. But I can't..." Cassie paused, feeling the tears sting her eyes as she tried to swallow the huge lump in her throat. "No, I take that back, Mother. I *won't* let you run my life any longer."

Lenora snorted. "And what's that supposed to mean?"

"It means that I *won't* stop seeing Nick, unless I decide myself he isn't the person I want in my life. I will *never* call Mark Winston and apologize for a damn thing. And I *can't* in good conscience go back to work for Grandfather after he told me I'd never been anything more than a necessary inconvenience to him."

"And what about your father?" Lenora demanded, pretending to sniff into a white linen hanky she'd produced from nowhere. "Howard's going to be absolutely crushed over this entire thing."

"Where *is* Father?" Cassie asked, suddenly realizing he still hadn't arrived.

"I left him in Italy and took the first available flight," Lenora said, sniffing again. "And thank God I did. Just thinking about poor Howard walking through that door and seeing a naked..."

Cassie cut her off. "I'll explain things to Father myself when he gets home."

Anticipating Lenora would fly into a screaming rage at any moment, Cassie held her breath. But instead, Lenora remained sitting on the sofa, expressionless. Cassie couldn't decide if Lenora was too livid to respond to Cassie's insolence, or if she'd fallen into a catatonic state of shock at having her normally obedient daughter disobey her orders.

Reaching out, Cassie took her mother's hand in her own. "I'm not trying to be unfair about this, Mother. It's just time for me to start making my own decisions."

"Well, isn't that just wonderful," Lenora huffed, withdrawing her hand as if she'd just been bitten by a viper. "I've devoted my entire life…"

"You've devoted your entire life trying to keep me from living mine, Mother!"

Far from catatonic now, Lenora jumped up from the sofa again and pointed her finger in Cassie's direction. "Then do as you please, young lady, but you won't do it here. Nick Hardin will never be welcome in my house. And neither—"

"And neither will I?" Cassie demanded.

Lenora didn't waver. "If you insist on seeing Nick Hardin, no, Cassandra, you aren't welcome here, either."

Cassie stiffened. This was one time Lenora had issued an ultimatum Cassie couldn't accept. "If that's the way you feel then, Mother, I guess I'll go pack my things."

"Fine," Lenora snapped. "I guess you've just made your first decision. I hope you can live with it."

They both rose from their seats at the same time, neither one looking at the other. Cassie headed for the stairs but stopped when the doorbell rang.

"I'll get that," Lenora informed Cassie. "It's John coming for Duchess."

Cassie's mouth dropped open as Lenora stormed past her. "Why is John coming for Duchess?"

Lenora ignored Cassie's question and swung the door open, turning into a perfect vision of sweetness and light when Duchess's trainer stepped into the foyer. "I really appreciate you handling this for me, John. And please be as discreet as possible. I'm already the laughingstock of the entire kennel club. The sooner you find a buyer for Duchess, the better.''

Cassie pushed past her mother and grabbed the handle on Duchess's crate. Glaring first at Lenora, then at the portly man who had taken a step in her direction, Cassie said through clenched teeth, "Duchess isn't going anywhere."

"Give John that stupid dog," Lenora demanded.

"She's pregnant, Mother," Cassie fumed.

"And whose fault is that?"

"Mine," Cassie shouted. "But don't take it out on the dog."

"I won't have that dog and her deformed puppies in this house," Lenora snapped, then motioned for John to take possession of the crate.

The man hesitated, then sent a nervous look in Lenora's direction and Cassie saw her chance.

Removing Duchess quickly from her crate, Cassie stomped past both the trainer and her mother, grabbed her purse from the hall table and slammed the door behind her. By the time her screaming mother and the overwrought dog trainer made it down the front porch steps, Cassie's silver Lexus was already squealing out of the driveway.

"Well, it looks like we're on our own, kids," Cassie told Duchess and Earl, but she didn't mention that she had no idea what they were going to do, or even where they were going.

The only thing Cassie knew for certain was that she didn't intend to finally win her independence from her mother, only to hand it over to Nick Hardin.

No, it was time she stepped back and decided what *she* wanted out of life.

11

DEE PLACED A SUITCASE stuffed with Cassie's clothes inside the door, then looked around the sturdy A-frame fishing cabin the judge had left Cassie when he died. "I'd forgotten how charming your grandfather's place was, Cass."

Cassie smiled, thinking the same thing herself. She had always loved everything about the cabin, especially the full-length glass windows that ran across the front and the big sliding glass double doors that didn't mar her perfect view of the mountains and the valley below. She had been more than relieved when she contacted the real estate agent who handled the place for her and found that the cabin hadn't been rented for the summer.

"I'm afraid it wasn't so charming when I came up here last weekend," she told Dee, holding up her reddened hands as proof. "Everything in this place was covered with at least two inches of dirt. It took me all week just to make the place livable again."

"Well it looks great now," Dee said, glancing around the room. "A bit too rustic for my taste, but it is rather cozy, and of course, it's a terrific place to hide."

Cassie ignored Dee's biting remark, already knowing her friend would deliver a stern lecture before she returned to Asheville. Hoping to postpone the inevitable, Cassie said instead, "I really do appreciate you bringing me some of my things. I stopped and bought the bare necessities before I left Asheville, but I can't spend the rest of my life in shorts and T-shirts."

"That'll teach you to take more than the clothes on your back the next time you run away from home," Dee teased, but her eyes traveled past the stone fireplace to the curved stairway that led up to the loft. "Hey, do you remember how we used to pretend to be Heidi when we'd come up here in the summer with the judge? He'd even let us keep the skylight open so we could go to sleep looking at the stars."

Cassie laughed. "I hate to admit it, but I've had the skylight open every night since I've been here."

Dee left the great room and walked out on the deck, then leaned against the railing. When Cassie joined her, she pointed to the swift stream running below the cabin. "Remember that summer the judge tried to teach us to fly fish?"

"Yes, and he finally got so frustrated with us that he sent us back up here on the deck."

"Which is where we wanted to be in the first place so we could sunbathe," Dee said. "Of course, we both got a sunburn from hell when the judge forgot about us and let us go to sleep all lathered with suntan oil."

The two friends laughed and remained leaning over the deck railing watching while Duchess and Earl scampered around the hillside chasing grasshoppers. "Did you see Mother?" Cassie finally asked.

"Thank God, no," Dee groaned. "Lenora's taken to her sickbed, of course. But Louise is there."

"That really doesn't surprise me," Cassie said, and sighed. "What good would it do for Lenora to play sick if she didn't have an audience?"

"Well, if it's any consolation Louise is so upset with Lenora for throwing you out of the house, that Lenora isn't getting pampered. Louise even said herself that she didn't know who Lenora was more concerned about at the moment. You, or your father."

"It has to be a shock having both of us defy her at the

same time," Cassie mused. "I still can't believe Father had the nerve to remain in Italy and finish out his trip."

"Well, I'm proud of both of you," Dee said. "It was time Lenora learned she couldn't boss you guys around for the rest of your life."

Cassie didn't comment, but after a few minutes of silence, Dee's voice turned serious. "Look, I didn't miss the way you sidestepped my remark earlier, Cassie, but you have to realize you can't hide up here in Spruce Pine forever. It's too damn far from civilization for one thing. And you'd never survive a winter up here with nothing but a fireplace to heat the place."

"Winter's still a long way off," Cassie mumbled.

"It's sooner than you think," Dee argued. "And look at all the fun we're going to have finding you a place of your own. There are some really great new condos out in Weaverville. You could still be in downtown Asheville in fifteen minutes."

Cassie raised an eyebrow. "Are you forgetting I no longer have an office downtown?"

Dee sighed. "Collins and Collins isn't the only law firm in town. There are a dozen firms out there who would snap you up in a minute if you showed a little interest."

Cassie ran her hand absently over her stomach, thinking that jumping into a new job was the furthermost thing from her mind at the moment. The nagging question that had her nerves frayed to a snapping point had yet to be answered.

"Earth to Cassie," Dee chirped, waving her hand in front of Cassie's face. "I think this solitude is bringing on a severe case of cabin fever, girlfriend. You haven't heard a word I said."

Cassie frowned. "Yes I did. You were talking about all of those law firms who were just dying to latch onto one of Senator Edward Collins's rejects."

"If I'd known this was going to be a pity party, I would have brought you a cake," Dee scolded.

Cassie stuck out her tongue, then walked to the edge of the deck and took a seat on the top step of the weather-worn planks that led down from the cabin. Dee followed suit, forcing Cassie to slide over. The second they were seated, both dogs darted up the hill, tongues and tails wagging, determined to get a little affection.

"Hey, little mama, you certainly are filling out nicely," Dee said, unaware that Cassie flinched at the *M* word.

"They both love it up here as much as I do," Cassie said as she accepted a few wet kisses from Earl. "We take long walks in the woods at least three times a day so Duchess can get her exercise."

Dee ruffled Duchess's fur, then turned her head to look at Cassie. "I take it you haven't talked to Nick since Lenora got a bird's-eye-view of his amazing attributes."

Cassie shook her head.

"He's stopped talking about the dogs on his show, you know," Dee offered. "He passed it off saying Earl and Duchess talked things over and decided they wanted their privacy while they awaited the blessed event."

Cassie bit her lower lip. "Has he gone back to making crude slurs about lawyers and veterinarians?"

"No. I think the upcoming elections are providing more than enough fodder to keep him busy. He's on a patriotic roll at the moment."

"I couldn't care less," Cassie lied.

"Yeah, I figured as much," Dee said. "That's why you're hiding up here in the middle of nowhere, because you couldn't care less about Nick Hardin."

Cassie's eyes flashed in Dee's direction. "And what would you have me do, Dee? Throw myself at Nick's feet a second time? He was the one who walked off and left me sitting by the side of the road crying. I didn't walk out on him."

"You said yourself you asked him for some time to sort things out," Dee offered. "Did it ever occur to you that he might be waiting until *you* called him?"

Cassie shook her head. "You didn't see the way he looked at me, Dee. And then when Earl wouldn't go with him, he completely lost it. He thinks we both betrayed him. And I guess in a way, we did."

"Hey, don't tell me all this stuff," Dee grumbled. "Tell Nick. He's the one you have to convince."

"And if he won't listen?"

Dee shrugged. "What can I tell you? Being in love sucks sometimes."

"Yeah, with a capital *S*," Cassie said.

Another few seconds of reflective silence passed before Cassie playfully poked Dee in the side with her elbow. She was determined not to let the visit from her best friend be overshadowed by the current problems she was having in the love department. "Hey, I promised you lunch if you'd do my dirty work and bring me some clothes, didn't I?"

"Yes, you did. But given your lack of cooking skills, I was hoping you'd forget the offer," Dee said as they both got up from the steps. "And besides that," she added, "aren't you taking this Susie Homemaker bit a little too seriously? I mean really, Cass. Scrubbing floors and cooking hot meals? You're beginning to make me extremely nervous."

"Who said anything about a hot meal?" Cassie pushed Dee through the cabin doorway. "I was under the impression that peanut butter and jelly sandwiches were always served cold."

CASSIE STOOD ON THE DECK of the cabin waving as Dee backed her red Porsche out of the gravel drive.

Waving back, Dee called out, "Now, get your butt in there

and call him, Cassie. I'm sure Nick is as miserable as you are.''

When the last puffs of dust billowing from Dee's car settled on the dirt road below her, Cassie marched back into the great room of the cabin and eyed her cell phone suspiciously. She hadn't let the cell phone out of her sight for more than a week now, hoping, praying and even begging it to ring and fill the line with Nick's husky southern accent.

Of course, it hadn't.

But could Dee really be right? Had Nick been waiting for *her* to call *him?*

Before she lost her courage, Cassie grabbed the phone and punched in Nick's number, then listened to her heart erupt in a machine gun pattern of rat-a-tat-tat. ''Nick?'' she said when he answered on the second ring, ''Hey, it's me.''

He paused for so long, his deadly silence reached through the phone and shook Cassie until her teeth rattled. Finally, in a voice far from friendly, Nick asked, ''So, how are things going?''

''Fine,'' Cassie answered, trying to sound as nonchalant as possible. ''I just wanted to let you know the dogs are doing great. Dee examined Duchess earlier today and thinks the puppies may come earlier than we thought.''

As she waited out another painful stretch of silence, Cassie cursed herself for believing Dee's stupid assumption that Nick had been hurting as badly as she was. It was obvious that he hadn't. She wanted to tell him how much she missed him, that she loved him, and even beg him to come to her mountain hideaway so they could spend a glorious night in each other's arms. But his cold reserve kept her silent.

When she couldn't endure his cruel punishment a second longer, Cassie's voice broke through the stillness. ''Well...'' she said, her voice trailing off.

''Well what?'' Nick snapped, his voice harsh and distant. ''I can't believe you have the nerve to call me rambling on about puppies while you've left our lives hanging in the balance for over a week.''

"Now, wait just a minute," Cassie began.

"No. I'm not waiting even one more minute. You asked for time to sort things out and I gave it to you. But I deserve an answer. Have you made a decision, Cassie? Or are you still teetering on the fence?"

Without warning, Cassie's temper zoomed out of its hiding place. "And what's that supposed to mean?"

"It means you can't be your mother's little girl and my wife at the same time," he growled. "Make your choice."

"Your wife?" Cassie shrieked. "If that's your idea of a proposal, Nick Hardin, it's certainly not one I intend to accept."

Nick's voice was quiet but lethal. "Then I guess that answers my question, doesn't it?"

Before she could respond, Nick broke their connection, leaving only the dial tone buzzing in her ear. "The jerk hung up on me!" Cassie's outburst drew curious glances from the two dogs who were currently cuddled together on the love seat that faced the fireplace.

Feeling the need to demolish something before she shattered into tiny pieces herself, Cassie almost threw her only link with the outside world against the stone fireplace. Instead, she stomped out of the cabin, pretending it was Nick Hardin's arrogant butt she was kicking instead of the gravel and sticks that soared into the air every time her shoe met the ground.

True to character, Nick had insulted her one minute, then proposed to her the next. *But what is Nick proposing?* Cassie kept asking herself as she marched down the trail. Did he really expect her to put an end to Lenora's lifetime of orders so *he* could start bossing her around himself?

If he'd really been that interested in her decision, he would have made an effort to call her. Maybe not at her parents' house, but a simple phone call to Dee could have told him where she was. Instead, he had acted no better than her mother. Both of them had issued her ultimatums, and had expected her to crumble under their demands without giving a thought to the fact that she might need a little support while she was trying to sort out the crazy events that had left her life in turmoil.

When the dogs raced past her, heading for the swift stream below the cabin, Cassie suddenly stopped dead in her tracks.

Oh, my God, she thought, her hand flying to her mouth. *I've fallen in love with a male version of my own mother.*

NICK RELIEVED *HIS* NEGATIVE energy by taking his vengeance out on the water as he made angry strokes back and forth across the pool. Damn, but that woman had him tied in a knot tighter than a fresh-packed pretzel. She'd driven him crazy for more than a week, while he waited like a doomed man hanging by his fingernails on the edge of a cliff. He hadn't been able to eat, much less sleep. All he'd accomplished was worrying day and night about whether or not he still had a place in her life.

And what had she done? Hell, she'd had the nerve to call him up as if the eight torturous days they'd been apart never happened, chirping happily about dogs and puppies. She hadn't said she missed him, hadn't mentioned whether or not she'd informed her parents that she *did* intend to see him. And she certainly hadn't sounded as if her previous concern over their possible baby problem was giving her an ounce of worry.

Which, of course, could only mean one thing.

Evidently, there wasn't going to be a baby, after all. And now that there wasn't going to be a baby, it didn't take a genius to figure out that the proper Miss Collins no longer needed to keep him waiting in the wings playing the role of the concerned father.

Swimming up to the side of the pool, Nick pounded his fist on the concrete as he labored to catch his breath. She was obviously still hell-bent on remaining her mother's little girl. She sure hadn't graced his doorway in more than a week.

Not a proposal I intend to accept, her royal behind, Nick thought as he pulled his nude body out of the pool. The little temptress hadn't seemed to care that he was lacking in social graces when she'd moaned his name over and over in the darkness of her bedroom. But now that Mommy was home, she'd suddenly turned into some Martha Stewart wanna-be, berating him for not conforming to a bunch of ridiculous formalities.

Storming into the den, he went straight for the liquor decanters on his well-stocked bar. Not bothering to scrounge around for a glass, he took a long swig straight from the bottle labeled Bourbon, then wiped his mouth with the back of his hand.

How could I have been so stupid? he kept asking himself. From the moment he'd met her, he'd known she'd be trouble. She'd bounced into his life, threatening to wield her legal ax in his direction one minute, and then she'd turned on her sweet southern charm, saying that she couldn't live without him.

Memories of another woman who had sent the same type of mixed messages prompted Nick to draw the bottle to his lips for a longer drink. He'd convinced himself that Cassie wasn't anything like his mother, but she'd finally shown her true colors. Like his mother, Cassie couldn't bring herself to put him first in her life.

He hated himself for loving both of them in spite of it.

And he did love Cassie. He loved her more than he ever thought possible. If he had his way, he would spend the rest of his life with her. But not if it meant taking a back seat to her mother. And not if Cassie expected him to pretend to be some stuffed-shirt social imbecile that he wasn't.

No, if Cassie wanted him, she could take him for himself or not at all. It was up to her now. As he'd told her earlier on the phone, she'd have to make a choice.

Knowing there wasn't a damn thing he could do about it if Cassie did decide she couldn't put him first in her life, Nick let out a long sigh and quickly drew the bottle to his lips again. At least his broken heart had taught him one valuable lesson.

He would never trust another female as long as he lived.

By the time he took his fourth swig from the bottle, Nick was wallowing in total self-pity. He did, however, pay one final tribute to the two furry culprits who had brought him and Cassie together in the first place.

In honor of Earl and Duchess, Nick promptly got himself *dog-eared* drunk.

12

CASSIE SAT ON THE DECK of the cabin with her legs drawn to her chest, watching the sun slip behind the shadowed mountains. She'd watched a similar sunset from the Blue Ridge Parkway once, curled safely in the circle of Nick's strong arms. But now that evening seemed like nothing more than a twisted fantasy. Especially since the days had melted into weeks and the stalemate between them still existed.

Letting out a long sigh, Cassie remembered how happy they'd been that day, talking about everything from ice cream to their favorite movies. They'd both laughed when they discovered each claimed *Gone With the Wind* as their favorite movie of all time. Of course, they promptly got into a heated discussion about Rhett and Scarlett.

Nick insisted Rhett Butler had washed his hands of Scarlett O'Hara with his famous "Frankly, my dear" line. Cassie, on the other hand, had argued that Rhett had taken Scarlett back the next day because he loved her too much to live without her.

The disagreement eventually ended in a fierce wrestling match, which turned much more serious the minute Nick managed to pin her beneath him.

The thought that she might never feel those strong, wonderful hands exploring her body again shattered Cassie's heart into a zillion tiny pieces. She loved him. She knew she did. But it had taken her twenty-eight years to gain her independence from Lenora. Marriage to Cassie meant a fifty-

fifty relationship. And from Nick's recent actions, Cassie doubted he had an equal partnership in mind.

Pulling herself up from the deck, she started into the cabin, but the flash of headlights coming up the dirt road below her steered her back to the deck railing. Hope drove her into madness as she gripped the wooden rail, but her optimism quickly vanished when the familiar black Lincoln bobbled up the gravel drive and stopped in the parking area just below the steps. Certainly in no mood for a family reunion, Cassie grimaced when her father got out of the car first, then walked around to open the passenger side door of the Lincoln.

Queen Lenora had obviously decided to leave her sickbed.

As her mother stepped from the car, Cassie watched Lenora automatically wrinkle her nose in disgust at the primitive surroundings. Leaving the railing, Cassie headed for the stairs, determined to guard the entrance to the cabin like a sentry on duty. Whether they were her parents or not, they were on *her* property now. And Cassie intended to stay in Spruce Pine until *she* decided it was time to leave.

In her multicolored jumpsuit with her matching four-inch heels, Lenora looked like an exotic peacock picking her way over the rough gravel drive. Cassie almost laughed watching her mother tiptoe toward the stairs with her pinkies held high in the air as if she were terrified of brushing up against anything even remotely wild or rustic.

"God, but this place is even more horrible than I remembered," Lenora groaned, then motioned for her husband to lend his hand for the trek up to the deck.

"If you came here for a fight, don't waste your time climbing the stairs, Mother," Cassie warned.

Still, Lenora continued, stopping only when Cassie refused to move from the top step. Raising her eyes to meet the mirror image of what she'd looked like herself as a young woman, Lenora pursed her lips for a moment before she shot an angry glance at her husband. "Believe me, this was your father's idea, Cassandra, not mine. And since Howard's already informed me that *he* intends to do all of the talking, there shouldn't be any fighting between us.''

This I've got to see, Cassie decided, and stepped aside so her mother could pass. When she turned back to face her father, she managed a weak smile. Howard Collins was still one of the most attractive men Cassie had ever seen. He was tall and lean, with just the right amount of gray tingeing the temples of his thick, dark hair. But it was his eyes that Cassie loved best. They were a soft brown flecked with gold. And they were always kind.

"It's good to see you, Father. I've missed you."

Howard Collins placed an affectionate kiss on his daughter's cheek, then took her elbow like the gentleman he was. "Let's go inside, princess. Your mother is behaving herself at the moment, but we both know that could change at any minute."

Exchanging knowing glances they entered the cabin to find Lenora shrinking back from the two dogs who were approaching her cautiously, stalking their intended prey.

"Can't you at least do something with *him* while I'm here?" Lenora wailed, taking another step back as she pointed in Earl's direction.

Cassie clapped her hands and pointed to the stairs that led up to the loft. "Go. Both of you," she ordered, feeling great satisfaction when both dogs obeyed and scooted up the stairs.

Lenora raised an eyebrow in Cassie's direction, then glanced around the room with as much disdain as she'd shown outside. "Well, at least you can take up animal training now that you've thrown your legal career down the toilet."

"Lenora, stop it!" Howard demanded.

Cassie gripped the edge of the love seat to keep from falling on her face. She had never heard her father raise his voice in his life, and especially not to her mother.

"Sit down, both of you," Howard Collins ordered, puffing his chest out a bit. "I have a few things I want to say."

Lenora sent a loathsome look at the tattered love seat, then let her eyes sweep to the two wooden rocking chairs flanking the fireplace. "I prefer to stand, Howard."

"I said *sit*, Lenora," Howard insisted.

Shocked for the second time in two minutes, Cassie watched in awe as Lenora tossed her head indignantly, but finally chose a rocking chair that evidently represented the least threat to her silk outfit. Cassie chose the love seat for herself, but suddenly wished she had a video camera. Lenora's phenomenal acquiescence was an event she felt should be accurately recorded for posterity.

"Let me begin by saying that I owe both of you an apology," Howard said, looking first at his wife, then at his daughter. "I've failed you both by not taking charge of my own household."

Cassie's eyes strayed from her father's face long enough to get a quick look at her mother and noticed that Lenora now had both arms of the rocking chair clutched in a white-knuckled grip.

"However, ladies, I'm here to tell you that those times are over." He paced back and forth in front of them. "I'm taking charge of our family, as I should have done from the beginning. And the first thing I intend to do is put an end to this silly feud that has everyone running around in circles."

Lenora started to protest, but Howard stopped her with a single glance. "Lenora, I will not allow you to destroy our family by trying to keep Cassie tied to your apron strings for the rest of her life. She's a grown woman who's perfectly capable of making her own decisions. And whether you agree with her decisions or not, Lenora, our daughter will always be welcome in our home, as will anyone else she cares to bring with her."

Cassie felt like cheering, until her father leveled his stare in her direction. "And Cassie, it's time you stopped acting like a child. You've always complained about your mother taking control of your life, but you never make any attempt to do anything about it. It's time you stopped hiding up here at the cabin sulking and make some plans for your future. I don't care whether you decide to straighten things out with your young man first, or find your own apartment, or get a new job. Just do it."

Turning on his heel then, Howard Collins started toward the door, but before he left the room, he stopped and checked his watch. "You girls have five minutes to patch things up," he said, then sent Lenora a warning look. "I'll be waiting in the car."

After Howard left, both Cassie and Lenora remained sitting inside the cabin with their mouths gaping open and their ears still ringing from his true, but extremely brusque words.

Cassie looked at her mother. Lenora stared back.

"I'm totally speechless, Mother. What on earth has happened to Father?"

Lenora threw her hands into the air, then popped out of her rocking chair. "Believe me, I have no idea, but Howard's been like this ever since he returned from Europe." Her voice was all breathy and excited. "And don't you dare tell your father, Cassandra, but I *love* it. Why, last night in our bedroom he even…"

Cassie immediately clamped both hands over her ears. "Spare me the details, Mother," she begged. "I know Father told me to start acting like an adult, but I'm still not ready to hear about your sex life."

"Then I guess we're even," Lenora said with satisfaction, "because I wasn't ready to know anything about your sex life, either, much less find him walking around naked in my foyer."

Cassie laughed in spite of herself. "I owe you a huge

apology for putting you in that situation, Mother. I'm really sorry.''

Lenora walked to where Cassie was sitting and gave her daughter a much-needed hug. ''I do love you, Cassandra. Maybe when you're a mother yourself, you'll understand how hard it is to stay out of your children's lives and finally let go.''

Cassie returned her mother's hug, but their happy reunion was interrupted when a loud horn blasted from the driveway. ''I'll go get Father,'' Cassie offered. ''I'm sure he thinks we've come to blows by now.''

''That won't be necessary,'' Lenora insisted. ''I'll tell Howard the war has ended.''

Cassie started to object, but Lenora delivered a quick kiss to the top of her head, then sashayed across the room in her classic fluid style. Turning when she reached the doorway, she sent Cassie a mischievous little smile.

''Oh, and by the way, dear. In case you *do* decide to drop by any time soon, you might want to give us a little warning first. You see, your boyfriend isn't the only one who's been running through the house nude these days.''

THE MORNING AFTER her parents' visit, Cassie woke and almost screamed when she looked in the mirror. Her father had been right. She'd spent so much time sulking in the wilderness, she'd stopped giving much thought to anything else.

Especially her own appearance.

Holding a strand of her once-silky hair close to the mirror, Cassie grimaced at the split ends, praying the damage could be repaired with the help of a good conditioner. It was then that she noticed her ghastly fingernails in the mirror. And when she finally got the courage, she looked down at her unshaven legs and the badly chipped polish on all ten of her previously manicured toes.

''Lord, I'm a mess,'' she mumbled under her breath, deciding if Nick could see her in her current condition, he would thank his lucky stars that she hadn't accepted his proposal.

All morning, her father's last words, "Just do it," kept echoing through her mind. And he had been right, of course. She had enjoyed the peace and solitude of the mountains long enough. It was time to face her problems instead of hiding from them.

After a quick shower, she walked out on the deck where both dogs were basking in the warm morning sun. "You'll have to stay by yourself today, guys," she told them. "It's time I made a trip down the mountain."

The dogs safely inside the cabin, she headed for the Lexus. As she started down the mountain, she began rehearsing in her mind what she planned to say to Nick when she saw him again face-to-face. They certainly had a lot of baggage to work through if they decided to stay together. Including Nick accepting the fact that she intended to be her own person. He might think he wanted a meek little wife who would jump the second he beckoned, but Cassie knew better. He'd even admitted that the main reason he'd been attracted to her was her ability to get in his face.

And she certainly intended to get in his face again as soon as possible.

Cassie picked up speed when she hit the main highway back to Asheville. She was on a mission now. A mission that would either make a life *with* Nick Hardin, or without him.

"HEY, NICK—an Attorney Collins is here to see you," the errand boy called out as he stuck his head through Nick's office door.

Nick felt himself go deaf, dumb and blind all at the same time.

Cassie's here? he kept asking himself. A range of emotions from joy, to relief, and then back to joy again rocketed through him like a wayward torpedo. Cassie showing up at his office could only mean one thing.

She'd come to her senses and decided to accept his proposal.

Jumping up from his desk, he started across the room. He stopped, however, when he came face-to-face with a tall, distinguished-looking man who was dressed in an expensive tailored suit. Nick's first impulse was to excuse himself and hurry off to see what was keeping his lovely bride-to-be, but the cool regard in the man's eyes told him he had jumped to the wrong conclusion.

It was obvious that the *other* Attorney Collins had stopped by to pay him a visit.

"Howard Collins," the man provided, and surprised Nick by extending his hand.

Nick felt like running and hiding under his desk. And why shouldn't he? He'd always known facing Howard Collins wouldn't be an easy task. After all, the man possessed the upsetting knowledge that both his daughter *and* his wife had seen Nick buck naked. Nick had planned to face the man eventually. But with a prepared speech. And maybe even with a revolver in his pocket for good measure.

Certainly not caught off guard like this.

Pulling himself together, he forced himself to shake the man's hand, then nodded to a chair by the side of his desk. "Have a seat, Mr. Collins. I'm sure you've come for an apology about the fiasco that happened when your wife…"

"And are you extending an apology for that fiasco, Mr. Hardin?" Howard Collins interrupted as he lowered himself into the chair.

Nick walked around his desk and returned to his seat. "Yes, sir, I am. That was an embarrassing experience for both of us. But I assure you it was completely accidental. I never would have…"

"I accept your apology for shocking my wife, Mr. Hardin, but that's really not what I came to see you about."

"Call me Nick. Please," Nick offered for lack of anything better to say.

"Okay, Nick. I don't have to tell you my daughter's reputation has suffered terribly since the two of you have become, shall I say, 'an item.'"

Despite the gut instinct that told him to pacify the man, Nick's humble demeanor instantly evaporated. "And you've come to make sure I never bother Cassie again," Nick said through clenched teeth. "Well, I hate to disappoint you, Mr. Collins, but Cassie has already made that extremely clear herself."

Howard Collins leaned back in his chair and templed his fingers across his chest. Looking up at Nick over the top of his fingers, he smiled slightly. "Pardon me for saying so, Nick, but I think this conversation would go a lot smoother if you stopped putting words in my mouth. I didn't come here to *discourage* you from seeing Cassie. I came to inquire exactly what your intentions *are* where my daughter's concerned."

Nick was speechless. "You mean…"

"I'm sure an unconventional man like yourself will think this sounds outdated and a bit old-fashioned, but you compromised my daughter and her reputation. And as her father, I feel I have the right to know what you intend to do about it."

An image of Howard Collins holding a shotgun to his back instantly flashed through Nick's mind. "If you're asking if I love Cassie, I do, Mr. Collins. I've even asked her to marry me, but she turned me down."

Howard's eyebrow shot up a notch. "You've seen Cassie since my wife returned from Europe?"

"No."

"Then you're saying you proposed to Cassie before Lenora came home?" Howard quizzed.

Nick tugged at the collar of his button-down shirt, suddenly feeling the searing wave of heat that came from sitting in the proverbial hot seat. "Not exactly," Nick admitted. "I more or less proposed during a phone conversation."

"A phone conversation?" Howard Collins repeated, his brows coming together in a frown. "You mean you asked Cassie to marry you on the telephone?"

"Well, yeah," Nick said, realizing how trifling it sounded when Howard Collins put it that way. "And she turned me down. In fact, I believe her exact words were," he added, raising his voice several octaves to imitate Cassie's female voice, " 'If that's your idea of a proposal, Nick Hardin, it's not one I intend to accept.' "

To Nick's surprise, Howard Collins threw his head back and laughed.

"Excuse me if I don't laugh along with you, Mr. Collins," Nick complained, "but I didn't find your daughter's rejection a damn bit funny."

Ignoring Nick's sullen look, Howard Collins rose from the chair and reached for the writing tablet on the corner of Nick's desk. Taking a gold pen from his pocket, he scribbled Cassie's address at Spruce Pine across the top of the pad, then handed the tablet back to Nick.

"I have enough confidence in my daughter, Nick, to know that she wouldn't give you a second look if she didn't think you were worthy of her affection. Don't make a liar out of her. Be the man she thinks you are and do the right thing."

As Howard Collins turned to leave, Nick called out, "Mr. Collins? Sir, does that mean you wouldn't have a problem with our relationship if we did work things out?"

Howard Collins turned back to face Nick and smiled. "As I said before, Nick, I'm confident Cassie will make the right choice. It's up to you to make my daughter an offer she can't refuse."

IT WAS DUSK WHEN CASSIE returned to the cabin that evening, arms laden with packages. She'd spent most of the day indulging herself in the finest luxuries money could buy. Her first stop, however, had been to the drugstore.

It was a trip Cassie knew was long overdue.

She'd tried to convince herself that her late period was only due to the incredible amount of stress she'd been under over the past few weeks. After all, her period had been late before. In fact, the same year she took her bar exam.

But you had nothing to worry about then, stupid, Cassie scolded herself, then let out a long sigh as the feeling of anxiety washed over her again. Of course, it would only take a matter of minutes to answer the burning question, now that she had the proper tools in hand. Provided, that is, that she could muster up enough courage to pee on the stupid pregnancy test stick.

"I'm home, kids," she called, pushing the cabin door open with her elbow.

In response to her call, Earl immediately appeared at the banister that ran across the top of the exposed loft. Cassie smiled up at him until it registered with her exactly where Earl was standing. "Hey, if you've been on my pillow again, you're in big trouble, Mister." She dumped her packages on the love seat.

Turning her attention back to the packages she'd bought to transform herself from a "mountain mama" into a total "femme fatale," she picked out a few items, then headed for the bathroom. She intended to pay Nick a visit the very next day. But she intended to look like a million bucks when she did it.

Once she had her magic potions lined up on the small bathroom vanity, she kicked her clothes off in a pile, then donned her faded pink bathrobe that had seen better days. Deciding she would let the magic work its miracles while she fixed a bite to eat, she promptly went to work.

"Ugh," she groaned as she massaged gooey, greasy hair treatment into her scalp. After her long tresses were saturated and tinted the color of coal tar, she quickly wrapped a towel around her head and immediately went to work on her facial.

Within minutes, she had the mint-scented mask smeared on so thick she looked like a lime-green mime.

It was the last box sitting on the vanity, however, that seemed to be staring at her from its place by the sink. Taking a deep breath, she grabbed the box, followed the instructions and hurried from the bathroom.

To wait a torturous five minutes for a plus or a minus to appear in the appropriate little circle was more than her rattled nerves could endure.

Hoping a nice cup of hot tea would relax her enough to face the answer that would soon be waiting for her in the bathroom, she filled her grandfather's worn-out teakettle from the faucet, lit the gas stove, then headed toward the remaining packages piled on the love seat.

"Let's see. I'll need cotton balls, polish remover and Hot Passionate Pink," she called out as she found the items, then took her treasures to the rough-hewn table in the dining section of the great room. After positioning both ladder-back chairs so they faced each other, she sat on one chair and propped her feet on the other. She had just finished the ritual of jamming a legion of cotton balls between all ten of her polish-chipped toes when Earl's shrill bark made her glance at the doorway.

Had a ghost appeared on the other side of the sliding glass doors, the apparition would have been better received.

Cassie jumped to her feet the second she saw Nick standing on the deck, and without taking time to remove the cotton balls, did a silly duck-walk across the cluttered room. Even after she slid the door open, she still couldn't believe her eyes. Standing on the deck looking like an advertisement straight out of GQ was Nick, dressed in a full-tailed tuxedo and holding a bundle of long-stemmed red roses nervously out in front of him.

"What are *you* doing here?" she demanded.

Nick raised an amused eyebrow, then walked past Cassie and entered the cabin without an invitation. When he turned back to face her, he took a deep breath, then thrust the roses against her chest, forcing her to accept them.

"Why am I here?" he asked, stalling for time.

"You heard me the first time."

"Well... Frankly, my dear," he began, "I'm here because I *do* give a damn."

"You do?" Involuntarily, she took a small step in his direction.

He closed the distance between them in a flash. His voice was raw with emotion when he said, "Cassie, whether you believe me or not, I do love you. And since you weren't too pleased with my first proposal, I decided to try it your way."

"Oh, Nick." She would have jumped straight into Nick's arms had he not surprised her by dropping down on one knee.

Kneeling before her, he looked up at her, then shook his head, obviously trying to regain his composure. "Cassie," he began, but he still couldn't keep a straight face.

Her eyes narrowed when he burst into robust laughter. "You were gaining big points before, but you're treading on real thin ice now, buddy," Cassie warned.

Nick's face turned solemn for a moment, but despite his best efforts he couldn't keep from laughing.

Cassie was livid. Throwing the roses on the floor, she stomped back to the door and pointed outside to the waiting deck. "You've had your fun, Nick. Now I think you'd better leave."

"Dammit, Cassie," he argued, still retaining his proper

groom-to-be position. "I'm sorry you don't seem to like this proposal any better than the last one…but it's hard to be serious when you're proposing to a woman with a green face."

Shock instantly replaced the anger in Cassie's eyes. She'd been so startled by Nick's arrival, she'd forgotten how silly she must look to her handsome Prince Charming, who was still down on one knee waiting for her unmanicured hand.

A lesser woman might have run from the room screaming, but Cassie lifted her chin defiantly and sent Nick a silly jack-o'-lantern grin. "No, you're wrong, Nick. I think I'm going to like this proposal just fine. Because if you're willing to propose to me when I look like this, then there's no doubt in my mind that you really do love me."

"I'll never give you any reason to doubt it," he said, holding out one hand.

When she stepped closer, Nick withdrew a small box from his inside jacket pocket and took her hand in his. "I love you, Cassie. Will you please be my wife?"

"Just try and stop me," she whispered.

When he slipped a magnificent marquee-cut diamond on her finger, he didn't even notice her partially broken nail.

Nick stood up then, took a handkerchief from his pocket and wiped most of the goo from Cassie's lathered face. Drawing her into his arms, he kissed her so passionately she didn't object when he untied the belt of her tattered robe and slid his wonderful hands over her quivering naked body.

"I've missed you so much," he murmured, but before Cassie could pull him in the direction of the loft, Earl bounded down the stairs, barking frantically as he made several laps around their legs.

Nick laughed. "Hey, buddy. Glad to see me?"

Earl darted back up the stairs to the loft, but when they didn't follow, he started his frantic barking again.

"Something's wrong," Cassie said, adjusting her robe and retying the belt.

"Where's Duchess?"

They started for the stairs at the same time, but Cassie jumped ahead of Nick and reached the top first. "Oh, my God, Nick, I think she's in labor," she wailed as she ran to the bed.

Lying on her side, with *her* head on Cassie's pillow, was Duchess, panting heavily and growling at Earl, who had hopped up on the bed beside her.

"Sorry, old man, but I've heard women get nasty at a time like this." Nick scooped Earl up and tucked him under his arm. "Maybe you'd better go back downstairs with me."

"Don't you dare leave me up here alone!" Cassie gasped.

"Shouldn't I go boil some water or something?" Nick asked and as if on cue, a loud shrill from the teakettle echoed from the floor below.

"How'd you do that?"

Cassie wasn't amused. "This isn't funny, Nick. Turn off the tea water and call Dee while you're down there," she instructed as he started toward the stairs. "Her office and home numbers are on the refrigerator. My cell phone should be on the kitchen counter."

After Nick disappeared down the stairs, Cassie turned her attention back to Duchess, whose panting sounded very similar to the Lamaze technique Nick had joked about on his program. "It's okay, sweetie," Cassie assured the little mother as she stroked Duchess's head. "Nick's calling Dee now. She'll get you through this."

"Hey, counselor, your phone battery's dead," Nick called from the floor below.

Cassie launched herself from the bed in a panic and hurried down the stairs, oblivious to the stubborn cotton balls that were still lodged between most of her toes.

"I can't believe this is happening," she moaned, rummaging through one of the kitchen drawers. "Dee left me a list of instructions on what to do if Duchess went into labor before she could get here, but we didn't expect the puppies for at least another week."

When she couldn't find the instructions, Cassie sent Nick a tearful look. "You're going to have to go get Dee yourself. Hurry, before something goes wrong."

Nick took her in his arms then, and let her cry softly against his shoulder. "You're getting all upset over nothing, hon," he assured her as he rubbed her back. "Duchess is going to do just fine. Besides, it would take me over an hour to get back to Asheville. And that still doesn't mean I could track Dee down when I got there."

"But...but..." Cassie sobbed, "how are we going to know what to do?"

He lifted her chin and forced her to look at him. "The first thing *you're* going to do is get your butt in the shower and wash that silly gunk off your face. I just asked the most beautiful woman in the world to be my wife. I'd like to make sure she's still hiding under there somewhere."

Cassie fiddled with the towel that was still wrapped around her head and managed a weak smile. "I'm sorry, Nick. I don't know what's gotten into me lately. My nerves are shot...and I seem to cry at the drop of a hat."

When Nick leaned forward and kissed the tip of her nose, she added, "Promise you'll stay with Duchess while I'm in the shower?"

"Promise." He turned Cassie around and pushed her in the direction of the open bathroom door.

"Just let me run up once more and check on Duchess," she begged, and headed for the stairs.

Struggling out of his tux jacket, Nick removed his cummerbund and practically tore the silk tie from around his neck. He'd just pulled his shirttail out of his pants when Cassie screamed his name. Bounding back up the steps two at a time, Nick broke into a wide grin. She was holding up a tiny black-and-white puppy that was the spitting image of Earl.

"Nice going, counselor. Looks like you're a better mid-wife than you thought."

"You'd better scrounge around out in the woodshed and see if you can find us a box," Cassie said, beaming proudly as she rubbed the squirming puppy against her cheek. "The babies are going to need their own bed."

"You bet they are," Nick said, catching her gaze long enough to give her the full meaning of his words. "I'm not going anywhere tonight until I've shown you what you have to look forward to the rest of your life."

"Is that a threat or a promise, Mr. Hardin?" Cassie asked, sending Nick a demure little smile.

"When you finish playing midwife I'll let you decide for yourself."

Cassie laughed, but another whimper from Duchess jerked Cassie's head back around. "Hurry, Nick. I think she's having another one."

Walking to the bed, Nick leaned over Cassie's shoulder at the exact moment Duchess decided to give another over-wrought push.

"Here comes puppy number two," Cassie said, watching in awe as the birth sac slid onto the blanket.

When she turned back to Nick, however, he was already hurrying toward the stairs with both hands clamped firmly over his mouth.

CASSIE SNUGGLED UNDER Nick's arm as they stood at the foot of the bed watching Duchess groom her two perfect puppies. Earl had even been allowed back on the bed. This time, however, he kept his distance, cocking his head in won-der every time one of the puppies made even the slightest whimper.

"Too bad I don't have a good cigar for me and my little buddy to share," Nick said as he bent down and scratched Earl behind the ears.

"A dog biscuit will do just fine for both of you."

"They are kind of cute, aren't they?"

"Cute?" Cassie huffed, admiring the tiny snow-white female and her black-and-white brother. "These puppies come from champion breeding stock, remember? And *cute* is definitely not an AKC-approved word for describing even half-champion puppies."

"Tell that to the kennel club when you try having the one that looks like Earl inducted into the doggy hall of fame."

Cassie laughed. "We'll keep them both, of course," she said, then looked up at Nick for his approval. "And I'm going to name them Romeo and Juliet."

Nick shook his head. "I don't know about keeping both puppies, counselor. Four dogs under one roof? I know I have a big house, but I'd planned on keeping some of those rooms available to raise our own champion brood."

The second Nick said the words, a thunderclap cracked in Cassie's head with such force she thought she felt the floor shake beneath her still-unpedicured feet. Ducking under Nick's arm, she ran for the stairs while a jumble of pluses and minuses flashed through her mind.

"Cassie? Hey? What's wrong now?" Nick yelled from behind her.

By the time she reached the bathroom, Cassie's knees were so weak she had to clutch the doorjamb for support. Mesmerized by the tubelike container that was still lying on the sink, Cassie took a step forward and forced herself to look at the carved-out circle.

"Hey, hon, what's wrong? Are you okay?"

When she looked in the mirror, Cassie saw Nick's reflection. She watched his eyes flicker from the pregnancy test box that was still sitting on the vanity to the tube she was now holding in her hand.

"Do you have something to tell me, counselor?" he asked in a shaky voice.

Cassie nodded and sent him a glowing smile. "How many rooms did you say you have in that big house of yours, my love?"

The Doctor Dilemma

Dianne Drake

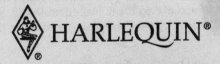

HARLEQUIN®

TORONTO • NEW YORK • LONDON
AMSTERDAM • PARIS • SYDNEY • HAMBURG
STOCKHOLM • ATHENS • TOKYO • MILAN • MADRID
PRAGUE • WARSAW • BUDAPEST • AUCKLAND

Dear Reader,

Welcome to my first journey into romance writing. As a longtime nonfiction writer who specializes in health articles, I always had the secret desire to write a little romance, and those who know me weren't surprised that my first time out is a medical story. I was a nurse, as was my mother and grandmother, and making Lacy Archer, the main character of my book, a nurse seemed a natural fit.

When it comes to nursing stories, the best ones were from my grandmother, Willie Pearl. You'll see her in these pages, and yes, what you'll read is definitely Grandma Willie all the way. She worked in a small-town medical practice, in an old brick building that wasn't up to medical office standards. But then, seventy years ago, things like that didn't matter so much. Neither did the fact that Grandma didn't have any official training, and the town doctor was actually a veterinarian. At any given time, their waiting room was filled with humans, hound dogs and pigs. And like Lacy Archer, my grandmother treated every patient the same, whether they had two legs or four.

Country medicine has changed since my grandmother practiced it, but the story that never changes is the romance between the doctor and nurse. I would like to thank Harlequin Duets, and my editor, Kathryn Lye, for allowing me to bring this one to you.

Wishing you health and happiness,

Dianne Drake

Dedicated to

Willie Pearl Holland, my grandmother.

Marva Wingard, one of the greatest romance fans
on this planet. Thanks for telling me over and over
and over that I should do this.

Joel, my husband,
for his continued support and encouragement.

1

LACY TILTED HER HEAD back, squinted at the July sun and let the cool water from a bottle marked Glacier trickle down her parched throat. It wasn't her home town, but it was close enough. And it wasn't her grandfather she was about to go to work for, but Dr. Washburn sounded like a good substitute, and at his advancing age, he was bound to be more like her grandfather than the doctors she'd been working for over the past decade. "I'm tired of the rat race," she said and then chuckled.

"Who was winning? You, or the rats?" Mayor Jed Lambert pushed a strand of sparse hair from his round face, then wiped away a bead of sweat. His gaze shifted to the Jeep Cherokee parked in the handicapped spot in front of the town hall, then to Lacy.

"It's either caught or be caught, Mayor, and one day I looked up and that big ol' net was slipping down over me. That's when I figured it was time to get away."

"Well, we're certainly glad to have you, Miss Archer, but…"

"Lacy," she interrupted. She didn't want formality here. She wanted to be part of the town, part of everyday life in Sunstone, Indiana, and that didn't fit with being called Miss Archer or Nurse Archer. After so many years and so many pretenses, now it was time to be Lacy. Just plain Lacy.

"Lacy. We're glad you took us up on the offer, but I'm afraid there's been a little change in plans."

"Really?" Lacy's heart clutched. When she'd read the ad in the nursing journal, she knew it sounded too good to be true. Adequate salary, great place to live, rural medicine. No big city hospital hassles. The nurse she was replacing probably decided it was too good a job to give up, and she couldn't blame her. But, Lacy really wanted the job. "What?" she asked. "Is the job already taken?"

"Oh, no. Nothing like that," the mayor interjected quickly, "but Doc Washburn had a heart attack last week."

"Is he okay?" She'd been marking off the days for a month, waiting for her duty in surgical intensive care to come to an end. And while she didn't slash off each date with a big red marker, she saw the imaginary slashes each time she checked the calendar. Somehow, it never crossed her mind that she should come up with a plan B in case plan A didn't work out.

"He's fine. It was only a minor attack, but he retired. It was quick, and we were so busy getting things straightened out we didn't have time to get hold of you, but we do have someone to replace him temporarily." The mayor glanced at the Cherokee. This time a frown broke his ruddy complexion. "A friend of Doc Washburn's grandson, from Chicago. Eminently qualified, so I'm told. His name is Jack Sutton, and he'll be here long enough for us to find a permanent doctor." He paused and kicked at a pebble on the sidewalk. "I hope." His attention focused on the rock as it skipped its way into the street, then he moved a hesitant and uncomfortable gaze to Lacy. "Look, why don't you go on in and meet him. He's waiting for me to come and take him to lunch. But since I'm sure you're hungry after that long bus ride, maybe the two of you could go across the street to the diner, grab a bite to eat and get to know each other." He took two steps backwards, smiled awkwardly and nodded an abrupt dismissal. "I'll go on back to the bus station, get your bags and haul them to my office, then after lunch, the three of us can sit down and figure out what's what." Before Lacy could blink, Mayor Lambert turned the corner and scooted away.

"Don't you think you should…" Lacy started, stopping her words when she realized the mayor wasn't about to turn back. "…take me in and introduce me," she finished under her breath. "Oh, well." She sighed, taking a long, hard look at the town hall, wandering what kind of ogre lurked inside that caused the mayor to quake in his boots. "You've come this far, Lacy. No turning back now." She'd sold everything, including her car, to come up with the little nest egg that would allow her to start over in Sunstone. Now that she was here, ready for her new life, she wasn't about to let anything change her plans, including the doctor she was about to meet.

The mayor's office was plain—plain metal desk, plain metal bookshelves, plain metal filing cabinets. Its singular inhabitant, however, was anything but plain, and Lacy recognized his type instantly. Impatient, judging from the long, exasperated sigh that escaped him and the frantic rhythm he tapped on the chair arm. And, he was too self-important to park his car in a spot that wasn't marked handicapped. No wonder the mayor was so anxious to escape.

She wasn't sure she wanted to introduce herself. That would signal the beginning of the working relationship, the beginning of the same thing she'd just left, and she wasn't ready for that. She thought about turning around and walking out without saying a word, but she also thought about how much she wanted this opportunity. And she *did* want it. And he was, after all, temporary. "I'm Lacy Archer," she finally said after the internal debate. "Your nurse."

"I'd like a cup of coffee, Miss Archer. Black." His voice

was flat and full of authority, like he was used to barking out orders and having them obeyed.

"I believe I saw a diner across the street, and I'll bet they make coffee."

"So did I, and I'm sure they do. So why don't you hop on over there and get me a cup?" Dr. Jack Sutton shifted in the straight-backed oak chair, wincing as he unconsciously tried to cross his right leg over his left. "Damn it," he muttered under his breath, cursing the golf ball that had shattered his knee.

"Are you okay?" She saw his cane propped against his chair and instantly regretted her thought about the handicapped parking space. "Can I help you?"

"You can help me by getting that cup of coffee—" he snorted "—and a sandwich, turkey on whole wheat, white meat only. Tomato, lettuce, a little mustard."

"I'm your nurse, Doctor, not your waitress."

"And my nurse sees to my lunch, Miss Archer. Oh, and have them put a dill pickle on the side. Spear, not slices. Kosher, if they have it."

Lacy drew in a deep breath to steady herself before she replied, and she held it for a moment before letting it out slowly and loud enough she was certain he could hear her exasperation. "No wonder the mayor was so anxious to run away. You scared him."

JACK TWISTED around to catch a glimpse of Lacy, but she stepped out of his sight line, and he had to content himself with watching her shadow on the wall across from him. Her movements, even though exaggerated in the tracing, were jerky, irritated, and if he'd been a betting man, he'd have bet there wasn't a cup of coffee in his near future—black or otherwise. No turkey sandwich, either, and definitely no pickle. "If you want to know the truth, Miss Archer, he scares me. This whole town scares me. From what I've seen so far, they're so backward, I'll bet they haul out the old hay wagon to use as an ambulance.''

''If the hay wagon works, what's the problem?'' she retorted.

''If it would haul you over to the diner for my lunch, then I guess nothing.'' He turned to face the mayor's empty desk and relaxed as much as he could, considering his condition. Might as well get used to it, he thought. Two months or until the real doctor showed up, whichever came first. That was the promise he'd made, and there was nothing he could do about it except endure. ''A small tossed salad would be good, too,'' he taunted. ''Low-fat dressing.''

''How high do they jump for you back in your big city hospital?'' she asked, biting the inside of her cheek.

''It's not so much a case of how high, but how fast.'' The hint of a smile tugged at him, but it was hard to smile and frown at the same time. And out here in the middle of nowhere, practicing medicine like it hadn't been practiced in fifty years, there was a lot more to frown about than smile. But Lacy Archer and her indignation did cause the corners of his mouth to turn up just a bit. And as that happened, the frown did soften. ''In fact, when I hire my nurses, part of the application process is to see how fast they take off from the starting line.''

Lacy folded her arms across her chest and let out another huffy sigh. He was like all the rats she was running away from. Too much ego, not enough compassion for the poor workers who got their toes crushed by his stampede to get to the top. He was probably one of those doctors who played God, and she bet secretly he even wanted to be called God. ''So, do you really intend to stick it out here with the hay wagon until a new doctor is found?'' *I hope not, I hope not, I hope not…*

"Only as long as I absolutely have to." He finally managed to twist all the way around to get a good look at the body that went with the deep, throaty voice. She was gorgeous—with raven black hair almost as short as his and bright, blue-violet eyes. Probably contacts. No one had eyes that color naturally. Instinctively, he rose to his feet, but his knee buckled, and he grabbed the chair for support.

"Let me help you," she said, flying across the office and grabbing him around the waist. He felt firm around the middle, like he worked out, and she snaked her hand a little farther around than she should have in her professional capacity. "Maybe you should sit down."

"I'm fine," he grumbled, pushing her away. Positioning his cane, he straightened himself, clearing his throat in embarrassment. "Since you're not going to get me a cup of coffee—"

"Or a sandwich," she interrupted. Definitely the Dr. God thing going on here.

"Or a sandwich." He ground the words out, unable to control his impatience. "Since you're not going to get me a cup of coffee or a sandwich, can we just get this meeting over with so I can get settled in?"

Backing away, Lacy shrugged. "That's fine with me, but I think the mayor wants to be in on it, provided you don't scare him away again." She bit back a cynical laugh, thinking about the contract she'd signed. The initial clause stated something to the effect that either she or the town could back away from the deal within the first three months for any reason. Good option. She was beginning to wonder if she should take it and run.

"Look, Lucy, I've—"

"That's Lacy, Doctor," she broke in. "L-A-C-Y, Lacy."

"Look, Lacy…" He accented her name, stretched it out belligerently and let it linger far too long on his tongue,

"I've been waiting for the mayor the past half hour. My knee hurts, I'm hungry and I'm tired. And I'm not in the mood to put up with—"

"How did you hurt your knee?" she interrupted, more as a diversion from where the conversation was headed than from caring. He was inconsiderate, pompous, arrogant, and she was going to be saddled with him for awhile, so there would be plenty of time ahead for the unpleasantries. All she wanted right now was to clear some sort of path to a working relationship, and since in Jack Sutton's mind it was all about Jack Sutton, she'd start by showing a little Jack Sutton concern. One thing she'd learned over the years was that big egos could be satiated by amazingly tiny strokes, and his ego leaned definitely toward the huge side.

"*I* didn't hurt my knee." Jack closed his eyes and saw the stupid little white ball heading right for him. It was like it was implanted with a homing device. "My knee was injured by a golf ball from a man who has no business playing the game. It was his fault, not mine." Huffing out a long, annoyed sigh, he emphasized, "He's the one who hurt my knee, not me." Gripping his cane in his right hand to offset his left knee injury—he hated it when people did that wrong, using their cane on the same side as the injury—Jack stepped away from the chair and headed to the door. "I'm staying in the Billingsly cabin just outside town. Tell the mayor if he wants to talk to me, I'll be there, trying to get—"

A doctor getting injured on the golf course? What were the odds? "You tell him," she interrupted. "It's lunchtime, and the only thing I intend to do is go across the street to the diner for a sandwich and a..."

"A cup of coffee?" His eyebrows arched, and the trace of a faint smile returned to his lips. Nurses didn't talk back to him, and a nudge of admiration for the one who did caught him off guard. "Black?"

"Iced tea, with artificial sweetener and extra lemon."

"Turkey sandwich, tossed salad with diet ranch?"

"And pickle on the side. Actually, that doesn't sound bad, Doctor. Maybe I will."

"So, are you buying?"

She couldn't fight the smile that brushed across her face. He had the persistence of a starving medical student hinting at a bite, or the whole meal, and she'd always been a sucker for one of those, usually offering up at least half of what she had. "I'll bet you were good while you were in med school." She laughed in spite of herself. She would have fed him if he'd come begging at her table. "Did anybody ever *not* fall for your feed-the-hungry-med-student routine?"

"You owe me, Miss Archer." Jack stepped forward and pushed the door all the way open, then gestured for Lacy to pass through it. "It is miss, isn't it? I mean, you didn't convince some poor, unsuspecting husband to come to this place, too, did you?"

"Yes, it is, and no, I didn't," she returned, brushing against him as she slipped through the doorway. Old buildings had tiny door openings, and the town hall was no exception. And Lacy suddenly shivered as her jeans briefly caressed his khakis.

"So like I was saying, you owe me, Miss Archer."

"How do you figure?" Lacy stepped into the hall and headed for the outside door as quickly as she could without breaking into a full-fledged run. She wasn't sure what had just happened in the mayor's doorway, but she knew she didn't want it repeated at the next door. So she hurried, listening to the clicking of his cane on the wooden floor as he tried to catch up to her.

"If I hadn't agreed to spend some time in this godfor-saken place, you wouldn't have a job with a paycheck coming in until some other doctor completely lost his senses and moved here. Judging from what I know about what nurses make, you probably couldn't afford that long a vacation. So you'd have to go back to wherever it is you came from, back to your big city hospital and big city doctors, and beg for your old job back. And as much as you seem to hate me and my kind…well, all I can say is that the least you can do is say thank-you and buy me some lunch. Hey, could you slow down a little?" He puffed. Even on a good day without a bum knee, he wasn't sure he could keep up with her. She moved like a spirited greyhound, sleek and faster than the wind. Only greyhounds were gentle creatures that didn't come with Lacy Archer's bite.

In spite of herself, Lacy laughed. "You've got quite a way with twisting a story. Ever thought about writing a fairy tale?"

"Hard truth to face, isn't it, that we've known each other for only a few minutes and you're already beholden to me."

"Beholden to you, Doctor? So, do you wear blue leotards and a red cape under your clothes?"

"That's what all the nurses ask." He chuckled. "The ones who are nice to me get to find out."

"Before or after you leap tall buildings?" Hitting the street a good thirty seconds before Jack, Lacy spun around to watch him exit the building. Tall, nice wide shoulders, he was certainly handsome. Of course, being a doctor, he probably used his good looks to his advantage. Charm the patients, lure the nurses. Turn on that perfect smile and watch his little corner of the world drop at his feet. "So typical," she muttered under her breath. *He thinks the universe revolves around him.* "If you want to show off your

long underwear to me, Doctor, you'll have to keep up."
Lacy laughed at the shocked expression from a little old
man seated on a bench by the curb, then doubled her pace
to the diner.

As she entered, she twisted around just enough to see
Jack on the other side of the street, making his way slowly
toward her. His limp was bad, much worse than she'd expected, judging from her first sight of him, and the cane
didn't balance it out well. Each time his left foot hit the
ground, his face registered pain, no matter how hard he
tried to hide it. Obviously he needed physical therapy, and
obviously he wasn't getting it. *Too stubborn for his own
good,* she thought. *Doctor knows best. But not, it seems, in
his own case.*

By the time Jack was halfway across the street, Lacy
was settled into a booth at the window, and her waitress
was almost finished jotting down the turkey sandwich,
tossed salad and iced tea order. "Glad to have you folks
here," she said. "It's been a worry, what with Doc Washburn leaving town." She was pushing sixty, with platinum,
poofy hair and lots of red lipstick. And her pink rayon
uniform might have fit her once, but her size was a little
too ample for it now, and it rode up well above her knees.
"Did you and the doctor come together?"

"Heavens, no," Lacy muttered. "And he's only here
temporarily, until someone permanent can be found." It
crossed her mind to ask the mayor for a hand in the selec-
tion, since she was the one who would have to work with
whomever was hired. "Which should be pretty soon, I
hope."

"Too bad. I wouldn't mind having someone that young
and good-looking take care of me." The waitress bent into
the booth to get a better look out the window at Jack.

"Gives you something to look forward to, if you know what I mean."

"Could I have lemon in my iced tea, please?" She looked at the waitress, who was still watching Jack. "Extra lemon. Three or four wedges."

"Um, sure, honey. And what do you think the doctor will want for lunch?"

"Hot dog. Lots of chili and onions, with some sliced pickles on the side. French fries, too, with gobs of melted cheese on them. And a large cola. Slap some chocolate syrup in it, if you would."

The waitress popped a wad of gum, then smiled. "Coming right up."

The Sunstone Café seemed efficient enough, not too trendy or decorated only to suit tourists. Plain booths that seated four lined the walls, their vinyl seats patched and repatched from years of use. Chrome tables and chairs, clean and standing up to the test of time, were scattered about the middle of the room. And a lunch counter with swivel seats overlooked a grill in plain view of anyone who cared to watch the cook. Lacy didn't see the jukebox, but she knew it was there somewhere, probably filled with records circa 1965.

She liked it. She liked everything about Sunstone that she'd seen so far, except...

"Did you order my sandwich?" Jack asked, slipping into the seat across from her.

"Waitress said it's coming right up." She grabbed the menu in her wobbly attempt to keep from laughing and feigned interest in the picture of the chocolate malt topped with whipped cream and a cherry.

"So, why do you hate me, Lucy? Have we met before? Did I dump you or something?" A smile hinted at the corner of his mouth again, and once again he fought to hold it back. He couldn't remember when he'd smiled that many times in a day, let alone in an hour. Something about Lacy made him want to smile.

"Lacy."

"Did you decide to hate the doctor before you got here, Lacy?" he teased.

"I don't hate doctors." She defended herself. "In fact, one of the people I love most in the world is a doctor. What I hate is what so many doctors become." Lacy slapped the menu down flat on the table and glared at him. "You expect me to wait on you—to throw my seven years of nursing education and ten years of experience right out the window so I can service you with a turkey sandwich. That's what I hate…that, and fetch me a cup of coffee, Nurse. I'll fetch you a syringe or gauze or a chest tube, but I won't fetch you coffee and a turkey sandwich."

"Should I have asked for egg salad and mineral water?" Settling back, he stretched his leg out under the table, then checked to make sure he wasn't cramping her room under there. Even though his leg was out of the brace, it still felt more comfortable stretched out, but it was a nuisance for the person sitting across from him. And, as mad as Lacy was, he wouldn't put it past her to kick him in his bad leg. Twice, if she could get away with it. "Egg salad, mineral water and a chest tube on the side?"

Grabbing a packet of pink sweetener from a plastic holder, Lacy ripped it open and dumped exactly two-thirds into her tea. "Be a nurse for a day, Jack. Just take off your doctor badge and…"

"Do I get to wear a white uniform, or will scrubs do?" He flashed her a mocking grin.

"Like I said," she continued, trying to stay calm, even though it wasn't easy with so much arrogance sitting across from her. "Tack an R.N. after your name and see how most doctors will treat you. They'll make every unreasonable demand they can think of, accuse you of the mistakes they make, and they'll expect you to read their minds and carry out an order even when they forget to put it in the chart. Sound familiar so far?"

The waitress interrupted Lacy with a turkey sandwich, then turned to Jack. "Yours is coming up in a minute, Doc."

"I have a feeling I just got mine," he said when the waitress was out of earshot.

"You know it's true," Lacy persisted. "Even if you won't admit it."

"And you want what from me? An inch of hide? An apology for every physician who's ever treated you badly?" Jack reached across the table and grabbed a wedge of cucumber off her salad plate. Dragging it slowly through the glop of dressing in the middle of her salad, he never took his eyes off her. And as he plopped it into his mouth he saw the comeback start in her eyes and spread to her face. Fire. Pure, blistering fire. *And me without an extinguisher,* he thought. Not that he really wanted to extinguish the exquisite burn. "Next time, try blue cheese," he said, licking a drop of dressing from his lips. "It has more bite than ranch, and you seem like a lady who loves a little bite." He looked out the window to hide his smile and stifle a chuckle. Another time, another place, he would have liked playing with fire. But Lacy was bent on being a country girl, and he was city all the way. And he didn't have the time or the inclination to sort out the differences, since he was in Sunstone as a favor to a friend and to let an injury heal. And nothing else. Nothing.

"Should I genuflect when I serve you?" Lacy muttered, visualizing his face, even though it was turned away. Nice eyes. Green. And in spite of his impossible attitude, she'd seen something she liked in them. Compassion, maybe? "Bow and curtsy? Kiss your…" She caught a glimpse of the smile that slipped from mocking into something more gentle. It was quick and half hidden, but she'd seen it even though he slapped his hand to his mouth to cover it. And it was a nice smile, really.

"My what, Lucy? Tell me what you're going to kiss."

"Lacy."

"Whatever."

The waitress, who had been edging closer and closer to the table, finally plunked Jack's platter of chili dog and cheese fries in front of him, along with a tall glass of soda. "Put in some extra chocolate for you, Doc." She beamed with pride over the little extra. "Refills are free, including the chocolate."

"What chocolate?" Jack said, turning to look at his food.

"In your cola."

His eyes rolled to look at Lacy, but she was hiding behind the menu again, and he could tell by its jiggle that she was laughing. "Thank you," he said without looking at the waitress. "This will be just fine."

"You told me to order, and that's exactly what I did," she said from behind the menu. "Anything else you'd like me to do for you?"

"How did you know this is my favorite meal?" he retorted, picking up a French fry and dragging it through the liquidy cheese. It was enough to turn a normal stomach, and his hadn't been normal for years, thanks to the hours he kept and the stress of his job. "You've been stalking me, or something?"

She laid the menu on the table and smiled openly as he put the greasy, cheesy fry in his mouth and chewed. Her food choice was perfect—he hated every bite of it. But she knew he'd eat it, just to keep her from thinking she'd won this round. But she had, even if he hadn't recognized it yet. The proof was in every gut-churning bite he forced down.

Next time, she knew he'd think twice before ordering her to order.

As he gagged down the last bite of hot dog, Lacy let her glance fall to his hands, specifically his left one. No ring, not even a telltale sign. She was used to doctors who conveniently slipped their wedding rings into their pockets, and she was good at spotting the slight indentation or change in skin coloring. But his hands were strong, no ring dents, no tan lines. "Are you married?" she blurted, already regretting being curious.

Jack picked up a napkin and wiped chili grease off his lips, then took a sip of the chocolate-tainted cola. "Are you interested?" he asked, gulping back a belch. He had to find a drugstore and grab some antacids pretty soon. Ten minutes ago he might have asked her to get them for him, but now he was afraid she'd bring back rat poison.

"Just want to know who I'm dealing with. That's all." She broke off a bite of her sandwich, then locked eyes with him. "And you asked first, didn't you? The way I figure it, you owe me." She popped the piece of sandwich into her mouth, then chewed ever so slowly and deliberately.

"Let me take a wild guess." He forced himself to stay focused on her eyes, not the way she was chewing. If ever anyone could make such a simple act look sexy... "You think I'm thinking about cheating on my wife, right? because that's what all doctors do. Let me clarify that. What all male doctors do. They cheat."

"Do you?"

"Of course I do. That's part of the master plan. I let some love-struck I-gotta-marry-a-doctor woman put me through med school while I slip into the linen closet with every good-looking nurse I can find. Once I graduate, I trade her in on a newer model, one who isn't tired and bedraggled from helping my career get going. But because I'm a doctor, I still cheat. Nature of the beast. Can't control it. Don't have to.'' God, those eyes. Never had anything so stunning stared back at him. And he was staring at her so hard, he was sure she could feel it. But he couldn't control it. Lacy Archer compelled him to stare.

''So you're not married.'' Lacy finally looked away from him. The way he was watching her made her nervous, and she couldn't take any more of watching him watch her, so she fixed her visual attention on two boys on skateboards in the street. Mayor Lambert was shaking his finger at them, probably telling them to get on the sidewalk.

Jack glanced quickly at what Lacy was watching, then at her. ''And what makes you think that?''

Lacy reached across the table and brushed her finger lightly over his ring finger. ''A good nurse doesn't fetch coffee for the doctor, Jack, but a good nurse does know how to read him.'' She removed her hand, placed it on her food bill and slid the bill under his hand. ''I'll see you in the mayor's office when you've finished with your lunch.'' She gave him a saucy wink, then disappeared out the diner door.

He looked at the plate full of greasy remainders, then shoved it across the table. ''Just a few weeks, Jack,'' Bo Washburn had said. ''My grandfather can't do the work now, and the town needs a good doctor until they can find one to replace him.'' Favor, indeed. Three hours in Sunstone were already three too many.

2

"WE HAVE a little problem about your office, Doc," Mayor Lambert mumbled before Jack was even in the door. "It seems we don't really have one for you yet. I'd assumed you two could work out of Doc Washburn's office for awhile, but Doc and his wife are heading out of town for a few weeks' R and R, and when they come back, they're going to turn it into a dining room. Anyway, we're hunting for something right now."

"Hunting for an office," Jack muttered. "Now that's an idea. Put the doctor in an office. You got anything to go in that office?" He'd left the sublime to come to the ridiculous, and they didn't even have a place for him to work.

"We've got the supplies and equipment," Jed Lambert returned. His voice called up the defense, but the look on his face was sheer offense. "Doc Washburn said you could have the stuff out of his office since he won't be needing it any more. That's a start in the right direction."

"The right direction, Mr. Mayor, is going to be down the highway to the next town that has a medical facility, because there's no way you can expect me to..." His focus turned to the slow, angry burn starting in Lacy's eyes. She wasn't going to hide anything. Not that she could, he guessed. None of those starched looks of indifference or unconcern coming from her. When she felt something, everyone around would know it. "...expect me to work under these conditions. So if, in my time here, you manage to rig up a medical office, let me know.''

Mayor Lambert shifted in his desk chair, and it let out a loud squeak. ''We'll get something going for you right away, Doc, even if we have to set up your clinic in the back room, here at city hall.''

''Please, don't call me Doc.'' He hated the term. It reminded him of one of the Seven Dwarfs—Sleepy, Grumpy, Sneezy, Doc. ''I prefer Dr. Sutton,'' he added.

''Well, Doc Sutton.'' An old voice chirped from the doorway. ''I found it, but it's going to need a good cleaning and some repair work before it's fit for sick people.'' She bounded into the mayor's office and dropped all five feet and one hundred pounds of herself into the chair across from the mayor's desk. At eighty, with curly white hair and wrinkled tan skin, Willie Pearl looked eighty, except for her eyes. They were sharp, full of spunk and forever young. ''Rented the old Fremont building. It's large enough, and with some work, it will make a fine office.''

''Willie Pearl was Doc Washburn's nurse,'' Jed Lambert explained, seeing the perplexed looks on Lacy and Jack's faces. ''She's getting married in a couple weeks and retiring, but in the meantime, she's offered to help you get your practice going.'' He ignored Jack's scowl and turned his attention to Lacy. ''This may solve your problem about finding a place to live, Lacy. The Fremont has a nice, big upstairs. It'll take some work, too, but you can live there, courtesy of Sunstone, if you'd like.''

''Are you the new nurse?'' Willie Pearl asked. ''And is that the new doctor?'' She nodded toward Jack without looking at him. He'd frowned at her on her way in the door, and she already didn't like him.

''I'm Lacy Archer,'' Lacy said, extending her hand to the older woman. ''And it's so nice to meet you...''

"Just call me Willie Pearl," the woman said, taking Lacy's hand. "Everybody does, since I've had so many last names and they can't keep up with the latest." She chuckled. "Last count, I think I've had five besides the one I was born with, six come two weeks from Saturday."

"Well, Willie Pearl, seeing that I'm homeless at the moment, perhaps you could show me where I'll be staying."

"Love to," Willie Pearl announced, springing up from her chair. "I suppose that one's coming, too, since he'll be working there." She nodded toward Jack, but didn't look at him.

"Why don't you ladies go hang some curtains and do whatever it is you need to do to fix the place, and call me when you need a doctor." Jack exited the room, and everyone listened to the sound of his cane hitting the floor. It was exaggerated and pompous, like his attitude, Lacy thought.

"Hold on, Doctor," Lacy called, once again biting out the word *doctor.* Sprinting down the hall, it took her only seconds to catch up, then she fell into his slow cadence, since he didn't stop. "We need to talk."

"I expect we'll have plenty of time to do that in the future, Miss Archer." He reached the door, pushed it open and stepped outside. "Let me know when you get that office ready."

"You don't intend to help?" she sputtered, following him to the parking lot.

"What I intend to do is return to the cabin and take a nap. I'll fix a little dinner later on, maybe some pasta, drink a glass of wine, take a shower, watch some television, then go to bed. What I don't intend to do is grab a mop and pail and get in on the cleaning brigade."

"Cleaning up an old building isn't anything I want to do, either," she argued, wedging herself between Jack and his car door, "but in the interest of getting this medical practice up and running…"

"Excuse me, Miss Archer. In Chicago, we hire people to clean the office. In fact, we hire people to set it up. That's *not* the doctor's responsibility."

"You're a long way from Chicago, Doctor."

"I'm paying off a favor here, Miss Archer, not setting up a new life, as you seem to be. So don't expect me to have the same level of enthusiasm you do, because except for treating patients, this really has nothing to do with me."

Frustrated, Lacy shook her head. "And to think I left the city for this," she snapped.

"Why *did* you leave the city?" He tried to squeeze past Lacy, but she wouldn't budge, and he didn't have the quick reflexes to come up with a tricky sidestepping maneuver.

"I left to get away from doctors like you, Doctor," she said bluntly.

"You're kind of stuck on stereotypes, aren't you? First I'm cheating on my wife. Next I'm big city pompous because the only thing I intend to do in Sunstone—and I mean the *only* thing—is treat patients until the real doctor shows up." The fire was back, burning almost to the edges of her. Bending a little closer to Lacy, he stared into her flaring eyes. Blue-violet for sure. No sign of contacts, but that color still couldn't be real. Probably the bright July sun casting too much glare. "Maybe you're sick of the kind of doctor you think I am, Lacy, but get this straight. Your problem has nothing to do with me. I wasn't there. I didn't do it to you, whatever *it* happens to be." What a beautiful mouth, even when it was pulled into a taut, angry line. He glanced down the length of her. Great hips. Great everything. Too bad her jeans hid her legs, but the way her body heaved when she was angry made up, a dozen times over, for what he couldn't see. "And I'm a good doctor, and will be even under these hay bale and pitchfork conditions. But that's all I'll be, Lacy. The doctor. Period. Don't expect anything more, because I'll be going back home shortly to practice modern medicine, and not the boiled root and berry poultice kind they have here.''

Lacy noted the obvious stare, his second in less than an hour, and tried to ignore the prickling sensation on the back of her neck. Twice in one hour for her, too. And she didn't understand, or like, the implication or her reaction. *He's not the first doctor to ogle me,* she reasoned, *and probably won't be the last.* But the involuntary shudder came anyway. One he saw. One that raised his eyebrows. ''So I take it you don't want to see your new office?''

''Doctor?'' A middle-aged man interrupted from his pickup truck before it came to a full stop in front of Jack and Lacy. ''I'm glad I caught up with you.'' He hopped out of the truck and grabbed a brown grocery bag out of the back. ''Since I never did get to pay off my bill to Doc Washburn, I thought I'd just settle up with you.'' He thrust the bag at Jack, then grinned. ''I think you'll be pleased.''

Without a word, Jack opened the bag and looked in. They were big—bigger than apples. And white. ''Turnips? You pay in turnips?''

''Not just turnips, Doc. Prizewinning turnips. I always take a blue ribbon over at the county fair for them.''

''And what am I supposed to do with turnips?'' Jack grunted.

''Same thing Doc Washburn did. Cook 'em and eat 'em.'' The farmer hurried to his truck and climbed in. ''I'll have the wife stop by your place tomorrow with your eggs. I didn't think there was any sense bringing them into town today, since you won't be using them until morning.'' He waved goodbye to the two, then drove away.

Jack thrust the bag into Lacy's hands, but she was quick

and shoved it right back. "Boiled and mashed with a little butter isn't too bad." She laughed. "My grandmother crumbles a little bacon in it, too, for seasoning."

"Then give these to your grandmother." He shoved the bag at her, and it ripped, sending a dozen healthy turnips rolling all over the sidewalk.

"There's an ordinance against that, *Doctor*," Mayor Lambert announced, stepping out of city hall.

"No turnips on the street?" Jack snapped, batting at one with his cane. It rolled a good ten feet down the sidewalk before it came to a stop.

"Littering, Doctor. Doesn't matter if it's trash or turnips. We don't litter in Sunstone."

Jack reached into his pocket and grabbed a five dollar bill, then waved it at the mayor. "Here's your littering fine, Mayor. Or can I pay it in turnips?"

"Fine's a hundred bucks for the first offense, Doctor. Either pick up the turnips or fork over another ninety-five."

"How about some jail time?" Lacy asked, laughing.

"Community service," the mayor responded. "In this case, probably street cleaning."

Jack fixed a cold stare on Lacy, then bent and picked up a turnip and tossed it at her. She caught it with all the skill of a first baseman, then lobbed it right back at him. "I get paid in cash, Doctor. Since you apparently do not, maybe you'd better hang on to this to tide you over until the turnip truck comes again."

Without a word, Jack threw the turnip at the trash can sitting next to the town hall's front door, but his pitch was wild and his solid, round vegetable sailed right through the front window, shattering glass and causing the mayor's secretary, Betty Parsons, who sat directly across from the window, to scream as if she'd been shot.

The mayor, who was shocked speechless, shook his head

while Lacy vaulted up the half dozen steps, right into Willie Pearl, who was tromping down them. "Who did this?" the old woman yelled, shaking the turnip at the crowd that was beginning to gather. "Which of you hooligans…"

Several people pointed accusing fingers at Jack, and a few muttered, "That man." Mayor Lambert, when he finally regained his wits, took his place next to the rattled secretary, who was mourning the loss of her favorite philodendron to the flying turnip, and pronounced, "Ladies and gentlemen, I would like for you to meet the new town doctor—Dr. Jack Sutton."

A few gasps went up, and several people backed away from Jack, like he was the devil incarnate. One mother pushed her child behind her for safety's sake. "Way to go, Doc," Lacy quipped as she stepped around him. "I'll bet no one will be bringing you turnips anymore." She glanced at the child, who was trying to peek out from his mother's skirts. His eyes were wide and frightened, like he'd never seen such a spectacle in his young life. "Or small children."

"The Fremont's two blocks south," Willie Pearl said, stepping up to Lacy and linking arms with her. "Why don't we go on over there while the doctor settles his score with the mayor and tries to ingratiate himself with the crowd." She whipped a small calculator from her pocket and handed it to the mayor. "I figured you'll be needing this to cipher all the damage he's done." She cracked a wide grin and continued. "And don't forget about Betty's philodendron." She made a cutting gesture across her throat. "It's a goner."

The short hike to the Fremont didn't take the two women long, and as they approached the two-story red brick building, Lacy saw the fuming doctor emerging from his Cherokee. The look on his face was black death, and his limp was more pronounced than ever. "Not good," she muttered to Willie Pearl. But so far, nothing about Jack Sutton was good in any way, shape or form. "You shouldn't be walking on that sidewalk with your knee as bad as it is," she called, still half a block away from him.

"I'm perfectly aware of what I should and shouldn't be doing about my knee," he called back. "And I've got better ways to spend my time than inspecting this dump, so can we get this over with?"

"In a hurry to get home and fry up them turnips, Doc?" Willie Pearl chuckled. "Got some greens in my garden that'll go good with them. Help yourself."

Lacy smiled. She hoped that in another forty-five years, she'd be just like Willie Pearl. Her mind conjured up an image of Jack in forty-five years. Still wildly handsome, his chestnut hair turned to sterling, his green eyes still sharp and his wide shoulders straight, not stooped from the years. But the sour expression on his face was still the same. Probably frozen there for eternity.

Stepping up to Jack, Lacy landed a taunting smile on him. "Glad you could make it, Doctor."

"Like I had a choice?"

"Life is full of choices, Doctor, and yours are all temporarily in Sunstone, so you might as well make the best of it. It'll make things easier."

"None of my choices are here, Miss Archer. Not the turnips, not this place and not the patients I'll see. Nothing."

Turning to avoid Jack's cold stare, Lacy gazed at the old two-story, Italianate, redbrick structure. A little on the plain side, but it was sturdy and lovely, with carved wooden cornices under the roofline and long, wavy-glassed windows. The limestone plaque in the eyebrowed arch over the second-story window directly above the front door read Fremont 1908, and it seemed that the time-honored Fremont 1908 might have a lot of good life left in it, with a little help from some friends. "It's a nice building from the outside, Willie Pearl," Lacy offered. "What did the Fremont use to be?"

"Feed and grain the first time around, then a hardware store," the old woman answered, pulling open one side of a double door. Its dark green paint was peeled almost down to the bare wood in spots, and it squeaked something awful on its hinges, but moved easier than expected, like it was warmed up and waiting for them. "Closed for about twenty years now. That fancy thing they call a home center, just across the county line, ran it out of business."

"It's going to be beautiful when we get it fixed up." Lacy ran her fingers lightly over the shutters. "Wonderful color," she said almost to herself, then smiled. Everything about the old building was wonderful, including the sudden vision of the medical practice she would help start within its walls. It was nothing like her grandfather's cramped little office, the one that had been her standard for what true rural medicine should be. It was better. Different, and better.

In spite of himself, Jack took a hard look at the building. "Someone should have torn it down years ago." He grunted.

"I'll welcome you to do better, Doc," Willie Pearl snapped. "Now, watch your step," she warned as they entered the building. "The floor's a little wobbly, and I wouldn't want you hurting yourself." She leaned close to Lacy and whispered, "With my luck, he'll trip, fall, hurt the other knee and end up staying longer than he already is."

"I heard that," Jack muttered, brushing a net of cobwebs away from the door. He glanced at the floor inside the main room, and he surmised wobbly meant uneven. The oak planks were worn with passage, dipping a little in some spots, a lot in others. "This place is a lawsuit waiting to happen, Willie Pearl. You know that, don't you?"

"You've been in the city too long, Doc," Willie Pearl replied. "People here don't automatically think lawsuit for every little hangnail and splinter."

"But the liability here will cost a fortune." He swiped some dust off the windowsill, stared at it for a moment, then rubbed his hands together to get rid of it. "And no one in their right mind will want to come here for medical treatment, even after it's cleaned up."

"Then I guess no one in Sunstone's in their right mind—" Willie Pearl snorted "—because they'll go wherever they have to when they need medical help. And that includes coming here to the Fremont."

"Go home, Jack. Nurse your knee. Read a book. Leave us alone," Lacy told him, wiping her face of the cobweb she'd just walked through. *And stay there until we can find your replacement.* "Willie Pearl and I can figure out what this place needs without your interference." She left him standing at the door and crossed the room to take a better look at the area. Her first impression, as she moved slowly around the room's perimeter, was that she liked what she saw, including the warped floor and the stamped tin ceiling panels hanging on, in places, only by a thread. She saw the dirt, the peeling paint, the dim lights, and knew the fix-up would require more than curtains and a good scrubbing. But she loved it all—its promise, its challenge. "It's magnificent," she whispered, forgetting momentarily that she wasn't alone.

"You're kidding, aren't you?" he asked.

"You still here?" she quipped.

"Like you'd let me live it down if I walked out right

now. And for your information, magnificent is a brand-new office with brand-new equipment. It's a state-of-the-art operating room, and even though your new country roots are deep, Lacy, you can't disagree with me. This place, no matter what you do to it, will never be the medical facility the people here need.''

"It's not the facility the people need, Jack," Lacy said. "It's the doctor. It's the way he considers his patients to be his friends and the way he'll take turnips instead of cash to save someone who can't pay from being humiliated."

"Turnips won't buy an X-ray machine." His knee was beginning to throb. His head hurt and dust was clogging his sinuses.

"You really don't get it, do you?" Her gaze followed Willie Pearl out the door. She couldn't blame the old woman for her quiet departure. Being around Jack wasn't exactly the highlight of anyone's day. "Medicine isn't always about the machines or the best office or any of the other trappings you consider so important. It's about—"

"I need to sit down," Jack interrupted. He scanned the room for a chair, found one that looked reasonably sturdy stashed under the stairs to the second story and pulled it out. He brushed the thick veneer of dust off the seat, then looked around for a towel to put on the seat before he sat. Finding none, he finally gave into the need to be off his feet, dirt or no dirt on his khakis. "Bo wouldn't expect this much from me, especially if he knew what was involved."

Lacy didn't reply. Instead, she watched a little brown field mouse scurry down the stairs directly behind Jack.

"Was it a love affair with a doctor gone bad?" he asked, shifting uncomfortably in the chair. "Or jealousy because I'm the doctor and you're not? Is that what accounts for your attitude?"

The mouse stopped almost directly above his head.

Watching him. She'd have given a week's salary to see that little brown vermin launch off the step and land on Jack's shoulder, but it just sat without moving. No movement. Not even a twitch.

"What are you staring at?" he demanded, refusing to twist around to give her the made-you-look satisfaction.

"Just a mouse."

"A…" He did look, and as he spun around he caught the movement of something scurrying away. "What the…" He bellowed, jumping up and knocking his chair over backward.

"Afraid of a mouse, Doc?" a big burly man asked, stepping through the door. He was huge, six-feet-six at least. Maybe even taller. And he was so well-muscled he filled the entire doorway. "I'll take care of it for you." Without another word, the man went outside, then returned in a few seconds, carrying a kitten in each hand. One was a calico, the other a solid white. "These babies will do the job, Doc. The mom cat is one hell of a mouser, so they should be, too." He dropped the kittens to the floor and both darted for the stairs, as if they smelled the trail of the fleeing rodent. "I heard you were moving into the Fremont, and since it's been empty for awhile, I figured you'd be needing a little exterminating."

"They're cute," Lacy offered, walking over to the man and extending a hand. "I'm Lacy Archer."

"The nurse," he answered, wiping his right hand on the back pocket of his jeans before he stuck it out. "I'm Wayne Bonham. Most of the folks around here just call me Ham."

"Good name," Jack muttered sarcastically, bending to pick up the chair he'd knocked over.

"Thanks," Ham said, grinning from ear to ear. He missed the sarcasm in Jack's voice or was ignoring it. But either way, he seemed genuinely happy to meet the new town doctor. "My mom gave it to me when I was born. She said I reminded her of a—"

"Let me guess," Jack interrupted. "A ham."

Ham grinned. "When I heard everybody talkin' about the way you threw that turnip at Betty Parsons, right through her window, I was a little nervous about comin' over here. But you don't seem as mean as they're saying you are. And since I owed Doc Washburn for Mama's last house call, I wanted to pay up."

"In cats," Jack said. "You're paying your medical bill in cats."

"Good mousers are valuable, Doc, and I know those two will do the job for you. Besides, with the way you threw Ken Howell's turnips all over the main street, I was a little afraid to bring you the sack of tomatoes I had set aside. They're not as dangerous as turnips, but they're a lot messier to clean up."

"Do the cats have names?" Lacy asked. She loved cats. She hadn't had once since she was a child, and then it was really her grandparents' cat, the one she visited every summer and on school holidays.

"No, ma'am. I've got about two dozen cats out on the farm right now, and I usually don't give them names."

"Do you think you could keep them for me for a few days until we get this place fixed up and I'm settled in?"

Ham moved toward the door, grinning. "I'd be happy to, and if you think you might need another couple, give me a shout. A building that's been empty as long as this one could have a lot more than two kittens can handle." He scooped up the kittens, who were busy chasing after a monster dust bunny, and took them to his truck.

"No cats," Jack snapped as soon as Ham was gone.

"Afraid you'll lob them through a window, too?" Lacy moved around the counter to the room that was directly behind it. Nice place for an examining room. Large, open, lots of light filtering through the curtainless windows.

"I didn't deliberately throw that turnip through the window, and you know it." Jack followed Lacy but stopped in the doorway. She was making plans. He could see it in the way she was looking around, touching the windowpanes, feeling the peeling wallpaper. And for a moment, all he did was watch her glide gracefully from wall to wall, taking in every inch of the room's detail as he was taking in every inch of her. Too bad they hadn't met in some city, somewhere. Too bad her transplant to the country had taken hold the minute she stepped foot into Sunstone. It was like she'd always belonged there, and the townspeople saw that, too, and accepted her because of it.

His world was so far away from this, his transplant was already in the height of rejection. And he wanted to go home—back where he belonged. Back where he fit, and where people paid his customary two-hundred-fifty-dollar office call in cash, not cats.

"That's not the story I heard, Jack," Lacy teased. That story would live on in Sunstone's infamous archive of rural legends forever. *Do you remember the day that doctor came to town and threw turnips through every window on main street? It took six men to wrestle him to the ground and get those turnips away from him. And he almost killed Betty Parsons, you know. She wasn't the same for weeks— for months. Even now she shakes whenever she sees a turnip.* "It's a good thing you won't be moving in permanently. People in these parts take their turnip tossing pretty seriously."

"This place is a mess, and it looks like you've got a lot of work to do." Jack backed out of the room and headed for the front door. For a moment there, he almost cared what the people thought about him—what Lacy thought about him. But those sentiments disappeared as quickly as they'd hit. No involvement. He'd promised himself when he'd agreed to come—no involvement with anything or anyone for any reason. Just do the job then get out of there. "I'm going home."

"Don't expect me to clean this place by myself, Doctor. It's your office, too." Lacy nodded her acknowledgment to two young men who'd entered through the back door. "At least for now."

"My office is a nice, clean suite back in Chicago...my *only* office."

"Where do you want this stuff, ma'am?" one of the boys asked.

Lacy turned her back on Jack as he headed for the front door. "Just leave everything out there in the back room, for now." No need to run after him, beg him to stay or try to argue him into it. He wasn't going to budge in his attitude or arrogance. And in two months or less he'd be gone.

She shut her eyes to visualize the clinic the Fremont 1908 could become—what she wanted it to become. It was clean, homey, a place people trusted. The waiting room was full, and the doctor standing in the doorway with a smile on his face and an outstretched hand to greet them was...Jack.

"No way," she said, trudging upstairs to see her living quarters. But the image fixed in her mind had Jack there with her. And his image growing there, in her dream for the future, wouldn't go away no matter how hard she tried to cut out the Jack Sutton part.

When she was halfway upstairs, the telltale squeak of the front door stopped her, and she spun to see if Jack had changed his mind and come back to help. She hoped he would, but she doubted he was capable of doing anything that didn't directly benefit Jack Sutton. So she wasn't surprised to find a young woman cradling a small, sobbing child at the door, instead of Jack.

"He cut his arm," the woman cried. "Doc Washburn's retired, and I didn't want to take Bobby all the way to the clinic in the next county." She pulled the little boy tighter to her, dipping her head to wipe a tear on the blanket bundled around him. "I didn't know what to do."

"Put him on the counter over there," Lacy instructed, pointing to the old display case. "Keep him wrapped up." She didn't want the child coming in contact with the dirt on the counter.

Lacy followed the mother across the room, then pulled the blanket from the child's arm and appraised the injury. It was a nasty gash, about two inches long. The bleeding was stopped, but Lacy knew it could start again easily. "How did this happen?" she asked.

"He was climbing over the fence." The mother sniffled. "And he fell off."

Lacy prodded the injury and smiled. Not too deep or serious. "He'll need a few stitches, but he'll be fine."

"Where's the doctor?" the woman asked. "Shouldn't the doctor be the one to do this? Doc Washburn always did."

"The doctor's out right now. I'm not sure when he'll be back." Or if.

3

"Go see what you can find in Doc Washburn's cabinet,"
Jack ordered from the door.

His calm, reassuring voice surprised Lacy. She hadn't
heard it before and was shocked he had it in him. This was
a voice she liked. Silky smooth like milk chocolate. One
that, without Jack Sutton attached to it, could seduce any
woman, anytime, anywhere.

"We need antiseptic, to begin with." Jack stepped up to
take a look at the cut, then gave Lacy a wink. "And I'll
just bet this young man's going to need some stitches,
Nurse Archer. The kind we give grown-ups, not the kind
we use on kids."

"Yes, Doctor," Lacy replied without question. Rushing
to the back room to check the confusion of supplies and
equipment still being carried in from Doc Washburn's office, she paused briefly to watch Jack talk to the child. The
more he talked, the less the child cried, until finally the boy
quieted down and flashed a hint of a wary smile. *Maybe
there's more to Jack Sutton than meets the eye,* she thought
as she gathered an armful of medical supplies. Any doctor
with the charm to soothe a wailing child couldn't be all
bad.

"I'll bet you can't guess how old this young man is."
Jack arched his eyebrows playfully when Lacy stepped up
to the old display counter. "Bet you won't even come
close."

"Thirteen...no, make that fourteen." She was amazed by Jack's gifted way with the child.

"He's six." With sterile gauze, Jack swabbed the wound, which was now seeping. His hands were gentle and fast. "But you sure could have fooled me. I would have sworn Bobby, here, was at least eight or nine." Bending to take a closer look at the cut, he whistled softly. "I've gotta tell you, Bobby, I've never seen a six-year-old with a cut as good as this one. You usually see something like this on someone who's at least eleven or twelve."

"I'm really six," the child said quietly. "Really." His lips quivered, and tears still flooded his eyes, but the fear was gone, replaced by total trust and admiration for Jack. It was the same trust and admiration Lacy had seen her grandfather's patients give him.

"And I'll bet when I'm done with you, you'll have more stitches than any other six-year-old in Sunstone." Jack turned his attention to the mismatch of supplies Lacy was spreading on a clean sheet she'd draped over the counter. "Now, this isn't going to hurt at all," he promised, cracking open a bottle of hydrogen peroxide, the only cleansing agent Lacy could find. Thankfully, the wound was already clean. Bobby's mother had washed it with soap and water immediately after the accident. But Jack knew that opting on the side of caution could prevent the little guy from getting a serious infection. "It's going to bubble up, right on your arm," he said. "But it won't hurt." Glancing sideways at Lacy, he said, "I'll need some topical, if you can find it." To Bobby he said, "A topical is a medicine I'll give you to take away some of the pain, but I have to give it to you with a shot. I'm pretty good with a needle, though, so it won't hurt too much."

Jack's hands were steady as he poured the peroxide over Bobby's arm. "Can you stay here with him for a minute?"

he asked Lacy when she returned with the vial of medicine. "I'm going to the back room to buffer it."

"What's that mean?" Bobby asked, his eyes following Jack.

"It means the medicine he wants to give you can sting a little, and he's got a secret way to get rid of the sting." Most doctors didn't bother with the procedure. They were either in too much of a hurry to take the time, or they just didn't care that the medication to deaden the skin often hurt worse than the wound.

A glint of admiration for Jack suddenly sprang up in her, and stuck. She wasn't about to back away from her original opinion of him, but she did yield willingly to the slight modification.

"How loud can you howl?" Jack asked, stepping into the room, hiding the syringe behind his back.

"Pretty loud," Bobby said. He wanted to cry when he saw the needle, but he squeezed his eyes shut instead, and waited. Doc Washburn had given him shots before, and they really hurt, but he always got a sucker afterward, two if he didn't cry, and he thought maybe this new doctor might even give him three, since he was so nice. So, after several seconds when he hadn't felt the shot, Bobby opened his eyes a crack and saw the syringe on the counter. "When will you stick me with that?" he asked, pointing to the dreaded object.

"Already did." Jack chuckled. "When you weren't looking. And wasn't I as good with the needle as I told you I'd be?"

"Wow. You were even better." Bobby cracked the first sign of a real smile. "That didn't hurt at all."

"Now let me hear how loud you can howl," Jack encouraged.

Bobby let out a little howl, then stopped. "Is that good enough?"

Jack shook his head. "Nope. You gotta do better than that."

The boy tried again and again, until the two teens who were still moving equipment ran into the room to see what was going on.

"We thought you were hurting him," the biggest one said. "I mean…"

"That's okay," Jack replied. "We were just practicing. Either of you guys ever had stitches?" he asked.

"Sure," one teen said. "Five, right here." He pointed to a tiny scar just above his left eye.

"Only five?" Jack chuckled. "Well, it looks like Bobby's going to beat you. He's getting ten for sure, maybe even fifteen. Isn't that right, Bobby?"

"Sure is," Bobby said proudly. "Maybe even fifty."

The first stitch went smoothly, and as Jack started the second, Bobby's howling got a little louder, then louder with each stitch, until finally, when number ten was anchored, Lacy wondered if they'd be treating the boy for strained vocal cords, too. "All done," Jack announced, stepping back to look at his work.

"Do I get some candy?" Bobby asked. "Doc Washburn always gave me some candy. Two if I don't cry, but he never did stitches, so maybe I should get three this time."

"It's in the drawer under the medicine cabinet," one of the teenagers called from the back.

"Looks like you're in luck," Jack said, standing. "And since I've got to give you one more shot, I think we should make it four."

"What happened to you?" Bobby asked, noticing Jack's cane for the first time.

"Got hit by a golf ball," he said.

"Did you get stitches?" The child held out his hand for the candy Lacy found in the drawer, and his eyes lit up as he took all four pieces.

Nodding, Jack smiled. "Lots of them."

"No kidding?" Bobby exclaimed, his eyes wide with amazement. "As many as me?"

"No kidding, Bobby. But you got the most," he lied, "and you'll have the best scar. And you howled a lot better than I did, too." He looked at Bobby's mother, a sympathetic smile crossing his face. "He's up to date on all his boosters, isn't he? Including tetanus?"

She nodded, pulling her son into her arms. "Doc Washburn always took good care of us. Called us when it was time to get those things done." Then she added, shyly, "We hated to see him retire, but we're awfully happy to have you here...especially the way you were with Bobby."

Leaning against the counter, Jack turned away before the blush rose from his neck, and he jotted some follow-up instructions on a pad of paper he'd found in his medical bag. Then he instructed Lacy to draw up a syringe full of antibiotic. "You've got a great kid," he said, handing the instructions to Bobby's mother, "and he'll be as good as new in no time. We'll need to see him in about a week to remove the sutures, though, so give us a call to schedule an appointment."

Bobby didn't even fret about the last shot, and as he followed his mother to the front door, he turned and stuck out his right hand to Jack. "Thank you, Doc... Hey, I don't know your name."

"It's Jack," Jack replied, shaking the boy's hand.

"Thank you, Dr. Jack," Bobby said, shuffling out the door to catch up with his mother.

After shutting the door, Lacy turned to face Jack. "Nice work."

"What?"

"You know perfectly well what I said, Doctor." A genuine smile crossed her face. His personality might be lacking, but she was glad he had good doctoring skills. Maybe the working relationship wouldn't be so bad, after all.

"TELL ME about your knee," Lacy urged as she began to clean up the makeshift examining area.

"Bo put in a new one." He dropped into a wooden chair and began to rub at the ache. The surgery was several weeks behind him, and the pain had certainly dulled into the nagging revelation that what he did to other people hurt like hell. It was a foreign concept to him until he'd been told his best option would be to lop out the old joint and put in a new one. He'd made the same pronouncement of impending surgery hundreds of times, all with the casual attitude that it wasn't a big deal. But it was when it happened to him. Thirty-six years old with replacement parts and a better feeling for what his patients were suffering. "Who would have ever guessed a ball half the size of your fist could do so much damage?"

"So this friend of yours did the surgery? Is he any good?"

"Next to me, he's the best."

"Which means you're an orthopedist." Absently, she dropped to her knees next to Jack, pushed his hand aside and began to rub. Over the years, she'd learned that a little attention and a good massage were often as effective as a pain pill. "I would have guessed that as good as you were with Bobby, you might be a pediatrician."

"Thanks," he sighed. "I've always liked kids, but..." His voice trailed off. Her touch was pure magic. Better than the handful of aspirins he usually popped when the aching began.

"My mom told me to bring this over to you," a young girl said, pushing open the squeaky door. She carried a bucket, a mop and a bottle of cleaning solution. "She said she'd be back in a little while to start cleaning this place, as soon as she can get Bobby down for a nap."

"I brought you some chairs," a woman said, stepping into the building behind Bobby's sister. She dragged two chairs in through the door, saw Lacy on her knees next to Jack and started to back away. "They're mismatched, from a couple old kitchen sets, but I never had the heart to throw them out because they were still good," she sputtered, casting a skeptical glance around the room. "Anyway, let me go out to the car and get the other two."

"I'm out of here for good," Jack said to Lacy. Too many people already coming around. Too social, and way too personal. He didn't want to deal with them or even know them in any sense unless they were sick. And he figured the next few would be coming through the door any minute, if not to bring some crazy form of payment, then to get a close-up look at what was replacing Doctor Washburn. His knee buckled when he stood up, though, and he dropped his cane trying to regain his balance, then teetered into his seat. Good days, bad days. He'd had them all, over the past few weeks, and this ranked right at the top of the bad list. The drive from Chicago to Sunstone was much too long for someone in his stage of healing, and he'd have certainly advised one of his patients recovering from a total knee replacement not to do it. But he'd done it, then spent too much time on his feet afterward. Now he needed sleep. More than that, his body needed time to rest and repair. "Lacy, go see what Doc Washburn has locked up in the way of pain meds." He grunted, not happy about giving in.

"You hurt that much?" she asked, crossing the room

and stopping by his side. His face was a little pale, and cold sweat dotted his forehead—the answer to her question.

"This place is giving me a headache."

"More than the one you're giving everyone in town?"

"Pain meds, Lacy?"

"Enough to take the edge off, or enough to knock you out?" She would have rubbed his knee a little more and tried to make him comfortable in some way—that was her natural reaction to someone in pain—but he was testier than a hungry bear, and not too discerning about whom he clawed. And she didn't have the time or the inclination to be clawed anymore today by Jack Sutton and his problems. "If you let me decide, Doctor, it's knockout time."

"Just get the pills," he instructed as he rubbed the cold sweat from his face with the back of his hand.

When Lacy returned with two generic acetaminophen tablets with codeine, Jack had moved to the stairs, and his legs were stretched out in front of him. And he was sound asleep.

In the next few hours, as Jack continued to snooze on the steps, several Sunstone residents dropped by, each bringing something different to spruce up the office or Lacy's apartment. Word of the new doctor in town spread fast, and word of the condition of Fremont 1908 spread even faster. So by the time Jack finally opened his eyes, he found himself surrounded by a dozen strangers, all busy scrubbing floors, washing windows and walls and arranging furniture.

"What's going on?" he asked groggily, trying to focus on Lacy, who was crawling by him on her hands and knees, toothbrush in hand, cleaning the crevices between the wood planks.

"We're cleaning up your new office, Doctor," she said.

"And by the way, everyone in town knows that you snore."

"Do I drool, too?" he asked, leaning forward to rub his knee.

"I didn't personally witness it, but if you did, I'm sure someone noticed, and they'll tell me." She chuckled. "So, how's your knee?"

"Better," he lied, watching the flurry of activity. "A little better." But the pain was increasing so much that he was thinking about calling Bo to ask if he'd put the damned new knee in backward.

"Good," Lacy said, straightening. She held out the toothbrush for him. "Want to clean something?"

Jack pushed her hand away, then grabbed the banister and tried to pull himself up, but he was slow and unsteady, and his knee felt like someone was shoving a hot branding iron right through it. "Seriously, Lacy," he grunted, fumbling for his cane. "I know it's none of my business, but if you really intend to set up a clinic in this relic, wouldn't you be better off hiring a professional cleaning team to come in?" He took a step forward, his knee wobbled, and he slid down to the step. "I mean, look at these people. They think it's a party. And they've brought food." He gestured to the crowd of people who were simultaneously laughing, eating and cleaning. "This pitch-in mentality isn't the way to establish a real medical practice, and you know it. It makes you one of them, and you can't afford to be if you want to take care of them. You've got to separate yourself. Set yourself apart. And allowing them to drag in fried chicken and scrub buckets is breeding a familiarity that's going to turn around and bite you in the…"

He shook his head and let out an impatient breath. It wasn't his practice or his office, but it frustrated him still the same. "You're establishing a precedent that any reputable doctor who eventually settles in here probably won't like." He stretched his leg out in front of him and winced. Time to go home, take a long soak in the Billingsly hot tub. Actually, they were only Sunstone weekenders, a day or two in the cabin every now and then, when the country life beckoned. Smart people, who knew when enough was enough and went back to the city. Setting him up in their cabin was the one good thing Mayor Lambert had done, because it had all the big city amenities. And no mice.

"Your opinion, Jack," Lacy said, shrugging. "And you're welcome to it. But you're missing out on something you'll never find in your kind of medical practice."

"Like payment in cats?"

"Friendships. Personal relationships. People who care about you as a person, and not as a medical object whose only purpose is to cure their ills."

"Medical object?" he asked.

"Kind of like a sex object." She chuckled. "And you can't tell me your patients see you as anything other than a medical object. That's the way medicine is today. It breeds unfamiliarity."

"I've had one or two look at me as a sex object," He defended himself, positioning himself for another try at standing.

Lacy watched him grip the banister, but before he could pull himself up she'd locked her grip around his belt to help steady him on his feet. "Now what?" she asked, when he was fully upright.

"Bathroom, then home."

"Now that could be a real problem, Doctor, since no one's had the time to clean it yet. Of course, if you'd care to…"

"Just get a damned bucket and help me get there," Jack growled. "And some gloves. I'm not cleaning a toilet without gloves." At least in the bathroom, behind a closed door, he wouldn't have to watch all those people having a good time cleaning, as if it were a major town festival. And he could lock the door and keep Lacy out for awhile. Out in the physical sense, anyway. In the mental sense, she was already squirming into each crevice of his brain. "Think we could move a little faster?" he asked quietly. "People are staring." Lacy's fingers burned into his side as she helped him walk across the room. Truth was, he liked the feel of it and didn't want to risk it any longer than he had to.

"I can run, Doctor, if you can."

Almost to the bathroom, Jack hoped the door was thick and the lock would hold tight. Even that, he was afraid, wouldn't stop Lacy Archer from intruding.

LACY GLANCED at the bathroom door. He'd been in there half an hour, and she didn't know if he'd passed out from the pain or if he was working. She strolled by casually about ten times, pressing her ear to the door. She heard nothing over the roar of the workers, who were busy with various chores or scoping-out all the casseroles, salads and desserts set out as a pitch-in dinner. It was hard to hear anything in there.

"Jack," she called, tapping on the door. "Are you all right?"

She heard a response but couldn't decipher it. Something between a bark and a word she wasn't sure she wanted repeated. It sounded strong, nothing remotely like, "Help me." So she figured he was probably just hiding out in the only semi-quiet place in Fremont 1908. And she couldn't blame him, after the way he'd introduced himself to the town that afternoon. No doubt he was still too embarrassed to show his face. And no one working at the Fremont 1908 seemed to care or even notice the conspicuous absence.

Glancing at the bathroom door again, Lacy drew in a somber sigh. He really should be at the cabin right now, leg propped up, doing whatever it was he did in his spare time—except playing golf.

Golf… The poetic justice couldn't have been scripted any better. But she did feel sorry for him, she had to admit. He was in a lot of pain, and if he didn't have a full recovery, his long hours of standing over the operating table would come to an end, and he'd end up doing nothing more than consulting work…which was okay if he wanted to be a consultant. But Jack was a surgeon, and surgeons operated. And she knew, without any proof of it, that Jack was a great surgeon.

Glancing at her watch, Lacy wondered if it was time to give him the pain pill she rustled up earlier. "Jack," she called. "Let me in. I come bearing drugs."

All noise in the room ceased as if on cue, then all eyes turned slowly in her direction. For one long moment, no one moved. No one even breathed. She could feel the burn of their scrutiny. "Pain pills," she explained uncomfortably. "For his knee. He had surgery." By the time the last words were out, no one was watching anymore. Attention was focused on work and food.

"You certainly aren't helping my image, letting everyone think I'm on drugs," he growled, opening the door. He grabbed her hand and pulled her into the cramped room.

"Do you care, since you'll be leaving?" Even though the tiny window above the sink was open, the room was stuffy, the cloying, minty scent of cleaning solution thick in the air, and Jack was scarlet red and dripping with sweat. His knit shirt hung on the back of a chair, arranged neatly so not to wrinkle, Lacy guessed. And his brow was beaded, matting locks of his brown hair to his forehead. He looked boyish and charming, and the sight of his strong, half-naked body doubled her heartbeat.

"Of course I care," he snapped. Spotting a smudge on the mirror, he swiped at it with a rag. "I don't want them thinking—"

"Missed a spot," she interrupted, pointing to a smear in the corner. She had to look at the mirror—focus on something other than Jack.

"I'm not a drug addict, and I don't want them thinking I am," he continued. "I may not be here long, but..." He turned his attention to the mirror. "Where? I don't see it."

"I see it, Jack, even if you don't." Behind that big city bluff, Jack was a caring physician. And she would have bet her first week's pay that he wanted them to care, too. Not that he would ever admit it.

"And what's that supposed to mean?"

"It means take your pill so you can put your best leg forward once you step out that door." She forced a paper pill cup into his hand then watched as he took only one from it and swallowed it without water.

"Just to take the edge off."

"You've done a good job," she said, watching him slide into the chrome kitchen chair Willie Pearl had dragged in there for him earlier.

"Of course I've done a good job. What did you expect? That I can't clean a toilet? I worked my way through med school cleaning toilets, and a lot worse," he added in a hoarse whisper. "Janitor. For four long years."

Lacy fanned herself with her hand. She'd seen too many strong, half-naked bodies to have that kind of reaction, but the more she looked, and the more she tried not to look, the harder her pulse pounded. Probably just a reaction to the mix of fumes and heat. "The sink..." It was half done, divided right down the middle. Clean and shiny on one side, brown and gritty on the other. "I'll finish it," she panted.

Shutting his eyes, Jack dropped his head against the wall and drew in a long, ragged breath. "How many of them are out there now?" he asked, suddenly too tired to care.

"About twenty, and I understand a few more are coming later," she said, glad to break the moment. "There's still plenty of food, with more showing up every few minutes, so I think they intend to work into the night." Instinctively, she reached out and brushed the back of her hand across his forehead to push away the damp hair sticking there, to see if the sweat was cold and clammy from pain. "How are you feeling, Jack?" she asked. "Tell me the truth. Is it getting worse?"

At her touch, Jack's eyes shot open, and he softened his customary gunmetal stare. His face was still a little stony, but his look of haughty condescension was completely gone. "I'll feel better when I get my chores done," he said. A slow, infectious grin crossed his face, and he leaned forward in his chair, grabbed the sink and pulled himself up. "So step aside, Nurse. The patient is waiting."

"I said I'd do it," Lacy insisted. She was pressed close to him in that tiny cubicle, and her pulse began to pound again. She felt the heat radiating from his body. Could he feel her heat; the heat he was causing? "You go out there and lie down. Someone brought a bed in awhile ago, and I think you should use it until I can take you home."

"I don't think this town is ready for their new doctor, looking like I do, barely able to walk, taking a nap in the bed in the middle of the room, snoring and drooling. Most people have a different image..."

Lacy grabbed the brush from his hand, poured a small amount of lime cleanser in the sink and turned away. She needed the distraction from being so close to someone that good-looking, to someone she wasn't even sure she liked but who attracted her so powerfully she couldn't have stopped her runaway libido even if she'd wanted to. She desperately needed the distraction because as hot as it was in there, her body wanted to melt against his. Her fingers wanted to twine through the damp, swirled hair on his chest. *Do the sink, Lacy,* her brain screamed. *Don't do the doctor.* "I think with a little more work this sink will be as good as new." Her voice sounded strange, husky, full of sex, and she hoped he didn't notice.

TOO TIRED, Jack thought. *Too tired, too close.* And his personal code. Never get involved with anybody at work. Not a nurse, not another doctor, not a therapist or technician and definitely not a patient. When those working relationships turned into romance and romance went bad, the working relationship couldn't be salvaged. And he needed this working relationship with Lacy, no matter how much his mind was filling with other things at the moment, because he had every intention of letting her run this hayseed clinic until the cavalry arrived and sent him back where he belonged. "Nothing will ever make this sink as good as new," he growled, taking the brush back from her. "Don't you think you should get out there and take charge, or something."

Lacy cleared her throat and turned slowly from the sink. "Willie Pearl's in charge." She stepped back from Jack, who was grateful for the bit of extra space. The squeeze was tight, though, and her breasts grazed his skin, drawing an involuntary shudder from him. And from her, Jack noticed. Her nipples pebbled, straining against her T-shirt, and a brief image of how they might look flashed into his mind. "She's got everybody working like a well-oiled machine, and I don't think I should interfere. Not that she'd let me, even if I tried.'' Lacy took two more steps backward, away from him, and was pressed to the door. ''But maybe I should go out there and see what's going on, anyway.''

Tight proximity and Lacy Archer weren't going to mix, Jack decided as he moved to the sink, careful not to brush against her again. ''Do you think you could run out to my Jeep and grab some clean clothes from one of my bags? At some point, I'm going to have to come out of the bathroom, and I'd like to look a little better than I do now.''

''Sure,'' Lacy sputtered, glad for the excuse to exit. ''No problem.''

Jack turned to lock the door once Lacy pulled it shut, then thought about banging his head against it to pound in some sense. He'd had his share of relationships, starting in med school, but they were convenient and blessedly short. No marriages of convenience like so many of his friends jumped into—marriages that lasted only the duration of medical school, then went by the wayside. He hadn't even come close. But he'd never met anyone to come close with. A few nice moments was all he ever expected and all he ever got.

And then came the ladder—the one that would move him up in his career. He was on track, in the right position, in the right practice. Continuing to move up the ladder was his only priority. Distractions not permitted. Not even for a second. He'd worked too hard for too long not to arrive, and he was finally at the place in his life where he wanted to be. Successful. Period. End of story. Jack Sutton had arrived.

And yet he also knew that Lacy had the oblivious power to distract him from everything.

4

JACK FINALLY EMERGED from the glistening-clean bath-room, glistening-clean himself in blue denim jeans and white T-shirt. Everyone was still busy, working, eating and chatting, and at least ten people had been added to Lacy's estimated twenty. All in all, it was a cozy scene. A little too cozy for Jack's tastes, since he had no intention of fitting in or even trying to fit. Two or three hours of routine office calls a day, plus emergencies, was his promise, and that's as far as it went.

"Want something to eat, Doc?" Willie Pearl called from the far side of the room. She had a mop in one hand and a chicken leg in the other. "We've got enough to feed everyone in town twice."

He glanced at the spread, all carefully organized on the clean counter that only hours earlier served as the exam-ining table for Bobby. He looked at the floor, too, and the walls. All clean, ready for paint. And what would probably be the waiting area had odds-and-ends chairs, some not-so-bad-looking curtains at the windows and a braided rug. An old desk sat crossways in the corner, overlooking the entire room. Probably for Willie Pearl, since her brass and plastic name plate was already sitting on it.

Declining the food, Jack pushed through the crowd into the examining room, hoping for some privacy, someplace to hide from the prying eyes. Lacy was there, feet propped up on an old crate. "They'll be back tomorrow to do this room," she said. "The day after to start my apartment upstairs."

"You really intend to live here?" he asked, shutting the door. "Work here, live here, make this old building the center of your universe?"

"Since the town's goal is to make this a real clinic, and not just an eight-hours-a-day, five-days-a-week office, someone has to."

"Which means you're putting yourself on call twenty-four hours a day." He pulled an old oak library chair next to Lacy and sat down. "That's a lot of work. I hope they're paying you enough."

"As a matter of fact, I'll be earning about half of what I did before. And as for the work, I ran an intensive care unit, so I'm used to it." She drew in a deep breath and let out a weary sigh. "And don't get nervous about being too involved, because I don't expect much from you."

"That's good, because I didn't come here to give much," he said, his voice carefully neutral.

"Like I said…"

"Look Lacy, I'm not setting up a life here, like you are. My reason for being here is to help out an old friend, and nothing else. Bo and I went through med school together, and his grandfather advised me on several occasions. So I owe him. As it happened, the timing worked out. I was forced into some time off, Henry Washburn had a heart attack and retired, and Sunstone needed a temporary replacement. That's all there is to it. Henry asked, and what could I say? But I'm not a country doctor. I don't want to be a country doctor. I'll do what's required, and that's all. And I hope my replacement will ride into town on his big white steed any day."

"Rural medicine and good doctors aren't mutually exclusive, Jack. You do know that, don't you?"

"Rural medicine isn't an option in medical school. You can study orthopedics, cardiology, trauma surgery and just about any other specialty that involves the human body, but rural medicine isn't listed in the program."

"And that's why it's dying," Lacy replied. "It's being ignored."

"It's dying because we go to college for four years, then do four more years of medical school, followed by an internship and five-year residency. And we expect more than a sack full of turnips and a dilapidated hardware store in return." Jack fell into a relaxed slump in his chair and leaned his head against the back of the chair.

"My grandfather didn't," she said quietly. "He said it never occurred to him to not go home after he finished med school."

"And what does he have to show for his lifetime of work?"

"More than you can ever imagine, Jack." Lacy smiled and shook her head sadly. Jack couldn't or wouldn't understand, and she was wasting her time and breath trying to tell him anything.

"Why do you want this so bad, Lacy?" he asked, reaching down to rub his knee. It had worked earlier, getting her to take over. Maybe…

She did reach across and begin the massage. It was the natural thing to do, something she would have done for any patient, she reasoned. What she wouldn't have done with any patient, though, was enjoy the massage in a way that tingled to the end of her fingertip nerves. "My grandfather is a country doc, retired now, and he had, and still has, a great life. After he retired, his practice was bought out by a bigger practice in the next town, and that was eventually assimilated into a hospital-managed practice. Now the people my grandpa knew by name, the children he delivered and gave booster shots to every year, spend hours sitting in a sterile, impersonal waiting room, waiting to see a doctor who doesn't know or care who they are. Sunstone is trying to stay away from that, and I admire them. And, I can help. I know the hours a country doc works, I know what one does, and with that, I can help build a small rural clinic, and let the people here have the medical care they want.''

"So why didn't you become a doctor?"

She sucked in a sharp breath. "All the good nurses get asked that question. It's like nursing isn't good enough, or the nurses who are really on the ball are wasting their time being only nurses.'' Exasperation filled her voice and filtered down to her touch. Her gentle massage turned heavy and pinching.

Jack laid his hand across hers and whispered, "Sorry. I didn't mean to..."

"Sure you did. You all do."

"The stereotype thing again," he said, pushing her hand from his knee.

"If it fits..."

"How can you know what fits, Lacy, when you can't look beyond your tight little rut? I only asked why you didn't become a country doctor because of what I hear in your voice when you talk about your grandfather. I wasn't slamming your choice to be a nurse, and I certainly wasn't implying that good nurses are wasting their time by not being doctors.''

"It was because of my grandmother," she said quietly. "She was my grandfather's nurse, and I liked the way she took care of her patients. She took time, got to know them.'' She moved her hand to his knee again and listened to the sharp intake of his breath. "I thought about med school and even tried it out for awhile. But I was a nurse—

am a nurse—and that's a part of me that won't change. I can give my patients something you, Doc Washburn and my grandfather can't.''

Jack smiled appreciatively. A lady with a mission and a passion. It had been a long time since he'd had a mission other than climbing the career ladder. And his passion died on the first rung of that climb. "I'm sure you'll make it work, Lacy,'' he said quietly. "If I can—" He caught himself about to offer his help and choked back the words. *No involvement, Jack,* he warned himself. *Not on any level.*

Lacy heard the almost offer and forced back a cynical laugh. People like Jack didn't know how to help, outside of giving a few suggestions or writing a check. The help she needed was tangible. A roll-up-your-sleeves-and-pitch-in effort. Something more substantial than cleaning a toilet. "Oh, I'll make it work, Jack. They want it, I want it, and now all we have to do is find a doctor who wants it, too." Straightening, she punched the button to illuminate her watch and saw that it was almost ten. "I'm going to drive you out to your cabin now and see if I can find someone to follow us and bring me back.''

"Why don't you stay with me until your apartment is fit for human habitation?'' he suggested impulsively. "The cabin has two bedrooms, and I'll just bet you'd like to take a nice long soak in the hot tub before you turn in.''

"I can wash off in the sink,'' Lacy said. "And since someone brought me a bed, I'd hate to be rude.'' The idea did sound wonderful, though, and her body was crying out for the luxury, but not in *his* cabin. There wasn't enough room under his roof for the three of them—Jack, his attitude and her. And what would the people of Sunstone think, anyway? For a moment, though, the image of drinking morning coffee together and looking across the table at his face brushed with an early-day stubble evoked an earthy emotion. But she didn't need earthy at this juncture in her life. And beyond Jack's obvious physical appeal, what else was there?

Nothing that she could see. Or wanted to see.

But he was a good doctor. That she would admit. Good and compassionate.

"Suit yourself." Jack shrugged indifferently. He didn't need her there, anyway. "But don't accuse me of not extending some good old-fashioned country hospitality." Five minutes later, he left with Ham, and Lacy glanced out the window while he climbed up into the pickup. She would have waved good-night had Jack glanced back. But he didn't.

He did clean the bathroom, she thought later, as she intentionally looked for a spot he'd missed. After stripping off her shirt and bra, she dipped a donated washcloth into the basin, then drew it up to her chest and let the cool water trickle down the valley between her breasts. Jack's hot tub would have been nice. Having him squeeze the trickle of water from the washcloth even nicer. The thought hardened her nipples, as they'd hardened when she'd brushed against him earlier, and she looked in the mirror, shaking her head in disgust. Jack Sutton, no matter how handsome, wasn't her type. For starters, he was city all the way, and she was shedding herself of that burden.

Although she usually slept sans PJs, for modesty's sake, Lacy pulled on an oversize T-shirt and a pair of dainty panties, then plodded to the bed that was sitting in the middle of the room. It would go upstairs when the upstairs was clean, but for now, it was the most prominent piece of furniture in the waiting room. She didn't care, though. The sheets carried the faint scent of soap and lilac sachet, the mattress was so comfortable it hugged her as a mother would, and the pillow was already dented for her head. What more could she ask?

Pulling the sheet up to her neck, Lacy finally relaxed and closed her eyes. One day down with Jack, one day closer to his replacement. The odd thought struck her, though, that she wasn't sure if that was good or bad.

LIGHT POKED through the curtains way too early as far as Lacy was concerned. She was an evening person, three to eleven. Never, ever crawled out of bed before ten in the morning. She'd worked that shift most of her nursing life, and it was imprinted on her body clock. Ten o'clock in the morning, a couple cups of coffee, a shower and some toe touches and she was ready to face the world—barely. And her body clock was telling her that she had at least three good hours of sleep left before she started her morning routine. But it seemed Sunstone was on a different clock, because its residents were starting her day for her. She heard them outside. Voices and hammering. Happy sounds from happy people who were happy to rise with the rooster and get to work.

Amazing work ethic, she thought, scooting down far enough into the bed that only the top of her head stuck out from under the handmade quilt someone had donated to her cause. Through the thick cover, however, she smelled the coffee, then moved up just enough to get a better whiff but not enough to admit she was on the verge of really waking up. Rich, wake-up aroma. Brewed. Brewed was good. She usually fixed instant, and the idea of waking up to freshly brewed coffee had a certain small town charm, despite the damnable small town early hour.

Settling under the quilt for a moment, Lacy shut her eyes and relaxed, but as her head began to clear of its early-day blear, and as the coffee smells, and the smells of what she thought might be fresh muffins filled the room and almost dragged her forcibly from her sanctuary, she realized she wasn't alone. Someone had invaded her stopgap privacy to fix breakfast, and here she was in the middle of it, barely dressed. Peeking under the covers to make sure she really was dressed, she found her T-shirt pulled immodestly above her waist and twisted in a knot, and it occurred to her that her breakfast bringer could have seen more of her than she cared to show. Admittedly, the black barely-there panties probably weren't the best choice, but she'd shredded the white cotton sensibles she always wore under her nursing uniform, since she intended to be a rural nurse in jeans.

"Hello," she called tentatively. "Who's here?"

"Just the hired help," Jack said, stepping out of the soon-to-be examining room.

Pulling her cover to her chin, she crouched in the bed. "Why?"

"I work here. Remember?" He held out a mug of coffee for her. "Black okay?"

She nodded, reaching for the cup. Breakfast in bed, served by Jack Sutton, was much more appealing than just smelling the coffee, and for a moment she wondered if it was actually a dream. Unfortunately, the Jack she was coming to know wasn't nice, like this Jack. And he certainly wouldn't have volunteered to come to town and serve her breakfast in bed. "Was there an emergency?" she asked. "Is that why you're here so early?"

No way he was going to tell her she'd been the first thing on his mind that morning. He didn't even want to admit that to himself. "Best hours of the day," he said. "Nothing better than getting up at the crack of dawn and getting to work. And the people outside who are already working on the building will tell you the same thing." He watched her unwillingly force her eyes open. Unless she slept in her contacts, that blue-violet was her real color. He'd never seen anything quite like it, and he was almost as intrigued by the color of her eyes as he was the black panties. And her stomach, her T-shirt pulled to her waist…the best way to start the day any man could have. But, with so many people already outside, he didn't like the idea of anybody else starting off their day with something so gorgeous, something he wanted only for his own memory. So, even though his first inclination was to leave her in her almost natural, totally sensational state, sensibility ruled, and he'd covered her. Good thing, too. Within minutes, Willie Pearl and her fiancé, Palmer Roark, had strolled in with coffee and muffins. Both tried to be quiet as they tiptoed by Lacy, but Jack did notice the look Palmer gave her—a true testimony to the phrase old, but not dead. Even though Palmer was every bit of eighty years, and then some, he still had a good eye.

"Hungry?" He held out a lemon poppy seed muffin, thinking he might like to crawl in beside Lacy. He'd already polished off two, and they were huge. Normally, three cups of coffee tided him over until lunch, but this morning, in spite of the pain, he was famished. "What kind of name is Lacy?" he added, pulling a chair up next to her bed.

"Are you practicing your bedside manner, Doctor?" she asked. She wasn't used to having breakfast in bed, or conversation to accompany that breakfast. She wasn't used to having people wander through her bedroom, either, or to sleeping in the middle of a feed-and-grain-turned-hardware store.

"No, I was just curious about what was happening here." His out-of-practice conversational skills were showing. Or was it that Lacy made him a little nervous? Maybe a combination of both. "Since I'm being forced into duty in this dump, I thought I should acclimate myself." Liar. He'd had Lacy on the brain for more hours than he cared to count, and this morning he was pushing on the door of the Fremont 1908 before he realized what he was doing.

Balancing the coffee mug and the muffin and at the same time trying to keep the sheet tucked around her chin wasn't easy, and Lacy really wanted to let go of the sheet and eat the muffin while it was still hot. But she didn't have three hands, and three hands were what she needed. "It's a family name," she said. "My grandmother is Lacy, my mother is Lacy and I'm Lacy. So now that you're acquainted with my family tree, would you please leave so I can get out of bed?" She liked his mood this morning. Before the pain set in, he wasn't so bad. But, watching him limp to the door, she knew the pain would soon follow. Too bad. He had a certain artless charm right now.

"You don't have anything I haven't seen before, so there's no reason for me to leave." His face remained an expressionless mask, but a hint of humor sparked in his eyes. "And when I say anything, I mean *anything*."

"Anything?" she questioned, clutching the sheet even tighter.

"Well, I'll admit those black panties were something new. Are they called G-strings now, or a thong?" His forehead wrinkled into a frown, but his eyes still sparkled mischief. "Black's a good color on you, you know. Of course, there was so little material in that…"

"Get out," she said. She couldn't, wouldn't move until he was gone. Couldn't even lift the mug to her lips for fear he'd see the way her hands were shaking. So what if he'd seen more than he should when he came in? Like he said, he'd seen it all before. He was a doctor. But he wasn't her doctor, and even her own doctor hadn't seen her in those panties. "And keep those people out of here until I'm up and dressed."

Jack turned his head slowly. "I wasn't the only one wandering through this morning. In fact, there was quite a parade, so I was told."

"I would have heard them," Lacy sputtered. "I'm not that sound a sleeper." She shut her eyes, and the vision of a long line of Sunstonians filing by her bed to pay respect popped into her mind. Mothers were clamping their hands over their children's eyes to protect them from the sight, and men were pausing for a longer look, removing their hats and saluting. "I don't believe you," she cried, not sure if she did or didn't.

"Then ask yourself how the coffee and muffins got here, because I sure didn't get up this morning and fix them." Grabbing his cane, Jack opened the door. "I've got to tell you you've made a heck of an impression already. Maybe it's something you should write up and submit to a nursing journal—*How to Impress Your Patients in One Easy Step*. Talk about a sex object."

"Get out," she said again.

Up and dressed took about half an hour, because after Jack joined the painting party on the sidewalk outside, Lacy hopped out of bed and paced the floor for ten minutes, trying to regain her wits. He had a lot of nerve, sneaking around her room like that, looking at her—at her... The thought of what he'd looked at, and what he claimed everyone else in town had looked at, too, made her blush, and she desperately wanted a long shower to wash away the embarrassment, then the means to slip down the drain unnoticed. The best she got, though, was a quick, lukewarm sponge off. Enough to keep her clean, but not enough to snap her mind back to anything but Jack Sutton and what he'd said. After pulling on a pair of jeans over lacy pink panties, ones he definitely would not see, Lacy chose a white tank top, wishing she owned a suit of armor. Or a nun's habit.

"You can come in now," she called tentatively from the Fremont 1908's front door. The paint was wet, its odor strong. The shutters were painted, too, almost the exact color they were in 1908. And the crowd of a dozen workers turned to Lacy and applauded.

"Oh, no," she sputtered, slamming shut the door.

"He put them up to it," Willie Pearl said even before she entered the room. She was in the back room, formerly the loading dock, taking inventory of the medical supplies in Doc Washburn's cabinet and making a purchase list. She stepped into the main room, a vision in lavender—lavender stretch pants, lavender flowered cotton shirt and a lavender bandanna. A clipboard was tucked under her arm, and she strode over to Lacy like a woman with a purpose. "You were all neatly and properly tucked in when Palmer and I got here, and I think the Doc did it since he was still standing over you with his face all red and his eyes bugged out like a man who hasn't seen a pretty behind for a long time. But he didn't let anyone else in, and if he's telling you differently, he's lying. Or trying to get your goat." Willie Pearl dropped her clipboard on the desk then marched to the front door. "And if you ask me, there wasn't a doctorly thought on his mind." She swung open the door and zipped outside, then grabbed a paintbrush and disappeared into the crowd of eager painters.

"Jack Sutton," Lacy said seething. She peeked out the window and saw him watching the front door, probably waiting for her to emerge and make a fool of herself again. His face was almost animated in anticipation—a dead giveaway. Willie Pearl was right. He *was* trying to get her goat.

"If you think you're going to get away with this, you are so wrong. So, so wrong."

"I think someone's coming to put in a phone," Jack said, finally poking his head through the door ten minutes later. Lacy had not gone outside, not even opened the door and looked outside, and he was feeling a little bad about the prank he'd played. Those practical joke days were over, put to bed after high school, and he didn't have a clue what it was about Lacy that took him back nearly twenty years. Her innocent optimism, maybe? Or enthusiasm in the face of an almost insurmountable obstacle? Maybe it was just her wide-eyed vision of the future—pack up your life and take it wherever you wanted to, go and do with it anything you chose. Whatever the case, she was evoking something that didn't have a place in his life anywhere. And he was going to have to be very careful. "Also, Bobby's dad said he has something to show you and that he'll be over about noon." As Jack stepped into the building, his knee buckled, and he grabbed the wet door frame for support before Lacy could sail across the room and help him. "Great. Just great." He grunted, pulling his green hand away from the sticky wood. His knee buckled again, and he dropped his cane, but this time Lacy was quicker than he and grabbed him around the waist.

"Are you sure that thing is healing like it should?" she asked, supporting his weight while she helped him to her bed.

"How should I know?" He pushed himself into a half-sitting, half-reclining position, and Lacy lifted his leg into a comfortable place. "It hurts like hell, and that's all I can tell you."

"Want a pill?" she asked.

"No."

"A shot?"

"Hell, no."

"A pillow under it?"

"Leave me alone."

Lacy picked up his cane and tossed it to him. "So tell me, Doctor, just when did you have this charisma bypass? It seems to have been more of a success than your knee surgery."

"Do you harass all your patients this way?" he grumbled.

"No, but then, you're not my patient." She sat in the chair he'd been sitting in earlier and reached across to untie his shoe.

"Just what do you think you're doing?" he snapped.

"Getting ready to take a look at your knee. Since you don't seem to know what's going on, I guess I'll have to figure it out." She pulled the white athletic shoe off and removed his sock. "Think maybe I'll lock the door and give you the privacy you didn't give me earlier, though." Lacy sprang out of her chair, flew to the front door, locked it, then moved past the bed to the back room. Several minutes later she returned with gauze, an elastic knee bandage, antibiotic ointment, a syringe full of a numbing agent, suture removers and a whole host of other supplies she'd found. She wasn't sure what she'd need, if anything, but she decided that because of Jack's back-and-forth bad mood, she should be prepared, because if she got started with the exam and had to go hunt for something else, he'd probably bolt right out of there.

Returning to the bed and the patient from hell, Lacy laid her supplies out carefully, then snapped on a pair of latex gloves. "Anything in your medical history I should know? Allergies, communicable diseases, personality disorders, mass murders?"

"I don't want you examining me," he said. "I have a *doctor* who can do that."

"Your doctor's not here, and I am."

"And you consider yourself qualified?"

She leaned over the bed to untie his other shoe, then yanked it off and tossed it on the floor. "Want me to go find Ham and see if he's had any medical training?" Lacy laid four suckers next to him. "If you're good, you can have those when we're finished. Now, would you like to take off your pants, or would you like me to take them off for you?"

"Don't you touch my pants," he returned, taking a protective hold of the button above the zipper.

Lacy took away one sucker, then sat down. "Let's play pretend," she said. "Let's pretend you're the doctor and I'm the patient, and I'm acting just the way you are. What would you do?"

"I'd send my nurse to handle the situation." He eyed his shoes on the floor, wishing he could find the strength to make a lunge for them. But right now, he didn't have the strength to make a lunge for Lacy, even if she were bare-breasted and straddling him. The pain was wiping him out.

"Well, I'm the nurse, and I'm handling it. So cooperate." She liked being a critical care nurse. Her patients were usually too sick to protest, and they almost always appreciated her attention and concern. Not like Jack, the classic poster boy for the saying, Doctors make the worst patients.

"Or you'll do what?"

"Or I'll call Willie Pearl to come in and hold you down."

Shaking his head in resignation, Jack slumped back into the pillow and shut his eyes. "You take them off," he responded grudgingly. Having his knee checked was inevitable, so he figured he might as well get it over with. Besides, something was wrong. He knew it, but he'd refused to look at the hideous thing himself. "And if you're even entertaining the notion of causing me bodily harm with that needle I will invite the whole town in to see your private spectacle next time it's unveiled."

"From Willie Pearl's description of the way you were standing over my bed leering, I doubt you'd care to have anyone see the spectacle *you* were creating over my spectacle."

"I'm a surgeon." He defended himself as the red-handed heat of humiliation started in his neck and rose to his face. "It's my job to be observant."

"Then why haven't you been observant about your knee? There's some kind of process going on in it and—"

"Just check the knee, Lacy," he sighed. "And hurry. I have other things to do today."

"No golf course in Sunstone, Doctor. I checked." The jeans were tight, but it took her only one tug to discover he wasn't a boxer man. On a body like his, boxers would have been a crime. His legs were long and sinewy, his hips narrow. Every inch of him, now that she had seen almost every inch at one time or another, was devilishly good looking, and it took every ounce of restraint to avert her eyes from the rich shape of his manhood outlined against the stretchy cotton fabric to the scar she was supposed to be examining.

"Now that you've taken a good look at everything, Nurse," Jack snapped, "don't you think you should get on with the real exam?"

"You owed me one, Jack, and now I've been repaid."

"But I didn't have to strip you down to have a look,"

he countered. "You had it all right out there for anyone to see."

"Anyone who had the nerve to barge into my bedroom while I was asleep."

"Not your bedroom. My waiting room, and that's the risk you take when you choose to sleep there, naked."

"I wasn't naked," she replied, throwing his jeans in a heap on the floor.

"Close enough that what I saw didn't count as clothes." He liked the way she blushed. It wasn't dainty and just barely pink. It couldn't be hidden or written off as anything but a full-out flush. Starting in the crimson patch he could see below her throat, spreading like wildfire all the way up her cheeks, Lacy's blush was hot and splotchy and sexier than any blush he'd ever seen. And, it was something she'd never be able to hide. Yes, he definitely liked that. "I'll bet you don't wear anything like that under your white uniform." He chuckled.

Stuffing a second sucker into her pocket, she retorted, "I'll bet you'll never have the chance to find out. Now, shut up, and bend your knee."

5

"YOU HAVE QUITE A WAY with your patients." Jack dreaded the task of moving his knee into position, and he winced when he tried. "Bet you got an A plus in your bedside manner class."

"Most of my patients were a little more helpful about their own recovery than you are, Jack." Polite way to put it, she thought. "And they didn't complain as much."

"Complain? You think this is complaining?" Bending his knee hurt like nothing he'd ever imagined, and as he moved it slowly upward, he shut his eyes and bit his lip. The movement was there, but way too difficult for someone in this stage of recovery.

"Let's just say you're on the verge of losing another sucker." Lacy supported his calf and straightened his leg. The muscles were already trying to contract, to tighten into a permanent bend. That was a sure sign he needed physical therapy. "Or something a lot more serious, if you don't start taking better care of yourself."

"I think the range of motion is pretty good," he lied. He knew it was lousy. So did Lacy. "It seems to be getting a little better every day." But each day, the pain was getting worse, cutting short the workouts he needed to make himself strong again. One of those catch twenty-two things. In pain if he did, in pain if he didn't.

"Yeah, well, in my opinion your range is way too tight," Lacy murmured. "You're not pushing yourself past your previous day's stopping point. If you've been exercising at all, that is.'' Her cheeks were still flushed, but they were beginning to cool down. Calm was finally beginning to spread throughout her body, allowing her full attention to snap to Jack's condition. ''I'll bet you've been counting on the think system—think it's better and it will be.'' Bending closer to the incision scar that sliced through the middle of his knee, two inches above and below, she marveled at the technology of a whole new joint. Years ago, with his injury, he might have spent the rest of his life in terrible pain or in a wheelchair. Today, the pain would go away eventually, and at worst he'd be left with a slight limp and a scar. That is, if he decided it was time to start cooperating.

''I'm not stubborn,'' he argued, gripping both sides of the mattress to fight the pain. ''I'm busy. And I haven't been thinking or visualizing myself healed. I know what's involved in a total knee recovery.''

''Maybe the doctor part of you knows, but the Jack Sutton part is stubborn, and he thinks he should be above the pain. But you're not exempt just because you think you should be.'' She prodded the red area around his knee, drawing another wince from him.

''You mean doctors are people, too?'' His hands were beginning to shake, and a fist of nausea was punching from the inside.

Lacy looked up and regarded his face. White and drained and beaded with cold sweat, it screamed pain, but his eyes were almost mellow, trusting. Did he trust her to take care of him, or was she just imagining it; maybe hoping for it? ''So why didn't you get this looked at before you came here? This infection didn't just start, you know, and I'm sure your own big city doctor would have—''

''None of your business,'' he interrupted. He knew her

probing fingers were gentle, but it felt like she was hammering nails through his flesh.

"You thought it would just go away, didn't you?"

"None of your business."

"What would you say to a patient who did the same thing, Jack?"

"None of your business."

"So, is that an admission that—"

"I'm not admitting a thing." He gave her a painful smile, then continued, "But thanks."

Lacy traced the incision with her fingers, then moved slowly and methodically to the surrounding areas. Sometimes the fingers picked up physical clues that were overlooked when the eyes were open and watching, and she often shut her eyes to gain that higher physical understanding of her patient. And what her fingers found was hot, swollen and tight. "You've got way too much inflammation going on. There's an infection in there somewhere." She bent closer to the scar and studied it with her eyes. Just as she expected, she found what she had felt with her fingers. Near the top of the scar, in the reddest, most swollen area, was a barely perceptible lump. On a cursory examination, just eyeballing the area, it would have gone undetected. But her grandpa had taught her to use all her senses when treating a patient, and his advice had never failed her, not once.

Jack's gasp of pain as her fingers pinched was her answer. She'd seen this happen dozens of times, in every kind of incision. Normally, it didn't cause a problem, but she guessed Jack had a particular sensitivity to the suture material used during his surgery. "You've got one stitch still in there, Jack, and it's infected."

"No way." He should have known it because the symptoms were right, and he was embarrassed that she had to be the one to make the diagnosis.

"Then feel for yourself."

"Just yank it out," he said, grunting.

"The skin's completely healed up around it, which means it's a little past the yanking stage."

"Then go get Doc Washburn and ask him to take care of it." Even though he wouldn't admit it, Lacy's diagnosis was a relief, because this was a curable infection, and everything he'd been conjuring up for the past eighteen hours started with another new knee and months of therapy.

"Doc Washburn's on vacation," Lacy reminded him, "so you'll have to do it yourself or trust me with the honors."

He shook his head vigorously. "Trust you with a scalpel—"

Before the rest of the words were out, Lacy swabbed the area with an antiseptic solution, made the tiny slice and pulled out the black thread. Then she prodded the wound to evacuate as much infected fluid as she could and finally held up the stitch as a trophy for Jack to see. Jack had his eyes squeezed shut tight, though. Tugging a sucker from her pocket, she set it beside the other two. "And if you're good while I'm bandaging your ouchie, you'll get the last one back, too."

Jack relaxed while she applied the antibiotic ointment, taped his tiny incision shut and applied gauze. "So deep down, you don't blame the big, bad doctor for wanting to practice somewhere that benefits him, like a real clinic or hospital, and not some makeshift country boy practice?" he asked, finally opening his eyes.

"No, not really. It's hard work, with little more than self-satisfaction to show for it, and most people aren't cut out to do it, and I guess that includes you. But don't condemn those who do want to be here, Jack. We're every bit as important to our patients as you are to yours." She took one last look at her handiwork, then stepped back. "If you promise to let me range that knee for you a couple times a day, I'll give you an extra sucker, and I won't tell Bobby what a baby you were."

"I can do it," he protested, but not too hard. The idea of having someone in his corner was nice. And he liked knowing that she would argue with him about his decision, because it showed that she cared—even if only in her professional capacity. "Now that the stitch is out, the pain should go away pretty fast."

"You can't wait for the pain to go away, Jack. You've neglected exercising already, and being an orthopedic surgeon certainly doesn't exempt you from the complications you're gong to have if you don't get going."

Her argument wasn't yet ended. He could tell from the rigid set of her shoulders. "So I'll fight through the pain and start this afternoon," he replied lazily. He enjoyed listening to the lilt in her voice and the creaking of the boards as she moved across the wooden floor. "There's a whirlpool in the cabin. Water therapy will do me good."

Lacy picked up his jeans and threw them at him. "That won't work for active range of motion exercises, and you know it." She scooped up her makeshift surgical supplies and carried them to the cabinet. "And if I were you, I'd write myself a script for some antibiotics just to make sure that localized infection doesn't spread," she called. "Something fairly strong, like…"

Jack listened to her prattle on for the next couple minutes about her medication choices and treatment advice. It really was nice to be cared for, for a change.

IT WAS ALMOST NOON when the work crew began to thin out. Many were headed home for lunch. A few had agreed to meet at the diner, and then there were those who chose to picnic under the maple trees outside the Fremont 1908. Surprisingly, Jack had spent the entire morning at Willie Pearl's desk, his leg propped up on a chair, watching, not saying a word. But at least he was there, Lacy thought as she scurried by him for the twentieth time in an hour. He was there, being seen, being part of the interaction, if only in the physical sense.

"Miss Lacy?" Mike Ross called from the door. "Could you come out here a minute?"

"Sure." She followed Mike out the door and over to his pickup truck.

"It's old, and the body doesn't look too good, but it runs well," Mike said, pointing to the patchwork truck parked in front of the building. The front end was an orangish-red, the doors a buffered, rusty yellow and the truck bed brown.

"That's nice," Lacy commented, not sure why Mike wanted to show her his truck.

"Gets pretty good gas mileage, too, but the ride's a little bumpy." He opened the door and pointed to the plaid blanket on the seat. "Since the vinyl's cracked, we put this blanket on. The color matches the outside pretty well." He chuckled. Leaving the door open, he strolled to the front and popped open the hood. "I changed the oil this morning and put in some new spark plugs. Walt Conners, down at the garage, donated the new tires since he still owed some on his bill."

"It looks like you've got yourself a nice ride," Lacy commented.

"No, ma'am. *You've* got yourself a nice ride. I fixed this up for you, since you don't have a car."

"A truck for me?" Lacy asked. "Are you sure you can spare it?" She'd never driven a truck, never driven anything larger than a compact car, and three compacts could fit in the behemoth being presented to her.

"I've got a new one, and this baby was just sitting around getting rusty. You might as well have it, and maybe it will help repay what you and Doc did to help Bobby yesterday."

"But I can't," Lacy protested. It sat higher off the ground than anything she'd ever ridden in, its floorboard looming several inches above her waist. "I really can't. I'm not even sure I can climb up in it without a stepladder."

"Don't worry about that." Mike laughed. "Once you get the hang of swinging yourself up, it won't be a problem. And besides, you need something that can get you off the road and through the fields if you're going to make house calls."

"We don't do house calls," Jack announced from the doorway.

"Doc Washburn did," Mike replied.

"And he's welcome to continue if he chooses, but I don't make house calls."

"And no one expected *you* would, Doc. But Miss Lacy here, she's different. We thought she would be willing to, if there's a need."

"And you were right, Mike. I'll be glad to make a house call in an emergency, and I appreciate the…the truck." She held out her hand for the keys, then climbed into the cab.

Twenty minutes later, after Lacy had taken her truck for a test drive up and down every one of Sunstone's streets, and a few rural roads to boot, Jack was alone in the Fremont 1908, listening to the roar of Lacy's truck engine as it came to a stop out back. Amazingly, the pain in his knee was already beginning to lessen, and he could feel the tight throb of inflammation decrease. But a different ache was setting in, a different throb, and as he'd paced the floor for those twenty minutes, peering out the window and waiting for Lacy to return, he knew it was an ache of the very worst kind. It was one that no amount of painkiller could touch.

"I didn't think you'd still be here," she said from the shadows of the back room.

"I was just on my way out the door," he lied. He had no intention of leaving until he saw Lacy march through the door, safe and sound. Each time he saw her speed past the Fremont 1908 in her new truck, practicing the gears or learning how to accelerate without leaving a black patch on the road, the chauvinist in him argued it was way too much truck for a woman and that Mike Ross should have known better. But the man who was getting to know Lacy much better than he wanted countered right back that nothing was too much for her, that she could handle anything, from a jacked-up four on the floor to him. "I don't think the gang will be back until tonight." He pointed to the phone on the desk. "We've finally got communication with the outside world, though."

"You were waiting for me, weren't you?" she asked. "You didn't think I could handle the truck, and you were waiting to patch me up after the accident." She knew he'd say no, but she held out a fragment of hope that he'd admit it, because she wanted him to care enough to wait and worry just a little.

"Actually, I was. You owe me a therapy session."

Lacy emerged from the shadows smiling. It wasn't the reason she hoped for, but it would do. "So, are you going to take off those pants, or am I going to have to do it for you, again?"

"Sorry to bother you Doc, Miss Lacy," Ham Bonham sputtered, stepping out of the back room right behind Lacy. "The door was open and I..." His gaze was welded to the floor, and he twisted his baseball cap nervously. "I didn't mean to barge in on you two like this, especially since you were about to..." He coughed nervously, dropped his hat then stooped to pick it up.

"She was about to give me physical therapy." Jack barked the words. "And doesn't that back door have a lock on it?"

Ham moved his eyes to look at Jack for a moment, then immediately looked at the floor. "Not for the last ten years or so, but I can get you one if you think you'll need it."

"I'd appreciate it," Lacy answered. Small town safety aside, she lived in the Fremont 1908 alone, and she didn't like the idea that anyone could wander in any time of the day or night. "As soon as possible." She saw the look of concern on Ham's face. His bloodhound eyes drooped, and the breaths he drew into his huge chest were labored.

Jack saw it, too. "Are you ill, Ham?" he asked softly.

"It's my mother, Doc. She's—"

"Where is she?" Jack interrupted.

Ham finally looked up, then a slow smile crossed his face. "You'll help her?"

"Just bring her on in." He turned and headed to the examining room and stopped just short of the door. "Lacy, maybe she needs help getting inside."

"Doc Washburn always came to the house," Ham said, his gaze dropping to the floor. "My mother has some special difficulties, and it's just easier to look at her at home."

"Difficulties?" Lacy asked. "Such as?" She was already preparing herself for the possibility that it was a house call she'd make alone, since Jack had made himself perfectly clear on the subject.

Ham nodded, then shrugged. "And right after lunch she got this awful pain. It scares me when she gets like that, but I just can't get her to leave the house."

"Where?" Jack asked.

"In the recliner, watching her soap opera."

"Where is her pain?" he persisted, letting out an audible sigh.

"It's private, and she won't tell me." Ham headed to the back room. "Could be one of those female things, but I don't know for sure. Whatever it is, though, Doc Washburn always knew just what to do to help her." He stepped onto the loading dock, then turned. "The house is two miles north of town, just straight up the road. Name's on the mailbox. And I'd be much obliged if you'd come and take a look at her right away. She gets so testy when she's not feeling well. I'll put on some good locks later today, to pay you, if that's okay."

"Locks are just fine," Jack answered. "Since we don't need any more cats."

The sarcastic edge in Jack's voice was obvious, at least to Lacy, but she smiled in spite of it. He was making a house call, something he vowed he wouldn't do. Maybe there was a little bit of the country life in him after all. She hoped so, anyway, since they would be experiencing the country life together for a few weeks. "Your wheels or mine, Doctor?" Lacy asked, opening the front door.

Mrs. LolaGertrude—all one word—Bonham was indeed watching a soap opera when Jack and Lacy pulled up to the paintless picket fence outside her house, and they could hear every word of it as plainly as if they were the ones sitting in front of the television in recliners. "Do you suppose her difficulty has anything to do with her hearing?" Jack asked as he climbed from the passenger seat in Lacy's truck.

"It's a good thing her nearest neighbor is an acre away." Lacy laughed and followed Jack up the steps.

Inside, the house was tidy. The furniture looked as if it had been around for fifty years, and the chairs and couch were covered with clashing flowered slipcovers and throw pillows, but everything was clean. And LolaGertrude looked as if she hadn't quite emerged from the 1950s yet herself. "Mama," Ham called over the racket. "This is the new doc. He's here to take care of you."

LolaGertrude didn't respond.

"She gets a little carried away when her story gets exciting," Ham explained. "She's watched this one every day since it came on in 1962."

Lacy stepped to the side of LolaGertrude's chair and saw an empty potato chip bag on a snack tray next to the recliner. Along with it was a box of vanilla wafers, three candy bar wrappers, two empty cans of pop, a bowl of mostly eaten popcorn and a still to be eaten snack cake. "Mrs. Bonham," she shouted. "Dr. Sutton and I are here to take a look at you." She was a bit on the hefty side, but not enough to make it a health concern. And she was also large in stature, which was to be expected, considering the size of her son. Heredity, in this instance, was certainly telling, because in addition to the size, she had the same bloodhound eyes Ham had. But her skin was porcelain smooth, placing her in the indistinguishable age range between sixty and one hundred. And she smelled strongly of baby powder and Chantilly cologne.

LolaGertrude looked up and smiled, then cupped her hand to her ear. "Speak up, dear. I don't hear very well." Her voice was robust, booming deeply over the sound of the television.

"Has she ever considered a hearing aid?" Jack shouted at Ham.

"She has a whole drawer full, but she doesn't like the noise they make." Ham shouted, too. "She says they make everything too loud." At that moment the program broke for a commercial, which was twice as loud, and Ham increased his volume and continued. "She's pretty set in her ways, and once she's decided she doesn't like something, you can't get her to change her mind.''

Lacy's ears were beginning to ring, and she noticed that a ceramic wall pocket vase filled with plastic flowers was vibrating so hard against the wall above the television it was probably sending out its own frequency of some sort. ''Could you please turn down the television sound?'' Lacy yelled, leaning in close to LolaGertrude in hopes that the woman could hear her.

''Not on your life, young lady.'' LolaGertrude bristled. ''Not while my story is still on. Everyone in these parts knows better than to disturb me when my stories are on.''

''Stories?'' Jack yelled.

''Just two more after this one,'' Ham returned. He walked to a small occasional table topped with dust-catching glass knickknacks and pulled open the drawer. Inside was a bag of brand-new squeezable orange earplugs. ''Doc Washburn always brought his own, but we keep these around in case of an emergency and for visitors like you who don't know my mama.''

Grateful for the small mercy, Jack squeezed one into each ear then handed a pair to Lacy. ''I can't wait until her stories are over,'' he shouted.

''Speak up, Doc. Those things are kind of deceiving. They make you think what you're saying is real loud since you can hear it so well in your head, but it's not. It usually comes out softer.''

''I can't wait until her stories are over,'' he repeated.

''Louder, Doc.''

''I can't wait…''

Ham made the same gesture his mother had earlier. He cupped his hand to his ear, then shook his head and shrugged.

''Damn it,'' Jack hollered, ripping out his earplugs.

"I heard that, Doctor, and we do not allow profanity in this house," LolaGertrude boomed.

Jack spun around and saw that the credits were rolling at the end of the woman's program. Seizing the opportunity, he grabbed the remote control off the snack table next to her chair and muted the sound. "Where does it hurt, Mrs. Bonham," he asked, handing the remote to Lacy before LolaGertrude had a chance to lunge for it. In a hand-to-hand battle over the television's control, he guessed he would be bested by her, and he didn't want to have the chance to find out.

"Doc Washburn always came after my programs," LolaGertrude bellowed. Even with the television silenced, her voice was at its loudest volume.

Jack cleared away a spot on the snack tray for his medical bag and set it down. "Now, Mrs. Bonham..."

LolaGertrude turned her head away from him and wouldn't look at him.

"Maybe we should come back later," Lacy said, grabbing Jack's medical bag. "Her programs will be back on in a minute, and..."

Jack yanked the bag out of her hands and dropped it on the snack tray. "We're here now, and we'll do it now," he said, his voice double its normal volume. "Sorry," he said immediately. "I didn't mean to yell."

Lacy grabbed his bag, clutched it to her chest and stepped back. "Just tell me what you want and I'll get it for you, Doctor," she said. Her voice was a little loud.

Jack snatched the bag back. "Why don't you take Ham outside while I talk to his mother."

"But..." Lacy began to protest. She shut her mouth when she saw the scowl on Jack's face. "Whatever you say, Doctor."

"I made a pitcher of lemonade for Mama, and she hasn't drunk it all yet," Ham said, pointing to the kitchen.

Lacy looked at Jack and shrugged. "If you need me, just shout."

"Now, Mrs. Bonham, what's your problem?" Jack asked, turning his attention to his patient.

"What?"

"Where does it hurt?" he shouted.

"Same place as always."

He waited for a little more instruction, but when none was offered, he continued, "Which is where?"

"Doc Washburn always knew without asking." Lola-Gertrude twisted in her chair and emitted a belch that started in the pit of her stomach and rumbled like a diesel engine all the way to her lips. Like everything else about the woman, it was big and loud.

Jack bit the inside of his cheek to keep from saying what was dying to slip out. "Did Doc Washburn give you any pills for that indigestion?" he asked.

"No. Just that chalky liquid, and I won't take it 'cause it tastes something awful." She eyed the television remote sitting on a credenza across the room, then pushed herself forward in her chair.

"Stay there," he ordered. "Let me listen to your chest and check a few other things before you get up."

"But my story is coming on."

"Your story will wait five minutes."

LolaGertrude slumped in her chair and harumphed in grand style. "Just make it fast."

Seizing the opportunity, Jack opened his bag and pulled out his stethoscope. Unfortunately, he saw Lacy's black thong tied to the end of it at the exact moment LolaGertrude did.

"Ham," she screamed, jumping up from her chair. "He's a pervert. Help me. Help!"

LolaGertrude's sprint was faster than either Lacy's or Ham's, because by the time they arrived from the kitchen, she was standing in the middle of her couch, bellowing, "Pervert, pervert," and lobbing throw pillows at Jack. "Just look what he shoved in my face," she screeched, pointing to Jack.

Lacy looked at Jack, who was standing next to Lola-Gertrude's recliner, trying to untie the panties she had tied to the stethoscope earlier. The look on his face was total confusion. "Come down from there before you fall and hurt yourself," Lacy coaxed, forcing back the laugh that was bubbling to the surface. "And calm down."

"Mama," Ham cried. "What did he do to you?"

LolaGertrude's response was a belch even louder than the first one, followed by two more in rapid succession.

Without a word, Jack crammed his stethoscope into his bag, grabbed his cane and marched straight to the door, then outside. He was leaning against Lacy's truck when she finally caught up with him. "Jack, about the panties…"

"Doc. Doc. Wait up," Ham cried from the front porch. He was waiving the black panties in the air. "You forgot these."

Jack's response was a black death scowl at Lacy.

Ham lumbered down the sidewalk and held out the panties for Jack. "I don't recall ever seeing a doctor treat a patient like you treated Mama, but she says it got rid of her difficulties faster than anything Doc Washburn ever did for her, and I thank you kindly."

The television started blaring from the house again, and Jack knew LolaGertrude Bonham was recovered and back to watching her stories.

"I'll come over and put in a good lock for you just as

soon as I fix Mama her afternoon snack,'' Ham announced. He thrust the panties into Jack's hands, turned and lumbered into the house—whistling.

Not a single word was spoken in the cab of Lacy's patchwork pickup on the ride back to the Fremont 1908.

6

"IT WASN'T LIKE you really waved them at her," Lacy said, finally breaking the silence before she and Jack plodded through the working masses in the Fremont 1908. She was still embarrassed, and her neck still bore traces of red splotches. And she was sure word of Jack's panty raid had made it to town a lot faster than she and Jack had.

"Next time I see your panties *anywhere,* I expect you to be in them," he replied.

His voice was so quiet, so deep, Lacy wasn't sure she'd heard what she thought she did, and she wasn't about to ask him to repeat himself. But what she thought he said caused her pulse to flutter a little faster, her breath to catch ever so slightly in her throat, and the telltale red to start its way up to her face. "Look, Jack, I'm really sorry…"

Jack bent to Lacy, brushing his cheek to hers, then whispered in her ear, "And stick to black, Lacy. It becomes you." Then he walked into the building and shut himself in the examining room.

Lacy wondered if he was angry and how close he was to his boiling point. He didn't seem angry, though. He seemed…actually, she didn't know what he seemed. She was getting good at reading his dark moods and anticipating his indifference, but this was so different, so…seductive. Seductive? Is that how he intended to pass the time in Sunstone, by trying to seduce her? Lacy's humiliation suddenly turned to anger, and everything she thought about him from the start came flooding back. Nurse chaser. Use 'em then dump 'em. Perfect plan, since his departure from country life was inevitable. "No way, Jack Sutton," she muttered. "Not with me you don't."

But when he closed himself off from the crowd, she raised her hand to her cheek and traced the spot where his cheek had brushed hers.

Turning her attention to the working crowd, hoping it would take her mind off Jack, Lacy watched the people of Sunstone wander in a few at a time, some bringing cleaning supplies, others food. Like the night before, they seemed happy to be there, to be a part of something important in their lives. It was nice to be part of that, she decided as she picked up a sanding block and took instructions from crew chief, Willie Pearl, on how and what to sand.

"He'll get over it," Willie Pearl chirped a few hours later. The old woman linked her arm through Lacy's and pulled her off the sanding detail, then pushed her toward the assortment of food spread out on the wooden sales counter turned examining table turned buffet. "'Course, I don't know a thing about him, so maybe he won't. Who knows."

"I remember a time when Willie Pearl embarrassed me like that," Palmer Rourke said. Palmer's voice was grave, and his wrinkles folded into other wrinkles. And he was in the process of filling two plates with enough food to feed at least four people.

Lacy smiled at the older man and waited for the rest of the story, but after half a minute she realized it wasn't coming, because Palmer carried his two overflowing plates to the steps leading upstairs, spread them out and began to eat in a methodical way. "Not very talkative, is he," Lacy finally commented to Willie Pearl.

"Oh, he talks, all right. He just doesn't air our dirty

laundry—or in this case panties—in public for everyone to see." Her laugh crackled like static electricity. "Or talk about. And believe me, they're talking. All kinds of speculations going on, you know. They're pretty sure the panties were yours, since LolaGertrude couldn't even get half of herself into those little things, but how and why they got in his bag is the big question. Must have had a dozen people ask me."

"So my panties are a topic of discussion now?"

"Them hanging on the end of his stethoscope is something worth talking about, don't you think?"

"What I think—" It didn't matter what she thought. No one cared. Opinions were already formed, conclusions already drawn. "...is that I'm really tired." Her version of the story wasn't relevant. "I'm not hungry, but I am tired, so I'm going to the back room and sit down and rest for awhile before I get back to work." And she did. Lacy retreated to the farthest, darkest corner of the loading dock, and dropped onto a wooden crate. She didn't feel sociable at the moment, and alone in the dark suited her mood.

"I come bearing chicken," a voice whispered several minutes later.

"And I'm sure the only thing on your mind is chicken. Right, Jack?"

Jack could see her obscure silhouette and nothing more, and he headed in her direction carrying a plate of food in one hand and his cane in the other. "Well, I'll admit I'm thinking about baked beans and brownies, too."

"Give me a break. You're thinking about sex and how to have it with me. Admit it." She heard thudding footsteps retreat from the dark room, and wondered who was taking that pronouncement to the workers in the next room.

"Want a bullhorn?" He chuckled, winding his way through a maze of medicine cabinets and boxes full of medical supplies. "I'm sure they're waiting for the details." Jack finally found Lacy and dropped onto a wooden crate across from her. "I'm afraid, though, that after what they heard about our visit with LolaGertrude, this may be a little too much. Don't you think?"

"What I think, Jack, is that you won't be here long so you've decided to get straight to the bottom line."

"You mean getting you into bed?"

"Isn't that what you want to do?" she asked.

"What I want to do right now is to share a little dinner with you," he said, taking a bite of coleslaw. "You ought to try some of this. Someone in Sunstone sure knows how to fix it."

"I'll bet if I offered, you'd take me up on it right here and now."

"Can I eat my chicken first? It's delicious. Nice crispy coating, not too greasy." He took a bite from a chicken leg, then held it out for Lacy to do the same. "Better than anything my mother ever fixed. Want some?"

Lacy swatted his hand away. "I'm not interested in food, Jack."

He took another bite of coleslaw, then spooned up a little more and offered it to her. "Get over it, Lacy. I'm not the one who seduced you, then dumped you."

"That's not the way it was," she defended herself.

"So I was right. You did get in on a little white coat lust." He picked up a chocolate-slathered chocolate brownie, took a bite, then held it out for her. "Here, eat this. Doctor's order. It will cure whatever's ailing you."

She pushed his hand away, then stood up. "It wasn't lust, and I didn't get dumped…not really. And it's none of your business, anyway."

"Let me guess. You were hell-bent on marrying a doctor, and he was hell-bent on working his way through the entire nursing staff.'' After popping the rest of the brownie into his mouth, he wiped his lips on a paper napkin, then unscrewed the cap on a bottle of spring water. ''Am I right?'' he asked.

''No,'' she admitted. Her anger toward Jack was rerouting itself as she remembered one of the most stupid mistakes in her life. She'd known it could happen, even seen it coming. But at the time, nothing could have stopped her from plunging headlong into the worst emotional disaster in her life, not to mention the most embarrassing. ''Not the entire staff. We had five male nurses on the roster that he didn't touch.''

''Pretty bad, huh?''

She nodded, even though he couldn't see it. ''I even took him to meet my grandparents.''

''Did you marry him?''

''Of course not.''

''Meaning…''

''Meaning I caught him with my—''

''Your best friend,'' Jack interrupted.

''Roommate. In my apartment.''

''Not in your bed, I hope.'' Jack held another piece of chicken for Lacy, and this time she took it.

''Everybody knew.'' She took a small bite, and after deciding it was pretty good, went after the rest of the leg.

''Including you?''

She mumbled something that Jack couldn't interpret and kept on eating.

''That's not what I want from you, Lacy.'' He was beginning to realize that what he wanted was something so much more he couldn't even put it together in mental imagery or cohesive thoughts. And that was fine, since he couldn't have it, anyway.

''No sex?'' she finally managed to ask between bites.

"Good God," Willie Pearl said, stepping into the doorway. "Then it's true. They're out there talking like you two are having a regular orgy going in here."

"No orgy, except on this delicious food," Jack returned. "Go back and tell them I'll only give them gossip fodder once a day, and the black panties were it for today."

"How did you do that?" Lacy asked, ignoring Willie Pearl's accusation.

"What?"

"Get me to tell you? I've never told anybody before." Not even her grandfather, and she usually told him everything.

"I'm good, I guess."

"So what do you intend to do with it?"

"What?" He was flattered she'd confided in him. The attitude had been a dead giveaway from the start, but that she had actually told him what was responsible for it made him feel...special. And needed. He liked that. Maybe it meant she trusted him. He hoped so.

"What I told you. Are you going to tell everybody you meet what an idiot I was, or just blackmail me when you want something?"

"Nothing."

"Nothing, what?"

"I intend to do nothing with what you told me. That's why you told me, isn't it? Because you trust me enough to know I won't betray you?"

Lacy finally sat, and spooned up some of the coleslaw he'd offered earlier. "I'm really sorry about the panties" she said. "I didn't expect...I mean, I thought you'd find them before you pulled them out and waved them at a patient. I really wanted to explain it to you earlier, but you shut yourself in your examining room and..."

"So you've been waiting for the accusation all this

time?'' He picked up another brownie and waved it under her nose. ''And for what it's worth, I was taking a nap on the examining table.''

She took the brownie and licked the icing. ''Then you weren't mad at me?''

Even in the dark, what she was doing was too much to watch. Lacy and icing, the makings of one hell of a great fantasy. Trying to blank out the images, he forced his attention to the baked beans on his plate. ''Mad? Why would I be mad? The town now thinks that besides being a stark, raving turnip thrower, I'm a perverted panty waver. Why would that make me mad?'' Too much temptation here. Way too much. And she didn't have a clue.

''Look, you two,'' Willie Pearl interrupted. ''You can kiss and make up later. But for now, Mrs. Johnson called and she says she's had terrible hiccups for the past two hours. She's wondering if you'll come by and wave those panties at her like you did to LolaGertrude. She's hoping that'll cure her.'' The old woman chuckled deviously, then backed out of the room.

Lacy smiled. LolaGertrude and the black panties—the making of another Sunstonian legend. ''Bet they're out there plotting how to get rid of both of us.''

''Or taking bets on what we'll do for an encore.'' Jack laughed. He reached down and rubbed his knee, then bent and stretched it a couple times. That ache was beginning to go away, thanks to Lacy, but a bigger one was rooted firmly, also thanks to Lacy.

''How is your knee, by the way?''

''Better.''

''Much better, some better, a little better? What?''

''I'm not ready to throw away my cane and start dancing yet, if that's what you're asking.'' Jack looked at the dab of peach cobbler on the plate and decided to leave it for Lacy. "But it's feeling a little better, I suppose."

"You hate to admit it, don't you?"

"Admit what?"

"It kills you, doesn't it, to admit that someone who isn't a doctor cured you?"

"There's that attitude again, Lacy. It always gets right back to your stereotype. It's either the big bad city doctor or your grandpa, and there's nothing in between. Well, I've got some news for you, Nurse…" He started to push himself up, but a searing hot pain stabbed his knee then retreated, and he dropped down beside Lacy. "Time for my antibiotic," he said, panting.

"And a pain pill?"

He shook his head. "The think system. I think the pain is letting up, so therefore it is."

Lacy stood, then offered him a hand. "What I think is that you should go home, soak yourself in hot water for awhile and go to bed."

"This time I concur with your diagnosis." Asking her to go with him and give him a little more of her magical therapy was on the tip of his tongue, and he did everything but bite down hard to keep the suggestion inside.

Smiling, Lacy headed for the medicine cabinet, pulled out a bottle of capsules and shook one out for him. "And you'll let me range it in the morning?"

Jack nodded. "Are you keeping score?" he asked. "How many times you're right and I'm wrong?"

"Just some hash marks on the medicine cabinet."

"And you're way out ahead, no doubt." When they both returned to the main room, all signs of dinner were put away, and the work detail was into it up to their elbows. The waiting room walls were being given a second coat of paint, and the tin ceiling was undergoing a close inspection.

In the examining room, the cleaning was completed, and the floor was being sanded and buffed in preparation for a good coat of varnish.

Lacy returned to her windowsill-sanding project, and Jack took her advice and went home. "The doc's looking a might peaked." Willie Pearl's voice boomed from the examining room. "Think maybe you ought to follow him on out to the cabin to make sure he's okay?"

All eyes turned to Lacy, and a scarlet blush blotched its way from her neck to her cheeks. "He took his pill, and he's going straight to bed. I don't need—"

"Is it true he tried to get LolaGertrude to put on those black panties?" someone in the crowd asked. "I heard he just threw them at her and insisted."

"No, that's not what happened," someone else said. "He just asked her if she liked them. I think they were a present for—"

"I heard he chased her around the room with them, waving them and yelling."

"And I'm sure you know that poor Betty Parsons is still jumpy after he threw that turnip at her. She has a headache that won't go away, but she's afraid to have the doc look at her."

"And she has nightmares."

Lacy blew the sanding dust off the windowsill and turned her attention from the gossip and to work. Nothing as exciting as Jack Sutton had happened to Sunstone in years. The town would miss him when he went back to Chicago.

So would she.

By ten that night, the waiting room looked sparkling new with its second coat of paint, and the hardwood floor glistened underneath its first coat of varnish. The examining room was clean, ready for paint and varnish, and Lacy was tired all the way down to her bones and then some.

"Since you're not going to cuddle up with the doc, where are you going to sleep tonight?" Willie Pearl asked, leaning against the examining room door. She'd been the hardest worker all day, and she still looked as fresh in her lavender as she had this morning.

"Jack and I don't have that kind of a relationship." Lacy sighed, trying to measure her words evenly so Willie Pearl couldn't read anything into them. "And I haven't figured out where I'll stay yet, but I'll probably just go outside and curl up in the truck so I don't have to sniff paint and varnish fumes all night." Cuddling up with Jack sounded pretty good, though. Too good...way too good. And for a moment, she was in bed with him, cuddling, warm, naked...

"You can come home with me," the old woman offered. "I can send Palmer on home for the night, and you can—"

"Thanks, but I'll be fine here," Lacy interrupted, hoping the splotches weren't returning to give her away. She had no intention of separating the two lovers, not even for the night. And she envied them. Naked in bed with Jack sprang to mind again, and she spun away from Willie Pearl to hide the obvious red creeping in. "Besides, if anyone needs help in the middle of the night, they'll expect to find me here, even if I am camped out in the alley."

And although people would talk about anything, tonight she'd be safe and snug in her truck alone, and there would be nothing to talk about. But she was keeping her fingers crossed for a good dream.

THE ROOM was beautiful, all timbers and earthy, just light enough to catch a vague glimpse but dark enough to create the mood. The whirlpool was actually a hot tub, but he knew the image of hot tub was something far beyond whirlpool. Hot tub was about two people sipping champagne on the edge of making love. Whirlpool was about therapy, to cure dull aches. Well, tonight the whirlpool wasn't going to cure the dull ache the hot tub would have cured. And he was in the hot tub, alone, turning it into a lowly, therapeutic whirlpool.

Drawing in a ragged sigh, Jack slipped into the warm water, trying to concentrate on anything but the image of the woman he wanted there with him. But that image wouldn't go away, and as he slid under the bubbling surface, steam rose, creating a mist, fogging the tiny windows above the tub. Enveloped by the emptiness of the room, a sense of dim loneliness settled over him. He'd started feeling listless the moment he left the Fremont 1908, and the listlessness had followed him home. And it was all wrapped up in Lacy. She wasn't like the rest. She didn't give in, not to her principle, not to him, not to anyone. He liked that, even though he wasn't sure he knew how to deal with it.

The tepid water, meant to soothe his tiredness, only irritated him, and he found himself wanting more than moderately warm in his life. So much for keeping everything in a rigid order. One sassy optimist of a nurse was overturning everything he wanted, everything he'd worked so hard to create for himself. But damn it. He couldn't stay in Sunstone. Not for Lacy. Not for anybody.

Leaning his head against the side of the hot tub, Jack closed his eyes and tried again to blot out the images. He was tired. His knee hurt. His heart hurt a little, too.

Soon dreamy images of Lacy mixed with the drowsiness embracing him, and Jack drifted into a far-off world of peace, contentment… "Lacy," he murmured, sliding down into the water until he was submerged to his chest.

The dream carried her to him, into his hot tub, and she bent over him to trace a delicate path, from his lips to his jawline. Moving from ear to ear, she lingered on his stubble, stroking it lightly with her thumb. "I'm glad you haven't shaved,'' she said, purring. ''I like my men to feel rough.''

She placed a light kiss just below his ear, then nibbled his earlobe playfully. Then her tongue darted in and out of the hollow recess, and she laughed softly as she backed away to enjoy his response.

Such a sensitive spot. Jack never knew how sensitive. ''I have one on the other side, too.''

''I'm aware of anatomy, Doctor. Of yours...of mine.'' Dipping her hand into the bubbling water, she drew some up and let it drip down her fingers to a spot just below his shoulder. Then she pressed a long kiss to the tender spot between his neck and shoulder, and pulled away just enough to tease his tingling flesh with her tongue. ''That's your clavicle.'' She dipped into the water again, letting it drip, this time, on his chest. Again, she bent to press her lips to it, and this time she swirled her tongue through the hair until Jack thought he would explode. ''And that's your pectoral, Doctor.'' The third time, she dribbled the water just at the line where the water's surface formed a plain across his abdomen. Slipping her hand under the water, Lacy opened her eyes wide in astonishment and smiled boldly. ''I do believe that's your...''

A phone rang in the distance, and Jack's eyes shot open. No Lacy. No hot tub. Only a whirlpool and a huge need for a cold shower.

''Damn,'' he muttered.

LACY TWISTED and turned in the front seat for an hour, bumping into the steering wheel, bruising her hip on the door handle. Finally, when she decided there was no comfortable position to be had in the truck's cab, she grabbed her blankets and pillow and plodded to the back of the truck, then climbed into the bed, grateful it had a sleeper shell on top. Not that she was opposed to camping out or anything. But in July, with mosquitoes out in full force, plus those pesky hard-shell flying beetles buzzing around just ready to pinch her when she moved, she was glad for the shelter.

When she finally found a semicomfortable position, sleep hit fast, followed by dreams of Jack. She was in his arms, in his whirlpool. Their lips were about to meet, and he was groaning her name in ecstasy. "Lacy..."

"Mmm," she sighed.

"Lacy, wake up." He shook her shoulder.

"The water's a little too cool," she said. "Can you turn up the heat?"

"Lacy, a man named Ben Dunbar just called. His wife, Louise, is giving birth."

Giving birth...giving birth. The words pierced her fog, and she opened her eyes to see Jack's dark shadow huddled in the back of the pickup truck with her. "Who's doing what?" she asked, trying to shake away the sleep. It had promised to be such a good dream, and she was royally irritated he'd interrupted it before anything happened. They hadn't even gotten their lips all the way together.

"Louise Dunbar is giving birth, and we have to get out to their farm." He turned on a flashlight, careful not to point it in Lacy's eyes. The last thing he needed was to blind his nurse on a night when he really needed her nursing skills. He hadn't delivered a baby since he was a student, and he was keeping his fingers crossed that Lacy had better obstetric experience than he.

Lacy sat up and stretched, her mind still fuzzy, and she took a quick look to see what manner of sleeping apparel he'd caught her in this time. Tonight she was in a pair of sweats, thank heaven. Plain gray and baggy. Sensible panties underneath. "Shouldn't she go to the hospital?"

"Apparently there's no time. Ben said she's moaning so loud he thinks she's about to drop any minute."

"Drop?"

Shrugging, Jack smiled. "I'm just repeating what he said."

Lacy fumbled for her shoes, pulled them on, tied them, then crawled to the tailgate. "I'll go in and get whatever obstetric supplies I can find," she said, "but I think you'd better get back on the phone and persuade Mr. Dunbar that there are people out there eminently more qualified to do this than we are." Lacy's feet hit the ground and she ran into the Fremont 1908 and directly to the supply cabinet, where she started to rummage for anything that might be used to deliver a baby. "Have you done this before?" she called to Jack, who was in the waiting room, dialing the Dunbar farm.

"Sure," he said, hedging. "Have you?"

"Sure," she called. Years before, she'd done a stint in labor and delivery for almost a week. She'd assisted in a half dozen births, which definitely did not qualify her to deliver Louise Dunbar's baby. And while the outcome was wonderful—a tiny new life—she'd hated the long, long hours that led up to it. It wasn't her kind of nursing, and she'd vowed never to do it again if she didn't have to. And she hadn't. But now she wished she'd spent another week or two there, and she kept her fingers crossed, hoping that Jack had more experience than she. Considering he was a bone doc, though, she doubted it.

She set aside the medical supplies she could find, emptied a brown paper bag filled with disposable plates, cups and napkins someone had brought for serving dinner, and crammed everything she and Jack would probably need into it. Providing it was a normal birth, Doc Washburn's meager medical supplies would suffice. She hoped so, anyway.

Poor Louise, Lacy thought as she grabbed the bag and took a good look at herself. Wearing sweats, carrying a brown paper bag—not exactly the stereotypical image of a nurse. Stereotypical. The word brought a cognizant smile to her face. Jack was right. She was hung up on it. Later, when there was more time, she'd tell him. "So did you convince him?" she asked as they were headed out the back door.

"It's breech, Lacy. He said her first two came out backward, and so is this one."

Lacy's face went ashen. "We can't do it, Jack. We don't have the right equipment." *Let alone the experience, both of us put together,* she thought.

"I called Life Flier down in Louisville, and they'll have someone there in about an hour. From what Ben said, though, I don't think Louise has an hour."

"Oh, no," Lacy murmured, following Jack to his Jeep. She suddenly understood the phrase "baptism by fire."

Taking one last look at the directions he'd scribbled to Ben Dunbar's farm, Jack handed them to Lacy. "It should take twenty minutes from here. Keep me on the right road, Lacy. We don't have time to get lost." Pulling into the street, he glanced in his mirror at the Fremont 1908. "And by the way, this is absolutely my last house call."

7

"WHY DIDN'T YOU CALL ME so I could just meet you there?" Lacy asked. She tapped her feet in an uneven rhythm on the floorboard. This wasn't what she expected when she'd agreed to house calls. Not even close. Sore throats, sprains and bellyaches, yes. Childbirth, no way. "You wasted a good half hour coming to get me."

Jack exited the two-lane highway and turned onto a dirt road. He slowed a little to get his bearings, then picked up speed once he decided he was on the right road. "I did, but you were in the truck. Ever heard of one of these for when you're away from the office phone?" He tossed his cell phone into her lap.

"I used to have one, but…"

"Let me guess." He chuckled. "You got rid of it when you moved to the country. Rural life and cell phones don't mix."

"Actually, my grandfather was never without his. He had other modern amenities, too—a computer, Internet access, running water…" Lacy squirmed when Jack hit a pothole that was so deep her seat belt locked around her.

"You okay?" He glanced over to see her fighting to keep the seat belt from strangling her.

"I lost it when I moved." She choked the words out, still wrestling with the belt. "Just haven't gotten around to getting another one yet."

"Well, tell the mayor you need one, and make the town

pay for it, since you're going to be on call for them twenty-four seven.''

The seat belt finally unlocked, and Lacy slid into a more comfortable position and sputtered, ''You need me out there, Jack, so don't try to strangle me until after we've delivered Louise's baby.''

He needed her, all right, and childbirth was only the half of it. Not even half of it, really. His need was growing in so many ways, he couldn't even begin to fathom them. And he didn't want to. Out of mind, out of heart. Yeah, right. She'd already bored so deeply into both only a deep coma would keep her out. And then she'd probably find some way to slip into his unconsciousness. ''Give Dunbar a call and see how Louise is progressing. Just hit the recall.''

''How many of these deliveries have you done?'' Lacy asked as she waited for someone to answer her call and at the same time tried to keep her focus tuned to the road landmarks scratched in Jack's typical physician handwriting. Nervously, she shifted her gaze from the written directions, to the scenery whizzing by, to the phone, then back to the directions. *Take left at foots burn.* ''What do you mean left at foots burn?''

''Left at Ford's barn.''

''And free pint means?''

''Fresh paint. The barn has fresh paint.''

''Okay. So we take a left at Ford's freshly painted barn.'' She glanced again at the directions. ''Then another left at the Buick... I can't even make out the next word.''

''Schoolhouse. Brick schoolhouse.''

''Okay, another left there. Then...I can read this one. One mile to Jay somebody's sill. Then—''

''Silo.''

''Jay somebody's silo—''

''Pollard.''

"To Jay Pollard's silo, then a hard right up the dirt…it looks like rod but I'm guessing it's road…to a spit hog fence."

"Split log, country girl. There's no such thing as a spit hog fence." He knew exactly where he was going. He'd memorized the directions when he wrote them down. But this was diverting her nervousness, and she needed the diversion, the way she was shaking hard enough to vibrate the Jeep.

"Next time let me write down the instructions," she grumbled. "This stuff you call writing won't cut it, and as best as I can decipher it, we could be heading into the next state."

"And you call yourself a nurse?" he teased. "I thought decoding was part of your training."

"What I was trained to do was call the doctor back to the ICU to decode his or her own handwriting. After you do that a couple times, they learn to be legible." Returning to the directions, she continued, "Follow till darn—"

"Corn."

"Cornfield. Dunbar house first on the left, end of darn…cornfield. Halt mine offroar. Is that German or something?"

"Half mile off road."

"Hello, Mr. Dunbar," Lacy said when Ben Dunbar finally picked up. "This is Lacy Archer, Dr. Sutton's nurse. I'm just calling to check on Louise." She mumbled a couple uh-huhs and an okay, then said, "We should be there in a few minutes. Try not to let her push until we get there. Okay?" She was silent for another few seconds, then said, "No, don't do that."

She clicked off, frowning. "He said Louise is getting close and that when the time comes, short of tying her legs together, there's no way he can stop her from pushing."

She tucked the cell phone in Jack's medical bag, then continued, "I know I'm not an experienced obstetrics nurse, Jack, but they don't actually tie women's legs together to keep them from delivering, do they?"

"Getting back to the question you asked earlier about how many breech deliveries I've done, the answer is one, after we get through with this one. And I can honestly say I've never seen a woman's legs tied together to keep her from delivering. Think maybe you should call your grandpa and ask him?"

"He's fishing somewhere in Canada, or I would." She looked out the window for a moment at the shadowy cornfields. "Have you ever even delivered a baby?"

"A few, during my labor and delivery rotation, when I was a resident, but that's been years ago, and—"

"And you were probably guided through the procedure by a well-trained obstetrician who saw your being there as an inconvenience…almost as much an inconvenience as you thought it was, since you were set on doing bones."

"Were you there?" He laughed. "Hiding in some baggy green scrubs, covering your face with a mask?" Had she been there, he would have known it, no matter how well her scrubs hid her. Something about Lacy cried out for attention—his attention—and that poor baby might still be waiting to be born if she'd been in the delivery room, distracting him.

And boy, she was distracting him more and more every minute.

"Not there, but it's the same story, Doc, different hospital. I worked with a midwife who could deliver a baby in her sleep. She put up with the student nurses, but only because she had to. If she'd had her way, we would have spent our labor and delivery time emptying bedpans and rubbing backs."

Jack chuckled. "So, how many breech deliveries have you assisted?"

"The same as you," she pronounced, slumping in her seat. "One, when we get through this one."

"I don't suppose you could get that midwife on the phone, could you, since Grandpa isn't available?" His Jeep hit another pothole and jerked to the side of the road. Banging his knee on the steering wheel, Jack swore under his breath, straightened the vehicle and decided to slow his speed. Neither his Jeep's front end alignment nor his knee could take too many more impacts without serious side effects.

In the distance, the Jeep's headlights outlined a big barn. Even in the dark, its fresh red paint blazed the way. "That's got to be the Ford barn," Lacy said, straightening in her seat. "So now you take a left on the first road after it." The first road turned out to be more of a path—one lane, and pitted with a series of tiny Swiss cheese potholes.

Passing the barn, they found the other landmarks easily enough, and even though their speed barely crept above twenty miles an hour, in the dark, in the state of nervous anticipation they were both experiencing, it seemed forever. So by the time they neared the split log fence, Lacy's nerves were as frayed as the bad end of an old rope. "Can't we go any faster?" she asked. "At this rate, Louise's kid will be entering kindergarten by the time we get there."

"We're doing good to hit twenty," Jack replied. "If you think you could—"

"I think we just passed the split log fence," Lacy interrupted. "Back up so I can see for sure."

"I didn't see one," Jack disagreed.

"Just back up." Lacy twisted around to look out the window behind her. "Even in the dark, I know that fence was made of logs."

"Whatever." Jack huffed, throwing his Jeep into Reverse. Two hundred feet back, he tromped on the brake, causing the vehicle to fishtail in the dirt. "It's a wire fence, Lacy. Look." Impatiently, he flipped on his brights. "Regular fence wire, and barbed wire. No split logs."

"What are those posts made of?" she asked.

Jack took a quick look before grinding the car into forward. "Logs," he grunted. "Straight logs, used as posts. Not split logs."

"So I'm not good at logs. Sue me."

"I thought you were a country girl." He spotted a real split log fence up ahead and released a deep, relieved sigh. They were almost there.

"I never said that."

"You implied it. All that stuff about your grandfather and how you know about running a rural practice."

Lacy looked at the log fence coming up on her right. No wire anywhere. "I said my grandfather was a country doc, and I do know how to make a rural medical practice work, since I spent most summers helping him." Taking another look at the directions, she went on, "Split log fence, starboard side, Doctor."

"You sure this time?" he teased, slowing the Jeep even more. The sky was overcast. He'd heard the earlier forecast for rain, and he hoped it would stay off until he could get Louise tucked safely in the helicopter and on her way to Louisville. If the storm setting in turned out to be bad, as was the case with so many Midwest summer thunderstorms, the chopper would be grounded, and that was something he didn't even want to consider.

"I'm sure. And when you get to the end of the cornfield, jog to the left then stay on that road until you come to the end of it."

"You know what corn looks like, Lacy?"

"Popped or creamed?"

Since the imminent storm blotted out the stars, there were no other lights but for his headlights, and everything looked the same. Glancing sideways at Lacy, he saw her bite her lip nervously. Just on her left side. Her face was creased into a frown, too. A cute frown. And he was beginning to like her short-cropped tomboy hair. It accented her soft features and those eyes. Once you got past the amazing color, you realized they were big, optimistic, full of expectation. "Did someone in your family have eyes that color?" he asked.

"Both of the Lacys before me. Only neither of them had such a deep color. I think the color of my mother and grandmother's eyes combined and settled in me. But both my dad and grandpa said the eyes are what made them fall in love with my mom and grandmother."

He understood that. It was hard to get past Lacy's eyes. "They're..." He wanted to say beautiful, stunning, the most exotic thing he'd ever seen, but the words stuck in his throat. "They're unusual," he finally managed to say.

"Most people think they're contacts."

"Any fool could tell the difference right away," he lied. "So, at the end of the road past the cornfield, where?"

"First road on the left. Halt mine offroar. Remember?"

"We're almost there, then? Maybe we should figure out what we're going to do."

Lacy looked at the bleak sky. "How's the helicopter ever going to find this place, Jack? They can't follow the landmarks like we did."

"They said they'll radio the sheriff and have him lead them out here."

"But they're still a good half hour away, aren't they?" Lacy's face creased to a frown again. A little more worried than cute this time. Between the doctor, the nurse and the patient, the patient was the one with the most experience, and that wasn't good. She was expecting qualified medical help, not a couple of first-timers.

"That's the best they could do, since this part of Indiana is a little off their beaten path." Slowing, Jack maneuvered the turn from the dirt road onto a gravel driveway. In the distance he saw the house lights blazing, as if to welcome the two of them. He only hoped the welcome wasn't too late. He glanced at his watch. It had taken a little more than the regular twenty minutes, and he was keeping his fingers crossed that the extra time hadn't turned into a problem. His mind flashed to an image of a pregnant Louise Dunbar writhing in bed, trying to give birth, her legs lassoed together. "We may have to do a C-section, Lacy," he said solemnly, maneuvering his Jeep to a stop in front of the house. "You run on in, and I'll be right behind you with the equipment." No time for her to wait for him. She could get there and get that baby delivered before he could even drag his sorry leg up the stairs.

Lacy gave his arm a reassuring squeeze. "This has got to be a lot easier than some of those complicated bone surgeries you do."

Jack smiled. "You'd think so, wouldn't you?"

"Glad you two got here, Doc," Ben Dunbar called from the side of his house. Rounding the corner, he motioned for them to follow. "She's down hard and moaning like nothing I've ever heard. It wasn't anything like this with her first two, and I'm beginning to get a little worried something might be going wrong. Since she got so big with this one, though, I have to think it's probably twins. Doc Washburn thought so, too. Said he thought he heard a couple heartbeats."

"Twins?" Lacy and Jack exclaimed together.

Ben shrugged. "She's been pretty swollen. And cranky,

lately. Wouldn't surprise me, at all. And her sister's dropped nothing but twins.''

After hurrying to the back of the house, Lacy vaulted up the steps the instant she saw them and dashed inside. Jack followed, cursing his cane every step of the way. "She's probably upstairs, in bed," Lacy said, heading down the hall. As they came to the stairs, they stopped for an instant to listen, and it was stone quiet. No moans, no groans. Not even a whimper. Not a good sign. "Jack, you don't suppose she…"

Before Lacy could finish the sentence, Jack pushed around her and took the stairs as fast as his bad leg would allow, wishing he could have taken them two at a time. At the top, he headed for the nearest bedroom. Empty. "Damn," he muttered. The second and third were empty, too. "She's not up here," he said, scratching his head as he exited the fourth and last bedroom.

"I didn't see her in the front room as we came through the hall, either," Lacy replied. "Let me run outside and ask Ben when she is."

Pushing through the back door downstairs, Lacy found Ben standing at the bottom of the steps, his arms folded across his chest. "I expect you two got washed up okay in the house, but you could have done it down at the pump."

"Where's Louise?" Lacy asked. Her voice was filled with dread for the woman she couldn't find.

"Where she's been all night. Down in the barn with Sally."

"You left her down in the barn?" Lacy exclaimed, then turned and yelled into the house. "She's out here, Jack. In the barn."

"Darn right I did. I was lucky to get her there," Ben said, seemingly unaffected by the urgency of his wife's impending breech birth. "She was out in the field when she started to drop, and she sat down, right there. Took me nearly an hour to coax her to get up and go. If I'd let her have her way, she would have done it right there. She's stubborn like that, you know.''

Jack hit the door and limped outside, gripping both supplies and cane. Too much. Too awkward. Starting tomorrow, therapy was going to be a new priority. Top of his list. The people here needed better than he was physically able to give. ''Take me to her, Ben.''

''WE'RE GOING TO NEED some clean sheets or blankets,'' Lacy called after the two men. ''You go back in and get them, Ben,'' she instructed. She was tempted to do the boiling water thing, too, one of the oldest known devices to get the man away from the scene of the birth. But, the full city block hike from the house to the barn would serve that purpose. Catching up to Jack, she grabbed the supplies from him and fell into step. The wince on his face with each step he took across the rutted barnyard told her how much he hurt. A misstep could cause a lot of damage. ''Slow down,'' she urged, grabbing hold of him to ease his pace. ''Louise has waited this long for us to get here, and another minute's not going to make any difference.''

''Can you believe he didn't carry her to the house, Lacy? I know farmers are earthy, rugged people, and farm wives are known for their hearty stamina, but this is ridiculous.''

''Maybe there's a nice room attached to the barn for the hired help to live in,'' Lacy offered. ''Or maybe she's stubborn, like he said, and getting her to the barn was the best he could do.''

''Or maybe he just put her in a stall with the goats because it was the easiest thing to do.'' Jack stepped around a couple of those goats and pulled Lacy into the well-lighted building. At least Ben had seen fit to rig the place with several drop lights. "Louise?" he called, not seeing the woman right away.

The only response came from the cows, so Jack called again, much louder, and a cheerful, smiling woman appeared from one of the stalls and motioned for them. "She's over here," she called, "and she's having some problems."

Instinctively, Lacy sprinted to the stall, then her mouth dropped open and she dropped her medical equipment to the clean straw floor. "You've got to be kidding." She choked the words out.

As Jack stepped to Lacy's side, his reaction was the same. "No way." Louise was in the stall, all right, sprawled on her side, mooing for all she was worth.

"I take it you're not Louise," Lacy said to the woman.

The woman laughed, then went into the stall and kneeled by Louise's head. "I'm Sally Dunbar. Ben's wife."

"We don't do cows." Jack snorted.

"Doc Washburn always did, when one of them was having a hard time."

"Call a vet," Jack replied. "And call me when *you* decide to have a baby, Mrs. Dunbar."

"Please don't leave her like this, Doc," Sally pleaded. "She'll die."

Jack took a couple steps toward the door, then turned back. "I'm sorry," he said, his voice softening, "but there's really nothing I can do for you." He lumbered across the barnyard and was halfway to his vehicle when Lacy caught up to him. "We've got to help these people," she cried. "They depend on that cow and her calves."

"Don't you think I know that, Lacy? But it's not my problem. I can't deliver a breech calf."

She grabbed hold of his arm, and he stopped. "They're counting on you, Jack. That's the way it is here."

"Well, I'm sorry, Miss Scarlett, but I don't know nuthin' 'bout birthin' no bovines."

"I'm sorry, too. I really thought I saw a little more compassion in you than that." Without another word, Lacy turned and ran to the barn. She didn't know anything about birthing bovines, either, but tonight she was gong to learn.

"Dr. Sutton's knee is really bad," she explained to the Dunbars, "and he's not up to this." Her words came out bitterly. She wanted him to help. She wanted him to be the kind of man who didn't make distinctions when someone needed him, and Lacy was disappointed in Jack, and angry. And, she was angry with herself for having such expectations. She had no right to them. She had no reason to softpedal Jack's refusal to help, either, except that something deep inside her forced her to try to make him look a little better in Ben and Sally's eyes. "He had surgery recently, and he's still in a lot of pain."

"That explains the turnips," Ben stated matter-of-factly. "I was wondering why a normal man would act like that, especially when we're talking about Ken Howell's turnips. They're prizewinners, you know."

Sizing up the cow, Lacy saw the signs that the birth was well in progress. "So, Louise," she said to the distressed beast. "I've delivered babies, but never cow babies, so this is going to take everything we've both got, and then some." She patted the cow on the rump and shook her head skeptically.

"She's too tired to push anymore," Sally said, sitting at the cow's head, stroking her gently between the eyes. "If we don't get the calves out soon, they'll all die."

"Then we'll just have to get them out right away," Lacy said, wondering how in the world she would do it.

"Those are the back feet coming down, ma'am," Ben

explained. "The front ones should be coming first. I do have calf pullers. That's why I called the doc, 'cause Sally can't—"

"Sure," Lacy interrupted, guessing what a calf puller was. "Go get them."

"Are you sure those are the back legs?" Jack asked, stepping up to the stall.

Ben nodded. "Pretty sure they are, though sometimes they can fool you. Thought your knee was hurting pretty bad, Doc," Ben said.

"I expect Louise is hurting a lot more than I am," he replied, rolling up his sleeves. "So where do we start, Nurse?" he asked.

Lacy's eyes locked with his briefly, and a flicker of understanding passed between them. She was grateful he'd come back, not only for Louise, but for her. "Turn the calf, Doctor. Cow Birth 101. Turn a breech delivery if you can."

"Not breech, ma'am," Ben cut in. "Breech comes in rump first, and that's a hard one. This is only backward, and you probably won't have to turn it. But you may have to help it slide on out."

"Which means I'm going to have to—" Jack's voice dropped abruptly as it fully dawned on him what it would take to help the calf slip out. "Anybody got an industrial-size drum of petroleum jelly?"

JACK LET OUT a resigned sigh as Ben returned with a giant economy-size jar of the lubricant. Maybe it was time he got prepared for all the rural eventualities, because Lacy wasn't about to let him out of a thing. "Guess it's time to go to work. Can you help me scrub?"

"Pump's at the side of the barn, Doc," Sally called.

"Thanks for coming back," Lacy said, cranking the

pump handle while Jack held his arms under the flow of water. "I was getting worried that it would take more than the three of us."

Dipping his arms to his elbows, then letting the water trickle off, he chuckled. Not exactly the sterile scrub room he was used to, but the scrub nurse was better than anything he'd seen in Chicago. "You'd have just called me later, and told me to come get you, so I decided to stay and save myself the extra trip."

"Why did you really come back?" She looked at him, and even in the dim barnyard light, she saw the answer written on his face. He cared. Dr. Sutton had an act he put on to distance himself professionally, but Jack Sutton couldn't be distanced. At that moment, if she could have reached up and kissed him, she would have, but the frightened moos from the soon to be mamma snapped her attention to the barn and the impending birth.

"I came back because you're not capable of delivering a cow by yourself, and you haven't got the good sense to walk away and let someone who knows what he's doing handle it."

"I thought maybe you were a little concerned for Louise."

"She's a cow," he protested.

"And somewhere way down in your dark soul you've got an ounce of true compassion, even for a cow, Dr. Sutton," she teased. "Admit it."

"Just help me get my shirt off," he grumbled, "if you want Louise to deliver those babies tonight."

"Do you have a T-shirt on underneath?"

He nodded. "It's got a big hole in it." He hadn't intended for it to be seen. It was an old favorite, more worn out than intact, and it was the first one he'd grabbed when he'd rushed out of the cabin. If he'd had even the slightest notion she would see him in it, he would have...

"Then it won't mater if it gets ruined," she said, reaching to unbutton his chambray shirt. She pulled it out of his jeans, started with the bottom button and worked her way to the top, her fingers quick and light as she tried deliberately not to make direct contact with anything but the shirt. As the shirt came off, he noticed her eyeing the hole and the crisp brown chest hair peeking through it. "Like the shirt," she teased.

"This isn't in my contract, you know," Jack said in a cool drawl. He watched her tie his shirt around her waist, and the gesture struck him as oddly intimate. He liked the easy way she took control, the way she just did without asking how or why. "Grab the bottle of antiseptic from my hip pocket and pour it over both arms," he instructed.

"Did your contract specifically spell out human patients, Doctor?"

"Guess I should have read the fine print. That mayor probably sneaked something in about cows and pigs." After his arms were scrubbed, he stuck two fingers in the jar of lubricating jelly and globed the slippery goo on his forearm.

"Higher," Lacy urged, laughing. "You never know how far..."

After several more dips into the pot, Jack was petroleum jelly from the tips of his fingers to his shoulders. "Now I know why I went into orthopedics." He snorted and walked to the barn.

Lacy carried his cane and watched him move. After he attempted several difficult, slow steps, she put a steadying arm around his waist. "Keep those greasy arms away from me," she warned, as they made their way to Louise's stall.

"Look, Doc," Ben said, holding onto a set of chains Lacy guessed to be the calf pullers. "I don't mean to question your judgment, you being a doctor and all. I mean, I got all those blankets and sheets, even if I can't figure out what they're for. But I did it, anyway. This helicopter, though, the one that just landed out front... I don't think we can get Louise into that thing. And I've got to tell you, the sheriff isn't too happy about leading that helicopter out here in the middle of the night, just so we can take Louise to some fancy vet hospital in Louisville."

Helicopter? He'd forgotten. Jack looked at his slick arms, then threw back his head and let loose a great peal of laughter. "You tell the good sheriff, plus the people on the helicopter, that everything's under control here, but thanks for showing up, and to please send me the bill. Now, if you'll excuse me, I have to go birth them bovines." As he walked away, he was humming a tune that sounded vaguely like "Old MacDonald Had a Farm."

"WELL JACK," Lacy laughed, "here's something to add to your resume." He was full of surprises. Hot and cold. Caring and uncaring. There was a lot of Jack Sutton to understand, and as Lacy watched him take his place next to the moaning cow, she wondered about the strange feeling coming over her. At times it was exasperation. Other times it was sympathy. Occasionally even admiration. Right now, it wasn't a feeling she knew too well, and she had the strangest little nagging sensation it was one she definitely didn't want to have for Jack. And that T-shirt, it was too much. Holes and all, it was sexy as hell. Keep your eyes glued in their sockets, Lacy. You're on duty. "Sally gave me a book," Lacy said. "It's got a chapter on delivering calves."

"Read on," he prompted.

"Okay. It says, 'Clean your arms thoroughly with disinfectant and…' We've already done that." She scanned the page, her finger running over the lines as a guide. "Here, this might be it. It says, 'Form your fingers and thumb in a cone and push them through the—' Well, you know what to push them through, don't you?"

"I can't, Lacy. The feet are presenting. Skip on down to that part."

Louise was in full distress, her moans growing weaker. In another few minutes it wouldn't matter, and it didn't take a veterinarian to figure that out. "What next?" he asked impatiently.

"Let's hook up the chains and get the poor baby out of there," Lacy said, studying the chain-winch contraption. It was like a jack, probably to be placed against the mother cow. Ben helped with the setup, looping the chain over the calf's back feet, while Jack, with his slippery arms, stepped aside.

"See if you can get an arm in there, Doc, to help move that calf on out. You slide, I'll pull." Ben began to pull the chain, and slowly, the feet and legs emerged in their fullest glory, all set and ready to kick. "You catch it when it's out," he told Lacy, "and treat it just like you would your own baby."

"My own baby wouldn't be pulled out by a chain," Lacy grumbled, trying to find the right position in the birthing process.

"If it's a big one like this, it would." Ben laughed.

The process went smoothly, with Jack easing the baby through the birth canal, trying to guide the feet so as not to injure the mother. And, within a few minutes, Louise produced a brand-new baby boy.

"It's dead," Lacy cried, trying to clear its mouth and eyes. It was limp and blue, its eyes glassy.

"Feel for a heartbeat, Lacy," Jack instructed calmly. "Just like you would with any of your intensive care patients. Ben, I have a small cylinder of oxygen in the supplies. Would you get it, please."

"There's a slight pulse," Lacy exclaimed. She pulled her stethoscope up to her ears and listened. "It's getting stronger."

"Stick a straw up its nose," Jack continued. "Lay the calf on its side and stretch his head out so he can get enough air in him, then tickle his nose with the straw."

Lacy looked at him, her eyes wide with amazement. Definitely full of surprises.

"Do it, Lacy," he encouraged patiently. "I've got another one coming down, and it's in a hurry." He moved into a kneeling position for the delivery, and Lacy could tell he was feeling quite a bit of pain.

"Here's the oxygen," Ben announced, setting the green cylinder next to Lacy.

Lacy stuck the straw up the baby's nose, as directed, and within seconds, the calf started to cough and sputter. Immediately, she cranked open the oxygen and held the clear plastic mask over the calf's snout as he coughed and sucked in air.

"He'll be up and ready to go in twenty minutes," Sally said.

"So will his sister," Jack pronounced, cradling the new baby next to his chest. "I mean, I guess this one's a she."

"I thought they taught you those things in medical school," Lacy laughed.

Twenty minutes later, dripping wet from a good hosing down, Jack and Lacy lay collapsed in a heap in each other's arms in the stall next to Louise. When Ben and Sally saw that Louise was bouncing back admirably after her ordeal and that brother and sister were doing fine, they went to the house to clean up and fix sandwiches.

"Maybe we should go hose down one more time," Lacy said, wearily. The twins were in the stall with them, though, and she really didn't want to miss their first steps. She was energized by the anticipation, and it was the first time she realized how exciting a child's first steps must be. She'd heard friends go on and on about the event, and turned a deaf ear. A few steps in an entire life were so insignificant, she never could understand what all the fuss was about. But with the expected event only minutes away, she suddenly understood. And she knew the excitement and joy of a baby's first steps had to be thousands of times greater than waiting for a calf to get up and walk.

How could it be that helping to deliver this calf had made her want a baby? But it had, badly, a desire she never knew she had in her.

"Instead of hosing off, I think sandblasting might be a better choice," Jack replied, plucking a piece of straw from Lacy's hair. His chambray shirt she'd tied so carefully around her waist had become a towel, his favorite holey T-shirt now owned several more holes, ones that would relegate the old favorite to the trash, and his jeans were something he'd probably never put on again. He was tired, exhilarated by the successful delivery and happy to have Lacy in his arms.

"Watch this," Lacy whispered, pointing to the first calf delivered. Bubba, as she'd dubbed him. "He's trying to get up." The calf moved to its front knees, then pushed itself up. He wobbled, tried to take a couple steps, then wobbled some more. But in no time, he was accustomed to his land legs and looking for mamma. "Isn't that amazing?" she asked. "All that effort to be born just a few minutes ago, and now he's up, walking around like it never happened." Sissy, as Lacy had named the other, followed suit minutes later, and as Lacy led both babies to their mother, she thought twins would be good. Bubba and Sissy Sutton.

Glancing over the stall at Jack, who was still stretched out in the straw, she wondered if he had twins in him.

8

BIG, COLD RAINDROPS dropped from the night sky by the time Lacy and Jack were winding down from their evening. They'd cleaned up a second time, at Lacy's insistence, then eaten a country share of ham sandwiches. Something about delivering twin calves in the middle of the night revved up huge appetites in both of them. And after they'd polished off the last of Sally Dunbar's homemade blueberry pie, they bade their farewells, took one last trip to the barn to look in on mother and children, then headed for Jack's Jeep.

"There's a blanket in back," Jack offered, when he saw Lacy shiver.

"You take it," she said, wearily, "and let me drive. You've been on your feet way too long."

"I'm not going to argue with you there," he returned, climbing into the passenger's side. His leg hurt, but surprisingly, not as badly as he thought it might have. "Did your grandfather ever deliver cows, or was he fortunate enough to be able to stick to humans?" Stretching out in his seat, Jack dropped the back to a reclining position and shut his eyes. Sleep was so close behind them he had to force himself to stay awake for Lacy's answer.

"There was a vet in town. He had a farm animal practice and..." She heard the gentle snore from under the blanket and smiled. He'd earned his sleep, tonight.

A CRACK of lightning split the night sky, followed by a single forge of thunder that echoed into a sustained chorus, and Jack jumped straight up in the front seat. "What the—" He choked the words out, trying to orient himself. It was pouring outside, and the low, continuous rumble made it sound like he was in a thirty-two-lane bowling alley. As best as he could tell, though, when he looked around, he was parked in the alley behind the Fremont 1908.

"Lacy?" he called, twisting to see if she'd crawled into the back seat. His gaze returned to what he could see of the storm outside, then followed a dim light trail to the back room in the old building. She was standing there, her face framed in a window, watching. It was too dark to see her features, but he'd memorized them a dozen times over. He knew the worried look on her face, and he could shut his eyes and picture the way she was biting the left side of her lower lip. "Oh, brother," he muttered, sliding lower in the seat. It was worse than his first real crush—Miss Nance, his third grade teacher. Apples, flowers, erase the blackboards every single day—all signs of true love. Then came the heartbreaker.

The storm he remembered that day was almost as bad as the one tonight, and then Miss Nance's fiancé showed up to drive her home. After that, Jack sat in the back row, sulking. A lifetime of plans down the drain because he fell in love with a woman with whom he could have no future.

"No wonder I'm such a screw-up," he muttered, still watching the face in the window. "I keep falling for women I can't have." He looked pensively at the rain beating against the windshield and pulled the blanket around his shoulders. No need going inside while it was still pouring. The only thing waiting for him in there was a reminder that his life didn't mix with hers. Similar dreams, opposite directions.

LACY PACED for an hour, stopping every minute or two to stare out the window at the Jeep in the alley. She could see the vehicle's outline, but not inside. Still, she was drawn back to that window to stare until her stare turned into a blur. Then she crawled into bed and willed herself to dream of anything, or anyone, but Jack.

She heard him creep in later, and guessed the rain was finally letting up. The distinctive thud of his cane on the wooden floor and the slight dragging of his left foot were muted, and she knew he was trying not to wake her. But she'd been awake the whole time, worried that he'd twist the wrong way in the Jeep and hurt his knee even more. "You can have the bed," she said quietly. She was on her side, her back to him, and she didn't turn over as he came nearer. "I've got enough bedding here for half the town, so I'll take the floor."

Tonight, she was glad the bed was only a twin.

"I'll take the examining table," he offered.

"You're too long for it," Lacy said, turning over. "And with your knee…"

"You'd like for me to take the bed and make you sleep on the floor so you'll have something to complain about in the morning."

"You'd like for me to sleep in the bed in hopes that I'm wearing something black and barely there." She sat up in bed and smiled. "But no such luck, Doctor. The only skin I've got uncovered is what you're seeing now, plus my toes." She held up her hands and wiggled her fingers at him. Her sweatshirt came down to mid-knuckle and the sweatpants right down to her ankles. "So take the bed and give your knee a rest." Tossing back the covers, Lacy hopped out on the side opposite Jack and motioned for him to take her place.

"Is there any point arguing with you?" he asked, dropping into the warm spot that still carried a trace of her scent. The thought of their first night together happened the minute he first heard her voice, but that fantasy hadn't played out in the front room of an old hardware store, he in a twin bed and she on the floor.

"Do you need to ask?" She grabbed a pillow from the foot of the bed, raised his leg and tucked the pillow under his knee.

"Would it make any difference if I did ask?" He liked her touch and thought about what it would be like if it was personal, not professional. A personal touch half as good as the professional touch he was getting would be the best he'd ever had.

"Depends on what you're asking, I suppose." She felt the muscle in his leg tighten as she tried to make him comfortable and fought the urge to offer him a pill. "And in which capacity—as Dr. Sutton or just plain Jack."

"What things do I need to ask you, Lacy? Make me a list." He pulled himself up in bed, then watched her lean down to rearrange his pillow. "Do I need to ask you if I can do this?" He brushed the back of his hand across her cheek and over her lips. "Or this?" He reached for her sweatshirt-covered hand and traced a light kiss across her fingertips.

"No," she said softly. "I mean, yes." Lacy stepped back. "I mean…"

"I never thought I'd see the day you were at a loss for words." He laughed. "Lacy Archer left speechless. What's this world coming to?"

"I'm not speechless," she spluttered, trying to catch both her breath and her whirling senses. "I'm just—just…"

"Just what, Lacy?" Jack coaxed. "Why don't you come over here and tell me what it is you are." He patted the edge of the bed and shifted as far to the other side as he could, which wasn't too far. It was going to be a tight fit, but one he welcomed.

Lacy took a step forward, then hesitated. The outcome couldn't be good, no matter how she framed the fantasy. That she would have no future with Jack was a given, but then, so were her growing feelings. How was it she'd spent a career resisting the advances of doctors, and here she was, second day on the job, in a new town, ready to jump at the first advance that came her way? *Not like you, Lacy,* she warned herself. Then she looked at the shadowed outline of Jack. *Not at all like you.* But it was Jack's advance, and she wanted it, and the feelings flooding her ruled out every possible angle of sensibility. "Oh, Jack, what are we doing?" she finally said, crossing to the bed.

Jack received her with open arms, and Lacy's slip into his embrace was a perfect fit. "It's been a long day," she whispered as her tongue teased his ear. "Perhaps we should call it a night."

Jack's arms encircled her, then he took hold of her bulky sweatshirt. "It's a night," he whispered, inching the garment slowly up and kissing every morsel of skin he exposed.

Lacy sighed, contented to savor his persuasive touch, and she arched into him, begging more and more. "Let me know if I hurt your knee," she said softly.

"What knee?" He took a painfully, deliciously long time with her bra. Tantalizing her nipples through the fabric with a light and possessive touch, then planting demanding kisses above the line of the lace, his ardor was surprisingly restrained, and Lacy gasped at the sheer delight of sensations he introduced to her. This wasn't her first time, but in the deepest, most profound sense it was, and she pushed all the doubts and fears of the future to the farthest corner of her mind. Tonight was the night. Maybe the only night. And she wanted it all.

Jack's hands found every pleasure point, and his search sent new rushes of desire through her each time he stopped to explore. His fingers burned into her quivering flesh as they slid across her belly and pressed beneath her sweatpants toward spots yet to be explored. Wanting nothing to hamper that which aroused her, Lacy stepped off the bed and wiggled out of her sweats, and as her navel was fully exposed, he leaned over to caress it with a light kiss. "You're wearing my favorite color," he growled into her belly.

"These are blue," she said. "Those were black."

"Got anything in red?" he asked. "You'd look sensational wrapped in red." He pressed a hard kiss below her navel, just above her panty line. "You'd look sensational out of red."

"Have you got anything wrapped in foil?" she asked.

By the time Lacy rejoined Jack, he was fully reclined in the bed, leaving only room enough for her to come to rest astride him. "Is this place locked up tight," he asked, "or should we be prepared for night visitors?"

"I have a sneaking hunch half the people in town have a key," she returned, moving her hands magically over his chest. "And the other half are just waiting for their copy."

Jack shuddered as she feathered her fingers downward. "Do you want to risk getting caught here like this?" As she stroked the hard lines along his ribs, her thumbs delicately taunting his nipples, he sucked in a more explosive shudder, then held his breath for a moment before letting it escape, rough and ragged. "Anybody could walk right in on us, you know."

Lacy bent low to trace the path her hands had followed

with tiny, hot kisses, then stopped at his pants. "It's up to you, Jack. Do you want to stop?" She pulled back and sat straight up. "Tell me what you want, Doctor. For one night, and one night only, following your orders is my fondest desire."

"Meaning?"

"Meaning tell me, Doctor. Tell me now, because to-morrow starts in just a few hours, and tomorrow doesn't come with a guarantee."

"Then make it coffee," he growled. "Black."

"Got no coffee, Doc," she stated huskily. "But will this do instead?" Lacy was shocked by her need, but not shocked enough to stop it. This was what she wanted, but she'd truly intended to hold firm in her resolve to stay away from it. However, what he offered and what she craved melted her resolve, and the Lacy that would not be seduced by any doctor wanted nothing but seduction from this doctor tonight. All the tomorrows could fall as they may.

She kissed him tenderly at first, trying to balance her weight on his good side. As she pressed harder, he moaned lightly in response, and she immediately jumped off the bed. "I'm sorry," she gasped. "Did I hurt you? Can I get some ice for your knee?"

"It's not my knee that's hurting right now," he panted.

"Oh," she said. "I thought...I mean..."

He patted the bed, inviting her back, and she moved tentatively, trying to find the right spot, trying not to hurt him. "Don't worry about me," he said impatiently. "If you hurt me, I'll get over it." Reaching around her waist, he pulled her to him, and this time she did land on his knee. In response he sat straight up, and accidentally knocked Lacy to the floor.

"I don't suppose you'd care for some ice this time,

would you?'' she asked, standing up then rubbing her backside.

''I'm sorry.'' He repositioned the pillow under his throbbing knee. ''Did I hurt you?''

Lacy smiled sadly. Her bold moment was gone, and she was back to the fact that it wouldn't work. ''No, but you would have.'' *More than you'll ever know.* She reached under the pillow and pulled out the foil packet he'd tucked there, then pressed it into his hand. ''I would have let you hurt me, too.'' She grabbed her sweats off the floor, then went to her pile of blankets behind the counter. ''And if anyone asks, I'll tell them you forced me to sleep on the floor.''

Yanking the covers over his head, Jack let out a quiet, frustrated moan, then tried to turn onto his side. His knee slid off the pillow, and started to throb even more. But that throb wasn't as bad as his other throb, the one that hurt so deep inside it kept him awake for hours.

JACK OPENED HIS EYES to the smell of coffee and saw Lacy sitting next to the bed holding a mug. ''Black?'' he asked, drowsily.

''Like mud.'' She watched him struggle to sit up, then handed the mug over. ''How's your knee? I heard you moan a couple times last night, and I wondered if you had hurt it turning over.''

His first sip down, he looked over the rim at Lacy, figuring she must have meant it when she said tomorrow came with no guarantees. It was tomorrow now, and nothing about her indicated what had almost happened between them. ''Coffee's good,'' he murmured. ''And the knee's not so bad this morning.''

"Good," Lacy said, jumping up. "Would you like your therapy before or after you clean up?"

"You're assuming I want therapy this morning?" Therapy would have been fine from Willie Pearl or anyone else willing to give his leg a good bend and stretch. But not from Lacy. Not now. Not after she'd touched him physically, personally, in a way other than a physical therapist would.

"Do you want to wait until later?"

"What I want is to take a nice, long shower, get into some clean clothes, read the paper, if this town has a paper, and drink my second cup of coffee."

"The coffee I can do. Some kind soul dropped off a coffeemaker yesterday. The rest you're going to have to scrounge for yourself."

Jack took his cane from the head of the bed, pushed himself up and headed for the shoes he'd left by the back door when he'd tried to sneak in. "What are you going to do with your half of the bull?" he asked. He had to get his mind off what almost happened and onto the here and now. Talk of cows would sure do it. But that's not what he really wanted to talk about.

"What *are* you talking about?"

"Bubba. He's our pay for the delivery."

Lacy stretched and headed for the wooden display counter upon which was sitting a white cardboard box full of warm doughnuts. Ellis MacNamara, the town baker, would be in later that day to have a couple stitches removed, and he'd prepaid his office call with the doughnuts. "You're kidding, aren't you? They're not really going to give him to us?" Lacy pulled out a glazed, ate half in just a few bites, then swiped at the frosted glaze on her lips with the back of her hand. "I mean, what would we do with him?"

Jack shrugged, keeping his eyes on his shoes, not Lacy. Most women would have wanted to talk about it, get it all out in the open, hash and rehash that miserable failed attempt, and it made him nervous that Lacy wasn't even hinting at it. Maybe it was just a one-night-only deal for her, after all. He'd hoped not, and somewhere in the back of his illogical brain he'd even conjured up ways to carry on a long-distance relationship with her after he returned to Chicago. It would last until he could convince her to move there with him. But now he wasn't sure what he wanted. One thing was definite, though. He didn't like being on the receiving end of a one-time-only deal. "Don't include me in that we, Lacy. Ben intends to deliver that little calf when it's weaned from its mama, and since I'll be gone by that time, I've decided to deed my half of Bubba over to you."

"I'll deed him back to the Dunbars, then," Lacy said firmly.

"And offend them?" Jack wandered over to the counter and reached for a doughnut from the box. "Ben said he always paid Doc Washburn by doing odd jobs around his house, and since everyone in town is doing odd jobs around here already, he thought we should have the bull. Just think of him as a big kitten."

Lacy walked to the front window and looked across the street. Gray day. The road was dotted with puddles, the clouds were swollen and waiting to open again, and she was too tired to think about what she'd do with her paycheck from her first home delivery. "Why don't they just keep him, and I'll go to visit on weekends or something. In fact, why don't I deed my half over to you, and you can take him back to Chicago for a house pet. Just think of him as a big kitten.''

"Sorry. No pets allowed in my condo," Jack said, polishing off his second doughnut. "You get the full bull, lock, stock and whatever else comes with cattle." He picked up his third doughnut and propped himself casually against the wooden counter. "Now, what have we got lined up for this morning?"

"We'll discuss the bull later." Lacy grabbed the appointment book off Willie Pearl's desk and looked at the day's schedule. "Sore neck first, then poison ivy."

"Patient names?"

She shrugged. "Willie Pearl's got the diagnosis penciled in, one for nine o'clock, then the other at nine-thirty, but no names to go with them. Only initials."

"With Willie Pearl to make the diagnosis, it doesn't look like I'll be needed here." He wrapped two more doughnuts in a napkin, filled his coffee mug then headed for the door. "I'm going home, Lacy. Gonna prop some pillows under my knee and relax. Call me if you need me."

"Looks like he's in another good mood this morning," Willie Pearl called from the front door. Jack gave her a quick nod as he passed her on his way out.

"We had a rough night."

"So I heard, and Ben and Sally are singing high praises of you and the doc this morning. They said for a couple of people who don't know one end of a cow from another, you didn't do a bad job."

"Did Doc Washburn have much of a veterinary practice?" Lacy asked. She plodded to the coffeemaker, poured a cup and handed it to Willie Pearl, then poured one for herself. Normally, she preferred tea, but this morning the bitter taste suited her. She was tired, too. Probably not as tired as Jack, considering his condition, but a night spent in cow birth wasn't anything she was conditioned for, not that she *could* condition herself for something like that.

"He took care of a few animals, but only in emergencies. There's a good farm animal vet in the next county, but folks depended on Doc when the vet wasn't available. So what's he in a snit about this time?"

"Like I said, we had a rough night. And I think his knee hurts."

Willie Pearl cast a skeptical glance at the bed still standing in the middle of the room. "You *are* talking about what happened out at Ben Dunbar's farm, aren't you, and not about what happened when the doc shacked up here afterward?"

"What else would I be talking about?" Lacy snapped. "And do you have this place bugged, or something?" News, any news, spread fast in small towns. And some news quite often took on new life as it was told from person to person. She wasn't surprised that word of Jack spending the night at the Fremont 1908 had spread, but she was a little amazed at how quickly.

"I've been around that block more times than you are years old, young lady," Willie Pearl cackled. She laid a hand on Lacy's arm and squeezed. "You have a choice, so don't mess it up. Do what you think is right and forget about everything else. Now, go get yourself cleaned up for work. We've got six people coming in so far, starting in about ten minutes."

"Six?" Lacy exclaimed. "Ten minutes ago it was only two."

Willie Pearl nodded impatiently, cradling the phone against her shoulder and holding up six fingers. Lacy wondered if she was getting ready to schedule a seventh appointment.

"And don't forget to get that bed pushed into the back," Willie Pearl called as Lacy disappeared into the bathroom. "Don't want the folks around here getting any ideas."

"Yeah, right. Like they actually need to get a look at the bed before the idea starts springing to mind."

"Must have been some night for you to be in the same snit he's in." Willie Pearl was laughing when she motioned in the first patient. It was Cherie, from the beauty salon. She was all decked out in her finest fringed jeans and denim jacket. The jeans were too tight, and the zipper looked like it could pop open at any minute.

Lacy's first thought, when she saw the woman, was, *How do you ever sit down in those?* And the fact that Cherie chose to stand and lean against the wall answered that question. Probably a good thing, since Lacy was sure she would have to be the one to hoist Cherie back to a standing position if she did manage to struggle herself all the way down into a chair.

"I hear he spent the night right here," Cherie commented, following Lacy into the examining room. "He sure does work fast. I like that in a man."

Lacy chose not to respond, and instead moved Cherie's neck from side to side. "How long has it been stiff?"

"Couple days. Think I slept wrong on it or something."

Lacy handed her a sample packet of over-the-counter pain reliever and a sample tube of muscle rub. "Try these," she said. "And if it's not better in another couple days, come back and have the doctor check you out. He may want to prescribe a muscle relaxer or something."

"But shouldn't the doctor take a look at me before then?"

"You'd like that, wouldn't you Cherie?" Willie Pearl called from the waiting room. "And I'll bet you won't be showing him your neck."

Shaking her head in obvious exasperation and letting out a befitting huff of air, Cherie turned and hustled to the door like a woman who was feeling no pain—in her neck or anywhere else. From the front window, Lacy watched the woman's departure, then turned to Willie Pearl "What was that all about?"

"She likes younger men."

"You mean…"

"All I can tell you is that they had to ban her from the high school." Willie Pearl laughed. "Good thing we're inland, because she'd haul herself out to the dock and wait for the sailors to come in, and she wouldn't greet them in the motherly sense. Five will get you ten that she's on her way out to the doc's cabin right now."

"Should we call and warn him?" Lacy asked.

Willie Pearl shook her head, picked up a pencil and crossed the first name off their patient roster. "Not in my job description, but you can do whatever you want."

Lacy could just see Cherie making her advances. Fending her off would give Jack something to do in his free time. "Maybe later, when we're not so busy." She chuckled, then opened the front door to greet the next patient, a man in his mid-forties. His wife was with him, and Lacy knew by the look on his face whose idea the appointment was.

"He's got poison ivy," the wife announced, then whispered, "on his privates, if you know what I mean."

"And I won't be taking my pants down for no nurse," the husband said, fuming.

"You will if she asks you."

Lacy gave Willie Pearl a cross-eyed look as she escorted her patient into the examining room. Ten minutes later, when they emerged, he had a smile on his face, a handful of sample packets of ointment, a bag of disposable gloves and a stern warning in his head that next time he pulled weeds, he was to wash his hands before he did *anything* else.

The next three patients had routine problems, nothing that required a doctor or even medication. The fourth had a sprained wrist Lacy bandaged in no time. And the last patient of the morning was Millie Ballard with an arthritic complaint. "It seems to be getting worse," she said as Lacy made her comfortable on the examining table.

According to Doc Washburn's chart, Millie was on the lowest possible dose of over-the-counter ibuprofen. Her joints didn't look swollen, and for a woman of seventy plus years she had remarkably good range of motion, but she wrung her hands nervously as Lacy went about the assessment and winced quietly once or twice in the exam. Lacy knew Millie needed attention more than anything and expected she would be seeing the woman on a regular basis. "I think we should increase your dose," Lacy said, patting the woman's hand. "Take one more pill at night, before bed. It will make getting up in the morning a little easier."

Lacy suddenly wondered if Millie had someone to get up with every morning.

"And Millie, schedule another appointment for next week. Have Willie Pearl set it for the morning so I can see how the new treatment is working."

"Thank you, dear," Millie said, sliding off the table. "Blueberries are in season right now, but I expect you had Sally Dunbar's blueberries last night. But pie cherries are in, too. So which would you prefer?"

"I'm sorry?" Lacy replied, frowning. "I'm not sure I understand what you're asking me."

"Why, your pie, dear. I always made Doc Washburn a pie as part of what I owed him for seeing me. I could go with peach, too, if you like peach. I heard they got a nice shipment in at the grocery."

"Peach sounds good," Lacy said. A truck in exchange for some stitches, a cow for a house call and a pie for an office exam—it was a good thing she was being paid by the town and not relying on income from the practice.

"Got one more before lunch," Willie Pearl said as Lacy showed Millie Ballard out the door. "This one may need the doctor."

This one turned out to be a ten-year-old girl with a serious ear infection. Lacy could hand out ointments and advice, but the child needed a heavy-duty antibiotic, and she couldn't prescribe it, even though a supply of it was sitting in the cabinet five feet away. "I'll have Dr. Sutton stop by your house to see her this afternoon," Lacy said to the distraught mother. "He'll bring the medication with him. And in the meantime, try to get fluids down her." The child's skin looked dry, and it didn't snap back into place fast enough when Lacy pinched it. A sure sign of dehydration.

"Can I have a sucker?" the child asked.

"You can have two," Lacy said, handing out the customary sucker. "But you've got to drink a little water, too. Promise?"

The girl looked at Lacy and smiled weakly. "I promise," she vowed.

"He should have been here for that one," Lacy said, dropping into a chair in the empty waiting room. It was almost noon, and she was getting hungry. "Do we have patients this afternoon?"

"Two, but not until later. A sinus infection and a belly-ache." Willie Pearl shut her appointment book and stood. "Want to walk over to the diner for some lunch?" she asked.

"Sounds good," Lacy returned. "Give me a couple minutes to clean up."

Lacy had the water running full blast when she heard shouting from the waiting room. Opening the door, she saw two men drag a third one in and drop him into a chair. "Got him real bad this time," one of the men said. "Won't let go no matter what we sing."

"What won't let go?" Lacy asked.

The two companions looked at each other in amazement, as if Lacy should know. Then they looked at Willie Pearl, who shrugged a halfhearted apology. "I told you boys it was time to get rid of Wilbur, but you didn't listen to me, did you? And now he's gone and got stubborn, and you know what that means." She stood, grabbed her purse and marched to the front door. "See you at the diner, Lacy, just as soon as you take care of Wilbur."

"Which one of you is Wilbur?" she asked, assuming it was the man with his foot wrapped in a towel.

The one with the towel responded. "I'm Danny Roy Jackson, and these are my brothers Bobbo and Elvis."

As she watched, the towel began to move, and something long and snakelike poked out.

"What is that?" Lacy gasped, stepping back.

"Wilbur." All three responded in unison.

Taking another step back, Lacy asked, "And what is Wilbur?"

"A snake. Just a common garden variety. Not poisonous." Then to prove his words, Elvis bent and pulled the towel off Danny Roy's foot to reveal Wilbur, who apparently had his fangs embedded in Danny Roy's big toe. "He lives in the walls and comes out to eat the mice and sometimes lay in the window and sun himself, but I guess he missed breakfast because he latched on to Danny Roy this morning and hasn't let go."

"And I'm supposed to do what?" Lacy asked, backing to the other side of the room.

"Make him let go," Bobbo said simply. "Danny Roy's toe is beginning to hurt him something fierce."

"Without hurting him," Danny Roy added. "He's better than any two cats when it comes to mousing."

Lacy thought of the two new kittens she would soon receive and was glad Ham had chosen felines as payment, instead of reptiles or anything else in the form of a three-foot-long scaly-brown Wilbur. "What usually relaxes him enough to let go?" she asked.

"Singing, ma'am," Elvis said. "He's partial to country music."

9

JUST GETTING AWAY from Lacy had the tension-kicking effect Jack needed, and by the time he'd seen to the little girl with the ear infection thanks to Lacy's call, then soaked his aching muscles, pushed himself through a grueling half hour of leg lifts and quadricep flexes he felt better physically and emotionally. And he was almost looking forward to an afternoon of patient care. That is, until he turned the corner and had to jam on his brakes to keep from barreling right into the crowd of spectators who were gathered outside the Fremont 1908. "Oh, no," he muttered, shutting his eyes and dropping his head against the headrest. "What's she done now?"

Tooting his horn, Jack caught the attention of the people standing in his way and waved them aside, then he moved forward inch by inch until he was in the parking space with the sign that said Doctor. "What's going on?" he asked Mayor Lambert, who was motioning for him to hurry.

"We called you out at your cabin but there was no answer," the mayor said, panting. "And Lacy has your cell phone, so that didn't do us any good." His face was red and sweaty, and Jack noticed he had a bullhorn slung over his shoulder. Crowd control? He spun around for a quick count, and there might have been sixty or seventy people there.

"She has my cell phone?"

"She sure does, and when we dialed your number from

your office phone, guess where it rang from?'' A devilish grin appeared on the mayor's face, and he tumbled into the next sentence before Jack could utter a word. "In her bed, that's where. Right under the covers.''

"Great. And I suppose everyone in town already knows…'' Jack turned abruptly away from the mayor and started to push his way through the crowd. He heard his name in passing several times. And unless his imagination was in overdrive, he saw the collective frown of disapproval. The worst of it was, he hadn't done anything to deserve it. At least, not to his way of thinking. Small towns. Everything was observed and recorded in some fashion for posterity. Give him the big city any day, where no one noticed or cared.

"It's ugly in there,'' the mayor shouted over the bullhorn to Jack as Jack tried to make his way to the front door. "Never seen anything quite like it.''

Jack stopped and turned around. "What's going on in there?'' he shouted. The rumbling crowd suddenly went stone silent, and the collective frown deepened.

The mayor shrugged and shoved Jack in the door. Before the screen door swung shut, Jack heard the mayor's announcement from his bullhorn. "The doctor is in now, so please calm down and be quiet. Mothers, please make sure your children are with you at all times.''

"Good heavens,'' Jack muttered again, taking a few steps into the room. The first thing he heard was the sound of a country song that had been popular twenty years ago, and it wasn't playing on a CD or even a radio. Gathered outside the bathroom door was a choir of twenty people, being led by an honest-to-gosh director. The harmonies were perfect, and it took him a full second to realize exactly what he was witnessing. "Who are they?'' he asked as he walked by Ham, who was standing just beyond the stairs, holding an ax. "And why are you carrying that?"

He stopped for an answer, but Ham gripped his ax tighter and fixed his stare on the choir.

Moving into the waiting room, Jack saw Danny Roy, Bobbo and Elvis. They were seated on the floor, holding cans of soft drink, tapping their feet to the music. He didn't know them and didn't care to become acquainted at the moment. So he moved in the direction of Willie Pearl, who sat on top of her desk, gyrating back and forth in some kind of motion that didn't match the beat of the choir. Her face was drained white, and for once she was speechless.

He recognized several of the other people who were standing like cement statues in the room. They were wide-eyed and staring, all speechless, all appearing to be polite, respectful concertgoers who always turned out for a good country concert at the medical clinic in the middle of an afternoon.

"Where's Lacy?" Jack finally asked.

No one answered, but they shushed him when he interrupted the music.

"I said where's Lacy?"

In one grand gesture, everyone in the Fremont 1908 pointed to the bathroom, and Jack followed their direction. As he neared the closed door the singers parted, and when he pulled it open he found Lacy sitting on the floor, singing the same song as the choir, with huge tears streaming down her face.

"Lacy?" he said, stepping into the bathroom. "What's wrong?" Two more steps in and he saw that she was not alone. A snake lay coiled in her lap, its fangs embedded in her left forearm.

"Wilbur," she said, batting at the tears. "He likes country."

"Country?" Jack slipped to the floor next to Lacy and put his arm around her shoulder. "I guess this it the dumbest question of all time, but does it hurt?"

Lacy nodded and sniffled.

"And the music is supposed to do what? I thought snakes couldn't hear?"

"Maybe he feels the vibrations." She smiled a little. "And country's his rhythm."

"Wouldn't a couple of tranquilizers do the same thing?" Jack tightened his hold on Lacy and pushed her head to his shoulder. "I don't suppose we could just take a scalpel and..."

"You can't. He's a pet, sort of."

"Cows are one thing, Lacy. But I draw the line at snakes. New clinic policy. We don't treat snakes. Okay?"

"Okay." She watched Jack grab hold of the snake's head behind its jaw. Man of many talents, including snake handling, it seemed.

And a man who was becoming too easy to love.

Minutes later Jack handed an unscathed Wilbur over to the Preston boys, and they carried him outside to greet a cheering crowd. The First Congregational church choir followed, quite elated. And when word was out that Wilbur, Danny Roy and Lacy were all doing fine, everyone returned to what they normally did in the middle of a Sunstone afternoon. Ham tossed his ax into the back of his pickup truck and went home to his mother, and Willie Pearl went back to the lunch that had been interrupted at the diner when, almost forty minutes earlier, Elvis had strolled in ever so casually and announced, "Got Danny Roy unhooked from Wilbur okay, but now he's hooked to Miss Lacy and we can't get 'em apart."

"What the hell happened?" Jack asked, applying a topical antibiotic to Lacy's arm. The puncture wounds were deep but clean. There was no serious tissue damage, and since the snake was not venomous Jack didn't see a need for much more treatment than common, everyday first aid. "And why was the whole town here to see it?"

"I think they thought that it was Danny Roy, not Wilbur, who was hooked to me."

"Conjures up some interesting images."

"Shush. The whole thing is embarrassing."

"If you think this is embarrassing, wait until you have to explain how my cell phone got in your bed. Just so you're warned, that's the next talk of the town." He laughed as he applied the bandage. "You'll have some tissue swelling and bruising, but it will go away in a few days, and all you'll have left will be the happy memories."

"I said shush." Lacy climbed off the examining table and began to gather the used supplies. "If you'd been here, like you're supposed to be…"

"But I did do my exercises." Jack took the supplies and trash from her and tossed everything into the can across the room, then pushed Lacy into a chair and kicked a crate over to her. "Now, sit down and put your feet up."

She obliged willingly. "I was scared to death," she said. "And now I guess I get to be humiliated beyond a reasonable facsimile of human life."

Plopping down at his desk, Jack opened the bottom drawer and pulled out a bottle of brandy and two paper cups. Pouring the first half full, he handed it to Lacy. Then he poured into the next half as much as he'd poured her and stashed the bottle in the drawer. He watched her take a swallow before he sipped his own. He liked the fact that brandy in paper cups was okay with her. She wasn't a snifter kind of woman—didn't want one, didn't need one, didn't even care. She drank her brandy from a paper cup as if that was the way it was meant to be, and she made it look as elegant as if she were drinking it from fine antique crystal. "So my question is, why the choir? I can understand Ham and the ax, Willie Pearl dancing up on the desk, the guys who own the snake and even the onlookers, but why the choir?" He took another sip of brandy, wadded up the paper cup and threw it away.

"The Reverend said it was the first time any church choir in Sunstone was ever called to help in an emergency, and it was their privilege to answer the call of duty."

"The whole damned choir." Jack laughed. "You got the whole choir. I'm impressed."

By the time Lacy's brandy was history, the waiting room was brimming with patients. Willie Pearl's efforts to scare up a few more at lunch were a monumental success, and she'd scribbled the order of appointments on napkins for the seven lucky afternoon patients. So after the two people who were previously scheduled were seen to by Jack, Lacy called, "Number One," and collected the napkin marked with a number one.

Surprisingly, the afternoon went quickly and smoothly. She and Jack worked well together. She did the preliminary exam, he did the follow-up exam and handed out the prescription or treatment recommendation. It was all routine, and surprisingly, several of the patients paid cash, something new to the Fremont 1908 clinic. Of course, there were also fresh vegetables, an afghan, a few dinner invitations and a wheelbarrow left in offering, too. And by the end of the day, after the patients were gone and all the other-than-cash payment was stashed out of the way, Lacy was ready for bed. And it was barely six o'clock.

"They're going to start on your apartment in a couple days," Willie Pearl said on her way out the door. She looked like she could go another straight eight without feeling it, and Lacy hated it because she didn't have enough left in her to push her bed into the waiting area. Tonight she'd probably just sleep on the loading dock.

"She's got a date with Palmer," Jack remarked, stepping out of the examining room. "Wanted to know if we care to join them for pizza and beer in a couple hours or so. I said sure."

"Have a good time," she moaned. "I'm going to sleep now." Lacy staggered to the dark loading area and dropped face first into bed, and she was almost asleep when she head Jack's telltale gait getting louder. "Go away," she whined. "I'm tired. Leave me alone. I don't want pizza and beer and I don't want to get back up."

"They're expecting us," he said, moving closer to the bed.

"They can expect you."

"You're the one they like." He dropped his cane on the floor, then bent over and rolled Lacy off her face and on to her back. "You're the one they want."

Too tired to resist, she allowed herself to be rolled, allowed herself to enjoy his touch. It wasn't professional like a doctor's, but friendly, almost intimate, and the touch points tingled. For a moment she thought about pulling him into bed with her, but what they'd started last night wasn't going to be finished. And pretending that it could be would hurt. It would have to be her only safety net—distance, both physically and emotionally. But she'd played out the scenario so many times—how to keep him there, how he asked to stay, how he told her he was more than happy to give up his upscale practice for a combo country doc, country vet gig. Yeah, right. "Then pretend you're me. Smile a little and be friendly. No one will notice the difference."

Jack lowered himself easily to the bed, kicked off his shoes, then stretched out on his back. He wasn't tired, but he felt the tiredness in her body as he gathered her into his arms. It was heavy, like it was under the power of an opiate. "Just sleep for awhile, and we'll talk about it later, when you wake up."

"For a few minutes," she murmured. She liked being in his arms, but more than that she loved that it was his move, not hers. As the last attentive breath escaped her, Lacy felt his kiss on her forehead.

"ARE YOU OKAY?" Jack asked, glancing at her out of the corner of his eye. She'd slept two hours then reluctantly agreed to pizza and beer with Willie Pearl and Palmer. But her sleep had been restless. She'd twisted and turned and muttered until he finally slipped from the bed, hoping that the extra room would let her sleep better. But when he'd given her a wake-up nudge on the shoulder, she came up swinging. Literally. And she looked twice as tired as when she'd started her nap.

So much for country life, he thought.

"I'm just tired," she lied. "Didn't get enough sleep." No amount of tired could make her feel the way she did. Everything she'd ever wanted was right there, but what was becoming the most important part had no intention of staying. And the dream had pounded her for those two hours in every imaginable form. He'd ridden off into the sunset on his horse, in his Jeep, in a golf cart. She'd shown up to work and found a hastily scribbled, chicken-scratch goodbye note tacked to the front door. She'd shown up and waited for hours only to realize he was gone without so much as a civil farewell. Those two hours of dreaming had done nothing for her physical fatigue or disposition and even less for her mental acuity, and she was beginning to wonder if, in the interest of doing her job, she should actively work to get another doctor into Sunstone so she wouldn't have to keep dragging her heart around to be stomped on. "And Jack, I really don't feel like going out tonight."

But no matter how she felt, she was on her way to a roadhouse just over the county line to eat pizza she didn't want and drink beer she didn't want, either. Jack's persuasion, as usual, had been masterful. It cut right through her iron-clad resolve like a welder's torch.

"I thought it would be good for you to get away for a couple hours. Have some fun. Take your mind off work."

"You don't have a clue what's good for me, and…" Her eyes shifted to a reflection in the bushes along the side of the road just ahead of them. She blinked and looked again, but it was gone. "Stop, Jack," she said abruptly. Pushing herself up in the seat, she twisted backward to look at the spot they had just passed. "Back there. Did you see that?" Before the Jeep came to a complete stop, Lacy opened the door and bolted out.

Shaking his head, Jack grabbed his cane and followed. It had rained again, and the oil and water puddled to form a slick on the blacktop. The grass was just as slippery. So between fighting his knee and the outside conditions, it took him an eternity to catch up with her. When he finally did, he found her ripping leaves and branches away from a camouflaged clump about fifty feet off the road. "It's a car," she cried. "Someone's in it. I can hear moaning."

Without thinking, Jack dropped his cane and moved forward at a clip he didn't know was still in him. Going to the side opposite Lacy, he took up the task of clearing away the vegetation, and within seconds a dented red car lay exposed. "Are you okay in there?" he yelled.

The driver, a large middle-aged man shook his head and pointed to his chest.

"Heart attack?" Jack called. "Is it a heart attack?"

The man nodded weakly and closed his eyes.

"We've got to get him out," Jack shouted, eyeing the locked door. "Before he goes into arrest." The man was gasping for breath, and his eyes were beginning to roll back in his head.

Lacy ran to the passenger door and saw that it was locked, but on her way around she noticed that the hatch-back lock was missing. "We're in," she shouted, throwing the rear entry door up and climbing in.

"I'm a nurse," she called as she crawled forward in the cramped vehicle. It was giving her a good case of claustro-phobia, and she wondered how such a large man could stand being in such a closed space. "And he's a doctor." She reached over the man's shoulder and unlocked his door, then unfastened his seat belt. "Can you tell me your name?"

He shook his head and grunted.

"That's all right. Just save your breath, and we'll figure it out later." Wedging herself into the front seat, she saw Jack taking the man's pulse and frowning. "Do you have any heart medication with you?" she asked.

He nodded.

"Where is it?"

"Lacy, I'm going back to the Jeep for my bag," Jack called. "Back in a minute."

She watched him for a second, then returned her atten-tion to her patient. "Where is your heart medication?" she asked again.

He picked up his hand and held it out to her for an instant, then dropped it onto the seat.

"Are you still with me?" she called.

When he didn't respond, Lacy pressed her fingers to the pulse in his neck to make sure he was still alive. The pulse and the breathing quit at the same time, and immediately, Lacy jammed the pad of her thumb into his mid chest, in

line with his heart, and initiated a hard rub. She knew the
sternal rub hurt like hell and always left a nasty bruise, but
sometimes it caused the patient to snap back. But, as she
pulled her hand from his chest and pressed her fingers to
his pulse one more time, she felt nothing.

Lacy scrambled out the passenger door, ran to the
driver's side and began to drag the man to the flat, wet
ground.

"Jack," she called, not sure if he was close enough to
hear. "He's in full arrest."

"On my way," he called, cursing his knee with every
slow step. As he got within sight of the wreck, he saw Lacy
give the corpulent body one huge tug, then end up flat on
her back in the mud with the man on top of her. "I called
for an ambulance."

"It's been a minute," she wheezed, trying to push herself out from under him. "And you get the mouth-to-
mouth."

"He looks more your type than mine," Jack commented,
dropping slowly to his knees. The impact of the ground
hurt, no matter that he'd tried to control the contact, and
Jack drew in a sharp breath.

"Are you okay?" Lacy asked, assuming a position to
begin chest compressions.

"Ask me in the morning," he grunted, grabbing an airway from his medical kit and shoving it into the man's
mouth. He forced in a couple breaths, was glad to see the
man's chest rise and fall, then waited for Lacy to do her
round of compressions. "Did you find his medication?"

"No," Lacy panted. Pumping a heart was tough and totally exhausting. And she was grateful for the split second
reprieve in which Jack did the breathing again. "Didn't
have time to look."

"Stop for a second." Jack felt for a pulse, then placed

his stethoscope over the man's heart. "Nothing. Keep going."

Lacy pumped again, and Jack breathed. "Wish we were in a hospital," she said.

"Or back at our place." Jack put his mouth on the airway and puffed in a couple more breaths. "Or even the vet clinic over in the next county."

Lacy's arms were beginning to burn. Normally, she would have asked Jack to change places, but she was about ten minutes on her knees, and she knew his knee wasn't ready for that kind of a beating yet. "You don't happen to have any epinephrine, do you? Or a portable defibrillator?"

"Hold off," he instructed, putting his stethoscope in his ears. He listened to the man's chest for a moment then placed the stethoscope in a different position and listened again. Lacy saw the scowl but couldn't tell if it meant bad news. She hadn't worked a resuscitation with Jack before and didn't know his style. And every doctor and nurse had a certain style when it came to emergencies. "He's back. You can stop the compressions."

Slipping to the side of the man's chest, Lacy looked at the heavens and said a silent thank-you, then smiled. "Good job," she sighed.

"All I did was breathe. You're the one who got the real workout."

Exactly thirty minutes from the moment Lacy first saw the reflection off the road, Jack closed the ambulance door and watched the vehicle speed away into the night. The volunteer fire crew had shown up along with the county paramedics and several town spectators, and by the time the full crowd had gathered, the patient, who turned out to be John Fremont, owner of their building, was uttering profuse and profound thanks.

"He said he'd have his lawyers get busy transferring the

building over to you first thing tomorrow," Jack commented, helping Lacy into the Jeep.

"Me? Why me?"

"Because you're the one who's staying." Jack pulled a blanket from his back seat and tucked it around her, then leaned over and brushed a tender kiss across her cheek, then an equally tender one on her lips. "We're a good team, you know. Medically. We work well together," he whispered. "Very well."

Sighing, Lacy slipped down in the seat, shut her eyes, blanked everything out of her mind but the kiss and didn't join reality again until the vehicle was stopped in front of his cabin. "I thought we were going for pizza and beer."

"Tonight, you deserve something a little quieter than a roadhouse and a little more private than a waiting room." He opened the car door for her and steadied her as she stepped out. Even he could see her exhaustion was complete. Her face was pale, she wrung her hands nervously, and there was a dull flatness behind her eyes. No spark, no life, no Lacy. "I thought maybe a nice soak in my hot tub and some wine, then a night in a real bed in a real bedroom."

"I've got to call Willie Pearl and let hew know where I am...."

"Done."

"And I've got to call Mrs. Glover and see how Emily's ear infection is doing."

"Will do."

"And Millie Ballard..."

"Tomorrow, Lacy. It'll all keep until tomorrow. But tonight the doctor prescribes rest." He guided her up the dozen wooden steps to the front door, wishing he could carry her, then fished for his key. It wasn't on the same ring with his car keys, since this was the Billingsly cabin and not his and he'd never gotten around to combining the keys. Somehow, commingling keys made Sunstone seem like a permanent situation, and he didn't want to give the Fates the slightest hint that, in a moment of weakness, he'd actually thought about staying there. Be careful what you even think about... So he'd kept his life and keys separate, and as he jammed his hand in his pants pocket for the third time, he cursed himself. The cabin keys were missing.

"No luck?" she asked, dropping wearily into a lashed-log chair. It was a large chair, low and comfortable, and the pad in it was thick. Not a bad place to spend the night.

"I'll bet I dropped them out there when we were resuscitating John Fremont."

"And you don't have an extra set?"

"In the cabin," he muttered.

Smiling, Lacy stood then wandered down the steps to the Jeep. She pulled the blanket out of the back seat and took it to the lashed-log chair with her, then pulled it over herself as she curled up. "Wake me when you know something." It was a nice night. Hot, but not too hot for July. The frog songs from a distant pond were soothing, and as Lacy drifted off to sleep she wondered how many of those frogs would find their true love tonight.

"SHE LOOKS LIKE she's asleep."

"Shh. Don't want to go waking her up if we don't have to."

The voices wafted through Lacy's dream. She was sitting next to the frog pond, wine glass in hand....

"She don't drool none. Not one little speck that I could see."

"Shh"

Jack was there, pouring the wine. They were on a blanket, and the night was clear. The stars in the sky above....

"Doc said he doesn't want her disturbed, Elvis, so keep your yap shut."

"I just said she don't drool none."

Strains of Elvis Presley were exchanged with the frog song. Love me tender....

"Think the doc already knows that—" Bobbo laughed "—or should we tell him?"

"You two better keep quiet," Danny Roy whispered. "Doc's not gonna like you waking her up."

Elvis... Wrong Elvis. Suddenly, Lacy blinked her eyes open and saw the three silhouettes huddled over her. "Where's Jack?" she asked.

"Emily Glover took a turn for the worse," Elvis explained. "Since we were already here to get the house open for him, he asked us to stay until he got back."

Lacy sat up and looked around. She was still outside. "You're my baby-sitters?" she asked, pushing herself to the edge of the chair.

"Not exactly, ma'am. We're just here keeping an eye on things until Doc gets back." Bobbo shined a flashlight in her eyes. "You do look tired, just like the doc said you were."

Squinting, Lacy turned away and looked at the house. The front door was wide open. "So why am I still out here when the house is unlocked?"

"You looked so peaceful, ma'am. Had a nice smile on your face," Danny Roy offered. "Real nice, like you were having a good dream."

"And you don't drool none," Elvis added.

Danny Roy shot his youngest brother an irritated scowl, then continued. "We just hated to wake you up."

"How long has Jack been gone?" she asked, standing.

"Most of an hour, now," Bobbo replied.

"And you've been watching me sleep for an hour?" She

dropped the blanket into the chair and headed to the front door.

"No, ma'am," Bobbo answered. "Took us a good five minutes to get through that lock."

"Didn't snore none, either," Elvis supplied.

Lacy stepped into the cabin, then turned around. "I think you boys can go on home now. I appreciate everything you've done." Except the part where they all watched her sleep, but she was going to save that for Jack. "Night."

The three brothers tipped their baseball caps then bounded down the front steps. By the time Lacy had the front door shut and locked she heard the rumble of their truck on the driveway. They were speeding, throwing gravel that clanked and pinged on the truck's rusty fenders, probably swapping drool and snore stories. "I owe you, Jack," she muttered as she headed to the sofa. It was large, overstuffed and a perfect place for the next installment of her sleep.

Sleep lasted ten minutes, and Jack's pounding on the door told her it was probably all she was going to get for the rest of the night. "How's Emily?" she asked, opening the door.

"Fever spiked, but it's down now. She's resting comfortably."

"More than I can say for me," Lacy grumbled. "How dare you leave me on the porch with those snake charmers to watch over me." She padded into the kitchen, yanked open the refrigerator and looked for something cold to drink. And a snack. She found bottled water and an apple and didn't even care that it was Jack's last apple and last bottle of water. Taking her midnight snack to the couch, she plopped down and kicked her feet up, more to make sure he didn't plop down there with her than anything else

"I go to sleep for five minutes and wake up with Elvis hovering over me talking about how I don't drool."

"I'm glad to hear that you don't." He chuckled.

She took a bite of the apple, then chased it with a drink of water. "If you had a medical emergency, you should have wakened me instead of leaving me here." She took another bite then wiped away the juice trickling down her chin. "How would you feel if you woke up and half of Sunstone was standing over you, watching?"

"Like Cherie?" He liked the way she bit the apple. Forceful. Without pretense. "She came by to see me, you know. Wiggled her way right into my bed."

"Naked?" Her eyes went wide as she looked at him.

"Cherie or me?"

"Either one." She took another bite.

"One of us was, one wasn't."

"Which?"

"Why do you care?"

"I don't. I'm just curious." Lacy finished the apple and handed the core to Jack. He lobbed it at the trash can in the kitchen, then picked up her bottle of water and took a long, slow drink.

"She likes her men much younger," Lacy continued.

"She wasn't wearing underwear." Bending down, Jack picked up Lacy's legs and moved them aside, then dropped onto the sofa with her.

"Then it was you." She pulled her knees up just enough to make a little room for him, then after he was seated stretched her legs out over his lap. "You were naked."

"It's my house." He eyed the white crew socks she was wearing, then inched them down over her ankles. Slim ankles. Beautiful. Then he took her left foot in his hand and began to rub. "I can be naked here anytime I want."

"Any…time…" she said.

10

"DO YOU LOVE what you do, Jack? Do you love your big city medical practice and your condo overlooking Lake Michigan?"

"It's what I've always wanted. I decided on my first day of medical school where I was going and how I would get there, and I stuck to my plan." He propped his leg on a hassock and leaned back. The familiar throb was back, but each day it was getting better. In another week or so he'd be as good as new and shortly after that on his way back home to resume his practice. Almost from the moment of his injury that was the only thing on his mind—putting his life back in order. But now that it was about to happen, now that his life was about to fall back into the same line as before, the line seemed to be moving too fast. "It's not a bad life," he defended. His words were hollow, though.

Lacy sat up, unsnapped Jack's jeans and slid them gently down his leg. "Maybe not bad, but I'm ready for great. I've lived not bad for a long time and I'm counting on there being a whole lot more to my life in Sunstone than that." Even the slight movement of inching his jeans down jolted his leg and elicited a muffled groan. "But I'm not you, and what's good for you isn't good for me," she said, trying to sound more rational and matter-of-fact than she felt.

Jack raised slightly to let his jeans slide smoothly over his hips, then sank into the sofa when they reached mid-thigh. "It's the only thing I know, Lacy. I don't want to make house calls and deliver cows for a living. That may have worked for your grandfather or Doc Washburn, but it won't for me.'' He watched the jeans slide over his ankles, and land in a heap next to the chair.

Dropping to her knees next to the sofa, Lacy studied the incision, then smiled. ''Inflammation's down. So's the swelling.'' She ran her finger lightly from the top to the bottom of the surgical scar, then looked up. ''It is a nice dream, though, isn't it?''

''Very nice, for you.''

She bent her head to his knee and placed a line of kisses from the top of his scar to the bottom. This was all there would be—the here and now. And even though she'd never been a here and now kind of a person, her heart was tugging her to take all there was, even if it was only this once. *Your choice,* Willie Pearl had said. And Jack was waiting for her to make that choice. ''Now that I've started your therapy session for today, would you care to finish it in the whirl-pool?''

''Not the whirlpool,'' he growled. ''The hot tub.''

''WHAT ARE YOU staring at?'' Lacy asked lazily several minutes later. She was so tired she could barely drag her eyes open, and the warm mist rising from the tub did noth-ing to help keep her awake.

''Might be the dark circles under your eyes,'' Jack drawled. Or maybe the woman he wanted to keep with him for the rest of his life.

''Thanks. I needed that,'' She said as she slid down in the water a little more. ''If you look really close, you might find a wrinkle or two.''

''If I look really close, it won't be for a wrinkle.'' She looked good in a pair of his silk boxers. Even better, though, was his T-shirt. Too bad he'd discarded the one with all the holes. Lacy in a wet, holey shirt... The thought caused him to moan.

His low, seductive moan brought her eyes fully open. "Is this the way you seduce all your nurses, Doctor? You work them to death, drop them in hot water then swoop in?"

"No one's ever objected, before." Jack reached over his shoulder for Lacy's glass of wine then dropped a foil packet into it. "Actually, I take that back. My scrub nurse did. She's sixty-two years old, with five grandchildren, but since she's been married to the same man for forty years, she wasn't thrilled with my come-on."

"Have you no shame, Jack—" Lacy laughed "—trying to corrupt a woman who's been married forty years?" She paused and studied the water for a moment. "Forty years. Can you imagine being with the same person forty years?"

Not until this moment, he thought. "I can't imagine being with the same person forty hours."

"Don't sell yourself short, Jack. I'll bet you've got at least forty-eight in you."

"Hours or years?" Carrying his stemmed crystal goblet of wine with him, Jack scooted around the perimeter of the tub until his side was pressed to Lacy, and he wondered, with every inch of the journey, if she would move away. But she didn't budge, didn't even flinch when his arm slipped around her shoulders. "Do you have forty years in you?"

"For the right man." Her voice was thick with drowsy contentment, and she dropped her head against his arm and closed her eyes. This was the first moment she'd allowed herself to relax since she'd met Jack, and it was the heaven she expected. No Fremont 1908 to clean, no patients, no Willie Pearl running the operation like a drill sergeant. She was comfortable with him, and happy, and the world was a million miles away for just a little while.

This was a feeling she wanted to keep forever…far past the time limit he'd imposed on anything they might have.

"And who is the right man?"

"Someone with a passion for life. Someone who…" She paused, searching for the right words, words other than, *You are.* Those words would hurt too badly, and she couldn't speak them. "Someone who doesn't measure success by his bank account or his golf game, but can number his successes in his heart."

Jack winced and rubbed his knee. "I worked hard on my golf game."

"And you worked hard out there rescuing John Fremont, taking care of Bobby Ross, taking care of me when Wilbur wouldn't let go. And even taking care of Louise. So which gave you the most satisfaction? Your golf game or what you've done in Sunstone so far?" She opened her eyes and twisted to look directly in his, to read the emotion, to search for the truth she hoped would be there. "Is a good game of golf better than what you've done today?"

Jack tried to ignore her stare, but he couldn't. It was boring right through to a place he didn't want discovered. There wasn't a future for them no matter how much he wanted it, no forty or forty-eight years. There was barely a tomorrow in this town, or, unfortunately, in his relationship with Lacy. He'd thought through all of it, tried to find a way to blend country and city, but it couldn't be done. And he simply couldn't kid himself into believing that he could cut it as a rural doctor, because it wasn't in him. He had to go home, back to his surgery. "It's apples and oranges," he muttered. "One has nothing to do with the other."

"But if you had to make a choice?"

"Then I'd choose this." Jack set his glass down and

pulled her to him, and a trickle of wine splashed from her glass down her arm. Gently, he lifted her hand to his lips and traced the heady trail from her fingers to the crook of her elbow. Slowly, deliberately, he savored each drop in his journey, taking time to enjoy every pleasure it offered, yet he was eager to move on. Her skin was warm, soft to his lips, and he knew she could hear his heartbeat as he savored every inch of his exploration.

Finally, when the sweetness vanished from her arm, Jack continued his upward path until he found the contours of her throat. Nibbling playfully at first, and eagerly, he pressed her with darting kisses, the kind that brought her to an involuntary shudder and groan. The sound of her need, of her response to him was more than he could bear, and he sought her mouth in greedy passion. "Could I have been the right man?" he finally asked, pulling back, searching her eyes. "Another time, another place, Lacy? Could it have been me?"

Lacy arched herself to him, ready for what he offered. "Yes," she whispered, turning her eyes sadly to the water. "It could have been you."

"And never the twain shall meet?"

"I don't know, Jack. I had everything planned."

"Like I did?"

She nodded and looked at him. It was a beautiful face. One that would break her heart in two, but one she was driven to take to her heart for the time they had. "Like you do," she corrected.

"So where does that leave us?"

"In a hot tub, in a borrowed cabin…" In a borrowed life, one she'd have to give back soon. "With tonight." She pulled the foil packet from her wineglass and opened it.

Moving to his side, Lacy pulled herself up in the water

to straddle him, taking care not to bring her weight down on his knee. "Say ah," she teased, trying to throw off the hopeless mood settling between them.

"Ah," he breathed, as she feathered her fingers across his lips.

"Again, only open your mouth a little wider."

"Ah," he said, parting his lips to kiss her fingers.

"Good, now let me see your tonsils."

"Got no tonsils, Doc." He groaned.

"Prove it."

Jack coiled a hand around her neck and pulled her face to his. "You prove it," he growled, grinding his mouth hard into hers.

As she took his kisses, they grew more urgent, and she devoured them with a fury that matched his. His dream come to reality. As in his fantasy, Lacy wore no bra under her shirt, and he could see her nipples grow taut beneath the thin fabric. They were a dusky rose, and he felt their friction on his chest as she bent down to him. "Take it off," he ordered, his voice rough and charged with need. He'd seen her in his fantasy, and now he had to see all of her in his reality.

"You do it," she directed, taking hold of his hand and guiding it slowly from the neck of her shirt to the hem.

The unhurried journey over the wet fabric was nothing he could have anticipated, even in his best dream. The feel of her breast and nipple in his palm, the way she deliberately pressed herself into the natural contour of his hand, the way she raised his other hand to experience the same journey—dreamland never came close to this.

"Don't stop," she pleaded, when he paused briefly to study her face.

"As if I would." He laughed, moving his fingers to the shirt's hem. It was time to be rid of the garment, and as he worked with the wet material, moving it up inch by inch, the words *with tonight* rang through his brain. Who was he kidding here? Certainly not himself. Tonight would never be enough with Lacy. An entire lifetime wouldn't be enough.

She'll follow me back, he thought. *She has to.*

"As if you *could* stop," Lacy corrected. Jack savored her flesh with all the moves of a well-trained surgeon, and Lacy knew he would pleasure Lacy methodically and precisely as if he were engaged in the most delicate of operations.

When the wet cotton yielded, inch by inch, he kissed the flesh beneath, and Lacy held her breath to keep from moaning. The more he exposed and explored, the harder it was to keep it inside, and as the fabric was pulled over her breasts and his lips sought her nipple, he was surprised by the pent-up groan that finally escaped her throat.

"Did I hurt you?" he asked. "Want an ice pack or something?"

"Define *something* before I decide." She lowered her eyes wickedly and oh-so-seductively.

"Remarkable, maybe. And important. So which would you prefer?"

"Definitely both," she uttered, starting a trail of kisses at the base of his throat.

Jack held in a strangled gasp while her lips moved from the hollow of his throat in a straight line downward. Natural and unbridled, Lacy was actually something he could not have created in his wildest fantasy, and all he could do was drink her in, study every curve, memorize the sweet ecstasy he'd never expected to find.

LACY FELT the anticipation racing within her. She retrieved her wineglass and tilted it so streams of the sweet beverage dribbled a course from his throat to his chest. "So messy, Jack," she teased, rubbing the sticky juice into his skin then licking it slowly off her fingers one at a time. She pulled her lips into a half pout, something she'd wanted to do all her life—with the right man. And Jack was the right man for everything. "Guess I'll have to clean it up." She followed the course with her tongue from the deep bronze just below his jaw to the thick dark hair on his chest, alternately sucking to draw out his deep groans, then licking lightly to hear his ragged breathing. She liked the sound of his desire. And reveled in all the surest signs of a man who couldn't turn back.

When the burgundy trail dribbled into the water, Lacy continued downward with her hand, still teasing him with playful kisses at the water's edge, promising him everything, then withholding it. "Would you like me to rub your leg?"

"That's not my leg," he growled.

"It isn't?" Taking delight in an exploration as new to her as were the feelings she had for Jack, Lacy was reluctant to stop, even when he gasped her name and called out that he couldn't take any more. As much as she wanted the completion and wanted to give him completion, she didn't want this to end. Her eternity was numbered in days, and she wanted to draw out every one of those days and experiences as long as she could. But as her hand stroked him beneath the warm swirling surface, and she felt him drive into her rhythm, pure, raw want of the man she loved pushed everything aside but that moment. Moving to find her place on him, thoughts of what they couldn't have were replaced with thoughts of what they had there and then. And for Lacy, there and then exploded in a shatter of stars and fireworks and a breaking heart.

She'd heard some women shed tears at the moment of

climax. A hormonal surge, probably. Her tears, the ones she didn't allow Jack to see, were something altogether different. Something remarkable. Something important.

LACY KICKED the covers off and sat up. Not even in Sunstone a week, and she was getting used to the new morning routine. Things had been pretty quiet after the interlude in the hot tub. They'd dried off, fallen asleep in each other's arms, then outside their professional capacity avoided each other like the plague for the next couple of days. Not exactly the afterglow Lacy had expected, but under the circumstances she understood, maybe even willed the cool distance between them. He wasn't gone yet, and her heart was already half broken. That cool distance was the only balm she had.

Today they had a full schedule. Nine patients in the morning, ten after lunch. Enough to keep her mind only on her work. This morning, before the town arrived at her doorstep, she would plod to her brand-new shower, stand under the hot spray for ten minutes feeling totally alone, then wander downstairs, put on a pot of coffee and wait for the day to begin.

"You up yet?" Willie Pearl called from the stairway. So far, there was no door separating Lacy's upstairs living quarters from the clinic downstairs, but she didn't care. There was nothing in her apartment, or life, that required privacy. "I called Doc Sutton's, but there was no answer," Willie Pearl continued now that she was upstairs. "Not on his cell phone, either. It wouldn't happen to be in your bed again, would it?"

She loved Willie Pearl dearly, but she wasn't in the mood for this. "I went out and saw Emily Glover last evening and took it with me. It's probably still in the truck."

"So where's the doc?"

Lacy saw the old woman's gaze trail to the bathroom door, then around the rest of the room. "I haven't seen him since yesterday afternoon." She wished that was a lie, that Jack was hiding in the shower or anyplace else in the Fremont 1908. The gloomy truth was she was alone. Except for his medical duties, Jack was all but gone.

Lacy dropped her feet over the side of the bed. "Is there a problem?"

"Don't know for sure. It's Sally Dunbar. She's having some cramping."

"What kind of cramping? Abdominal? Muscle?" Lacy stood up and wandered to the armoire that served as a closet. She pulled open the door and yanked out a pair of jeans and a denim shirt.

"Uterine. She's about three months along. That's why she couldn't help you with birthing them calves. Too strenuous for someone in her condition."

Lacy spun around, grabbed a handful of underwear and said, "Can she make it in here?"

Willie Pearl shook her head. "It's taken her and Ben years to get pregnant, and she's too scared to move."

"Call them and tell them I'm on my way." Lacy scrambled into the bathroom, took a two-minute shower and was pulling on her clothes as she bounded down the steps. "Call around and see if anyone's seen Jack this morning," she yelled, vaulting out the back door to her truck. First thing this afternoon, she was going to buy her own cell phone.

She knew the way to the Dunbar farm and waved the sheriff off as he pulled alongside her speeding truck, his red lights flashing. She was dong fifty in a sleepy thirty-mile-an-hour zone, and she wasn't about to stop or slow down.

"Fall in behind me, Lacy." She heard his voice over a

loudspeaker. "Willie Pearl called and told me to escort you out there. She said this time it isn't about the cow."

She slowed enough to let the sheriff pass, then gunned the engine to keep up with him as he sped ahead, and the twenty-minute drive to the Dunbar farm was cut almost in half.

"Where's the doc?" Ben Dunbar called, sprinting out the front door.

"Haven't seen him this morning," Lacy replied, pushing past him into the house. "Is she upstairs?" Her mind raced to the first time she was there and the frantic search for Louise. Human she could handle today. Cows and pigs, definitely not.

"Second door on your right." Ben stayed at the bottom of the stairs, looking up.

"She's good at her job," Sheriff Turner reassured, patting Ben's shoulder. "You should have seen her the other day helping John Fremont out on the highway. The way she took care of him—getting him out of that sardine can he drives, singlehanded—any woman who can do that will take good care of your wife."

Ben Dunbar nodded absently, his eyes still fixed on the top of the stairs, second door on the right.

"Tell me what's happening, Sally," Lacy said, setting her bag of medical supplies on the nightstand at the side of the bed. She carried a duffel bag arranged neatly with everything she needed, instead of the grocery sack full of medical odds and ends. "When did the cramps start?"

"About two hours ago. They're not too bad, and I didn't say anything to Ben at first. But I had one that seemed worse than the others." She looked at the clock on the nightstand. "It's been an hour now. And Lacy, it scared me so badly I told Ben to call for help." Sally stared at the floor, a slight blush crossing her pale cheeks. "I know we should have called you, but we're so use to calling Willie Pearl or Doc Washburn, we just didn't think.''

Lacy patted the frightened woman on the hand. ''Don't worry about it. Willie Pearl was pretty quick to let me know. So, Sally, how far along are you?''

''Three, maybe four months.''

''Have you been checked by an obstetrician?''

She shook her head. ''We've wanted this so bad, I was afraid to even admit it was happening for fear something would go wrong.''

''Any cramping now?'

''No, not for about twenty minutes.''

''Any heavy bleeding or spotting?''

''No.''

''Vomiting?''

''Yes, some. I figured it was morning sickness.''

Lacy took her pulse and temperature, then listened to her lungs. ''So far, everything seems fine,'' she said, fastening the blood pressure cuff to Sally's arm. She squeezed the black rubber ball to pump up the cuff, then let the air out slowly and listened through her stethoscope. ''Your blood pressure's a little high,'' she said, pulling the stethoscope out of her ears. ''Any history of blood pressure problems?''

''Doc Washburn always said I was as healthy as a horse, except for the fact I couldn't get pregnant.'' Sally's voice caught in her throat. ''I'm not going to lose the baby, am I?''

''I'm going to do everything I can to make sure you deliver a healthy little Bubba or Sissy when the time comes,'' Lacy reassured. ''Now, can you lie back, prop up your knees and let me take a peek?''

Ten minutes later, Lacy met an agitated Ben Dunbar pacing a hole in the carpet downstairs. ''She's feeling better, and the cramps haven't come back. But I want her to be seen by an obstetrician right away, so I called for an ambulance.''

''But she's okay?''

''For the most part, yes. She's not bleeding, which is a very good sign, but her blood pressure's high, and since she's almost forty and this is her first baby, I want to be safe.''

''But she didn't lose the baby?''

Lacy smiled sympathetically and shook her head. ''I'm going to ride in the ambulance with her, if you don't mind.''

The thirty-mile ride to Louisville went quickly and without complication, and Lacy was glad she'd overruled Sally's decision to make the trip in Ben's pickup truck. An hour after pushing through the emergency room doors, a young man who looked like he should have been in high school stepped out to the waiting room to tell Lacy and Ben that Sally was doing well. ''It's a touch of the flu, actually,'' he said, then added, ''but since she's a little dehydrated, and her blood pressure's still slightly elevated, we're going to keep her for observation, just to be on the safe side.''

''Thank you,'' Ben said, pumping the young doctor's hand. ''And thank you, Lacy.'' Tears streamed down the man's face as he hugged her. ''We owe you so much.''

''Not another bull.'' Lacy laughed. ''One's enough.''

''What?'' the young doctor asked.

''Rural practice, Doctor,'' Jack said, stepping up behind the trio. Turning to Ben, he continued, ''I talked to the people in obstetrics and got a good recommendation for someone to take Sally's case. She's with her now.''

''I owe you, too, Doc,'' Ben said.

''Believe me, half a bull is enough.'' He watched the young doctor shrug, then walk away. ''These city docs just don't have a clue," he said, grabbing Lacy's arm and pulling her toward the consultation room reserved for doctors who need a private moment with a patient's family. "And Ben, you can go see your wife now. Through the double doors, down the hall, third door on the left."

"How did you get here?" Lacy asked as he shut the door.

"I was already here, visiting some old friends."

"I could have used your help," she said stiffly.

He dropped his cane and pulled her into his arms, then planted a quick kiss on her lips. "You feel good," he whispered.

"For a temp," she snapped.

"And what's that supposed to mean?"

"Nothing," she said, pushing away from him. "Nothing at all."

"That wasn't nothing in the hot tub, Lacy. It was everything, and you know it."

"And so do you," she cried.

Jack turned and walked toward the door. Laying his hand on the knob, he said, "We're not going to resolve this thing here, and I need to go look in on Sally. Can I drive you back to Sunstone?"

NUMB AND CONFUSED, Lacy wandered out the emergency door to the parking lot and sat on a cement wall. It was almost noon. The sun was hot, the sky clear. She turned her face to the sun and whispered, "What are we going to do?"

"About what?" Jack asked, dropping down next to her.

Jolted out of her momentary reverie, Lacy jumped. "That was a quick visit."

"Sally was getting an ultrasound." He shook his head,

then put a consoling arm around Lacy's shoulders. "I never meant for this to turn into such a mess."

"You should have stayed grumpy, like you were when you got to Sunstone. Then I'd have probably led the parade to get you out of town."

He leaned into her and touched a light kiss over her lips. "If I thought you'd survive in Chicago I'd tie you up and take you back, but you won't."

Raising her fingers to trace the kiss, Lacy shut her eyes to ponder the right words. "So we just end it right here? Chalk that night in the hot tub up to a medical experiment that failed and move on?"

He brushed a tear off her cheek, then ran his thumb along her jawline. "It's not like this is coming as some big shock. You knew my position when I got here, and it hasn't changed."

"How long, Jack?"

"End of next week, if things go the way I'm planning."

"And what's going to happen to Sunstone's clinic?"

Jack looked at the sun, squinted and shrugged. "Times are changing, Lacy. Like it or not, the day of the good ol' country doc is over."

"Not." She snapped the word.

"So are they going to name the baby Lacy if it's a girl?" he asked, deliberately trying to change the subject.

The thought made Lacy smile. A baby girl. Baby girl Dunbar...Lacy Dunbar. Little Lacy Dunbar was the reason big Lacy Archer was in Sunstone— Little Lacy Dunbar and Millie Ballard and Danny Roy, Bobbo and Elvis. This was what she wanted. It was what she had chosen, and it was as important to her as Jack's Chicago practice was to him.

Firm resolve, she thought. Firm enough to be admired. But that resolve wouldn't wrap its arms around her when the nights became lonely.

11

"YOU DID WHAT?" Jack barked the words.

"I scheduled us for a radio interview later." Lacy adjusted the curtains at her bedroom window, then stood back to make sure they were hanging straight. The apartment was almost done, and her life was on the verge of settling into a routine.

"And what if I don't feel like being interviewed?" He stood directly behind Lacy and watched her align the valance. Like everything else she did, it was perfect. The ruffles were evenly spaced, and each pleat fell into place just as the one on either side had done. Even in this insignificant chore Lacy had a design, an order to the way she accomplished her goal. So perfect, and he wanted perfect so badly he could feel the knot start to twist in his gut the instant he thought about being without her perfection.

Lacy adjusted the tiebacks before she answered and purposely kept her back to him. He was used to this because she'd purposely kept her back to him for the past two days. And whenever she didn't, every time she looked at him or their eyes made contact, he saw the goodbye there. The final curtain on their act was coming down, and there would be no curtain calls.

"Then I'll do it for the both of us."

He was leaving at the end of the week. Yesterday, he knew, she'd overheard a phone call about his surgical schedule for next week. He was already making plans, al-

ready back in the surgical rotation. Then there'd been another couple of phone calls discussing patients—patients
who did not live in Sunstone. He was halfway back to
Chicago, and they both knew it.

"No one really expects you to be part of it, anyway."

LACY GLANCED out the window and saw Ben Dunbar fast
at work building a corral in the ten-acre field that went with
the Fremont 1908. Bubba's home. Lacy and Bubba and the
two kittens Ham had delivered the day before. "You're
leaving, Jack, remember?"

"And if I want to be interviewed?" Jack challenged.

"It's a local show, Jack. It only goes out to the county,
and no one in Chicago will hear it, so what's the point?"

"The point is you said you'd scheduled both of us, and
I've just decided that I want to do it. So where's the radio
station?"

"In a tent at the fairgrounds. Founder's Day celebration." Throwing herself onto her bed, Lacy opened her eyes
too fast and watched the ceiling spin overhead. Round and
round, just like her life. Round and round, just like her
feelings for Jack. Tumultuous was the word. Agitation of
the mind or emotions. In her case, both. "The other day,
when we made love in the whirlpool—"

"Hot tub," he corrected.

"When we made love in the hot tub, you asked me if,
given another time and place, you could have been the right
one, and I was honest with you. Now it's your turn, Jack.
I need an answer. Another time, another place, could I have
been the right one?"

He crossed the room and sat in an overstuffed floral print
chair. It didn't fit the wood and brick motif, but then, neither did Lacy. She was a country cottage with a white
picket fence, tulip and daffodil beds and lace curtains. She

was a dreamer, an idealist for the perfect life, and nothing he could offer would be the perfection she deserved. "Another time, another place..." He stopped when the downstairs door squeaked open. "I think we have a patient," he said, pushing himself up.

"Just in the nick of time," Lacy muttered. "But don't think you're off the hook." Lacy waited until he was all the way down the stairs before she followed. Another time, another place. Another Lacy, another Jack. She wasn't going, he wasn't staying. *End of story. Get on with your life.*

BY MIDAFTERNOON, the clinic was deserted. Everyone in Sunstone was either at the Founder's Day celebration or getting ready to go. Everyone but Lacy, and she wasn't in the mood. In fact, all she really wanted to do was go upstairs, pull the covers over her face and sleep for a week, until Jack was gone and she could focus her thoughts and energy on all the good reasons she had for coming to Sunstone. And staying there after Jack was gone. But the night wouldn't creep in for several hours, and she did have that blasted interview to do later on, so she decided to tidy the office, take an inventory and find another few mindless tasks to keep herself occupied until then.

The only problem was, even the mindless jobs at the medical clinic took concentration, and she had none to give. "I hope the next one's older than dirt," she moaned aloud, thinking about Jack's replacement. "Or happily married with a dozen kids. Or gay. Or a woman."

Jack's replacement. Somehow the only face she could picture in the Fremont 1908 was Jack's. His was the only stethoscope. His hands the only ones to examine the patients. His words the only medical advice she could imagine hearing. "Lacy," she said aloud as she dropped onto the chair next to the front window. "Stop it. Just stop it." She twisted to look outside, then leaned her head back and closed her eyes. "Get over it," she said. "Get over it, get over it…" She chanted the mantra for several seconds, but it didn't work. The more she fought to put it out of her mind, the more it stayed there and hurt. She loved Jack Sutton. She loved Sunstone, too, but she couldn't have both. And the hard choice was going to be hers to make very soon.

"Whoever said you could have it all, anyway?" she moaned. Pushing herself up, Lacy headed for the front door. She wasn't ready to join the Founder's Day celebration, since her mood was anything but festive. But she didn't want to stay alone in the Fremont 1908, either. It held some remarkably vivid memories for a building that had been in use for only a few days.

Sunstone's streets were nearly empty. An occasional car drove by, honking a greeting to her. She wasn't even close to knowing all the people yet, but they knew her, and she waved back at them. Halfway through town, Lacy found herself peering in the diner window. Two old men sat at the counter, sipping coffee. She saw one pull a tiny flask from his pocket, look around to make sure no one could see him, then pour a small portion of the liquid from the flask into his coffee. The other man nudged him, and he too, got a little sip of the good stuff in his mug. Cherie was there, too, checking out the two men's so-called secret caper, then looking away, disinterested. They were much, much too old for her. "Good for you, Cherie," Lacy said. "At least you've got the guts to go after what you want."

A block away from the diner marked the end of the downtown section. Lacy crossed the street and decided to change her scenery from the north side to the south as she walked home. She gazed in a dress shop window for a minute, then moved on to the shoe store. The next store-front was empty, and the next was an antiques shop, open, according to the sign in the window, on weekends and by appointment.

When Lacy finally dragged herself back to the Fremont 1908, it was still light out. Another hour to go before she had to head out for the interview, so she went about re-arranging the waiting room chairs for the third time that day. She pulled them into a musical chairs configuration in the middle of the room, then put them back in the same spots they'd come from originally. Then she checked the regulator clock on the wall and double-checked to make sure it was still running. "Now that was five minutes well spent," she said, heading for the examining room.

Inside, she flipped the light switch and watched the place go from night to day. For an instant, it reminded her of her grandfather's office...everything well used and friendly. Then she began to see the details...a few of Jack's books on a shelf, his white lab coat—the one she'd never seen him wear—flung over a chair, his medical diploma hung temporarily on the wall. She looked at the gold writing on the diploma and blinked. His name wasn't even Jack. It was Jonathan Andrew. Jonathan Andrew Sutton, M.D.

There were so many things she didn't know about him. Glumly, Lacy dropped into Jack's desk chair and picked up the phone, then dialed Chicago. "Hello, Marian," she said after she drummed her fingers through four rings. "I'd like to talk to you about that job opening in your intensive care unit...."

"THIS IS Mayor Jed Lambert coming to you live from the Founder's Day celebration. I have with me here today Dr. Jack Sutton and Registered Nurse Lacy Archer. As most of you already know, they've taken over Doc Washburn's medical practice and are in the process of setting up a clinic in the old Fremont building. And just for your information, John Fremont is up and doing fine, and he says to tell everyone that he regrets to inform you that he'll no longer be judging the homemade pie contest at the county fair next month. Doctor Sutton's orders.'' The broadcast booth was a tent, complete with horseflies and one-hundred-percent sticky, dripping humidity, and the official broadcast board was a wobbly card table set up with a microphone. There was a sound engineer in a van outside the tent, but he was more interested in watching a shapely young woman decked out in short shorts and a way-above-the-belly-button T-shirt serve ice-cold cherry slushes to a small crowd than he was running his boards. ''Today, we're going to discuss Sunstone's medical future with Dr. Sutton and Miss Archer, and if there's time, you all can come on down to the tent and ask them some questions in person.''

Lacy watched Jack ease into a metal folding chair, then take a swig of his cherry slush. She shook her head when he held up the cup and offered her a drink, then turned her undivided attention to the mayor, who was prattling on about coming attractions in Sunstone.

''We need to talk,'' Jack whispered. ''Something just came up and I...''

Lacy shook her head and leaned away from him. She bumped the card table, and it teetered, and Mayor Lambert uttered an expletive as the microphone fell off and hit the dirt floor. Without a thought, Lacy dove after the microphone then planted it on the table. ''Sorry,'' she mumbled.

''That was Nurse Lacy Archer,'' the mayor announced as he pulled a white handkerchief from his pocket and dabbed at his brow. ''Would you say a few words to the audience, Lacy?''

''What?'' She choked. ''I can't...''

Her protest was in vain, because before the words were out of her mouth, Mayor Lambert was passing through the tent flap in search of fresh air, a cherry slush and a cool spot in which to rest.

"You're on," Jack mouthed, pushing the microphone in Lacy's direction.

She shook her head violently and shoved the microphone at him. His response was to lean back in his chair, pick up his cherry slush and take a long, long drink. "Dead air," he finally said. "Not good."

Lacy looked at the microphone as if it were a Wilbur, poised to strike, and finally leaned in to it a little. "Hi. This is Lacy Archer," she sputtered. "Coming to you from the broadcast tent at the Founder's Day celebration."

Jack took another drink of his slush, nodded and gave her the thumbs-up sign.

"Filling in for Mayor Lambert. I'm the nurse, uh, at the Fremont 1908. Office hours Monday through Friday, nine to five." She drew in a breath of relief and pulled the microphone a little closer. "And emergencies. I'm always there for emergencies. I mean, I live there. Upstairs. Of course, you all know that since you've been fixing up the building…including my apartment, for which I'm grateful. Thank you." She swiped at the sweat sliding down her face, then wiped her hand off on the leg of her jeans, wishing she'd chosen shorts instead. "It's, um, coming along nicely, so stop by any time for a tour…of the medical clinic, not my apartment. And thank you for all the food, too. It's been delicious. I'll have to, um, get some of the recipes, not that I do a lot of cooking, but I do, um, like to cook sometimes. So bring me those recipes."

"Bring me those recipes," Jack mimicked. "Good dialogue."

Lacy swiped at her face again and took in a deep breath,

then shoved the microphone across the table at Jack. Much to her surprise, he took it. "So what do you do for that embarrassing prickly heat in this hot July weather, Nurse Archer?" He handed the microphone back to her and grinned.

"Same thing you do for your embarrassing jock itch, Doctor. Keep the area dry. Apply medicated powder." She frowned at Jack. Prickly heat and jock itch were the last things she wanted to talk about on the radio. "Anything that can absorb moisture. Wear loose-fitting clothing...light cotton."

"Ointment?"

"There are some topical treatments that will work. So, ladies and gentlemen, if you think you have prickly heat or jock itch, Dr. Sutton will be available for consultation tomorrow morning starting at nine. No appointment necessary. Just show up—" she smiled triumphantly at Jack. "—with your prickly heat and jock itch and Dr. Sutton will take a look at it. Now, Dr. Sutton has a few words for you on that old summer favorite—mosquito bites. Dr. Sutton?" She shoved the microphone at him and picked up his cherry slush.

"They itch," Jack responded. "And burn, if you scratch them."

"So what do you recommend, Doctor?" Lacy's voice went husky, and she gave him a suggestive smile.

"Don't scratch."

"And how do you suggest not scratching something that itches?"

Jack leaned back in his chair, and a slow, lazy smile crossed his face. "Some itches have to be scratched, Miss Archer, or they'll drive you crazy for a lifetime. They get under your skin, and you think about them all the time, and you know there's no cure, that the only thing you can do is give in."

"So you're saying give in to your itch?"

Jack leaned forward and pulled the cherry slush across the table. "Depends on the itch, don't you think?"

"So how would you go about—" Lacy's words died when the power went out and the broadcast tent was thrown into pitch black. "What happened?" she asked.

"I guess someone didn't like our itch discussion and pulled the plug."

"You're right Jack, we've got to talk," Lacy said, pushing aside the microphone. "I did something you should know about."

"Does it have anything to do with my favorite panties?"

Lacy stood and walked around the table, then sat on Jack's lap. "It could, if you'd like to see me in them every day." She lowered her mouth to his, and her lips were fire. "Since we have some time to kill, want me to range your knee…or anything?" she asked wickedly. "Give you a little therapy to make things feel better."

"Which things?" he growled.

"Anything you want, Doctor."

Body pressed to body, Jack's mouth crushed hers with a kiss that started the trembling in all her nerve ends. "This is the therapy," he whispered hoarsely. "The only therapy I need."

The tent was growing hotter by the minute, since the two ventilation fans shut down when the power went out, and Lacy felt the sweat trickle between her breasts. "Let me get you out of those clothes, and I'll show you some real therapy," she said.

"Right here, Miss Archer? In the middle of the Founder's Day celebration? That's a bit bold for a country girl, isn't it?"

"You don't have a clue what country girls are about, Doctor." Her hand slipped into his shirt and slid down his sweat-slicked chest, stopping just briefly to tease him. She drew a groan from him and a shudder, then whispered huskily, "I can do better than that, and as soon as we get back to Chicago or your hot tub—whichever comes first—I'll prove it."

"Chicago? What…"

"I took a job, Jack. Not in your hospital, but—"

"You can't," he said, choking. "Lacy, you can't go to Chicago."

The words stung as if he'd slapped her, and Lacy jumped off his lap. "So it was just a fling in the hot tub. Doctor gets nurse to take off her clothes for one night of fun, then dumps her." Tears welled up in her eyes and mixed with the sweat beading her face. "I guess I'm pretty stupid, Jack. I really thought there was something more than sex between us, but I guess I was wrong." She batted at the tears and sniffed. "It was great, though. Best sex I've had since I can remember when. If I ever get to Chicago, I'll look you up."

Turning, Lacy intended to exit the tent, but it was too dark inside, and she didn't have a clue which way to go, so she struck out blindly.

"Lacy, it's not like that," Jack called in the pitch black. "You can't go to Chicago, because I'm not going back to Chicago."

"What?" she sputtered.

"I just resigned. What I want isn't there anymore." He reached out his hands to find her, to pull her into his arms, but she wasn't there. "I love you, and I want to stay here with you."

"So you're staying in Sunstone?" She moved toward Jack's voice. "You love me?"

"Even before the hot tub."

"Even before you saw me in my panties?"

"I fell in love with you the moment I looked into those eyes."

"I love you, too, Jack." She stepped closer to him, suddenly unsure of her footing in the dark. "That's why I don't mind going back to Chicago with you. I mean, you can't stay here. You're a surgeon…"

"I'm a surgeon with a new job in Louisville. I was there looking it over, trying to put together a deal that would allow me to stay here with you the day you took Sally to the hospital. It's on a limited basis, at least for now, so I'll have a few hours a week to keep the Fremont 1908 up and running." He stepped forward and bumped the table. "And I've recruited a few moonlighters who would love to come and see how country doctoring works. That is, if you can work with city doctors again."

"I can work with anyone, if that means keeping you here." Lacy finally found Jack in the dark and slipped her arms around his waist. "It's perfect, Jack. Absolutely perfect."

"So will you marry me?" He turned and pulled her into his arms. "You and Bubba and the kittens?" He bent to kiss her, then whispered, "And are you wearing those panties now? The black ones?"

"Yes, and yes."

Outside the tent, a spontaneous round of cheers split the night, and Jack and Lacy sucked in a sharp breath and held it. "You don't suppose…" He picked up the microphone and tapped it. "Testing, one, two three. Testing… Do you think this thing is on?"

Another wave of cheers outside the tent answered his question.

"WHAT DID YOU DO to rate this picnic lunch?" Lacy asked Jack, following him to a grassy spot in the meadow behind the Fremont 1908.

"I made a house call at Emma Cathcart's this morning, right after the one I made on you."

"I hope you weren't as friendly with Emma as you were me." Lacy laughed, latching onto Jack's arm.

"Well, that's between my patient and me, but she did offer turkey sandwiches in return. And when I stopped in to see Millie Ballard, she insisted I take a fresh peach pie." Jack stopped on a bluff and dropped a blanket to the ground. "The iced tea I made myself."

"Yourself?" Lacy asked, skeptically.

"Well, I carried the thermos over to the diner and filled it up all by myself." He produced a plastic bag from the picnic hamper. "The waitress told me extra lemon."

"And I'll bet you gave her an extra big tip for that little piece of advice." Lacy watched Jack lower himself to the blanket. One week married now, and life was good. Jack had a surgical practice again, plus the Fremont 1908 was coming along as the clinic she knew it could be. Their apartment upstairs was turning into a real home, too, and at the end of every hectic day, no matter what their medical duties had required of them, they went to bed—together.

Perfect.

"You mean ten dollars is too much to pay for advice that will keep me in your good graces for the rest of my life?" He poured the iced tea and squeezed two lemon wedges into it.

Settling into Jack's arms, Lacy let the warmth of the sun wash over her. It felt wonderful. Everything about her life felt wonderful. Like Willie Pearl had advised, she made her choice, the one that was right for her. To be with Jack, wherever he was. Perfect choice. "Do you really think you can survive here? I mean, what about your aversion to rural medicine?"

"It has its moments."

"Enough moments to keep you happy?"

"As long as I can work with the perfect rural nurse."

Lacy smiled, fighting back tears of happiness. "Make sure, Jack."

"I am sure. As long as I have you, that's all I need to make me happy." With the hand that was not entwined around Lacy, Jack opened the basket and pulled out a sandwich. "Food's worth staying around for, too."

"And what else?"

"There's Bubba to consider. He's going to be needing two parents pretty soon. Especially a father to teach him how to play baseball and take him fishing."

"Bull." She laughed.

Jack raised his index finger to his lips. "Shh. Don't let Bubba hear you say that about him," he warned. "It would hurt his feelings."

"Any other reason for staying?"

"There are the goats to consider."

"Goats? We don't have any goats."

"Didn't I tell you? I stopped by the Wilson place the other day to check on Charlie Wilson's gout, and he gave me—"

"Goats." Lacy tilted her head back, squinted her eyes at the July sun and let the iced tea trickle down her parched throat. Sunstone was her home now. Sunstone and Jack. And someday Bubba and Sissy Sutton. "I'm wearing those panties, Doctor, if you'd care to take a look."

"I'd love to—" Jack's words were interrupted by the sputter of an old pickup truck.

"Sounds like it's time for the doctor to be in." He smiled, placing a quick kiss on her forehead.

"Doc Sutton," Ham called from the loading dock at the back of the Fremont 1908. "I know you two don't want to be disturbed, but this will only take a minute. I've got my pig in the truck, and if you could just take a look at her…"

Harlequin truly does make any time special.... This year we are celebrating weddings in style!

A Walk Down the Aisle
WEDDING CELEBRATION

To help us celebrate, we want you to tell us how wearing the Harlequin wedding gown will make your wedding day special. As the grand prize, Harlequin will offer one lucky bride the chance to **"Walk Down the Aisle" in the Harlequin wedding gown!**

There's more...

For her honeymoon, she and her groom will spend five nights at the **Hyatt Regency Maui.** As part of this five-night honeymoon at the hotel renowned for its romantic attractions, the couple will enjoy a candlelit dinner for two in Swan Court, a sunset sail on the hotel's catamaran, and duet spa treatments.

A HYATT RESORT AND SPA

Maui • Molokai • Lanai

To enter, please write, in, 250 words or less, how wearing the Harlequin wedding gown will make your wedding day special. The entry will be judged based on its emotionally compelling nature, its originality and creativity, and its sincerity. This contest is open to Canadian and U.S. residents only and to those who are 18 years of age and older. There is no purchase necessary to enter. Void where prohibited. See further contest rules attached. Please send your entry to:

Walk Down the Aisle Contest

In Canada
P.O. Box 637
Fort Erie, Ontario
L2A 5X3

In U.S.A.
P.O. Box 9076
3010 Walden Ave.
Buffalo, NY 14269-9076

You can also enter by visiting www.eHarlequin.com

Win the Harlequin wedding gown and the vacation of a lifetime!
The deadline for entries is October 1, 2001.

HARLEQUIN®
Makes any time special ®

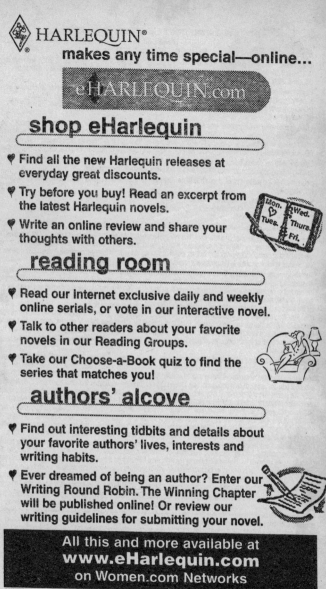

Harlequin invites you to walk down the aisle...

To honor our year long celebration of weddings, we are offering an exciting opportunity for you to own the Harlequin Bride Doll. Handcrafted in fine bisque porcelain, the wedding doll is dressed for her wedding day in a cream satin gown accented by lace trim. She carries an exquisite traditional bridal bouquet and wears a cathedral-length dotted Swiss veil. Embroidered flowers cascade down her lace overskirt to the scalloped hemline; underneath all is a multi-layered crinoline.

Join us in our celebration of weddings by sending away for your own Harlequin Bride Doll. This doll regularly retails for $74.95 U.S./approx. $108.68 CDN. One doll per household. Requests must be received no later than December 31, 2001. Offer good while quantities of gifts last. Please allow 6-8 weeks for delivery. Offer good in the U.S. and Canada only. Become part of this exciting offer!

Simply complete the order form and mail to:
"A Walk Down the Aisle"

IN U.S.A	IN CANADA
P.O. Box 9057	P.O. Box 622
3010 Walden Ave.	Fort Erie, Ontario
Buffalo, NY 14269-9057	L2A 5X3

Enclosed are eight (8) proofs of purchase found in the last pages of every specially marked Harlequin series book and $3.75 check or money order (for postage and handling). Please send my Harlequin Bride Doll to:

Name (PLEASE PRINT)

Address   Apt. #

City   State/Prov.   Zip/Postal Code

Account # (if applicable)   **097 KIK DAEW**

HARLEQUIN®
Makes any time special®

Visit us at www.eHarlequin.com

PHWDAPOPR2

*Three sizzling love stories
by today's hottest writers
can be found in...*

Midnight Fantasies....

Feel the heat!

Available July 2001

MYSTERY LOVER—*Vicki Lewis Thompson*

When an unexpected storm hits, rancher Jonas Garfield
takes cover in a nearby cave...and finds himself seduced
senseless by an enigmatic temptress who refuses to tell him
her name. All he knows is that this sexy woman wants him.
And for Jonas, that's enough—for now....

AFTER HOURS—*Stephanie Bond*

Michael Pierce has always considered costume shop
owner Rebecca Valentine no more than an associate—
until he drops by her shop one night and witnesses the
mousy wallflower's transformation into a seductive siren.
Suddenly he's desperate to know her much better.
But which woman is the real Rebecca?

SHOW AND TELL—*Kimberly Raye*

A naughty lingerie party. A forbidden fantasy. When Texas
bad boy Dallas Jericho finds a slip of paper left over from
the party, he is surprised—and aroused—to discover that he
is good girl Laney Merriweather's wildest fantasy. So what
can he do but show the lady what she's been missing....